LUPE

LUPE

GENE THOMPSON

RANDOM HOUSE NEW YORK

Library of Congress Cataloging in Publication Data

Thompson, Gene.
Lupe.

I. Title.
PZ4.T4685Lu [PS3570.H614]   813'.5'4   77–6000
ISBN 0–394–41988–X

Grateful acknowledgment is made to Citadel Press for
permission to reprint excerpts from "Chaldean Incantation"
and "Incantation Against Malefic Demons" (pages 265–67)
from Treasury of Witchcraft, edited by Harry E. Wedeck,
pages 21 and 22. Copyright © 1960 by Philosophical Library,
Inc. by arrangement with Citadel Press, a Division of Lyle
Stuart, Inc., Secaucus, N.J. 07094.

Manufactured in the United States of America

9 8 7 6 5 4 3 2

FIRST EDITION

To my wife

Be it enacted, that if any person shall use, practice or exercise any invocation or conjuration of any evil and wicked spirit, or take up any dead man, woman or child out of his, her or their grave, to be employed or used in any manner of witchcraft, enchantment, charm or sorcery, whereby any person shall be killed, or destroyed, wasted or consumed, that every such offender, being of any of the said offenses duly and lawfully convicted and attainted, shall suffer pains of death.

—Statute Against Witchcraft,
Massachusetts Bay Colony, 1693

Acknowledgments

I am profoundly grateful to the following for their unflagging encouragement and professional advice: Shelly Wile of Adams, Ray & Rosenberg Literary Agents; Robert and Susan Lescher of Robert Lescher Literary Agency; my editor, Robert D. Loomis at Random House; Bernard Resnick, M.D., for reading the manuscript for medical accuracy; and Martin Z. N. Katz, for his conversations with me on the law. In addition, for their unfailing enthusiasm and understanding, my heartfelt thanks are due to Gloria Stuart Sheekman; Rheta Resnick; Professor Jeremy R. Azrael of the University of Chicago; Professor W. I. Matson of the University of California at Berkeley; my wife, Sylvia, and our ever-faithful and perceptive David, Benjamin, Dinah, and Amanda.

LUPE

1

The house was Victorian. It stood at the end of a steep street in Pacific Heights and had an unspoiled view of San Francisco. David wanted the house as soon as they saw it. From the bedroom, they could look out over the Presidio and across the straits to the brown hills of Marin.

"Honey, it's a bargain."

"Because it's falling apart."

"We'll fix it up. Okay?"

"It'll cost a fortune."

"Doctors are rich. Haven't you heard?"

After five years in practice, David had only begun to do well. She felt they ought to invest. But his mind was made up. And she had never been able to refuse him anything. She tried to smile, to agree. Something made her hold back. She felt uneasy, trapped. The truth was, she was almost afraid of the house. She stood looking up at it, rubbing the palm of one hand against the back of the other.

"What's the matter, baby? Is it the money?"

She didn't answer.

"Well, don't worry about it!" He took her in his arms. She hoped he would see, would understand. All he saw was the house. "Please, Emmy?"

"All right."

It turned out the house was solid. True, there were broken treads on stairs, rotted shingles, shutters hung askew and the window sashes were warped. The garden behind the wrought-iron fence was overgrown, and all the paint had blistered and peeled.

3

It was an estate sale, and the broker told them the executors did not know the true value of the house. When the place had been sandblasted and a crew of workmen went over it, the structure turned out to be perfectly sound.

Furnishing it would cost a great deal. Emily and David moved in with almost nothing. The rooms were spacious and airy but smelled of paint, so that they had to sleep their first night in the house with the windows all open, a heavy fog chilling them to the bone. Three nights later, Emily was awakened by a noise. She shook David.

"What is that?" He looked at her, puzzled. She described it. "Plumbing. Goddamn it." David was irritated because the plumbing was the one thing he had taken for granted. It was all copper and doing it over meant tearing open paneled walls.

"I didn't know plumbing made noises like that."

"Just hope that I'm wrong."

They got up and checked all the faucets in the house, even checked the meter with a flashlight, but there were no leaks. The sound was intermittent, distant.

"Is it air in the pipes?"

"Maybe."

The sound had begun around one in the morning. It stopped abruptly at two. When it continued for three nights running, David called a plumber, and when that didn't solve the problem, he rang up the architect who had offices in his building and got in touch with a plumbing engineer. The engineer came out to the house with testing devices, including a stethoscope. Emily had been shopping and came in the back way when he was there. She overheard him talking in the kitchen with David.

"It isn't the plumbing."

"Well, don't tell my wife. I'd just as soon she thought it was the plumbing." The sounds made Emily nervous and David knew it.

"What does she think's causing it?"

"Who the hell knows?"

They were trying to have a baby and she was anxious. She had had a miscarriage the year before. She knew David didn't want her to be upset and it touched her.

4

"Well, these old houses are funny," the engineer said. "Things happen and you never know why. It could be a draft somewhere."

"Every night?"

"Search me."

The next day, Emily introduced herself to old Mrs. Prentice, who lived down the street in a redwood house Maybeck had built for her, a place full of beveled glass double doors, Oriental carpets, and hand-carved furniture that smelled of lavender polish. Mrs. Prentice, leaning on a cane, showed Emily into a garden full of ancient roses. Emily wanted to ask about the sounds in the house. She was hesitant, waiting for a chance, meanwhile admiring the flowers. Mrs. Prentice pointed at them with her cane.

"Austrian Copper . . . 1590. That's how roses looked then, like little peonies. Over there, Madame Eglantine. Fourteenth century. Chaucer mentions it. This one is *Rosa damascena bifera*, praised by Virgil and Ovid. The Romans liked it because it blooms in fall. Over there? Helen Traubel. Modern. Disease-free and that's all I'll say for it."

They got around to the subject of Emily's house. Emily took a deep breath and mentioned the noises. No, replied Mrs. Prentice, there had never been any trouble with the house.

Then Mrs. Prentice looked at her narrowly and asked, "Like a loud knocking, is it?"

"How did you know?" Emily was surprised. To her, plumbing noises generally meant moanings and shudderings.

"Probably an elemental."

"A what?"

"If you don't encourage them, they go away. There." Mrs. Prentice clipped a Peace rose, handing it to her, then tottered back inside.

Marianne came to see the house, coughing and laughing, flop-flop-flopping around in her loose handmade sandals. Emily told her about the noises at night. Marianne was fascinated.

"Seen anybody going widdershins around the house?"

"Oh, stop it!"

"I want to hear the noises."

"Well, come back at one in the morning."

"Can I?"

"Come on. I'll show you the upstairs."

"Is that where the noises are?"

"Do you want to see the rest of the house or don't you?"

"If I were you, I'd put a knife under the doorstep. Keeps away evil."

"I keep telling you, it's the pipes. I don't care what the plumber says. Everybody's got some crazy theory. The old lady down the street says it's an elemental."

"Well, don't laugh. Jung believed in them."

"I don't even know what it means."

"Look it up."

"I don't want to look it up and I really don't want to talk about it any more."

"Well, you don't have to snap at me."

"Sorry. What's in the bag?"

"Bread and salt. For luck. You should pardon the expression."

After Marianne's visit, Emily did not hear the sounds for another week. Then when Emily heard them again and woke David up, he became annoyed.

"I don't hear anything."

"Well, it stopped!"

"Emily, you're *imagining* it."

They quarreled about it. Briefly. Irritably. Then he was sorry because he had upset her. He put his arms around her and soothed her with love-making.

The plumbing engineer sent them a bill for fifty dollars. Everything cost them a great deal. The house was expensive to maintain. David named it The Millstone but he loved it.

He knew that she was uncomfortable. At first, he had been sure it was the rapping, but after the strange noises stopped, she still felt the same way. He decided being alone there bothered her and got Emily to hire a live-in maid—squat, smiling Esmeralda. And, of course, having her own things around would make a difference, so they began buying furniture. Esmeralda took pride in her work. The house was immaculate. David liked that.

"How's Emphysema? She working out?"

"Don't call her that."

6

"I thought you said she didn't understand English."

"A few words. But I never know which ones."

"Well, as long as you're happy with her." She didn't say anything. "Honey? What's the matter?"

"Nothing."

"Come on."

"She's fine. It's just that . . . well, she lies."

"How do you mean?"

"You know that majolica pitcher? That big one?"

"No."

"Yes you do"—she described it in the air with her hands—"the big one I never use."

"Oh, that thing. I hate it."

"That's why I never use it. Well, anyway, the other day I went into the kitchen and found it in pieces all over the floor. She was sweeping it up. I asked what happened and she said she didn't know."

"Get to the part about the lie."

"David, she broke it! She wouldn't admit it. She said she came back from the market and found it that way."

"Maybe she did."

"David, it was on the top rack of the baker's stand. All the way at the back. It couldn't have fallen off."

"Maybe the cat did it."

"We don't have a cat."

"We could get one." She made a face. He said, "Honey, it's just a pitcher."

"No, it isn't. She breaks things all the time. And she always says she didn't do it. Marianne says it's a cultural thing. That to them it isn't lying. It's just a matter of avoiding the unpleasant, whatever that distinction may mean. Anyway, she said not to corner her."

When Marianne had first come to San Francisco, Emily was delighted. It had been almost seven years since they had seen each other. Under the banter, Marianne seemed troubled. Understandable. The year before she had lost her husband.

Once Emily had said, "If you need anything—" But Marianne had waved away the suggestion.

"I can manage," she said. And that was the end of it. Marianne was the same as ever.

Emily tried to remember where they had met. She was sure it was at an Army party at the *Schloss* in Heidelberg. Everybody was drunk. Brother officers were taken, vomiting and apologizing, to the snow-caked grounds high above the frosty glitter of the town and walked in relays back to sobriety. Women on sofas in alcoves wept openly with friends they had wronged. The faithful and unfaithful exchanged glances, secret pressures. A general had been seen to urinate in a potted palm in the anteroom of a crowded toilet. A woman sang "God Bless America" a consistent quarter-tone above the band. They had all formed a ring, arms around each other's shoulders, and sung songs.

"We met there," said Emily.

"No."

"But I know we did! We were together at that party. I remember."

"But that's not where we first met."

"Well, where *did* we meet?"

Marianne grinned, refusing to tell her. Emily could just search her memory. It was an old game by now. They had played it for a year.

Marianne had introduced her to David seven years before, in Heidelberg. Before meeting her, David had asked what she was like and Marianne had answered, Wagnerian. Not telling him that Emily was beautiful, a blonde with creamy skin and dark-blue eyes.

When Emily found out about it, she was nettled. "Why did you say 'Wagnerian'? I didn't think I looked that big."

"I didn't mean that. You look the way Iseult is supposed to look but never does. I think it's all that singing. It gives them huge diaphragms, so that their tummies always stick out and they always eat. It must be something about singing, but those women have incredible appetites. I guess you need to stoke up a big furnace to sing all those *Yo-ho-to-ho*'s. No, I meant you

8

look like the legend. Part of it is the way you sit. You almost never move, do you know that? Doesn't anything ever take you by surprise?"

Emily laughed. But her white hands remained folded in her lap.

"You're afraid of something in yourself, aren't you? What do you really think would happen if you let go?"

"Do you mind if we don't talk about it any more?"

Emily, lost in her thoughts, went into the kitchen and started dinner. David came in. "What are you thinking about?" he asked.

"Marianne. And . . . you know. Those days."

He looked at Emily, remembering that he had taken her on their honeymoon to the Alps. He remembered skiers at Kitzbühel schussing down slopes at dusk, yodeling in harmony. Emily in his arms in front of the fire.

"Dinner," she said, handing him plates. It was Esmeralda's night off.

"Let's make love."

"I have to watch the vegetables."

"Let's make love down here."

"On the cold linoleum?"

"We'll stand up." He took her in his arms.

"God, you're huge!"

"Come on!"

"I'm not ready."

"You want dinner to spoil?" He lifted her up, then penetrated her. She gasped.

The phone rang. He picked up the kitchen extension. "Hello?" She put her hands over her face. He held her with his left arm, bracing her against the sink. "My wife? She's right here." He offered her the phone. "It's about insurance," he said. She just stared at him. "She's busy right now," he said into the phone. "Can you call her back? Of course, if you want to wait—" Emily stretched out a hand and broke the connection.

"You idiot! Why do you do things like that?"

"You don't know how it feels when you laugh." David hung up the phone, then embraced her passionately.

9

"Now?"

"Yes. Yes, now."

The gynecologist had thought that perhaps it was a question of tension. If they were more relaxed . . . ? But nothing worked. They both underwent the usual examinations. No, everything was all right. Emily thought, It's anxiety. She had hidden it very well but there it was. They had each other. And David had his house. Somehow it became more and more expensive to maintain. David started going to the office on Wednesdays. They had the kitchen done over, Japanese tile with concealed lighting above shoji ceilings. They bought Oriental carpets. He began to work late.

One night, he came home shaken. She found him in the library, pouring himself a stiff drink. He hadn't even called out hello. She went to him, kissing him tenderly.

"What is it?"

"Nothing."

"Tell me."

"Remember Stevie? That kid? I lost him." Stevie was a patient he had seen four years earlier, a teenager with a rare form of skin cancer. He had gone into remission from chemotherapy. The boy had seemed cured, but his immunological system was shot from the treatment. Just the night before, David had been called to the hospital to see Stevie and confirm a diagnosis. Yes, it was true. The boy had chicken pox. Chicken pox, the boy's father had said. Well, hell, that's nothing. But the boy had no resistance left. Not even enough to fight a childhood disease. It was generalized. He was moribund. There were tubes everywhere. The boy couldn't speak. His eyes kept following David around the room.

"I'm sorry, David," she said, stroking his hair.

"Thanks."

They had dinner late. He seemed vulnerable in a way she had never seen before. She wanted to talk about it.

"How do you tell a patient he's going to die?"

"We don't tell patients that."

"But if it's something like . . . well, melanoma."

"There's a new technique now. For early diagnosis. We have an eighty-six-percent cure rate."

10

"Oh."

"I mean, it's not so frightening any more."

"Oh."

Bullshit. A young woman he knew was interning in pathology but after an autopsy revealed that the tumor weighed more than the patient, she changed over to another specialty.

"Everybody has only one fatal disease." He was trying to brush it away with a joke but she wouldn't let him. She felt it was something he needed to talk about. When she pressed him, he said impatiently, "I treat skin diseases! Most of my patients have nothing worse than acne!" She had touched a nerve. David never wanted to talk about death.

The next morning, he arrived at the office early but the waiting room was already full. Later, his secretary would have figures about "patient load," a term he disliked but an index to his success. He went in to put on his white coat and caught one of the girls heating buns in the sterilizer. The week before, he had found her cleaning junk jewelry in the sonar box. Remembering, he started to grin. Then he caught sight of the Ostend boy in the waiting room, and his expression changed. Nell Ostend, that was his name. Scrub-faced. Early twenties. Complexion marred by what looked like flea bites, blond hair cut in the style of the forties. He was smoking a cigarette and reading an old issue of *Science*.

Yesterday's biopsies had been delayed. They were in now, along with a lab test on the Ostend boy. David glanced at the report only long enough to have his own judgment confirmed, then put it down slowly.

"Send in Mr. Ostend, please."

The blond boy followed the nurse into an examination room. He was still puffing on his cigarette and reading *Science*.

"Here's Doctor now, Mr. Ostend." She closed the door behind her.

"Sit down, please."

Flea bites. That's what they looked like. The boy had come in hoping to hear that's all they were, knowing better. By coincidence, he worked as a technician in a ward where they treated leukemia patients. He knew the signs himself. That made it easier to talk to him.

"I know what you're thinking, Nell." Funny name. He must have gotten it in Holland. Was it from his mother? "But people recover. You know that. Don't forget it."

Nell nodded, thinking. Statistics. A thin, thin margin of hope. David could see it beginning to happen already. By the next day, the boy would see himself as one of the lucky few who survive for no reason, clutching at hope like a man gasping for breath. It always happened.

After Nell had gone, David went into his private office and sat down in the visitor's chair opposite the desk, as if he had come there for advice. It was a classic case of leukemia. A death sentence. There was nothing more he could do. Christ. Two in twenty-four hours. You get used to it. That was what doctors always said. Bullshit.

At noon, he went out alone. It began to rain heavily. He went to the new place where Solari's had been and found there would be a half-hour wait. Impatiently, he hurried through the downpour to the crosswalk, sloshed across the puddles on Post Street to the St. Francis and headed for the grill. The room was dim, the air full of men's voices. The headwaiter came toward him. Suddenly, he had no appetite. He turned and left.

Death. He walked in the rain, thinking about it. But behind the word, there flickered the implied reality of life. As real as death was, life itself was that real. Flamelike, it burned through the body which it consumed, shone in the eyes, vibrated in the voice and, in the very fact of death, was seen as departing, escaping somehow into the charnel air. He looked up, tried to imagine some lightlike form dissolving into the ether, some sign of life. But life was function. Death was no more than the end of an arrangement. He walked back through the downpour, returning early to the office without lunch.

That was how he met Jennie. She had simply walked in at twelve-thirty without an appointment. Yes. Send her in. A cloud of red hair. Silvery perfume. Like incense. White, white skin. Big tits. A nice ass. Hard, round. So? Jesus, there were ten thousand women like that. What made her special?

12

"It's just contact dermatitis, which doesn't mean anything more than a skin irritation. Change detergents and it will go away. You won't have to come back."

She was looking at him steadily. He always said no—no to the frank look of invitation, no to the suggestive pressure of a patient's hand on his arm when he bent over to examine her, no to a hint.

"Six o'clock," she said. "My place."

He shook his head slightly.

As if reading his mind, she said, "It's the car, isn't it?" He had a recognizable car, a classic Mercedes. He wondered how she knew. "All right, Union Square parking lot, third level. We'll go in mine."

"I can't."

"After six. And don't keep me waiting in all those fumes."

Later, she took him back to the underground garage.

"Will you call me?"

"No."

"You mean, that's it?"

"That's it."

He was not going to call her again. But he did. The next time he showed up at her house on Russian Hill, he had sex with her without ever saying a word. Afterward, he said, "You know something? I don't even like you." She only smiled. After that, he constructed a completely alienated relationship for both of them. He looked on her as something he was trying to get over, like an infection.

2

On Thursdays, he went to the hospital for lunch. Half a dozen doctors always sat together. One Thursday, they nudged each other as a man came toward them, carrying his tray.

"That's him," somebody said. "That's the guy."

He was a psychiatrist whose treatment consisted of having sex with his patients.

"Men and women," said somebody.

David made room for him, half rising to shake hands. The psychiatrist looked young, handsome, and tired. His name was Mercy. Hearing it, David choked on his coffee. Dr. Mercy talked constantly, even diagnosing this trait in himself as compensation. He used a term: hate-fucking. David was surprised not to have thought about it. He turned it over in his mind, as if naming it would release him.

Instead, he found himself wanting her constantly. He was trapped, afraid. He made love to Emily to keep her from finding out.

Emily knew something was wrong. She told herself it was the hours he worked. That must be the reason. The house again. Everything was the house. She didn't feel well. She had come home late from the university, where she took graduate courses in anthropology, after spending the afternoon in the library. They were reading Jung, and she looked up "elementals" and was amused to discover that he had only described them as "the former stages of our own evolution," whatever that meant. You ought to look it up yourself, she imagined herself saying to Marianne. But another source, Tondriau, said, ". . . they become

14

immortal by having sexual relationships with humans." Impatient, she slammed shut the book and went home, feeling queasy.

Marianne had guessed that Emily was pregnant. Emily talked to her on the kitchen phone, cradling it on her shoulder as she peeled potatoes and carrots under the running water.

"What do you mean, David hasn't said anything?"

"I haven't told him." She felt uncomfortable.

"For chrissakes, he's a *doctor!*"

"What do you think he does, give me a pelvic every night when he gets home?"

"Yeah, but if *I* can tell—"

"Well, sometimes he's preoccupied. He's been working late." She really didn't want to talk about it. How could she explain that after her miscarriage, she was almost superstitious. David wanted children. Of course, they both did. If she could only give him a son . . . But talking about it was like tempting fate. She had made up her mind. She would keep it a secret as long as she could. She could hear Marianne talking, complaining. Then Marianne said abruptly that she had something important to tell her.

"Lady—" said a voice, interrupting.

"Just a minute," she said to Marianne.

"What?"

"Sorry. There's someone here." She looked around and called out, "Who is it?" She didn't see anyone. She heard Marianne's voice scratching over the phone: "Emily? You still there?"

"Sorry. It must be someone outside. One sec." Emily put down the receiver and went to the open window. "Yes?" she called out, turning around. There was no one in the walled garden. She looked around, puzzled, closed the window and turned back toward the kitchen. "Esmeralda!" The maid surfaced.

"*Sí, señora?*" she said, smiling her gold smile.

"Is someone in the house?"

"*No, señora.*" Esmeralda padded away. Emily frowned, glanced around the dining room and wondered whether Esmeralda could be lying. What did she mean, there was no one in the house? She walked into the dining room from the breakfast room, and then went into the living room. Empty. Shrugging, she went back to the phone and picked it up.

"Nobody."

"What's going on?"

"I thought there was somebody here but there isn't."

The door from the dining room into the living room suddenly slammed. Hard. She had closed the window. There was no draft. Anywhere.

"One second more, okay?" Emily put down the phone again on the passthrough and marched over to the door. She felt herself hesitate, then shiver. What's the matter with me? Reaching out and grasping the large porcelain knob, she turned it firmly, flinging open the door. The living room was exactly as it had been, the door into the entry hall closed, the windows all shut. Sighing with irritation at herself, she banged the door closed, glanced around at the breakfast room, dim in the failing afternoon light, and flicked a switch. The fluorescent tubes above the shoji ceiling sprang into life, flickered, then burned steadily, making the kitchen copper and warm yellow Japanese tile glow. She picked up the phone.

"It's me again."

"What's going *on?*"

"Nothing is going on! A door slammed, is all. So what else is new?"

"Nothing."

"You said you were going to tell me something."

"Did I?"

"Yes. You said it was important."

"Well, I don't remember what it was."

"You're lying, Marianne. I can always tell when you're lying. Now, just what were you going to tell me? Marianne?"

"Lady—" said the voice again. It was a young voice, soft, clear.

"Who is it?" She was confused, even alarmed.

"What is going *on?*"

"Marianne, did you hear it?"

"What?"

"A voice!"

"No."

"There *is* somebody here! Wait a minute, please. Don't hang

16

up." Emily put the phone down again and went through the kitchen to a door opening into a corridor off which doors gave onto a pantry, a broom closet, and Esmeralda's room. At the rear of the corridor were the back stairs. Quickly, she opened the broom closet door. The closet was empty. At the pantry, she hesitated, then yanked open the door. Empty. "All right, who is it?" she demanded. Silence. She walked to the foot of the stairs. No sign of anything amiss, no one anywhere. She felt the skin at the back of her neck prickle. "I said, who is it?" No answer. "Esmeralda!" she called out. Esmeralda's door opened and Esmeralda padded out, barefoot, heavy-breasted. She had obviously been resting.

"*Sí, señora?*"

Of course! The television! "Are you watching television?"

"*No, señora.*"

"Esmeralda!" Her tone was half teasing, half angry. She walked quickly past Esmeralda toward the door of the servant's room, put her head inside. The television was not only off, it was unplugged. Esmeralda unplugged everything all the time—lamps, radios, television sets, appliances—because she was convinced electricity leaked into the house, was damaging to human beings. Emily turned. Esmeralda was looking at her, her wrinkled brown face perplexed.

"*Qué manda, señora?*"

"*Nada. Lo siento,* Esmeralda." No, she did not command anything and she was sorry. At a loss, Emily gave her a brief smile and went quickly back to the phone, snatching it up.

"Are you playing jokes on me, Marianne?"

"What?"

"Well, somebody's called me twice and there's nobody here."

"What are you talking about?"

"I told you! Somebody said 'lady' and then a door slammed and then somebody called out 'lady' again and I've searched the damn house and there's nobody here. I know I heard it!"

"It sounds just like Boniface the Eighth!"

"What's that supposed to mean?"

"He was a Cardinal back in the thirteenth century who wanted to get rid of Pope Celestine the Fifth because Celestine was a

17

simpleton who took the Bible literally and was giving away all the Church property to the poor, so Boniface drilled a hole in his bedroom floor down through the ceiling of the papal bedroom and let down a speaking-tube at night, calling Celestine's name and saying it was God speaking and he wanted Celestine to resign. Incidentally, it worked. Celestine the Fifth is the only Pope who ever unpoped himself, if there is such a word. Maybe David's trying to tell you something! . . . Emily?"

"I'm here." Emily was annoyed.

"Look, I'd better let you go."

"No, please. It's all right. I have hours before David gets home and, to tell you the truth, I feel rotten. I think I've got a temperature."

Marianne was surprised, concerned. "Shouldn't you go to bed? I mean, Christ, you could have the flu!"

"I suppose."

"Will you ask David to look at you? I mean, Jesus! Promise?"

"Yes." She thought suddenly of how Marianne looked, the blowsy hair, the square Baltic face; Marianne with the dirty wash-dresses she always wore, the impossible sandals; Marianne coughing and laughing; Marianne who knew Greek, Latin, history, everything. There was something unspeakably comforting about her.

"Marianne?"

"What, honey?"

"Nothing. I guess I'll go upstairs."

"Talk to you later."

Emily hung up the phone, remembering too late that she had forgotten to find out what Marianne really wanted to tell her. Emily went back through the dining room and living room, then opened the door into the hall, looking around. Everything was in perfect order. In David's house. She felt giddy and steadied herself for a moment, a hand on a table. She started upstairs. On the landing, she caught sight of a figure and it made her jump. But it was only Esmeralda, who had come up the back stairs with fresh-ironed clothes. Esmeralda smiled at her, holding open the door to the bedroom for her. She went in, surprised to see the bed turned down.

18

"Hay mala?"

"Poquito." Boy, do I feel bad. The maid knows it, everybody knows it. Why the hell doesn't David?

Emily walked unsteadily toward the bed. Esmeralda put down the laundry and came over, helping her out of her clothes. She got into bed in her slip, huddling gratefully between the crisp sheets and under the billowing quilt. Esmeralda lit a fire in the parlor Franklin. A green twig sputtered. Emily drifted off. When she awoke, it was dark. Esmeralda must have come in, for she could dimly make out the fact that the curtains had been drawn. She could see the tea in its little Queen Anne silver service that David had long ago bought for her. She glanced at the lighted face of the clock. What time was it? The clock said nine-thirty. David hadn't come home, she had slept for five hours, and she felt disoriented, depressed.

Then it happened. The same voice said, "Hey, lady!" She screamed. She couldn't help herself. Flinging herself toward the table, she switched on the lamp. The room was empty. Nothing moved. Moments later, Esmeralda hurried in, her lined face full of concern, drying her hands on her apron.

"Señora?"

"There's someone in the house, Esmeralda!"

"No, señora!"

"Yes! Yes! I heard someone! God damn it, I heard someone in this house three times!" Why didn't she understand? Frightened, she tried to tell Esmeralda what had happened. Esmeralda comforted her, saying it was only a dream. Emily got up, putting on her robe. Had her husband telephoned? *No, señora.* Emily walked toward the window, pulling back the curtain and looking down at the garden, glowing in the lights from the breakfast-room windows. Where the hell was David?

"It's cold in my room," she said lamely to Esmeralda in the kitchen. She sat down, rubbing her arms. Well, Christ, it was no lie. She was absolutely freezing! Esmeralda nodded, frowning. Jesus, what was the matter with Esmeralda, anyway? The weather and the temperature of the house were two of her favorite topics of conversation. But now she avoided Emily's eyes, poured tea. Emily thought, I have a temperature. That explains everything.

19

She put a hand to her forehead, couldn't be sure. Emily drank her tea, picked up the phone and dialed Marianne. Roberta answered in her piping voice. No, Mommy was out at the movies with a friend. Emily put down the phone, annoyed that Marianne should have two friends on an evening when she herself felt as if she had only one.

She got a thermometer and put it in her mouth for a minute, then, remembering that it went up to ninety-something percent of where it was going in almost no time, she took it out. She tried to see the scale. Her eyes blurred. Then she saw the numbers quite clearly: 103°. No wonder she felt as if she had a chill! She went into the bathroom. Catching sight of her reflection, she was shocked at herself. And David thought she looked like a Vermeer painting, David, who said she never needed to wear make-up. She went back into the breakfast room and turned on the radio, willing to listen to anything.

That same sense of depression was still in the air, as if it waited patiently for nightfall, the way the fog waited outside the Gate, then, at the day's end, possessed the city. Yes, that was it. She herself was not the one who was depressed. Rather, the depression was an atmosphere, a disturbance. It was something that waited for her. No, it wasn't the house. She saw that now. The house was simply where it had found her.

She began to feel worse. Maybe David would want her on antibiotics. She picked up the phone and telephoned his office. The exchange answered. Had he left the office already? The girl at the exchange didn't know. Emily said impatiently, "I'm sure he's still there. He works late on Thursdays. Ring through, please. This is Mrs. Blake."

The phone rang a long time. Finally, the girl came back on the line with an apology. An error. She should have looked more carefully. Dr. Blake had left his office at six o'clock.

Emily put down the phone slowly. It was so obvious, it had never occurred to her. She remained sitting in the breakfast room until after eleven, when David finally returned. He came into the room, not realizing she was there.

"Who is she?" asked Emily.

20

He had been drinking. Heavily. She knew it as soon as she looked at him. Silence.

"I asked you a question," she said.

"All right. Her name is Jennie." He thought, She must realize that the only reason I'm telling her is that I love her. He stared at her, waiting for some reaction.

She sat there, motionless. She tried to think, couldn't. Part of her mind kept repeating the name he had blurted out. Her mind closed around it.

"Emmy—"

"It's all right."

Silence. It wasn't all right. Suddenly, he couldn't bear any more. "Emmy, I'm a doctor! Women come into my office and take off their clothes. I handle them. And don't let anybody give you any of that bullshit about how it's different when it's a doctor-patient relationship. You're still a man and she's still a woman and when you've got her stretched out naked on that table—"

"Don't."

"It's just that you know when she wants it and, for me, lots of the time, that was something I just had to have. That's as far as it went. Until this."

"Do you love her?"

"I just wanted to fuck her!" His speech was slurred. He was aware of it but couldn't help it.

"Don't."

"That word, baby, is in a class by itself, a cut above 'shit,' for which there is nonetheless much to be said."

"Don't." She felt deathly ill but couldn't bring herself to tell him about it.

"That's a great word. There's a tribe somewhere that yells it out at funerals, defecating in unison."

"I don't want to hear about words." Couldn't he see that she wasn't well?

"Shakespeare is words. The Bible is words."

"How long has this been going on?"

"Three months."

21

"That long."

She got up slowly and walked unsteadily away from him. He thought, All right, so I played around. Christ, I told her the truth! Her composure unnerved him. He couldn't deal with it. He felt angry at everything, the situation, himself, her.

"Is it over?" she asked.

He tried to answer. Lately, there were times when he had only to say something for the truth to run out of it. She turned and looked at him levelly. He lost his temper.

"I don't know whether it's over!"

"I want it to be over."

"Oh, *you* want!" Her composure began to infuriate him. "Well, I want a lot of things I can't have! A son, for instance!"

"David—"

"Go to hell!"

He turned away, strode to the door and left the room. She felt weak. Sick. And he hadn't noticed. She stood very still, trying to push away what she could not bear. She looked around the clean kitchen, at the sparkling surfaces, at the black oblong of the uncurtained window giving onto the little garden. To the left was the baker's stand with majolica they had collected in Italy, carrying it back on their laps in a crowded plane. Above it on two nails hung a majolica mask of Bacchus. David had bought it for himself in a little town—Viterbo—on the Amalfi drive, and he had laughed at himself, saying how ugly it was. Perhaps because in some way (neither of them had seen this at the time) it looked like him.

In the other room, David hesitated, wanting to go in to her. Then he heard a splintering crash and a cry. He ran toward the kitchen, shoving open the swinging door, and saw Emily down on her hands and knees, picking something up piece by piece, very carefully—brightly colored chunks of earthenware. He glanced up at the wall almost involuntarily and saw the bare nails where the mask had hung. Emily looked shaken, white. He ran to her, knelt down behind her, and seized her by the shoulders, trying to turn her around. He pulled her toward him. Her curled hands were filled with broken pieces of his mask, which she held out to him like a guilt offering.

22

"David, I'm *sorry!* Oh, God, David, I'm so sorry!"

"Honey, it's nothing! Honey, it doesn't matter to me at all. Emily, baby, the only thing in the world that matters to me is you, don't you know that?" He crushed her to him. "It's over baby, honest to God, it's over."

Slowly, she let him help her to her feet. He took the pieces from her and laid them on the sink. Comforting her, he led her from the room. He said, "The hell with it! If it made you feel better, I'm glad you broke it!" She looked at him with fear-struck eyes.

The mask had suddenly been flung across the room with terrible force, smashing itself to pieces against the wall.

I can't tell him, she thought. He won't believe me!

They went upstairs to bed.

He was awakened about an hour later by Emily screaming. He switched on the lights, grabbing her. She wrestled free of him, tried to get to the bathroom. David stumbled after her, holding on to her.

She shook him off, yelling, "I'm losing it!"

"What are you talking about?"

"I'm pregnant!"

Sirens. An ambulance. That strange, abrupt lateral motion of a stretcher. Injections. This was the hospital room. David wanted a boy. David had always wanted a boy. It was over. No, nothing. I can't. Take it away. I don't care. I'll eat tomorrow. No, it wasn't a nurse but a doctor. Hers. He patted her shoulder. Then she heard herself whisper, "Was it a boy?" and when he only nodded, she turned away and wept into her hands.

3

Marianne entered. She stood inside the curtains for a moment. Emily looked at her blankly, as if she didn't recognize her, and Marianne wondered if Emily was sedated. Marianne went to her, embracing her, leaning over the high hospital bed, conscious that Emily was being fed intravenously, that there were tubes. They both cried.

Then Emily said, "I found out. That's what you were going to tell me on the phone, isn't it?"

"We'll talk about it later, okay?"

"It's over," Emily said. "He told me it's over."

"Listen," Marianne said, ignoring her, "have you seen my earrings? Those diamond ones? I had them at your house that night after *Figaro*. Remember, they hurt and I took them off?" Emily vaguely remembered. "Well, what I want to know is, does your maid . . . um . . . take things?"

"Not so far as I know."

"Well, they're gone." She began describing them, explaining about the old-fashioned rose cut, how valuable they must have been in Lithuania, that they had belonged to her great-grandmother. She realized Emily was staring at her. "I'm sorry. I'm so stupid."

A nurse came in, holding open the door with her back, a tray of medicines in her hands. Visiting hours were over. Marianne kissed Emily lightly, then hurried out, went downstairs and got into her car.

The doctor insisted on keeping Emily in the hospital for observation, saying something about "retained products." The term was so distasteful to her, she couldn't bring herself to ask

24

him about it. She simply did as she was told, let them run tests, forced herself to eat and tried to catch up on her class reading about the Kwakiutl Indians. When the white settlers found them in the 1880s, they still hadn't invented the wheel, having no need for it. They went everywhere by water. Did they have the ritual dream of the bear? Probably. It was circumpolar, her text said. And the shaking booth? She couldn't remember. They had something, she was sure of it. Every culture had its own ways of manipulating the supernatural. Why? I mean, God, if they hadn't even invented the damn wheel! She looked at a picture of a demon in her text. The usual demon. Wild-eyed. Half-animal. Claws. No, wait! Not the usual demon. A witch! A witch's ride! But why a witch's ride in pre-Columbian America? Jesus, this wasn't only before Columbus. It was before Leif Ericson, before anybody! Her mind drifted. It was the sedatives they were giving her.

David came every day, sitting beside the bed, holding her hand. He seemed abstracted. He loves me. I don't care about anything else.

After three days, the doctor let Emily go home. She felt oppressed by a sense of guilt for having lost the baby. Absurd, but there it was. Worse, she blamed herself for what David had done. Some part of her whispered that she had failed him. The idea frightened her. She tried to put the whole thing out of her head. But David was her world, her reason for being. She would give him anything. All she needed to know was what he wanted.

His birthday was Friday.

She said to him, "Let's go out to dinner, okay? We'll get all dressed up and go to some place special."

"Honey, it's just one more birthday."

"I want to. Please?"

"All right."

He promised to be home by seven to change. But she wasn't going to take him out to dinner. He loved parties. She would surprise him with one. She spent an entire day on the phone, inviting what began as twenty people and ended as fifty. Remembering a mariachi band he had liked at a small Mexican restaurant, she hired them and got a caterer. They would need parking boys, not just because of the number of guests but to hide the cars.

The days raced by. There were a thousand things to do. The study floor was bare and she searched for an Oriental rug, first choosing a Sarouk, then a Kashan and finally settling on a Bokhara. It was delivered the day of the party, after David had left the house for the office. Suddenly, she thought she understood everything that had gone wrong between them. In some way, their lives had grown commonplace. He wanted excitement. She felt it now and that she could give it to him.

She had invited the guests for six-thirty, making them all promise to be on time. She had found herself a huge antique paisley shawl from Scotland and had a caftan made from it. Her thick gold hair was plaited in a crown on her head, encircled with a wreath of poppies and daisies.

The guests arrived, the women glittering in jewels, the men elegant in dark suits. A bartender filled their glasses with champagne while the mariachis sang. The room was full of warmth, laughter, and talk. The lights were low. Men took turns playing lookout. Every time a car drove up, there was a quick signal for silence. The room would go quiet with a lot of rapid shushing sounds and the lights would be switched off.

She heard Marianne's voice raised, laughing, telling stories.

"Words can be frightening. The Indo-European word for 'prick,' for example, was so dangerous that it was repressed completely out of existence."

A woman tried to change the subject but Marianne was not someone who could be interrupted.

"We must all be more careful with words. They can die on you. Take, for example, what happened to 'fuck' in the Army."

She was drunk. Emily eased her way through the crowd trying to get to her. Marianne trumpeted on:

"The art was to use it without any conceivable meaning. We said things like 'I perfectly fuck don't care.' Toward the end of my stay in quaint Heidelberg, it had even worked its way between syllables. If I ever go back to school, there's a fit subject for my thesis: On the Pejorative Use of 'Fuck' in the Armed Forces. And while I'm at it, where the fuck is David?" Emily forced a smile.

Emily knew some people would be late. They were. They

26

arrived shamefaced, mouthing excuses, expressing relief that David had not yet arrived. No one really expected him to be on time. Doctors were always late. Everybody knew that.

Besides, Maria Kodaly was there, and everybody was sure that she would play. She was a small woman in her seventies, with a cloud of blue-gray hair, resplendent in a silver lamé suit from Maison Mendessolle. Now she was holding court.

"Listen to me something! When I was a child, I was prodigy. They take me to the house of a famous man, very old. He plays a scale. I hear this outside and think, He's an old man. He doesn't know any longer how to play. He was Leschetizky, Chopin's star pupil. Every day, he practiced childish things. I had the first lesson and he said to me, 'To play the simplest thing perfectly is the most difficult thing in the world.'"

Someone asked her to play. She made a gesture. "I am retired." Everybody began insisting. Smiling, she made a reference to a famous but elderly French violinist whose recent performance had been a disappointment. She said to Emily in an undertone, "It was like stale French perfume, you understand?"

Her protestations were drowned out by demanding applause. Shrugging, she went to the piano, sat down and played Ravel's *Jeux d'Eau.* The room was filled with a multicolored rain, a downpour of iridescent sound. Then it was over. There was a roar of appreciation. It was eight o'clock. Emily slipped away to call David's exchange. He wasn't at the hospital. He had left the office two hours ago.

Emily returned to her guests with a glittering smile. She said, "I'm afraid David has a surprise for *us!* He has an emergency! Can you believe it?"

She knew they didn't. But it would give them something to pretend about. She moved among her guests, conscious of little eddies of silence surrounding her.

The caterer's maids were now serving the buffet. The conversation had softened. The note of excitement had somehow gone out of their voices. Emily made the rounds, making sure she talked to everyone. Aware that their eyes were following her, she tried to force herself to eat. Madame Kodaly came up to her, glancing at an emerald-studded watch, exclaiming at the time. It was only nine o'clock, but she had to leave. So did others.

Now there was no longer any pretense at surprise. The parking boys were bringing cars to the door. Emily's face ached from an evening of smiling.

By ten o'clock, most of the guests had left. When David drove up to the house and a parking boy ran up to help him out of his car, he knew what had happened. He went inside. Half a dozen guests were still there. They had all had a good deal to drink. They turned to greet him. A bartender hurried up, asking what he would like. One of the guests, a dentist who specialized in cosmetic work and dropped actors' names at parties, ran a hand through his thick wavy gray hair and said weakly:

"Surprise!"

Another man murmured, "I'll bet!" Then, realizing his voice had carried, he made a hurried excuse about having to leave, and the others immediately began asking for their coats. Emily saw them all to the door. When she went back into the living room, David was standing at a window, his back to her. She stood waiting.

Then she said, "I thought it was over."

He turned. "You don't understand."

"Don't I?"

Setting his mouth, he put down his glass, walked quickly out of the room and went upstairs. She thought, I've lost him. But those were just words. She could not lose him. She could not conceive of such a thing. Jennie was an abstraction, something in her way.

She went into the kitchen. Marianne hadn't left. She was sitting at the breakfast-room table drinking an Alka-Seltzer. Emily said with a helpless gesture:

"I can't give him up. I'll do anything to get him back. Anything."

Marianne looked at her steadily, saying nothing.

4

Marianne came by for her the next day. She said she had somewhere to go and wanted Emily's company.

"To go where?"

"Oh, some awful part of town."

"I don't want to go to some awful part of town."

"What do you want me to do, go alone?"

"Will you please tell me where I'm going?"

"I'm worried about those earrings. I'm beginning to think Roberta took them. I've simply got to know the truth."

Emily tried to get her to explain, but Marianne refused to say any more.

They drove in silence, Marianne taking advantage of stoplights to put on make-up. Then, with a quick look at Emily, she said, "You ought to talk to somebody. How about a marriage counselor?"

"No."

"Why don't you see a lawyer? That might shake him up."

"Marianne, *please!*"

"Emily, you've got a problem. You're going to have to decide what to do about it. I don't think you even know what you want."

"I want him back. But I don't want to talk about it any more." She was sorry she had ever said anything.

Marianne parked the car on a dirty street below Mission, and they got out and started walking, Marianne leading the way. They passed porno bookshops and an adult movie house. Next door, a girl of about fourteen lounged in a doorway. She wore shorts and built-up shoes and looked sullenly out at the passers-by, arms folded over big breasts, while a sign over her head flashed on and off, spelling out "Oral Love." A sailor from some foreign country walked by with a rolling gait, an earring in one ear—to protect him, Marianne said, from drowning.

"How far is it?"

Marianne consulted a piece of paper. "Another block."

They walked past a liquor store with a display window full of cheap wine. Two teenagers hurried past them, boys of about sixteen, giggling and pushing each other, their hair bleached, their eyebrows plucked and penciled. Ahead of them, the way was blocked by a group of boys and girls, heads shaved except for a kind of pigtail. Wearing long peach-colored robes, they danced back and forth barefoot, some banging on tambourines, others clapping rhythmically, chanting.

"Hare Krishna, Hare Krishna,
Krishna, Krishna, Krishna,
Hare Hare, Hare Rama,
Hare Rama, Rama Rama . . ."

Marianne pushed past them, pulling Emily behind her. As they reached the corner, they heard the squeal of brakes. Emily turned. People were running toward a stopped car. The driver, a boy in his twenties with dark, pockmarked skin, was scrambling out of the car, yelling and gesturing at the crowd, trying to explain. One of the boy dancers lay in the gutter unconscious, his eyes open and glazed, blood beginning to seep through his thin robe. The others continued dancing back and forth, oblivious. Emily tried to rush toward the boy. Marianne grabbed her arm. Trying to pull away, Emily said, "They didn't even see!"

"Come on!"

"We can't leave him there!"

"Honey, there's nothing we can do. And there's a squad car. See?"

They could hear the siren. The police car was already on its way down the street. Marianne yanked her away, then hurried them both down a side street lined with dilapidated old houses. Marianne, looking down at her paper, stopped in front of a flight of stairs. An old woman wrapped up in several different-colored sweaters sat on a broken kitchen chair on the sidewalk, feeding pigeons bits of popcorn which she pulled out of a bag and put between purplish lips. Pigeons fluttered around her. One sat on her breast. There were droppings on her clothes. The air was filled with rustling and cooing.

"Come on."

Marianne, a firm hand on Emily's elbow, trotted up the outside stairs, opened a heavy door. Inside, the stench of garbage. They climbed linoleum-covered stairs to the second floor. Marianne stopped at a door. They heard the crying of children, and from other apartments, loud music from different radio stations. Marianne knocked. The door opened a crack and a dark eye looked out at them.

Marianne said, "I'm Mrs. Milner. Jimbo sent me."

"Who's Jimbo?" Emily asked.

Marianne didn't answer. She pulled a bill out of her purse, gave it to the woman. The eye continued to stare at her. Quickly, she fumbled in her purse and pulled out another bill, thrusting it toward the crack in the door. Dark fingers snatched it. The door still remained open only a crack, the eye stared at her unblinkingly. Marianne hesitated, then thrust a third bill at the grasping hand. The door slammed shut. They heard the rattling of another chain. Then the door slowly opened on chaos. They walked in. The apartment was a shambles. The woman who had opened the door was Mexican. She had black hair, brownish skin, discolored teeth, and a face wrinkled into premature old age. There were half a dozen children in the room. From a television set, they heard applause and laughter and voices in Spanish. The woman led them toward a hanging curtain, pulling it aside and showing them into a cramped alcove with two broken wicker chairs and a little table with incense burning in a souvenir brass ashtray. The woman left, dropping the curtain behind her. Marianne sat down. Emily was reluctant, but Marianne made an insistent gesture at the other chair. The sound of voices crying and quarreling and the Spanish voices from the television set continued. From the next apartment, they heard the faint insistent sound of acid rock. Emily looked up to see one of the children, a young boy, standing in front of them. He was thin, barefoot, and dressed in ragged clothes. His dark, expressive eyes avoided her glance. Marianne said:

"Are you Lupe?"

Emily looked at Marianne, startled. The boy looked at Marianne blankly, not answering. The woman pushed aside the heavy curtain, coming back into the alcove, a baby balanced on her hip.

"You make fast, huh? Lupe, he tired today."

"Can you help me?" asked Marianne.

"He's only a boy! He can't be more than ten years old!"

"Eleven," said the woman. She padded away.

"What is this, anyway?" Emily got to her feet, raising her voice. Lupe looked at her, eyes fixed on her. "I want to get out of here!" she said loudly.

"Please. You're just upset."

"All right, I'm upset! Because I never thought you were such a fool!"

"Oh, stop it! You'll make him nervous and he won't be able to do anything." To Lupe, she said, "You see, I've lost a pair of earrings—"

"I want to leave! Now!"

"Jennie?" the boy asked Emily. It took Emily a moment to realize what he had said. Then she turned angrily to Marianne, who was staring at Lupe with her mouth open. "What did you tell him?" She demanded loudly.

The woman pulled aside the curtain, gestured. "You go now. Bad time. Later, okay?"

"I haven't talked to him yet! He hasn't said anything to me!" Marianne said. Swiftly, the woman slapped Lupe's face with all her strength. He began to cry, sobbing into his hands.

"*Hablas!*" she hissed at him, then turned and left, jerking the curtain closed behind her. Emily got up and went to Lupe, kneeling beside him, putting her hands on his thin arms.

Emily said, "I'm sorry. It's all right. It's all right, Lupe." He looked at her with a tear-streaked face. Now she saw for the first time that he had the hint of a harelip. His eyes were soft and luminous with long lashes sparkling with tears. Leaning toward Emily, he whispered:

32

"Bring me—" He stretched out a grimy hand, touching Emily's hair.

"Hair?" Thinking. Then she heard herself say, "A lock of hair?"

Lupe nodded, then whispered, "I fuck you good. Then I get rid of her. Okay, lady?"

She drew back, staring at him, incredulous. Had he really said it? His face was a child's face, trusting, yet fearful. He looked at her with profound innocence. No, he couldn't have said it. She sensed at the same time that Marianne hadn't reacted but she realized how close their faces had been, hers and Lupe's, and that he had been whispering to her. She looked at him, nonplussed. *Had* he said it? He brought his face as close to hers as he could. She caught the hint of a grin. Then he put his child's arms around her neck, his head pressed against hers, and whispered:

"I eat you, okay?" He licked her ear. A stab of unreal excitement went through her. She struggled to her feet, her hands shaking. The curtain was yanked aside, brass rings rattling. Annoyed, Marianne gave up and let the woman push them out the door.

On the stairs, she said to Emily, "Otherwise, she won't let us come back."

They went to a piano bar on Nob Hill, looking around after their eyes had adjusted to the dark to realize they were the only customers. A tired bartender switched lights on behind the bar. Bottles on mirrored shelves became visible. Music and darkness enfolded them. The room was rotating. Emily remembered that this was the Circus Bar. The motion made her dizzy and she tried not to look at the stationary walls. Marianne was pulling things out of her purse, searching for cigarettes. They ordered martinis. The bartender started to make small talk. Marianne ignored him. Emily couldn't bring herself to look at him. He trailed off, withdrew.

Emily said, "You told him!"

"I've never seen him before!"

"You told somebody." Then, when Marianne shook her head

slowly, studying her through a cloud of exhaled smoke, Emily locked her fingers together to keep her hands from shaking.

"What did he say to you?" Marianne asked. Emily didn't answer. She was trying to remember something. Had she met him before? "He whispered something to you," Marianne insisted. "What was it?"

"Why did you take me there?" Emily's voice rose. The bartender came toward them.

"Let's not talk about it any more, okay?"

"I want to talk about it. I want to know what the hell you thought you were doing."

"Two martinis straight up," said the bartender, setting down their drinks. Marianne paid him. "Everything all right, ladies?"

Emily didn't look at him. She was trying to remember something. Then it came to her and she got to her feet abruptly, her eyes wide, unseeing. "It's *him!*" she said loudly.

Marianne jumped up, taking hold of her firmly by the arms. "Sit down!" Shaking free of her, Emily said loudly:

"It's him! It's him!"

"I want you to sit down!"

The bartender said, "If you ladies got a problem, take it somewheres else, okay?"

"Shut up," Marianne said to him shortly.

"I'm just trying to tell you, polite like, that if you ladies can't keep it down—"

"Get your ass out of here," Marianne said.

"Lady, act nice or I throw you and your girl friend the hell outta here."

"Fuck you and the horse you rode into town on."

"That's *it.*" The bartender threw down a towel. Marianne took him by the arm and steered him away.

"Look, she just lost her baby. We're the only two people here. Now, why don't you be a good boy and go watch the ball game?"

"Try to keep it down, okay, lady?" He went away. Marianne went back to Emily, who was standing up, rubbing her hands together.

"Baby, will you sit down and drink your drink?" Emily didn't answer. Marianne pushed her back into the deep, upholstered

34

circular seat in the booth, sat down next to her, thigh to thigh, and lifted a glass to Emily's lips, making her drink.

Then Emily said, "I should have known right away. I guess it was just too disorienting . . . I mean, being there and talking to a boy—what is he, eleven—but he's the one. I know it!"

"What one, Emily?" Emily didn't answer. The bartender had turned up the Muzak, humming. Marianne watched Emily, smoking and drinking, silent. They heard the strains of an old Beatles song. Orpheus-like, it won back dead yesterdays.

Their eyes met. Emily said:

"You don't believe me."

"What one, Emily?"

"The voice I heard when we were on the phone! The night I lost the baby!"

"Emily!"

"You know I'm right. You know I'm always right about things like that!" True. If a voice came on television when Emily was in the other room, she would call out the name of the actor, even if it was a voice from the radio dramas of her childhood. Her memory for voices was infallible.

She asked, "Have you ever seen him before? Are you sure?"

"No, never."

"I know it's crazy, but could he have gotten in?"

"You know how David keeps that place, Marianne. We were locked out once and David himself couldn't find a way to get in! Besides, even if that weren't true, what the hell would the kid be doing in *my* house? I never heard of him. I didn't even know where we were going and the whole thing was last-minute anyway."

Marianne watched her, silent. Emily studied Marianne's expression. "You don't believe me."

"Would it be a favor to you if I were to say yes?"

Silence. A war of glances. Then:

"You heard what he said. *How did he know her name?*"

"For chrissakes, Emily, he's a *sensitive!*"

" 'Sensitive' is not exactly a word I would have thought of in connection with him." When Marianne looked blank, Emily said, "Then, you didn't hear what else he said to me."

"What else *did* he say?"

"Never mind." She took a deep breath, then a big gulp of her drink. Frowning, she asked Marianne, "How did you find out about him?"

"I told you. Jimbo."

"Who's Jimbo?"

"Jimbo was off the wall. He was a big, beautiful black—some kind of prince or something from Nairobi. I knew him at Berkeley. Then he turned up in Heidelberg. Funny. You wouldn't expect someone like that—I mean, with his background and being a medical student and all—to talk that way."

"What way?"

"He was superstitious. But he didn't seem to be. What I mean is, he made everything sound very reasonable and scientific, so that you didn't know until you were halfway into one of those crazy conversations that he sort of believed in all those nutty things. Anyway, that was when Matthew shot himself. God, it was insane. He wrote me a suicide note and mailed it. He *mailed* it! Then—bang. He was conscious when they got him to the hospital. You know what he said? 'I botched it.' The doctor tried to stop him from talking. I think they do that because of the bleeding. He went right on. He said he had remembered to feel for the heartbeat with his fingers. And then, he just died. After that, I broke up with Vince. I just didn't want to see him any more. He looked different. Just different. That happens after you stop loving somebody. It really happens. Well, I was beside myself. I had the insurance and Roberta, and all I wanted to do was come home. Anyway, Jimbo came by the night before I left and a lot of us went to the Bar Nach Ocht together and Jimbo said if I ever needed help here, to go see this boy. That's when he gave me the address." Marianne stubbed out her cigarette, snapped her purse shut. "Come on, drink up. I've got to get back and pick up Roberta."

Crazy Marianne. Lovable. But crazy. She had left her husband in Berkeley, where he was finishing up a seminar, and gone on ahead with Roberta to Heidelberg, getting work with the Army so they could live abroad for a couple of years. She had gone off the deep end and gotten involved with soldiers. "I was the Daugh-

36

ter of the Regiment! Jesus Christ!" Laughing and coughing, she had described herself as the *cloaca maxima* of Heidelberg. Then her husband came to town.

"Poor Matthew," said Marianne, remembering.

"You let him walk into it."

"What could I do?"

"Tell him . . . Why didn't you?"

"I kept thinking somebody else would. Isn't it ironic that the one time the wife hopes somebody will tell the husband, no one does?" Then, when Emily bit her lip, she said, "I'm sorry."

"It's all right." David. After Marianne had introduced them in Heidelberg, they had traveled. The Alps, Spain, everywhere. She remembered a plain outside Seville where the wind was so hot they said it could kill a man without blowing out a candle. David.

Marianne got up and Emily followed her out. In the car, Marianne held out a hand.

"Friends?"

"Friends." Emily hesitated. Then: "That boy . . . You won't go back there again?"

"I just thought he could help you."

"Help *me?* Do you mean to tell me—?"

"All right, I blew it! I took you there thinking he might be able to do something. I suppose I just made a fool of myself. I certainly didn't accomplish anything."

That night, when Emily got home, she found Marianne's rose-cut earrings lying on her nightstand. In plain sight.

5

David slept. Emily put out a hand, resting it on his shoulder, lying close to him, comforted by his smell. She whispered his name. His breathing continued deep and regular. She touched his cheek, running her squarish fingers over the rough stubble of his beard. He did not stir. She lay awake, trying to think. Had she lost him? She felt herself suffocated by fears. At the same time, she was afraid to let him see how she felt, knowing it could drive him away. She got up quietly and went to the bathroom, closing the door softly, then sat down in a slipper chair, trying to be calm. She thought of the boy. What was his name? Lupe. Yes. All right, she was hallucinating. But wait a minute. Jennie. He had said, Jennie. And Marianne heard it. Was she hallucinating, too? Quiet. Shh. But her mind wouldn't listen. A lock of hair. A lock of *hair,* for God's sake! And what the hell did he mean, he'd get rid of her?

She did not fall asleep until it was already light outside. When she awakened, David was gone. She began thinking. About David. Her mind raced. It was as if everything that had ever happened between them were being played back on a monitor at high speed. At the same time, it seemed as if she were listening to a rapid, incoherent voice somewhere in her head. Shut it off! Impossible. No, I'm not hungry, Esmeralda. She didn't go to her classes. She couldn't sleep. Her skin prickled, her flesh crawled. At first, she was stern with herself, almost sadistic, then weak, desperate, like a child. She would go into David's closet and bury her face in his clothes. She thought often of suicide. It was an anxiety attack, and it lasted for three days. Then, unable to bear it any longer, she picked up the phone and called a psychiatrist whose name she knew, Dr. Lambert Jones. She said to the service, "Yes. It's an emergency."

She arrived twenty minutes early for a three o'clock appointment, and when she was shown into his office, her hands were ice-cold. He was a small man with tinted glasses and a thin mustache. His voice had almost no resonance at all. She did not like his looks and wondered whether that would keep him from being of help to her. He gestured at a chair, placing himself opposite her in another chair, no desk between them. She felt vulnerable, exposed. As with the impossibility of measuring simultaneously the speed and position of an electron, analysis deflected an emotion from its course. One could not really put what one felt into words. Still, she had to have help. She plunged in and told him everything. Then she said:

"I want you to tell me what's the matter with me."

"Well, if names help, it's what we call 'obsessive rumination.' "

"Why am I doing it?"

"As a way of not thinking about something painful. We all exhibit neurotic behavior from time to time. In this case, I'm quite sure it's temporary. We have to remember that a neurosis always has a function. It's self-protective. I think what your husband told you about himself triggered something in your unconscious, something you do not want to think about, so that the greater the pressure from the unconscious, the greater the effort of the neurosis to cover it up. Or, as we say, to repress it."

"I don't feel I'm hiding anything from myself."

"Then the neurosis must be very successful."

Answers like that made her impatient. "What about the voice?"

"Let's leave that for a moment."

"I don't want to leave it. I heard that voice before I knew."

"Or before you allowed yourself to admit you knew."

"And the boy? Lupe?"

"He offered you a magical solution. Isn't that why you consulted him in the first place?"

"I did not consult him at all." Wasn't he listening? "I went there because Marianne took me. And she heard him say 'Jennie.' "

"She told you that?"

"Yes!"

"Because you wanted to hear it, perhaps?"

Circles. Bullshit. "I want to see her. That woman."

"Jennie?"

"Yes."

"I thought you told me you didn't know her."

"I could find her."

"I wonder if that would be wise."

"I want to see her." She got to her feet suddenly.

"We still have some time left," he said.

"I have to go now." She left the office, closing the soundproof door firmly behind her.

She would do it on Thursday, when he pretended to stay late at the hospital. He would know her car. She went to Hertz and rented a different one, waited in the lot where he kept his Mercedes. At six-ten, he came downstairs. Heart pounding, she started following him. Absurdly easy. She followed him in the fast-moving line of cars on Pine, staying right behind him, perfectly sure he couldn't see her.

At the foot of Russian Hill, he turned right. Here, there was less traffic and she followed him at a greater distance. Then she saw him turn down Lombard. Steep, red-bricked, it was a street that serpentined for a long block past beautifully landscaped terraced gardens, behind which stood squarish houses. The street was impossibly difficult to drive. Only a tourist would turn down it, unless, of course, one were going to one of those houses.

Quickly, Emily drove to the corner, made a U-turn, and doubled back along Hyde. At the intersection of Hyde and Lombard at the top of the hill, she glanced to her left and saw David's car parked a few houses down. She could see the address. She wrote it down carefully.

The next day, Emily went to City Hall and checked the tax rolls. The house was listed as belonging to Ludlow, Ms. Jennie. Ludlow. She thought for a moment, then went to the Legion of Honor Museum, where she was a docent, and checked their private list of contributors. Anyone living in such a house was probably on it. There it was. Ludlow, Jennie. Following the Lombard Street address was an alternate one: the Western Women's Club. Emily herself was a member, though she hadn't been there in years. But on the list was a familiar name: old Mrs. Prentice who lived down the street from her. And Mrs. Prentice was abroad. Conveniently.

She thought, I have to see her. I have to meet her. Home again, she brushed her long hair, twisting it into a loose knot, powdered her face, touched up her lipstick and put on her Chanel suit. Then she got into her car and drove to Jennie's.

She walked up the wooden steps, rang a jangling old-fashioned bell. A maid answered the door.

"I'm Mrs. Geiger," said Emily. "Mrs. Prentice from the Western Women's Club suggested I call."

She was shown into a sitting room. The blinds were drawn. She waited. Her heart began to race. She had trouble breathing. She thought, Why am I doing this? She wanted to leave. But it was too late. She heard a door open.

"Mrs. Geiger?"

A slender, cool white hand. Red, red hair. A mass of curls. What was she, twenty-five? She found herself unable to take her eyes off the cloud of red hair. "Mrs. Geiger?" she heard Jennie say again.

"Mrs. Prentice sent me."

"I didn't know she was in the country."

"She isn't. Before she left, she helped us draw up a list. We're collecting for Muscular Dystrophy." Emily herself collected for it. She took one of her own collection forms out of her purse and offered it to her. "I collect in my own neighborhood. We just need someone for your block." Jennie took the form, glancing at it. Emily's eyes fastened on her greedily.

"It must be a mistake," Jennie said. "We already have someone here collecting for it."

"I'm sorry!" Emily took back the form, looking at her with a fixed smile. Her eyes studied the white skin, the light-blue eyes.

"I wish I'd known you were coming. We could have had a drink."

"Another time."

41

"It's just that I'm having some treatments for my face—"

She's meeting him now. She knew she must have turned pale because Jennie looked at her and said, "Are you feeling all right?"

She clutched her purse, realizing that it was full of credit cards, personalized checks, letters, and everything said, Mrs. Blake, Mrs. David Blake. She turned abruptly, starting toward the front door. She closed her eyes for a moment. She felt a cool hand touching her forehead.

"Normal. You looked like you had a temperature."

She forced herself to open her eyes, to smile. "I'm quite all right, thank you."

The hand touched the side of her head. "Your hair is so beautiful," Jennie said.

"So is yours." Emily's eyes were riveted on it. She stretched out a hand, unable to help herself, and twisted a lock of it between her fingers.

"I hope we meet again."

"I'm sure we will."

In the car she regained her composure. She waited. Then she saw Jennie coming out of her garage, driving slowly down the red brick road. She turned right toward Pine. Emily followed her. At a distance.

Jennie parked in the Union Square garage. Emily followed her on foot, sure she was headed for David's office. But then Jennie surprised her, turning to go into a building with a large red door. Elizabeth Arden. Treatments for her face. She meant a facial. Then, Jennie must be meeting David later. She was obsessed with the idea of confronting them together. She would have to wait, follow her when she left. Waiting, she window-shopped on Post Street. She watched the door to Elizabeth Arden very carefully. Jennie did not come out. An hour passed. Emily was sure she had missed her. Turning, she walked toward the beauty salon, clutching her purse. She would go into Elizabeth Arden herself. She would make sure.

The receptionist was on the phone. Thank God they're always on the phone. She stole a quick glance at the appointment book, chose the last name on the page.

"I just want to say a word to my friend Mrs. Schwartz," Emily said, going on inside. It didn't matter to her whether Jennie saw her. She would simply say, What a coincidence! and then go on outside and keep waiting. She had to confront her with David. That was what mattered.

She walked down a corridor, cubicles on either side. Then she heard Jennie say, "I don't know why I'm letting you do this. I only came in for a facial."

"But it *has* to be done." A man's voice with the familiar, unmistakable cadence. David once told her someone had devised a way for a computer to pick it up on a voiceprint.

The voice said, "Comfy?"

"With you? Always."

"Eunuchs. We're just playthings. Fun but safe."

An answering laugh. Out of the corner of her eye, Emily saw snipped red ringlets on the polished floor. Suddenly, her throat was so dry, it hurt. The curtain was drawn. She reached down, snatched up a red lock of hair and stuffed it in her purse. Afterward, she would never be able to explain, even to herself, why she had done it. She walked quickly back, left the place and going to the garage, called Marianne.

"I've got to see you. I've just made an awful fool of myself. Can I come over?"

"I'm leaving in about ten minutes to pick up Roberta. It's half-day today. And after that, I promised to take her to Blum's."

"Hell."

"Why don't you meet me there?"

"Blum's?"

"She may change her mind. There's some new place she's been talking about. Meet me at the school. Half an hour."

Emily arrived at the convent school before Marianne. She sat down on a bench to wait. Across the playground, she could see a knot of children playing on a Junglegym and swings, supervised by a nun. Roberta came running toward her on thin, gangling legs, arms outstretched, and gave her a kiss.

"Hi, doll."

"Hi, Aunt Emily. Did you come instead of Mommy?"

"No, she'll be here. Any minute."

43

"She promised to take me—"

"I know. Can I go, too?"

Grinning, Roberta threw her arms around Emily. Emily picked her up, hugging her. "My! Such a big girl!" Then, over Roberta's shoulder she caught sight of one of the children across the playground standing apart from the others. He stood quite still and he was looking at her. It was Lupe. There was no doubt about it at all. What was he doing here? Slowly, she put Roberta down. "Honey—"

"Mommy!" Roberta had caught sight of her mother and, wresting free, raced away in the opposite direction. Emily turned. Marianne was coming toward them. Scooping up Roberta, Marianne strode toward her.

"Am I late?"

"I just got here. Marianne, look—" Emily turned back toward the playground. Lupe was gone. The Junglegym and swings were surrounded by a wide apron of lawn. Emily's eyes raked the grounds. He was nowhere in sight.

Marianne said, "Look at what?"

Roberta ran off to get her book bag. Emily said, "That boy. Does he go to school here?"

"What boy?"

"Lupe."

"Of course not. What are you talking about?"

"He was standing over there. With the other children. I just saw him."

"It must have been someone else."

"It was *him!* He was just standing there, watching me."

"I don't know what on earth he'd be doing *here*. This is a private school. And he lives miles away."

She started to say something, then caught herself. If she insisted, Marianne would give in. Marianne would shrug and say, All right, I believe you. ("Because you wanted to hear it, perhaps?") She let it go.

It turned out Roberta did have another place in mind, Ghirardelli Square.

"That's all the way downtown!"

"Mommy, you *promised!*"

44

"I guess I wasn't listening. I say yes to anything for the sake of peace. That's the story of my life."

They went to Blum's anyway, and over ice cream and coffee, began to plan Roberta's birthday party for the following week. It had to be a picnic and it had to be at the beach. Roberta was adamant. Marianne took out a stub of pencil and started writing on the back of an envelope.

"You're going to be ten and that means ten little girls. Now, let's make up a list."

"I want Aunt Emily!"

"Thanks, honey."

"Next? What about Sharlene?"

"I don't like Sharlene."

"She invited you to her party."

"I didn't want to go."

"You have to ask her." Marianne started to write down the name. "How do you spell it, with an 's' or a 'c'? It looks wrong both ways."

The waitress came by with the check.

"My treat," Emily said. She reached for her purse, then remembered she had left it in the car. They had come in Marianne's. "My purse," she said.

"I know. I just hope you remembered to lock the car."

"Don't worry. I did."

Afterward, they went back to the convent school for Emily's car and Emily followed them home and had a drink with Marianne while they listened to records. Marianne played an old record of Schwarzkopf singing "Voi Che Sapete." They sat on the floor next to the stereo, listening. Tears came to Marianne's eyes. She said, "Isn't it awful? I know every note of that music but when I open my mouth, this awful cawing comes out. Look at me! I'm thirty-two and all I can do is make my own Christmas cards!" She began crying, then coughing.

"Honey, it's all right. It's all right."

Marianne stopped crying. Emily reached in her purse for a Kleenex, handing it to her. She frowned.

Marianne said, "What's wrong?"

"Nothing."

45

Marianne wiped her eyes and blew her nose. "There! Now we've both made fools of ourselves! Which reminds me—what did *you* do?"

"Oh, nothing."

"Come on."

"I don't want to talk about it."

"Let's put it this way: tell me or I'll break your arm."

"I really don't want to talk about it, okay?"

The phone rang. Marianne struggled to her feet.

"Make yourself a fresh drink."

"No, I really have to go." She left quickly. When she got to the car, she searched her purse, finally emptying everything out on the seat. It was no use. It was gone. The lock of hair.

6

The day of Roberta's party, Emily had a class in the morning. Professor Hindley, a somber-suited man with pince-nez and a limp, who had studied under the anthropologist Elkins from Sydney, Australia, was doing a paper on psi phenomena among aborigines. He needed a control group, and several of the students in Emily's class were chosen, among them Emily.

The test was simple. It was conducted in two different rooms. When Emily's turn came, she found herself seated alone at a table in one room. There was no means of communication except for a buzzer which she was to push when she was ready for the professor in the next room to concentrate on a playing card. These cards had been taken out of a sealed packet and put into a machine which selected them one by one at random. There were twenty-five cards divided into five symbols: a cross, a star, a circle, a square, waves. Professor Hindley talked to her about standard deviation, critical ratio, and probability. She did not understand what was being said to her, and paid very little attention. Excusing himself, he went into the other room.

There was a tablet on the desk in front of her. She pressed the buzzer, wrote down the first card that came to mind (circle), and then continued doing this for fifteen minutes. Her mind was a blank and she wrote down the names of the cards as fast as she could—pressing the buzzer, writing down names, pressing the buzzer, writing down names. After fifteen minutes of rapid work, she was exhausted. The door opened and Professor Hindley smiled, thanking her.

She called Marianne afterward to make arrangements to pick up Roberta.

"How did you do?" Marianne asked.

"I flunked."

"How can you flunk?"

"Do I know? Listen, I guessed something like six hundred lousy cards and I was about ninety percent off!"

"How much do they pay if you win?"

"They don't pay anything. All in the interests of science."

"Fuck 'em."

Emily's score was so abnormally low, Professor Hindley examined the results with interest. Altogether, there had been 625 trials. Mean chance would have given Emily a score of $1/5 \times 625$, or 125. But Emily had scored only 16.

Professor Hindley tried displacement. Perhaps there had been some kind of a lag, and if he measured her guesses against the *previous* card, the score would more closely approximate chance. He ran a check on that and was rewarded with the discovery that the score was 121, well within the framework of chance. That was the answer. For some strange reason, Emily must have been guessing the previous card at the time when she was supposed to be guessing the one that he was concentrating on.

An associate named Eleanor Hayes, a bespectacled spinster, meticulous about her work, noticed something odd. She went over the results again, trying *forward* displacement. The professor was just putting on his coat to go out to lunch when Miss Hayes called him over, saying, "You're not going to believe this."

She showed Professor Hindley a different score. It had been arrived at by measuring Emily's guesses against the card the random sorting machine *hadn't yet selected.* Taking this tack, out of 625 cards checked against Emily's notes, *601 of her guesses were accurate.*

They checked everything over together several times, working in absolute silence. There was no doubt about it. They had no explanation. But the statistical odds against such a performance were almost incalculable. They ran into the trillions.

Professor Hindley said, "You understand what this means. We were testing her for telepathy. There isn't any telepathy involved here, since the machine hadn't yet selected the card, so there was no way I could have thought of it."

"Yes. It's precognition."

The professor thought of the results Rhine had achieved with Gloria Stuart and Shakleton. They had been remarkable. This far surpassed those records.

"I want to get her back immediately," he said. He was quite excited.

Later, Emily went by to pick up Roberta for the party. She waited in the marble lobby of the convent, hearing nuns' voices raised in a Gregorian chant. Sister Serena rustled toward her, saying, "Could you possibly wait? Just for fifteen minutes? The children are finishing an examination."

Sister Serena escorted her out. Emily turned, seeing a workman with a bucket of soapy water scrubbing with a brush at the convent wall, where somebody had crudely scrawled something, a cross surmounted by a circle.

"What is that, Sister?"

"Oh, you know how people like to scrawl on walls."

"I mean, that design. I've seen it before."

"Nothing but an old superstition."

Celtic. Of course. Now she remembered. It was like an ankh, yet different. "But what does it mean?"

Sister Serena was hesitant. Someone had been playing pranks. The night before, flickering lights had been seen in the churchyard next door, and when a priest went to investigate, he found a charred circle of broken crucifixes. "I guess that's why someone drew on the wall."

Now it came back to her. "It means 'God have mercy on us,' doesn't it?"

"Yes." With a little nod of her head, the nun went back inside. Emily descended the stone stairs, looking around. The fog was coming in. She was sure it would be the same down at China Beach and felt annoyed that Marianne had insisted on going through with the picnic anyway. She was getting some of the children, as well as the food. Emily was to pick up Roberta and three others at the convent.

Emily shivered, folded her arms, looked briefly down at her watch, and then walked to the red brick Romanesque church next door. It was empty, filled with pale light from the high, clear windows. She herself was no longer a practicing Catholic but still felt more comfortable entering as a worshiper rather than as a sightseer. A side door opening onto the little walled cemetery was ajar. She went toward it.

Outside, the grounds were dense with yew trees. Fog was beginning to obscure everything. Then she heard it, the sound of an instrument, rather like a flute playing softly. She stopped, entranced. The music had the character of an ancient melody. She listened, rapt. Six notes up, three notes down. The melody was repeated. It stopped. She looked around. There was no one there.

She walked slowly among monuments and tombstones. Behind a hedge was a marble bench. She looked around, seeing a small stone vault with a heavy rusted metal door. She walked toward it, curious, her footsteps crunching in the gravel. On both sides of the old doorway were carved stone angels, each with a fell of moss. The face of one was shattered, the other was defaced, so that what had once been a smiling angel now had a strangely offensive look. The door to the tomb, covered with graffiti, was slightly ajar. Emily reached out and touched it. The door opened inward with a creaking sound.

An oblong of light made the worn floor visible. In a moment, her eyes would adjust to the dark, and she would be able to make out the marble shelves. The tomb must be abandoned. No coffin would ever be left in a crypt with an open door. She remembered something (superstition or fact?): that the original purpose of gravestones was to keep the dead from rising up again. Then something moved in the light and she was overcome with a dread such as she had never felt. Lupe was standing there, grinning up at her. He opened his fly.

"Good place, huh? Come on, nobody see."

She thought, He followed me! No, that was impossible. She had come there on impulse. And she knew the place. There was only one way in. The gates had been locked for years and the walls were very high. An almost liquid terror flooded through her.

"Hey, you like my cock?" He had pulled it out of his pants, and now stood there in front of her, stroking it and smiling up at her insolently. She looked at the boy, incredulous. "You like it, huh?"

50

It was huge, erect, and straining. She could almost see the throb of a pulse beating along the swollen veins. No, it wasn't possible, not in a boy that age. She would have to ask David but she was sure—no, she couldn't ask David, what was she thinking of? But a boy like that, if he said anything, if people knew that she had once been to see him . . . ?

Her knees felt weak. It was absolutely necessary to stop him from talking. She tried to speak. The words wouldn't come. She would be reasonable. Why was he following her? He looked thin, undernourished. Money. That was it. He wanted money. She would give him money, tell him that he had misunderstood. After all, he came of another culture. She tried to avoid looking at his hand. How could he keep doing that?

The place stank, as if from a memory of . . . what? Putrefaction? There was a chink of light. Her eyes, accustomed now to the dark, made out his goat's face. The harelip was marked. When she first noticed it, she had shrugged it off. Now it was different. His face was disgusting, lascivious, the face of evil. She couldn't look away. His lips moved.

"You like it, huh? Hey, you really like it, right, lady?"

She tried to speak, tried to shake her head. When he spoke, his breath was foul—rotten teeth, sour stench, rancid oil. From under the thin green sleeveless undershirt, the stink of sweat.

"Come on." He backed into the tomb, motioning to her, jerking his head.

Suddenly, a cat mewed, rubbing itself against him. The cat had a dirty blue velvet collar and a silver bell. Tinkle, tinkle.

"Hey, you got me that hair. Now I'm gonna fuck your guts, and after that I take care of everything."

Then, as if she had broken free of invisible bonds, she turned and ran, stumbling through the churchyard, back into the church, wrenching open the door. There was someone coming out of the confessional, an old woman. She turned, uncertain. There was no one else anywhere. She didn't know what to do. She had to tell someone. She looked at the confessional, then ran toward it, pulling aside the curtain, kneeling her way into the booth.

"Father," she said. "This isn't a confession, but I simply have to speak to you. Something quite terrible just happened." She

51

waited. "Father?" No answer. She hesitated, rapped on the closed wooden grating, then emerged from the confessional and went around to the other side. Someone must be in there—an old woman had just made her confession. "Father?" She glanced at the other side. The curtain was open. There was no one there.

Sister Serena helped Roberta into a hooded coat, three other little girls clustered nearby. Emily forced a smile.

"We'd better hurry, honeybunch, or we'll be late." She thanked the nun. They hurried out. She had to talk. She would talk to Marianne. Yes.

Marianne was spreading out a cloth on the damp beach near the fire, taking food out of a hamper, asking why in hell they had to go to the beach on a day like this, as if the whole idea had been Emily's. Emily said, "At least, the wind isn't up."

"Hungry?"

"No. Thanks."

"What's wrong?"

The girls were out of earshot. Emily said carefully, kneeling on the wet sand next to Marianne, "I saw him again."

"Who?"

"That boy. Lupe."

"You went back?"

"Back where? No, I didn't go back." Make her meet your eyes. "At Roberta's school."

"In the playground again?"

"No! In the cemetery!"

"Cemetery?"

"I had to wait. For Roberta. I went next door. And there he was!"

"In the cemetery?"

"Yes!"

"What was he doing there?"

She doesn't believe me!

Marianne took hold of her hands gently, eyes on hers, those gray, wise eyes. "Emily? What was he doing there?"

"Do I know?" She forced herself to laugh.

"Well, what happened?"

It was as if she were in a trap. It was all senseless. She thought, I must stop thinking. I must try to think about nothing until I am calm.

"Emily, what's *wrong?*"

"I wish everybody would stop asking me what's wrong!" She turned away and, plunging her cold hands into the pockets of her coat, walked down the beach. Above her were rocky cliffs. Gulls screamed. Emily turned and saw Marianne and the children in the distance, a huddle of bright colors around a pale fire on the cold gray stretch of sand, fog blanking out the straits, only the grayish waters visible near the shore, lap-lapping, lap-lapping. Then she heard it, the sound of an instrument like a flute, playing very softly. It was the same ancient melody as before. Emily craned her neck, trying to see where the sound was coming from. Above her, she saw what looked like the mouth of a shallow cave. Marianne came up behind her, carrying a hot dog and a soft drink. She held out the food, asking, "Sure?"

"No, really. Listen."

Marianne listened. But the music was drowned out by the sound of girls running toward them, playing kickball.

"What?"

"Wait."

One of the girls kicked the ball hard in the opposite direction, and they all ran away again, their yelling growing fainter.

"Listen."

Marianne listened, frowning. "I don't hear anything."

"It's stopped."

"Roberta, *don't!*" Marianne ran toward the girls. The flute-playing began again. Emily listened. When it stopped, she walked back toward the group, the melody still in her head, repeating itself.

She thought, He's watching me. She was afraid. She stayed very close to Marianne, unable to bring herself to say anything.

At four o'clock, she saw with relief that it had begun to drizzle, and the party broke up. She drove three of the girls to their houses, then went directly home. Only when the door was locked did she feel safe. The sound of the phone made her jump.

It was Professor Hindley, calling to explain about her score on the test. At first she did not understand what he was trying to tell her. She listened while he repeated his explanation, her mind elsewhere. Then she reacted to a single word: precognition.

"There must be some mistake."

No, there wasn't any mistake, Professor Hindley assured her. Three professors had gone over the results together. She did not want to discuss it with him. At all.

"Of course, we're very eager to make more tests—"

She declined. Firmly. He did not understand. If it were a question of schedule, they would be more than happy to adjust to hers. A nameless fear tightened in her throat.

"I'm sorry. It's just not something that would interest me."

"But if one has a real gift, Mrs. Blake—"

"I don't have any gift," she said quickly. What he was saying disturbed her in a way she could not explain. She pretended someone was at the door and put an abrupt end to the conversation.

She waited, living only for the moment David came home, the David who never met her eyes any more. He didn't return until eleven. Then he went straight to bed, saying he didn't want anything to eat. He could not bear hurting her. She read pain in his eyes. He had a hunted look. She thought, Oh, God, if I could only help him. But there was nothing Emily could do for David. Except let him go.

She went into the bathroom, locked the door and knelt down on the floor, pressing her head against the cool porcelain of the sink, running the water so he wouldn't hear her crying. When does it end? she thought. When do you stop caring?

7

The next day, she went shopping. Aimlessly. She walked up Grant Avenue and then into the florist's to have a look. At first, she didn't realize someone was calling her because the voice had said, "Mrs. Geiger." Then she turned and saw Jennie smiling at her.

"You remember me?"

"Yes. Yes, of course I do."

Jennie was wearing a sort of turban with a wimple that half covered the right side of her face. It was pulled under her chin and around her neck and gave her face a narrow mediaeval look.

"I *knew* we'd run into each other again. Isn't that funny? How's Muscular Dystrophy?"

"Fine. Just fine."

"I was worried about you the other day."

"I'm quite all right. Really." The aisle was narrow. She waited for Jennie to give her room to pass. Flustered, she realized she was supposed to say something. Gesturing at the dogwood, she exclaimed, "Isn't it fantastic? Every year, I come in here to look. In fact, I come in here every time I pass by. The flowers are simply *incredible...*" There. Now she could get by Jennie on the pretext of looking at something. But Jennie stopped her.

"Then I just have to show you something." Jennie took her elbow, steered her toward a kind of humid dark grotto, then pointed to a thick, fleshy plant with a greenish flower like a cymbidium. "Look! Did you ever see one?"

"Dionaea muscipula," murmured a clerk, crowding past them, his arms filled with a dense, curly fern.

"You know what it is, don't you?"

55

"No."

"A Venus-flytrap! See that sticky part there, like a tongue? It eats flies! It actually *eats* them. Look at it."

Jennie stretched out a delicate hand. Emily's eyes fastened on the lacquered nails. At the same time, she thought, Why is her hair covered? Emily turned away then, feeling suddenly closed in.

"You don't like it?"

"Not really." Emily shuddered. "I prefer violets!" she said, catching sight of some.

"Violets it is!" Before Emily could stop her, Jennie had picked up a little fragrant bunch and was pinning it to her lapel, saying to the clerk at the same time, "Just put this on my bill. And I'll take this." Jennie reached out to another plant, breaking off a small blossom.

"Don't!" said Emily.

"What's the matter?"

"It's nothing."

Jennie looked at her, puzzled, putting the blue blossom on her own lapel. Emily caught sight of the manager talking to someone. If he saw her, he would address her by name. Trapped, she averted her face, stepped behind a palm frond.

"Is something wrong?"

"It's so close in here. I think I need some air."

The manager had gone behind the counter. Emily saw her chance. Swiftly, she walked toward the entrance, then out onto the street. Jennie followed her, a concerned look on her face.

"You look pale again."

"I'm really quite all right."

"You ought to sit down."

"It's nothing. Honestly." But her knees were weak. She told herself it was the strain of pretense. "I'll just get some coffee."

"I'll go with you. May I?"

There was no way out. Emily started toward Sutter, Jennie alongside her. There was a coffee shop a block away. But she was feeling quite strange. She knew that she was walking very slowly.

"You don't need coffee. You need a drink."

Emily almost laughed. It was certainly true. Jennie steered her into a dark Oriental bar and they sat down in a booth. When they

56

had ordered, Jennie pulled off her gloves and said, "May I tell you something? You have the loveliest hair I've ever seen." Emily felt an absurd impulse to laugh, stifled it. Jennie noticed, said, "What is it? Did I say something funny?"

"No. No, not at all."

"I suppose you're going to tell me it's a wig."

"No, it's perfectly real."

A girl in a gold mandarin jacket brought them drinks. Sitting back, Emily sipped her martini, studying Jennie.

"Feeling better?"

"Yes. Yes, thank you." Watching her, Emily unaccountably found herself enjoying the role she was playing. A kind of hectic excitement rose in her. They talked about flowers, about the countryside, about Europe, shopping. Suddenly, she wanted to know everything about her rival. Anonymous, she felt light-headed. She sat in a bright, empty shell of expectation. She felt she had to find out something, anything.

There was a pause. Emily said, "Do you do anything? It isn't possible. It must take all your time to look that lovely."

"I'm not so lovely today." Jennic untied the chiffon from around her neck, pulled away the wimple and exposed three wide ugly gashes running down her cheek, from the corner of her right eye all the way to her chin. Emily gasped.

"My God!"

"It was a cat. I don't know how it got into the house. I gave it cream. It kept purring, rubbing itself against my leg. I bent down to pet it. The purring was so loud, you wouldn't believe it. It put its cold nose right up to mine. Then, all of a sudden, *this* happened. I was so frightened. But I'm all right now. Thank God it's not going to scar."

Emily tried not to look at Jennie's blue flower. It was a periwinkle, flower of death, with which the condemned were garlanded in mediaeval England, on their way to the gallows. "A stray cat?"

"I don't think it was a stray. It had on a sort of worn-out blue velvet collar and a silver bell."

Emily got up, almost spilling her drink.

"I have to go now," she said. "Will you excuse me?" She made her way to the door very slowly. All she could think was, I have to stop him. My God, I have to stop him!

She had trouble finding where he lived. It was off Folsom, wasn't it? No, Mission. Near Onondaga. Yes, that was right. This was the street. They had parked somewhere and walked. Why? Because Marianne hadn't been sure of the address, that was it. She turned right, recognizing the houses, and parked the car. She got out and looked around. The street was deserted except for a drunk sprawled in a doorway, moaning.

She went toward Lupe's apartment house and was about to climb the stairs when she heard whistling. There was something eerily familiar about it. Then it struck her that it was the same melody she had heard before, played softly on a flutelike instrument. The whistling came from an alley alongside the building. There was a rusted wrought-iron gate with a sign that read "Tradesmen" still fastened to the top. She touched the gate, sure it was locked, and was surprised when it yielded to her touch. The whistling continued. She walked toward it, curious, strangely drawn.

Making her way down a narrow dirty strip of paving between the blank unwindowed brick wall of the house next door and the side of the house where Lupe lived, she looked around, saw nothing. The alley was covered with corrugated sheet metal so that it was not visible from the windows above. At the end of it, she could see an ugly, overgrown garden. Cats mewed, gathered around garbage cans. The air was thick with the stench of rotten food and stale urine. The whistling stopped abruptly. She thought, I shouldn't be here. No one can see me. She was afraid. When a hand touched her arm, she reacted in terror.

Then she saw that it was Lupe, looking up at her. She told herself that she shouldn't be afraid. She musn't let him see any sign of fear.

"Hey, so you finally showed up."

"Lupe, listen to me—" She felt suddenly quite sure of herself. He was only an eleven-year-old boy; there was nothing to be afraid of. *Eleven. My God!* "Lupe, remember that lady you mentioned to me?" He nodded. "I want you to forget all about the lady."

"You take it easy. When I get through with her, she ain't worth shit."

58

His words chilled her. Now she knew she was right. For some bizarre reason, he wanted to help her—by hurting Jennie. She had to stop him, make him understand.

"Lupe, I want you to leave that lady alone."

"She got that motherfucker by the balls, you know that, don't you? But she no get away with it 'cause I gonna help you." He said something under his breath in Spanish, looking at her with his dark-lashed eyes. Then he winked at her, laughed, and started to open his fly.

"Stop it!"

"Hey, easy, lady! I'm just taking a piss!"

He began to urinate against the wall, a strong stream like an animal's. She opened her purse. "I'm going to give you some money," she said, wondering how much would be enough. Too much and he might come back for more. She decided on ten dollars. Pulling out a bill, she offered it to him, saying, "I don't know how all this started but I do not want you to do anything else, do you understand me, Lupe?"

He had finished urinating, and now he shook out his penis in front of her, looking at it, frowning, alternately retracting and releasing the foreskin. "Look, you take your money. Me, I don't want no money from you at all."

She snapped her purse shut. If he wouldn't take the ten dollars, she would just leave it there on a garbage can. She waited for him to get out of her way so she could edge past him. Somewhere, a window banged open and a woman's shrill voice called out. He threw back his head and yelled out, *"Vengo!"* Then he looked at her with one of those extraordinary changes of expression she had seen before. Now, with a thin shaft of sunlight crossing it, his face looked angelic. His eyes had an incredible clarity. They were luminous and gentle and even sad, and the dark hair falling in curls around his neck and over his wide forehead framed his face, so that it reminded her suddenly of a haunted child's face from an El Greco.

A cat mewed, rubbing itself against his leg. He kicked it savagely, hatred flooding his face. The cat yowled, flung by the force of his leg against the brick wall.

"Bitch! I sent you there to take out her fucking eye!" Then

Emily saw it. Unmistakable. The frayed blue velvet ribbon with the little silver bell. She backed away with a frightened cry. Lupe looked at her, a sly smile twisting the corners of his mouth. He started away toward the back of the alley. He pushed open a metal cellar door, inviting her to follow him with a grin on his child's face. Emily said, desperate:

"I want you to go away!"

He looked at her. "Hey, we got a deal! I'm gonna fuck the shit outta you!"

She turned, stumbling, with a little cry, trying to get away. She heard him call after her, "Hey, watch out for the rats!" as she ran blindly down the length of the alley, struggling with the gate, forgetting it would only swing inward, then stumbled along the street to her car, trying not to look at the drunk still lying in the doorway. He had stopped moaning. She was just getting into her car when a slight sound made her hesitate, turn. For what seemed like forever, she stood there, unable to move, just staring. The man's eyes were open, fixed. And something horrible was happening. Unspeakable. She thought, He's dead. Panic seized her. She got into her car and drove away, her flesh crawling. She began to tremble uncontrollably. She drove home, telling herself she would call the police from the house and tell them a man was dead. Yes, and she would tell them about Lupe, too. Everything. But in the end, she did not telephone at all. She sat alone in her room, the door locked, unable to banish the memory of the dead man, eyes vacant, fixed, being eaten by rats.

David did not get home until after midnight. When he came into the bedroom, she threw herself in his arms.

"David! Oh, David!" She had made up her mind to tell him everything. She started sobbing. He gripped her shoulders. "I've got to talk to you!" she gasped.

"It won't do any good. You know it won't do any good." He let go of her, walked away. She covered her face with her hands, choking down sobs. *I can't lose him. It isn't happening!*

Late that night, she woke up feeling thirsty and went downstairs to get a glass of milk. Through the window, the garden was white in the moonlight. As she opened the refrigerator and started pouring the milk, she heard a sound. She looked around, thinking she had dropped something. Then it was repeated. She recognized it. A light tapping. She whirled around and saw Lupe, face pressed against the window, grinning in at her. The glass of milk fell from her hand, shattering on the floor. She yelled, "You get out of here or I'll call the police!"

David, hearing her, raced downstairs in his pajamas. At the same time, she saw Lupe run toward the dark shadows of the pergola at the back of the garden.

"What is it?"

"There's someone out there! A boy!"

David grabbed a heavy flashlight from a drawer, unlocked the door, started out.

"Don't!" But he was already outside. She called out to him, "Be careful!" David searched the small garden, pointing the flashlight everywhere. There was no sign of anyone. He came slowly back into the breakfast room.

"You were seeing things. Come on back to bed."

"I wasn't seeing things!"

She was beside herself, helpless, afraid. Locking the door, she went back to bed, lying there sleepless, vigilant.

8

The next morning, Emily went to the police station to register a complaint. She said to the woman deputy at the desk, "I'm being annoyed by someone."

"How do you mean, 'annoyed'? Telephone calls?"

"I'm being followed."

"Is it someone you know?"

"Not really." She took a quick breath. "It's a little boy. A friend took me to his house. He tells fortunes. But she wanted him to find her earrings."

"He tells fortunes?"

"He didn't tell *her* anything at all. As far as I'm concerned, she just wasted her money. But he said something to me that was so crude—"

"Is that what you mean by 'annoyed'?"

"Well, that's part of it."

"How old is the boy?"

"I think he's about eleven."

The deputy paused in her note-taking, then put down her pencil. "Eleven."

"Yes."

"I would think that the best thing to do is stay away from him."

"I don't think I'm making myself clear. I didn't go to see him in the first place. My friend went to see him. I just went with her. I have never tried to see him again and don't want to. But evidently, he doesn't feel the same way. He's following me. I want it stopped."

"How do you mean, following you?"

Emily told her the whole story but said nothing whatever about Jennie or the lock of hair.

The deputy bit her pencil, thinking. Then: "We can send a couple of officers by to talk with him. Is there a parent there?"

"He lives with his mother but I don't know how much English she understands."

Looking at the name on the piece of paper, the deputy said, "We'll send along someone who speaks Spanish."

"I'd like to go, too."

The deputy studied her note-pad doubtfully. "I don't think that will be necessary."

"I want to be there. I want him to know that I'm not afraid of him."

It was arranged that Officer Marshall, a big-boned red-headed man, and Officer Beltran, who was small, dark, and wiry, would meet her at Lupe's in half an hour. But after glancing at the deputy's notes, Officer Beltran asked if they could stop by the Blake house first, to look at the garden.

"Yes. Yes, of course."

They followed her to the house and she showed them around the garden, leading the way as they all walked along the path to the sitting-place under the pergola at the back. The men looked up at the high garden walls.

"Any ladders around here?" Beltran asked.

"The gardener brings his own."

"I guess the kid must have gotten out the way he came in."

"He was right here. I saw him run to this place."

"Well, he must have run back."

"He couldn't have. I was watching from the kitchen the whole time. There was a very bright moon last night. I could see everything in the garden."

"How do you suppose he got out?"

"I don't know how he got out any more than I know how he got in! I'm getting tired of his comings and goings. That's why I want you to talk to him."

They searched the house. There was an odor in the cellar.

"You got mice, lady?"

63

"I don't think so."

"Better check."

She made a mental note to call an exterminator. Then the officers left and she followed them to Lupe's. As they drove up, she saw an old-fashioned hearse with beveled glass windows parked in front of the building. The officers gave it a quick look, then the three of them went up the stairs together.

At the end of the hall, there was a notice in English and Spanish posted on the door of Lupe's apartment. As they walked toward it, the door opened and two sallow men dressed in black struggled into the hall, carrying a stretcher with a body covered with a shroud strapped to it. They heard the sound of crying. Emily started forward but Beltran put out a hand to stop her, saying in faintly accented English:

"Better stay here, ma'am."

"There must have been an accident." Emily said.

"That sign says quarantine."

A tall, balding man with sad, pouched eyes and a heavy growth of beard came out into the hall carrying a small black bag. Beltran went up to him and said something in Spanish. The man answered. Emily pressed herself up against the wall to allow the men with the stretcher to crowd past her. Officer Marshall went up and stood a few feet behind Officer Beltran. The conversation in Spanish continued. Emily caught snatches of it. Disease. Death. Then the talk became animated, almost disturbed, and she had trouble following it.

Finally, Officer Beltran motioned to her, the doctor opened the door to the apartment and murmured something. Beltran said, "Now, I don't want you to go in there, Mrs. Blake, but can you tell from here if you see the boy you were telling us about?"

Emily looked. The black-haired Mexican woman, the baby on her hip, shot Emily a look of hatred. Children crowded around the woman, clinging to her grubby skirts. Then the woman walked over to the alcove and lifted the curtain aside. A bed had been made up on a couch, and Emily could see Lupe lying in it, his face very pale. He rolled glazed eyes in their direction. There was no sign of recognition in them.

64

"Look, this is no time to have come here—" Emily began.

"Just tell us if you can see the boy you described to us at the station, will you do that, ma'am?"

"The boy is right there."

"Where?"

"Lying on that couch in the alcove."

"*Gracias,*" he said to the woman. "*Lo siento.*"

"*De nada.*" The woman looked at Emily and spat. The door was slammed shut by a barefoot child. Officer Beltran led Emily down the hall away from the apartment.

"Mrs. Blake, there must be some mistake."

"What do you mean?"

"These people, they have sickness in their house."

"I would never have come here if I'd known that."

"The sister, she died last night."

"Oh, no!"

"This here is Dr. Calderon."

"How do you do?" she said.

The doctor acknowledged the introduction with a murmured reply and a slight bow.

"Dr. Calderon says they have the diphtheria here. These people, they never got vaccinated. The girl, she died, but he vaccinated the others, he thinks just in time. Lupe, he's got a temperature of a hundred and four. He really ought to be in the hospital, but these people, they're afraid of something like that."

"I'm so sorry."

"Well, they think the worst is over. It looks like the boy, he's going to make it."

"We should go now," she said.

"Yes, well, what the doctor here wants me to tell you is that he's been here every day for the last week, and Lupe—he's been too sick to move."

"That isn't possible."

"Talk to the doctor here."

"There must be some mistake."

"It looks that way, lady."

But in the last week, she had seen Lupe not only in the garden

65

but in the alley. She had talked to him! But they didn't know that. She couldn't tell them. How could she explain why she had gone there?

The three men were all looking at her. She felt the weight of their glances, and it oppressed her so that she only wanted to get away. "I'm awfully sorry. I mean, to have caused you trouble." She turned, walking quickly toward the staircase. Once more on the street, she unlocked her car, deliberately keeping her mind blank, and drove home quickly. Esmeralda was in the kitchen, washing windows and singing. The garden was full of sunlight.

Methodically, Emily went through the house from cellar to attic, checking all the windows and doors. The cellar itself was solid masonry, and the windows were heavily barred. The coal chute had been bricked up. Upstairs, all the windows had burglar catches on them. Everything was secure. She even checked the attic. It was in perfect order. Vents in the roof let in fresh air, and the windows were nailed shut. There was simply no way anyone could have gotten into the house, and there was no other way into the garden, where the walls were all fifteen feet high.

That night, she waited up for David as usual. It was almost midnight. She remembered with a pang the late hours he had kept when he was interning. But how different that had been. He would come home to her worn out, stinking of formaldehyde, so tired that it was all she could do to help him undress and get him into bed. In those days, all he wanted was sleep, so much so that he used to make jokes about how they learned to doze off while waiting for the hospital elevator, sometimes while they listened to long-winded patients on the phone. She sat on the little sofa in her bedroom, shivering in her pink quilted robe. The fog had come in. It would be hard to drive. She worried about an accident. She tried to read. The phone rang. She ran to it, snatching it up.

"David?"

"Hey, what is it with you, lady? I do you a favor and you try to fuck me up. What is this shit, coming here with those asshole cops?"

Lupe! But now the voice was different, suddenly deeper. Then she saw the whole thing. Blackmail. They were all in it together,

66

the whole family. She said, trying to keep her voice steady:

"I've had enough. I'm calling the police." She broke the connection and started to dial the operator but the phone rang again. Flustered, she said, "Hello?"

"Listen, lady, I don't like dames hanging up on me, understand?" It made no sense. She had just broken the connection. He wouldn't have had time to dial again. Unless, of course, he had access to equipment.

Suspicious, she asked, "Where are you?"

"Come on, lady, what are you—testing me?"

"Are you afraid to tell me?"

"Afraid? Listen, I'm so close, I can see everything you do. Hey, I like that little pink robe you're wearing." She hung on to her senses. It was a robe she often wore. Lucky guess. "But you must be cold, standing there barefoot. How come you let the fire go out?" A thrill of fear went through her. "But I'd like to warm you up. You know what I'd like to do to you?" He began whispering obscene suggestions.

"You're *crazy!*"

"Think I ought to go to that doctor you went to see? That lousy shrink?" My God, he even knows about that! "He ain't no good to you, lady. He's gonna die. From that pain you get in the stomach. You know, when they cut you open? He's gonna die. But you and me, lady. That's a different story." Softly, he began to describe the things he wanted to do to her. His voice was low, hurried; in a bizarre sense, the rapid murmuring reminded her of the *Aves* and *Pater nosters* of a penitent, but everything was disgusting, unspeakably vile. Carefully, she set down the receiver on the rug, then ran downstairs to the other phone they had in David's study.

"This is an emergency. I want you to trace a call." After a moment, she was switched to the desk of a sergeant at the police station. Desperate, she tried to explain. She could hear an intermittent beeping on the line, indicating that what she said was being recorded, and it made her self-conscious. The sergeant laughed softly. She felt like a fool. He wanted to send a couple of men by.

"No. Listen, do this much. I'll give you the other number. Call

67

it. Have them break in on the line. I want you to verify what I'm telling you."

"You said you left it off the hook upstairs?"

"That's right."

"Then it's busy!"

"Break in on the line! That boy is threatening me!"

"Wait a minute."

An eternity. She sat down in David's leather desk chair, head in her hands, elbows on the desk. Then the sergeant's voice said:

"Line's clear now, lady."

"I see. All right, thank you."

"Sure you don't want us to come by?"

"No. No, I don't see the point of that."

The next day, she went down to the security office of the telephone company and demanded help, knowing that if the city had a bomb scare, the phone company would damn well find a way to monitor calls. Finally, she was successful. A trap was put on her line. If the caller rang up again, she had only to dial a certain number and ask the man at the other end to trace the call. She didn't even have to hurry because so long as she left her own phone off the hook, the caller couldn't break the connection. That night, she went to bed feeling secure. Waiting. But there was no call that night, nor the next, nor the next. After a week, the phone company apologized but explained that they could not keep the trap on the line any longer. Once it was removed, the phone rang again at night. When she answered it, there was no one on the line.

That happened three nights in a row. Then the calls stopped. But now she was sure Lupe was watching her constantly.

Panic in her eyes, Emily seized David by the shoulders and said, "Listen to me! There's this boy! He's following me! I'm afraid of him!"

"What does he want?"

"I . . . don't know."

He was trained to listen for the wrong note. Patients never told the whole truth. Sometimes, they told outright lies. What was

68

that story of Osler's? A patient had said to him, "I am afraid my friend has syphilis. I wonder what should be done for him?" And Osler had answered, "Take your friend out of your pants and let's have a look at him." No, she was not being entirely truthful. Why?

"David, *listen* to me!"

But the anxiety itself was very real. He was concerned about her. "I *am* listening."

"He keeps *following* me. He's only eleven and he makes these *obscene* suggestions. And, David, nobody *believes* me."

He wanted to ask if she had told Dr. Jones about any of this. That was sure to make her mistrustful. He would wait his chance. He said, "You've gone to the police, let them handle it."

"David, you do believe me, don't you?"

"I know that you would never lie to me."

The next morning, he called her psychiatrist to find out whether or not she had mentioned the boy. He received the expected bland noncommittal answer. It irritated him.

"Doctor," he said, "my wife happens to have a serious problem. All I am asking is, do you know about it? Now, I want a definite answer: yes or no?"

"I am aware of the problem," Dr. Jones said, after a pause.

"Thank you. That's all I wanted to know."

He had been planning to go away with Jennie for a weekend. Now he found himself reluctant to leave Emily alone.

69

9

"I didn't tell you the whole truth." This time, she sat on a sofa, and he sat a few feet away from her in the same chair, hands folded, saying nothing. His silence began to weigh on her. She wondered about the couch. He hadn't mentioned it, and it seemed odd to go into someone's office and lie down without invitation. The idea struck her as funny and she tried not to laugh.

"Why are you laughing?"

He didn't know. Suddenly, he seemed human. "It's nothing," she said. She waited for him to ask questions, to guide her. When he didn't speak, she began to feel oppressed, then irritated. "I didn't tell you because the whole thing seemed silly and embarrassing. But since I last saw you, it's gotten worse. The boy I told you about keeps following me around. I don't know how he manages to do what he does, but frankly I can't stand it any longer." She told him everything. Finally, she said, "I suppose you're going to tell me I'm crazy."

"Why? Because a boy is following you around?"

"How could he be in my garden when he was home?"

"Perhaps he has a twin brother. Perhaps he wasn't so sick as they thought. Perhaps he sneaked out. Boys have been sneaking out at night for years. To protect him, the first thing a family would say is that he was home."

"Yes. Yes, that's perfectly true. But how did he get into the garden?"

"I don't know. I have a patient in the locked ward at the hospital. She's dangerous. All the nurses and interns have been warned not to let her out of their sight. Yet she escapes repeatedly. She has a way of making herself invisible."

70

"Are you serious?"

"Yes. But that doesn't mean she does something supernatural. Houdini did things no one could explain. But they were all tricks. He exposed every medium he ever met. Isn't it possible the boy's playing tricks on you?"

"And the telephone?"

"More tricks."

"How does he play tricks like that?"

"I don't know. But then, I don't know how Houdini did what he did. Isn't that the whole nature of a trick? To keep you guessing?"

"I suppose it is."

"Do you think you've given him any encouragement?"

"What are you talking about?"

"You told me you went to see him a second time and then again with the police—"

"But that was to stop him from following me."

"People who play tricks want our attention. If we give it to them, it's a form of encouragement."

"But you don't understand what it's like to have someone know things he shouldn't know, when you don't even know how he could possibly have found them out. He even knows I've seen you! He told me they were going to cut you open!"

" 'They'?"

She described what Lupe had said, adding, "I think he was talking about appendicitis."

"It's interesting that he should have chosen appendicitis." When she gave him a puzzled look, he said, "It's rare today. Nobody knows why. That happens with diseases, ailments. It's rare *here*. But it isn't where he comes from."

"You mean he chose it because it's familiar to him?"

"Possibly." He glanced at the clock. She got quickly to her feet. Rising, he went to consult a pad on his desk. "Would you like to make another appointment now?"

"Do you think I need one?"

"You're going through a difficult period, Mrs. Blake. Perhaps if we examine these fantasies—"

"*Fantasies!* Then you don't believe me?"

"By 'fantasies,' I mean your reactions to what the boy says."
He flipped a page. "I want to see you in a week. On Monday."
He wrote down the time and date of the appointment on a little
card and handed it to her.

She said to David timidly, stroking the back of his hand and
giving him a brave smile, "Since I'm seeing somebody, would you
be willing to come with me? Just once?"
"It's no use."
"I beg you. Give me that much."
"All right."
"I'm seeing him next Monday."
"Monday's fine."
"Well, it's at nine in the morning."
"Any time is fine."
She was surprised at how quickly he had agreed. David, how-
ever, had no intention of going with her. The idea of speaking
openly to a stranger about his feelings had somehow crystallized
what he had known all along: he wanted Jennie. He wanted to
live with her. He would speak to her about it.

She said yes. There was an awkward pause. Jennie was watching
him with a half-smile on her face.
"Are you coming tonight?"
"Well, I'll be by."
"I mean, when are you moving in?"
He thought, rubbing his knuckles across his mouth. "Well,
Friday I'm going to Los Angeles for a few days . . ."
"Shall we set a date?" she asked, that same smile at the corners
of her mouth.
"I have to tell her first. You know that."
"Well?"
"It isn't easy."
"Write her a little note."
"Oh, for Christ's sake, she's in love with me!"
"You're sure of that."
He stared at her.
She shrugged. "She could have somebody else, too."

72

"Don't be ridiculous."

"You don't know women."

"Emily isn't 'women.' She couldn't pull a trick like that. She couldn't pull any kind of a trick. She's incapable of it."

"Oh."

Friday afternoon Jennie came to the office for a slight rash. Followed him down the narrow corridor to his private office. And saw the silver-framed picture on his desk. Emily's picture.

"Oh, my *God!*" she cried out. "It's her!"

"What is it?"

"She told me her name was Mrs. Geiger!"

His face mottled with anger.

She came home early, having cut class to see David off. It was just a symposium, but she wasn't used to having him away. He was in the bedroom packing, putting things into a large suitcase. He had three suits, two sports jackets, some sweaters and shirts, and several pairs of trousers on the bed. She looked at them.

He said in a tight voice, "I'm moving out—*Mrs. Geiger.*" She turned her back on him and went into the bathroom, closing the door. He knocked. "I have to come in. For my things."

"You can come in."

She was in the shower. He packed his toilet case, then stood there for a moment. She turned off the water.

"Yes?"

"I guess there isn't anything left to say."

"No. No, I guess there isn't."

Once he had gone downstairs and she heard the front door slam, she became hysterical. Grabbing at the phone, she called her psychiatrist. The exchange said he couldn't be reached. She ran downstairs in her bathrobe to David's study, went through an address book he kept in a drawer and found Dr. Jones's home number. She called him there. His wife answered the phone.

"May I speak with him? This is Mrs. Blake. It's an emergency."

"I'm sorry. He isn't here now."

"I have to reach him!"

"Are you a patient of his?"

"Yes."

73

"Well, I'm awfully sorry. There's no way I can reach him. If you'll call his exchange, I'm sure he has someone covering for him."

"I want to see him. What do you mean, you can't reach him? I'm sure he'll talk to me."

"I can't reach him by phone, Mrs. Blake. He's off back-packing."

"He's what?"

"Back-packing. In the Sierras. Really, Mrs. Blake, if you'll call the exchange—" She was used to disturbed patients, had learned to be matter-of-fact.

"Is he *alone?*"

"Well . . . yes."

"You've got to send someone after him right away! He's going to have an attack of appendicitis!"

"Really, Mrs. Blake—"

Emily tried to explain. When Mrs. Jones only countered with reassuring interruptions, Emily lost her head and screamed at her, "I'm warning you that if you don't do what I tell you, your husband is going to die of peritonitis!"

"Well, let's hope for the best, shall we, Mrs. Blake?"

Emily said goodbye, putting down the phone, feeling she had made a fool of herself. An utter fool. Somehow, it was sobering and she managed to get through the weekend on her own. She was determined not to ask anyone for help.

Early Monday morning, she received a telephone call from a Dr. Van Steen. He explained that he would be seeing a number of Dr. Jones's patients and offered either to keep Dr. Jones's appointment with her or to refer her to someone else, if she preferred.

"I don't understand . . ." She was not quite awake.

"Dr. Jones passed away over the weekend."

"Oh, my God, I am *sorry!*"

"Thank you. Now, as for today's appointment—"

Then the truth hit her. Her eyes filled with horror. "Was it appendicitis?" Then, when he didn't answer, she almost yelled into the phone, *"Was it appendicitis?"*

"Yes, it was."

"Oh, my *God!* My *God!*" She put down the phone slowly.

Lupe. How had he known? How could he possibly have known? She thought. Very carefully. Her eyes moved. But if he were capable of knowing *that,* what else might he know? And what might he be capable of doing?

She was not herself. She knew it. She caught sight of herself in the mirror. The face seemed to belong to someone else. The expression was odd, off-center.

Suppose he actually could get rid of Jennie? Make her go away?

It made no sense but Emily did not care any more. She would pay any price to hold on to her husband. She drove downtown and withdrew a thousand dollars from her savings account. That was what he had been after all along. A lot of money. No wonder he hadn't touched the ten-dollar bill she had offered him. She had been a fool. He could do things. And he wanted to be paid for them. Paid well.

She drove toward the Mission. At five-thirty, she parked the car a block away from his house and started walking. Ahead, in the middle of the street, a dozen ragged children, some barefoot, were playing a game. She saw Lupe at the far end of the group. He seemed even smaller than she had remembered. She did not like the idea of being seen by the other children but there was no way out of it now. She thought, Well, he'll see me and when he comes this way, I'll just start walking back toward the car. If he followed her, perhaps she could just meet him around the corner.

She turned her back, took a compact out of her purse and began powdering her nose, watching the reflection of the children over her shoulder. Lupe had disappeared. She turned quickly, then saw him walking rapidly in the opposite direction, on the other side of the street. Snapping shut her compact, she began striding down the sidewalk in the same direction.

At the end of the block, he turned the corner and began going down a narrower street. She ran awkwardly, trying to keep him in sight. She clutched her purse, worrying about the amount of cash she had in it. The neighborhood was strange, perhaps dangerous. She told herself it didn't matter. Far ahead, she saw him stop under a locust tree and light a cigarette. Exhaling a cloud of

75

smoke, he looked back in her direction but gave no indication that he had seen her. When she got closer, he began walking away.

She knew now that he wanted her to follow him, and she walked more slowly. The neighborhood here was unfamiliar to her. It was old and shabby, full of wooden cottages with shingled roofs and overgrown gardens separated from the broken sidewalk by wrought-iron fences. The road got steeper. Then she saw a stone wall rising from the top of the hill.

The street up to the wall was paved with cobblestones. She came to an iron gate set in the wall and through it, she could see headstones. He had led her to an old cemetery. She looked around for him. He was nowhere in sight. But the road ended at the gate, which was locked and fastened with a rusty chain. She tried it anyway. There was enough give for her to squeeze through. A steep path led to the unkempt grounds.

The yew-screened cemeteries she had visited, with landscaped lawns rolling down to the edge of the hills south of the city, had the well-tended look of suburban developments. But here, on this unvisited weed-choked mound of forgotten dead, this walled eminence, she felt an extraordinary sense of desolation.

"Lupe?" she said. There was a peculiar stillness in the air. She waited a moment, then called out his name again. The stillness reached everywhere, so that her voice seemed small, ineffectual. No answer.

She walked around. Under a tangle of ivy and myrtle were visible, like a ruined city, the fallen headstones. On a rise near the cliff descending to the city street, from which the burial ground was divided by a line as sharp as that separating an Algerian metropolis from a casbah, rose the stone houses of the dead, their low bronze doorways, through which one was obliged to go with bent head, still proof against the salt air. Breathless, she leaned against the barred door of a crypt. Narrow apertures were pierced at the top into the perpetual night of the burial chamber and she could feel the unexpected chill of the tomb's air.

Then she saw him, as before, standing in the open doorway of a crypt. He stretched out a child's hand, the nails broken, dirty, warts on the knuckles. She opened her purse. She took the money she had brought with her. He flicked a glance around, standing

76

there on the worn steps that descended to the crypt, seeming in some fey sense to be a part of the place. Behind him was a wall cf crude drawings, and she sensed the intertwining of the morbid and the lustful, almost imagined she could hear the music of an ancient obscene dance, performed moonlit in churchyards . . .

No! She felt herself seized, dragged forward and flung onto a cold marble slab. His strength was astounding. She thought, feeling the panic in her throat choking her, *I mustn't move. Maybe he has a knife!* She couldn't see anything. He had shoved the heavy door of the tomb closed. A child's hand with incredible force held her down while another ripped off her underclothes. Her eyes, accustomed now to the dark, made out his goat's face. He lay on her now, his little boy's face close to hers. His eyes were different. Now they were bloodshot, glazed. He grunted, breathing a foul breath into her face, pushing himself against her.

Abruptly, the head jerked away. She felt the cool of his bare shoulders against her thighs, the brush of his thick curls. He seized her vagina in his mouth. She felt as if she were being devoured alive. Her hands clutched at his hair, trying to pull his head off her. She heard panting and gasping and the sounds of sucking and licking, felt his tongue deep inside her. She could feel it happening to her. She couldn't help herself.

Then she felt him start to enter her. She thought, *My God, I'm having intercourse with a child!* Without warning, he penetrated her completely, with a penis that was extraordinarily long and icy cold.

"You like it, huh?"

She was gasping for breath, struggling with the hand on her neck, trying to cry out.

Suddenly, it was over. He was gone. How had she gotten out of the place? Had she walked all that way back? She did not remember. Here was the car. She reached into her purse for the keys. The money. *It was still there.* Thank God. Crying, sobbing with relief, she got into the car, thinking, *It didn't happen! None of it ever happened!* Then she realized that her underclothes were gone, her dress was ripped and stained. Now she remembered.

I came. Jesus God, I came.

She drove home erratically, her stomach knotted. Nothing

77

made any sense. Her hands shook so, she couldn't get her latchkey into the lock and had to ring for Esmeralda. Brushing by her, she ran upstairs, locking herself in the bedroom, trying to think. She couldn't.

Then the horror of the whole thing burst upon her. She could almost feel what was going to happen. She had to act, to do something. Snatching up the phone, she dialed Jennie's number, praying that Jennie was home. Ring. Ring. Ring. Then the silvery voice answered. Tinkle-tinkle.

"Hello?"

"This is Mrs. Blake," she said unevenly. "Mrs. David Blake. I have to tell you something." She had to stop him. She simply had to stop him.

10

At about ten-fifteen that night, residents on the serpentine block of Lombard Street were awakened by the sound of a woman screaming in agony. Lights began to go on in all the neighboring houses. Windows banged open. A woman in curlers appeared at an upstairs window next door. Her husband, wearing pajamas, appeared beside her.

"What the Christ—?" He ran to the phone, getting the operator. "Get me the police! . . . You don't need my goddamned phone number! This is an emergency!"

Outside, three men in pajamas tried to force open the door of the house from which the screams were coming. An older man ran up, calling out: "Around the back! You can climb over my wall! Try the door back there!"

A squad car pulled up. Two policemen scrambled over the wall with the help of a garden ladder and struggled with the back door, trying to force it open. They banged, yelled, as if someone inside could help them. The agonized screaming began to fade away. The air was filled with the sound of sirens coming closer.

A police photographer was taking pictures in the living room of the house, now brightly lit. A fingerprint man was at work, going over all the furniture. Lieutenant Fonner, a barrel-chested man in his middle forties, unaware that his pajamas were showing underneath the trousers of his suit, strode into the living room, beckoning to a young police detective named Skopos, who came toward him carrying a small open book.

"Nobody in. Nobody out. No statements." Fonner started away.

"Look. Diary. Names her killer. Anyway, the person she was afraid was going to kill her."

"Inadmissible evidence."

"You're kidding."

"No. That's the law. We can use it. But the prosecution can't."

"Christ, it's dated today! Jesus, she was practically on her damn deathbed!"

"Dying declarations admissible. This, no." Fonner crossed the room quickly. Ambulance attendants had wheeled in a stretcher. He held up a hand. "You guys hold it." He crossed back toward a window seat where a sickly-looking man in his sixties, wearing a dark suit, was snapping shut an old-fashioned black bag. He was the coroner and his name was Viterbo.

Fonner said, "What have you got?"

"I'll let you know."

"After the autopsy. Sure. Only, I don't think you've got much to work on."

Fonner turned to glance at the body sprawled in a wing chair, charred almost beyond recognition.

"Who was she?" the coroner asked.

Fonner consulted a notebook. Smudged. "Ludlow. Ms. Jennie. I think. But for all I know, it could be a Buddhist monk. Finished?" And when Viterbo nodded, Fonner said to the attendants with the stretcher, "All right, move it." Then to Viterbo, he said, "Well?"

"Later, okay?"

Fonner turned, seeing something, and reacted. He touched Viterbo on the sleeve. The two of them walked toward the wing chair as the gloved attendants put the body in a sheet and swung it up onto a stretcher.

"Look at the chair."

"Scorched," said Viterbo.

"But not burned."

"Okay, somebody killed her, set fire to the body to conceal the cause of death and then threw it in the chair. That what you're thinking?"

"You tell me."

"All I can tell you is how she died, and maybe, with the help

80

of the right dentist, who she was . . . Wait a minute! Didn't you guys have to break in?"

"I want a lid on that."

"You had to break in, right? I heard the guys talking. Every door was bolted. Every window locked. Correct?"

Fonner looked at him, not answering. He chewed on a cuticle. Viterbo said, "So how did whoever did it get away?" And when Fonner shrugged, not answering, Viterbo said, "Bothers you, doesn't it?"

Fonner said, "I don't believe in locked-door mysteries." He slipped the diary he had been given into an envelope, then walked away.

David remained sitting in the chair behind his office desk, staring up unbelievingly at Fonner.

"Dead?"

By way of explanation, Fonner threw down a police photograph of the charred remains sitting in the wing chair. David looked at it, and all the color ran out of his face. Fonner took back the photograph. Skopos made notes of their conversation.

"Do you mind telling us your whereabouts last night, Doctor?"

"I was at a symposium in L.A."

"Any witnesses?"

"About three hundred. I was delivering a paper."

"When?"

"The symposium went on from eight until about eleven-thirty. Then a few of us went out and had something to eat." When Fonner's eyes still remained locked on his, David pulled a prescription form toward him and scrawled down an address. "Here—Cedars–Sinai."

"And the names of the men you were with afterward?"

David put the prescription form down on the desk again and wrote out three names. "I'm not sure of the spelling of the last one," he said.

"They all doctors?"

"Yes."

"That's all right. When did you return?"

"I just got here."

"We talked to your nurses. They said you weren't expected until tomorrow."

"That's right."

"Mind explaining why you arrived this morning?"

Silence.

"Doctor?"

"I—uh—decided to come back."

"Why?"

"I wanted to see my wife."

"Is your wife sick?"

"No."

"Why did you want to see her? I mean, so that you just cut your visit a day short?"

"I just wanted to see her, that's all!"

"And have you seen her?"

"No. She wasn't home."

"We'd like to see her."

"Why?"

"We'd like to talk with her about this thing you had going with the deceased. How long did it last?"

"A little over three months."

"Your wife find out?"

"I told her."

"You think that's why your wife tried to kill her?"

"*What?*"

"Diary of the deceased said she was afraid of your wife."

"That's crazy!"

"Your nurse tells us decedent came into this office about five o'clock Friday for something called"—he consulted his notes—"Cleocin. Seems you prescribed it for her, the pharmacy didn't have any, and she knew you had some samples here in the office."

"Yes."

"What's Cleocin?"

"A lotion. She had a slight rosacea. Just a little inflammation of the skin. It's a perfectly conventional treatment. Look, I don't know what this has got to do with—"

"It's only the fact that that's what brought her here. While the nurse hunted for the samples, she went into your private office with you. Deceased was then heard to cry out"—he consulted his notes—" 'Oh, my God! My *God!*' " Fonner indicated David's own office in which they were now meeting. "Nurse glanced in and saw decedent holding a framed picture of your wife." Swiftly, Fonner picked up the picture of Emily from David's desk. "This picture. Nurse reports that decedent said, 'It's her!' Nurse says she overheard decedent say, 'She told me her name was Mrs. Geiger!' Decedent then went home, and wrote in her diary that your wife had visited her pretending to be someone else. She indicated that she was afraid of your wife. Can you tell me why?"

David sat down. He was very pale and he knew it. "Are you accusing my wife of murdering her?"

"No, sir. But we'd like to talk to her."

David nodded, then picked up the phone and asked his secretary to call Emily. When he heard Emily's voice on the phone, he said, "Honey?"

"David? Where are you?"

"At the office."

"Then you heard?"

"No. Not until I got back. The police told me. They're here. They want to talk to you." He looked up at Fonner for confirmation. "Can we come out now?"

"David, you will come with them?"

"Of course I will."

"David, I'm afraid."

"Don't be afraid."

"One more time, Mrs. Blake. You found out who 'Jennie' was by following your husband to his rendezvous with the deceased, then you called on her pretending to be a Mrs. Geiger."

"Yes."

"And you say you did this out of curiosity?"

"Yes."

"How many times did you see Miss Ludlow?"

"Twice. The second time, I ran into her by accident at Podesta's. I was . . . afraid she'd find out who I was."

"And that's all there was to it?"

"Yes."

83

"You have no idea why she might have been afraid of you?"

"No."

Fonner nodded, saying nothing at all about the details which Jennie had written in her diary. His face was impassive. He studied Emily for a moment longer. Then:

"All right. Thank you." Unexpectedly, Fonner shoved his notebook back into his pocket and ended the interview at that.

David showed Fonner and Skopos out, then came back into the study and took Emily in his arms, holding her with all his strength. Everything had changed. He could not explain it. He said, "Emmy, don't leave me. I'll do anything but don't leave me."

She was trembling. She pulled away from him. He didn't understand. "I'll make it up to you," he said.

"It's all right."

"Emmy, I don't know what happened to me but it's over. I can't even mourn. Emmy, *please—*"

"It's all right." She was standing by the desk, rubbing her arms. He went to her, putting his hands on her. She was rigid.

"Emmy, what is it?"

"David, I killed her."

He stared at her, incredulous. She repeated the words softly, almost without emotion. He grabbed her by the shoulders, turning her around. "What are you talking about?"

"It was that boy!"

"What boy?"

She told him the whole story, breathless, terrified, leaving out nothing. He listened, never taking his eyes off her. Then, when she got to the end, he said in a hard voice:

"You mean, he raped you? Are you telling me that the boy actually *raped* you?"

"Yes."

"When?"

"Late yesterday afternoon."

"In that cemetery?"

"Yes."

"My God!" A beat. Then: "Okay, where do I find him?"

84

"I don't want you to go anywhere near him, David!"

"Tell me where he lives. Emmy, tell me where he lives or I'll go to the police or Marianne and get the address from them, so there's no point in playing games with me. Now, where does he live?"

She told him, then saying, "David, don't do *anything!* I beg you not to do anything!"

"I want you to wait here for me, understand?"

Two hours later, she heard David's key in the lock and ran to the door. He gave her a kiss and led her into the study.

"Sit down, Emmy. I'll fix you a drink. What do you want?"

"I don't want anything." He went to the bar and got down a martini pitcher.

"I think we both need a drink." He mixed martinis in silence, taking his time. He had a way of doing that when he had something important to tell her, as if he required a little island of silence. Then, handing her a glass, he sat down on a footstool in front of the armchair where he had put her. They sipped their drinks. She waited for him to begin. He took a deep breath.

Then he said, "Emmy, you know I love you."

"Yes, David."

"I went a little crazy. God knows why. But it's over now. I'll always love you, Emmy. Do you understand that?"

"Yes. Yes, I understand that."

"So, if what I say is upsetting to you, I want you to trust me, I want you to trust me no matter how scared what I'm going to say makes you feel. Are you going to trust me?"

"Yes, David." She leaned forward, touching her cheek to his. He took her glass and set both glasses aside, then put his hands firmly on her shoulders and looked deep into her eyes.

"Emmy? Emmy, listen. Lupe is dead."

"Oh, Christ, God."

"No, no, wait. Listen. He died of diphtheria."

"He what?"

"He died of diphtheria. A week ago. It's a matter of public record. Family's gone. Moved away. God knows where."

85

"He died *when?*"

"A week ago." She began to shake her head slowly. "Emmy? Can you handle it? Are you okay?"

"You mean I imagined the whole thing. That's what you're saying, isn't it?"

"Honey, remember, there were no witnesses. Now, isn't that the God's truth, baby?"

"Marianne! Marianne heard him say Jennie's name!"

"All right, all right. Maybe the kid was a mind reader. Who knows? But the whole thing was a fantasy, sweetheart, and it happened because I was driving you out of your mind and I'm sorry, God in his heaven knows how sorry I am and I'll make it up to you, I swear it on my life, baby!"

"It never happened?"

"No, doll."

"It never happened?" She put her hands over her mouth and stared at him with wild eyes. "But Jennie's dead."

"But Lupe never happened. Do you understand? I want you to repeat after me, It never happened."

"It never happened. Oh, David, it never happened."

She threw herself into his arms, wanting never to be out of them again.

That night, she went to bed early. She wanted to wait up for David but she was exhausted. As soon as her head touched the pillow, she fell into a deep sleep. She was awakened some hours later by a gentle stroking of her legs. She turned onto her back, opening her arms.

"David."

Then, as a face pressed close to hers, she felt the downy softness of the cheek, smelled the odor of garlic. She opened her eyes. It was Lupe. The child's face hovered over hers. She could make out, even in the dim light, every detail of the luminous eyes, the long, child's lashes, the harelip pointing down to the lascivious smile, the crooked teeth. Her heart began to race wildly. Now it beat irregularly, trilling, fluttering like a bird in her breast. She gasped for breath, feeling his broken nails dig into her shoulders.

"Please, lady, I'm cold."

A voice said, "What do you want?" Was it her voice? She

86

couldn't be sure. She was in an agony of fear.

"Lady, I got nowhere to live. See, I used to live with this guy, Mr. Duray, but oh, Christ, lady, he was a awful bugger. Hey, how about I come live with you?"

Her breath sobbed.

Suddenly, he ducked his head and began sucking on her breast with such passion, she felt as if she were being devoured alive. She tried to cry out. She could neither move nor speak. Then she felt a sensation of trickling, an obscene wetness inching down her breast. She thought, *He's dead. This is a dream. I'm insane. This is how you dream when you're insane.*

Then she heard him say, "You know what I want."

"I don't know what you want."

"Don't shit me. I got some stuff a guy gave me. You come through for me, lady, or I smear it all over my cock and I fuck you to death, you hear me, what I'm saying?"

Then it was over. Somehow, he was gone, she was asleep. It was a dream. Of course it was a dream. She lay in her bed unable to move. David came home. He kissed her tenderly, stroking her. Then his hand hesitated. He turned on the bed lamp, looking at her.

"What happened? Did you scratch yourself?" He went to the bathroom and brought out some hydrogen peroxide to put on her breast. She took it from him quickly, saying she would do it herself and hurried into the bathroom. She could not bear the idea of being touched. By him. By anyone. She waited for a few minutes, then went back to bed. Not lying near him. Her mind said, I scratched myself. Oh, please, God, let me believe that I just scratched myself.

That night, her period came on. She missed the next one. And a few weeks later, a test confirmed the fact that she was pregnant. David kept holding her, saying, Baby, baby. When she put a hand to his cheek, it was wet with tears. Her heart was full. She had him back at last.

11

In the morgue, Fonner walked down the wet tiled floor of the basement with Viterbo, the coroner, who was very angry. His stringy neck was red. He said, "What's this bullshit in the papers about her smoking in bed?"

"Christ knows."

"Bed wasn't burned. Nothing was burned. When something like that happens, victim sets fire to the mattress. Drunk, most of the time. Overcome by smoke. This is nothing like that."

"Get to the point."

"I'm the coroner, understand? My reputation is involved. I don't mind your putting a lid on the case but I fucking-A well mind statements that make me sound like a fucking jerk."

"I'll take care of it."

"Yeah!"

"So what's the big deal?"

"No wounds. Toxicology report indicates no poison." He thrust papers at Fonner. "So nobody set fire to her to conceal any crime. She burned to death."

"Just like that."

"Soot in trachea."

Fonner looked at him, not understanding. Viterbo repeated it slowly.

"Soot in trachea. She was breathing while she was burning. Get it? Also, she was screaming. According to the neighbors, she was yelling her cunting head off."

"Yeah?"

"Cause of death—well, shit, her blood boiled."

88

There was a long pause. Then Viterbo continued, asking, "You call the fire department?"

"Yeah. But there were no fires."

"Jee-zuz!"

"What?"

"Cremation occurs at about fifteen hundred degrees Fahrenheit. Takes about two hours. This dame was barbecued in seven minutes—maybe eight and a half—and, according to you, the fire was out when you got there. Sure of that?"

"Yeah."

"Bullshit."

"Bullshit, who says?"

"Bullshit I say, because it's impossible!"

Over the protests of Dr. Viterbo, Fonner decided an inquest was in order. The coroner's jury met, and the circumstances surrounding Jennie Ludlow's death were explained. The six members of the jury were at first skeptical, then impatient. Dr. Viterbo resented the whole proceeding and let Fonner know it, since he suspected his own testimony made him sound like a fool. He decided to make short shrift of the whole thing.

"Look," he said to the jury, "we know the cause of death. It wasn't natural. That leaves three possibilities: misadventure, suicide, or foul play. We have no evidence to support any one of those three hypotheses."

The jury was getting restless. If the coroner couldn't tell them anything, how were they expected to bring in a verdict? A cadaverous-looking civil servant in a worn dark suit said in a querulous voice, "What do you want us to do if we can't decide?" Dr. Viterbo pretended not to hear the question. The civil servant persisted. "Can't a fella say he just don't know?" This provoked laughter, but Viterbo was now obliged to say that they were indeed free to make such an answer. The members of the jury murmured together. It took them only moments to return a simple verdict of "Undecided."

Since, in Viterbo's view, this made him look ridiculous, he promptly reconvened the jury the following day with new instructions. Because, he said, there was no evidence whatsoever that the

89

deceased had ever been suicidal and because "misadventure" would close off all further investigation and thus they would learn nothing, he was directing them to bring in a verdict of "foul play by person or persons unknown." This done, Viterbo forwarded the revised jury verdict back upstairs to Fonner, taking grim satisfaction in the thought that Fonner would now end up with an unsolved homicide case on his hands to mar *his* record. He'd teach Fonner a trick or two. After thirty-five years, Viterbo knew how to thread his labyrinthine way through the Byzantine politics of the civil service.

Red-faced and impatient (after all, he had only been trying to do his job), Fonner buried the records of the Jennie Ludlow case in a bottom drawer. But the following week, the office of the district attorney, finding the report of a fresh, unsolved murder in an in-basket, sent down word to ask for reports of progress.

Lieutenant Fonner, newly promoted, suffering from chronic indigestion, decided he would investigate the case personally, sure that he could prove the whole thing accidental and thereby give Viterbo a black eye.

Fonner began his investigation that day. He had an ax to grind. Not satisfied with the report of the arson squad, he authorized funds for an electrician and had all the wiring checked in the Ludlow house. It was in perfect order.

He said to Skopos, "I want to invent an accident that will fit the facts. I don't care if it's wrong. Let's just invent one, then we'll go from there."

"Spontaneous combustion."

"I looked into that. It just means something reaches its flashpoint. In this case, the only thing that did that was the deceased. Nothing else was burned."

"Chair was scorched."

"Big deal."

Skopos was a sergeant. He was young, dark-haired, with a handsome squarish face and a burly frame. Women found him attractive. He knew it and he liked to go to a singles' bar and sit there, waiting for the women to come to him. It was almost five-thirty. He had been sitting in the squad room trying to decide which bar to go to when Fonner sent for him. Skopos was ambitious. The lieutenant liked him. He put the thought of bars out of his head.

"Lightning," said Skopos.

"I thought of that. You check the weather reports?"

"Yeah. It was a clear night. But, you know, sometimes you get freak weather. Christ, they don't report every drop of rain."

"I thought of that, too. But she had these drapes. That kind that's fastened at the top and bottom. The lightning would have had to pass through them—not to mention the window—and they weren't even singed."

Skopos sighed, shrugging. Fonner said, "Okay, tell me something impossible. Anything."

"Okay. There's this trap door. A guy comes up and kills her with a flamethrower. A blowtorch. Anything?"

"There's no trap door."

"Okay, so let's pretend he came down the chimney."

"I been there, too. By now, the guys in arson must think I'm nuts. But I checked it out. No chemical residue. And anyway, those damn things can cut you in half. Besides, it's a physical impossibility."

Skopos frowned. "Anything like this ever happen before, Lieutenant?"

Fonner shoved a sheaf of papers at him, descriptions of similar events from the Boston *Sunday Globe,* the Dallas *Morning News,* the Blyth *News,* the Madras *Mail,* and the *Journal de Médecine* in France. It went on and on. In one case, the woman had been incinerated but *the clothing of the victim had not even been scorched.* Skopos was shaken. Fonner said, "Skopos, I want you to get into this with me. I want to know everything about Jennie Ludlow. Hour by hour. Day by day. Everybody she knew, everywhere she went. Let's start with that."

They worked together. Nothing made any sense. After five weeks, Fonner developed a dry, hacking cough. When he took his temperature, he discovered he had a fever. His wife, a thin rail of a woman with rimless glasses and a tic born of the fact that they weren't comfortable, which caused her to wrinkle her nose and squinch up her eyes, became irritable. "Look at your eyes, burning in your head like two coals, and you think I don't know?

91

It isn't as if you got any overtime, not one cent. Will you please look at me when I'm talking?" His joints ached. He had come to the end of his rope. He decided to drop the whole investigation and bury his notes in a file due to be retired.

Then he got a call from the district attorney's office requesting a progress report. Fonner tried to beg off. There really was so little to go on. Well, an oral report would be acceptable. When he demurred, saying he really hadn't been able to give the matter sufficient time, the surprised response made him realize his error. On his time sheets, he was obliged to put down the code numbers of his cases. By now, the hours devoted to the case of Jennie Ludlow must be quite impressive.

Fonner arranged for a meeting with the district attorney. With the insight of despair, he saw that his conduct would seem nothing less than obsessive. Gathering his notes, he went upstairs, convinced he would never make captain.

The reception he got surprised him. He was complimented on his diligence. Passing over the fact that Fonner had no clear line to pursue, the district attorney asked him to obtain the answers to certain questions. Fonner was puzzled.

"Just do it, Lieutenant."

Fonner did as he was told. A week later he was given more questions and told that the answers were to be kept confidential. He pursued his inquiries. He was then directed to ask further questions. He delivered the answers but they puzzled him. Back in his office, he pulled open a drawer, took out some antacid tablets, chewed them up and took a sip of water.

A buzzer sounded. He depressed a key and said, trying not to belch into the machine, "Yes, Helen?"

"He's on line one."

"Okay."

Releasing the intercom button, he picked up a phone, punching a button. "Fonner."

The soft, familiar voice gave him instructions. He listened, stunned, then said, "You're kidding." He listened a while longer, and then, his expression changing, answered, "Okay. Yes, sir. Right. Right. Right. I understand." He got up from his chair slowly, trying to think. Then, pressing his intercom button, he

92

said to Helen, trying to keep his voice casual, "Get Skopos for me."

That day, a Tuesday, was Emily's museum day. David had to drive up to Sonoma for a consultation. He said, "Can't you get off?"

"I'm a docent, honey."

"I'll tell you what. I'll rent a car and turn it in there. You drive up. We'll stay at the Mission Inn and then spend Wednesday in the wine country. You want to?"

Her face shone. She thought of something. "Remember Brittany?" She was thinking of a place where sheep grazed in the marshes, so that their flesh was salted. They had stayed in a timbered, whitewashed inn at the edge of the sea. "I saw a picture of a house like that where dinner is supposed to be marvelous. Do you want me to call up for reservations?"

"Yes."

"I love you, David."

There were only a few visitors that day at the Legion of Honor museum. Detective Skopos passed several people clumped together on the broad, shallow steps, a stout man talking to them in French and gesturing at the façade of the Palace, at the broad, sweeping lawns, at the straits below.

Inside, Skopos walked quickly from room to room. In a large gallery hung an exhibit of weaving. Several spectators looked at works on the wall, meanwhile consulting catalogs. They walked out in a group just as Skopos walked in. The exhibit room was deserted. Then someone entered from the other doorway. He glanced at a picture he had taken out of his pocket, then walked up to the woman, whom he recognized from having met once.

"Mrs. Emily Blake?"

"Yes?"

Skopos took out his identification and showed it to her, shoved the wallet back into his coat pocket and pulled the jacket around his barrel chest so that the shoulder holster wouldn't show. He said, "I have a warrant for your arrest for violation of Section One Eighty-seven of the Penal Code."

93

Looking at him blankly, Emily said, "What?"

Skopos pulled a card out of his side pocket and prepared to read from it. He cleared his throat.

"I am now going to read you your rights. 'You have the right to remain silent. Anything you say can and will be used against you in a court of law. You have the right to talk with an attorney before we question you and to have him present while we question you. If you cannot afford to hire an attorney, one will be appointed to represent you free of charge, if you want one. Do you understand each and every one of these rights as I have explained them to you?' "

Emily looked at him in complete bewilderment. He said, "Ma'am? Do you understand what I've just said to you?"

"Well, yes, of course."

Swiftly, he took a pair of handcuffs from his belt, fastened Emily's hands behind her back and led her out the main entrance to the museum. Several people stopped and turned. Skopos led her down the long flight of steps, thinking, Why the hell didn't I have the car at the back, where you can drive up to the door? Meanwhile, Emily, dazed, was calling out to people passing by, asking for help.

"There must be some mistake! Could you call my husband? Hello? I wonder if you could call my husband?" People looked at her, then looked away quickly.

Skopos put her in the back seat of a police car which had been specially shuttered, first nodding to the driver, then getting in beside her. The car started. A heavy wire mesh separated them from the front seat. The doors in the back seat had no handles, nor had the windows, and Emily thought wildly, If anything happened to the driver, we'd be trapped back here, and then she turned and looked open-mouthed at Skopos, utterly at a loss, as they raced along Geary Boulevard. Skopos neither spoke to Emily nor looked at her for the entire trip. He had been given his orders and made to repeat them.

12

Skopos led Emily toward the police station. She was trying to be calm but she stumbled on one of the steps, frightened because her hands were locked behind her, and he had to catch her. She was trembling and very pale. He started to say something reassuring, then remembered the orders he had had to repeat. He led her inside in silence.

Daly was at the desk, a thickset sergeant in his fifties who had his thinning hair cut so short, it almost looked as if he shaved his head. Glancing up, he hastily covered the paperback book he was reading (a "dirty book," by his own description; he got them from a pornographic bookstore he protected, going in once a week and saying to the two-hundred-and-ninety-five-pound boy in his early twenties who sat behind a low screen on a high platform from which he could watch the whole store, "Okay, what kind of filth are you selling today, kid? Let's see the dirtiest thing you got"), scratched his pockmarked face and looked at Skopos. Skopos pulled out a legal document, handing it to Daly.

"Book her."

Daly frowned, then beckoned to Skopos and said, without moving his lips, speaking in a low voice that had no carrying power, "What's going on?" He had glanced at the legal document.

"I said, Book her, Sergeant. Orders."

"You've got a right to interrogate her first. Maybe she'll talk. Once I book her, she gets to call her lawyer, he'll tell her to keep her pretty mouth shut and my guess is, that's what she'll do. Hell, you know all that. Go on. Take her inside."

"Orders. Book her. And don't talk to her."

95

"What's coming down?"

"Nobody talks to her."

"Who says?"

"Fonner."

"Okay." He picked up a phone. "Send Theale out." He took out an envelope and put it down on the desk, saying, "Valuables in here."

Mildred Theale, a policewoman in her mid-forties who had a businesslike expression and a heavy cold, came out and started toward Emily, snuffling. Skopos whispered to Officer Theale. Mildred Theale listened without changing her expression, then moved toward Emily, putting a hand on her arm.

Emily said, "Would you help me, please?"

Ignoring her, Mildred Theale took Emily's purse, emptied it onto Daly's desk and then began itemizing the contents as Daly made a list.

"One gold-plated Cross ball-point pen. One brown leather wallet containing"—she looked inside—"ten, fifteen, seventeen dollars in bills. Wait a minute. Let's get the jewelry out of the way first." Mildred took the watch from Emily's wrist. "One gold Omega watch, crystal scratched. See?" Mildred Theale held it up for all of them to see. Then she examined Emily's hands, which were still handcuffed behind her back, pulling off a gold ring and putting it down on the counter.

"One gold wedding band. Eighteen-karat. Inscription: AVO. I'll search her inside. Let's get back to the purse. Wallet containing photographs and credit cards as follows . . ."

Emily began to cry silently.

A barred door was slid shut with a banging sound. Emily felt the handcuffs removed and then watched unbelievingly as she was fingerprinted. She said to the officer who pressed her fingers down onto the inkpad, trying to smile but obviously frightened:

"Excuse me but could you tell me what One Eighty-seven is?"

He didn't answer.

Lights flashed as someone photographed her while Mildred held a number in front of her. Mildred turned Emily's head to the side, then full-face, trying at the same time not to sneeze. Emily started to laugh for no reason.

The photographer said, "Would you ask the subject not to smile, please?"

In a changing room, Emily stood naked by a bench, clutching her clothes, as Mildred stepped forward.

"Put the clothes down. Turn around. Now spread your cheeks."

"I think I'm going to be sick."

"You get sick, you get to clean it up."

In a prison dress, Emily stood at a wall telephone, Mildred beside her. She dialed a number slowly, then waited. A voice said, "Doctor's office."

"This is Mrs. Blake. Could you possibly reach my husband? He's in Sonoma."

"Doctor is between locations now, Mrs. Blake. I'll have him call you the moment I hear from him. Are you at home?"

"No. No, I'm not at home."

"May I have the number where he can reach you?"

"The number? It's—" Emily hesitated, looking up at the number of the pay phone.

Mildred said, "You can't use that number."

Emily tried to control her voice as she said into the phone, "I'm at—" and then, wetting her lips, she changed her mind and said, "Just tell him I'm—" She felt herself growing faint. Mildred, ready to give the message, reached for the phone. But Emily was too quick for her. She broke the connection. To Mildred, she said, "I don't want them to know. I mean, it isn't a good thing for him professionally. You can understand that, can't you?"

"You are allowed two completed calls. You've made one of them. Do you want to call an attorney?"

"I don't know an attorney."

"Do you want to call a bail bondsman?"

"I don't even know what I'm here for! Can't you tell me that much? I mean, don't you have to?"

Call Marianne! But how could she? Marianne was away with Roberta. On a retreat.

"Under the law, I must ask you again if you want to call a bail bondsman."

97

She thought, I must wait and let David handle it. "No," she said finally.

"This way."

"Why am I here?" She realized that her voice was very loud.

"I am not allowed to have any conversation with you."

She was in a women's holding cell now. She looked around with horror at the six other women. Two were obviously prostitutes. Their hair was dyed in exotic unreal colors. Three were older women, all drunks. One sat on the floor, staring into space. Another, about sixty, sat on an iron bed, sobbing. The third was vomiting into the toilet. Another woman in her late forties was hysterical. She kept banging her head on the bars of the cell and screaming. She was bruising herself and obviously unaware of it.

One of the prostitutes said calmly to Emily, pointing at the hysterical woman, "Nuts. Kept trying to kill herself. Know how she tried to do it? Put her head down the toilet and kept flushing it. That went on all night. Jesus!"

Emily ran to the bars and grabbed the arms of the hysterical woman, trying to help her. The two of them struggled. Emily said, "You're hurting yourself! Can you hear me?"

The cell door banged open and two orderlies entered with a strait jacket, forcing the hysterical woman into it as she screamed. They dragged her out.

Then Mildred entered, followed by Fonner, who looked in Emily's direction without meeting her eyes, then turned to Mildred and said, "I said, isolation."

Mildred took Emily's arm. Emily tried to hold back, a pleading look on her face.

"I'm trying to be cooperative but if you'd just tell me—"

Mildred twisted Emily's arm expertly. The pain caused Emily to cry out. Her knees buckled. The second prostitute spat in Mildred's face. Mildred, without letting go of Emily, aimed a kick at the prostitute that sent her sprawling across the cell with a howl of pain. Mildred dragged Emily out.

A cell door with a tiny, barred opening clicked shut. The cell was like a closet. It had a very high ceiling. It was almost too small to lie down in. The walls and the floor were padded. Her shoes

98

had been taken away. For the first time in her life, she felt the terror of claustrophobia. She threw herself against the padded door, pressing her face to the opening, and cried out for help. She could see nothing except a blank wall. There was no sound anywhere. She sank to her knees, then into a crouching position, holding herself with her arms. Her mind kept imagining a way out. It was absurd, as if her mind kept escaping. Repeatedly. Her body remained a prisoner. Overhead, a camera was focused on her and a microphone picked up even the faint sound of her breathing.

Hours later, Emily sat on the floor of the cell, combing her loose hair with her fingers and humming to herself. She began to sing, La la la, comforted by the sound of her own voice.

David returned to the inn shortly before six to find that Emily had not arrived yet. He waited an hour in their room, then called their house. Esmeralda told him in slow, careful English that the *señora* had not come back there from the museum. He thought, Well, something came up. She's late. He called his service, wondering if she had left any word for him. A relief girl told him there were no messages. At eight o'clock he began to get worried. He called his service again and found that Emily had called him around three, leaving no message. That led nowhere. He became convinced she had been in an accident and he called the highway patrol. They said they had no record of any such victim. He began checking with them every half-hour. Unable to reach Marianne, he called the Legion of Honor. Yes, she had been there. No, she had left. They could give him no information about her. He called half a dozen hospitals in San Francisco. No one knew anything. He gave them all the number where he could be reached and then sat down on the end of the bed, at a loss as to what to do next. He was torn between wanting to drive back and search for Emily himself and wanting to stay by the phone in the inn, since that was the number he had given everyone. He felt trapped, helpless. It was utterly unreal. Perhaps nothing was wrong. Impossible. He was on the telephone all night. He had called the San Francisco police and been transferred to a number of different precincts with no clear reason and with no result.

The next morning, he called San Francisco police headquarters downtown again, and this time they told him that Emily was there. Yes, said a voice, she was quite all right. He sagged with relief and gratitude. Then he asked what she was doing there. Had she been in an accident? They refused adamantly to give him any information. When he insisted, the connection was broken. Furious, he rented another car and raced back through the low hills of the wine country toward the city, arriving at the jail around eleven.

David lunged at Daly, grabbing him by the front of his shirt and smashing him up against a wall, yelling out:

"What the fuck is the matter with you guys? All damn night I've been going out of my skull searching for my wife, and now you tell me you've got her locked up in your stinking jail and you won't even tell me what for!"

"Take your hands off me."

"Take my hands off you? Listen to me, you bastard, you give me help or I go to the papers with a list of every fucking cop I've ever treated for clap that you guys have gotten from every working girl in town that you've hustled, after which your jobs won't be worth Jack Shit and you'd better believe it!"

"You got a lawyer?" Daly's voice was low, almost gentle. David looked at him, bewildered. Daly said, with a pleading note in his voice, "Get a lawyer."

"I want to see my wife!"

"Sorry. Orders."

"What's the charge?"

"P.C. One Eighty-seven." Then, as David looked at him blankly, Daly said softly, "Murder One."

13

Dr. Samuel Adams was not in a good mood. Malpractice insurance had been raised again. Dr. Adams, now sixty, had always intended to work half time during the last few years of his practice. That, however, was no longer possible, owing to the rising cost of his premiums. He knew now that he would be forced either into retirement or into maintaining the same schedule that had already begun to exhaust him in his fifties. But Cade Burr, elderly, acerbic, had been shown into his office. Dr. Adams enjoyed Cade. He decided on a genial tone.

"Want to take a pee, Cade?"

"That's what I'm here for." Cade dropped his trousers. Dr. Adams sat down on a stool, gesturing at the chair opposite him. He was a thin, tall man, perfectly bald, with taut brown skin. A pretty nurse entered, wheeling in the equipment. Cade turned his lion's head in her direction and said, watching her, "Fine-looking ass. Damn few women you can say that about." When the nurse did not react, Cade said, "One of the pleasures of being eighty-one. You get to say exactly what's on your mind." Sitting down opposite Adams, who began inserting a catheter into him, Cade said to the air, "When I was a boy, I can't tell you how many things I didn't do. I thought I was moral. Now I realize I was only squeamish."

"You have a blockage."

"I *had* a blockage. That was sixty years ago."

Ignoring him, Adams asked, "When are you going to let me operate?"

The nurse answered a telephone. "Yes?"

"Friend of mine had that prostate operation. Fella told me he

101

ended up with a hard-on that wouldn't quit. Now, at eighty-one, that sounds mighty attractive. But twenty-four hours a day?"

"I'm afraid he can't talk now."

"It won't be like that."

"Bullshit."

"I understand that, sir, but if you would just call back—"

"Who is it?"

"Dr. David Blake. For Mr. Burr."

Cade beckoned to her. She brought the phone to him. He began to pass water. The strain went out of his face.

"Davey? Sam and I are just taking a leak. It's one of those things we get together on from time to time." Listening. A look of concern. Cade scratched his big head with a big hand, rumpling the thick thatch of white hair. "Davey? What's the matter?" He listened again, then interrupted. "You don't know what's happened? Uh-huh. Yeah. Now, just take it easy." Adams and his nurse could hear the scratching sound of David's raised voice. Cade interrupted him again, saying, " 'Course you do. You need one right away. Now, I'll give you some names." The scratching voice went up a few decibels. Cade said impatiently, "Son, you don't need an old man eighty-one years old can't even take a piss by hisself, what's the matter with you?"

They could hear David's voice, earnest and incoherent. It sounded almost as if he were crying. Cade said, "Now, you cut that out, hear? Billy Blue Hill, get the hell on over here and let's talk sense!"

There was a click. Cade handed the phone back to the nurse. The stream was stronger now. Cade sighed, smiling at the nurse. She smiled back. He said, "Christ, that feels good. From where I sit, a piss is as good as a fuck any day."

"Cade! Oh, Cade!"

"Now, it's all right, Emily."

They sat in the small cell where Emily had been brought to meet him.

"Where's David?"

"Just easy now. At the moment, seems I'm the only one they'll let in here."

"Cade, what's *happening?*"

"They didn't tell you why you're here?"

"All they told me is a number! Can you imagine that? All they told me is P.C. One Eighty-seven! I've been saying it over and over to myself all night. It's as if the whole world has gone crazy! Cade, what is that number?"

"They've accused you of murder, Emily."

She got to her feet unsteadily, at the same time going completely white, so that Cade, who was waiting for her reaction, got up and held her by the arms, afraid she would faint. Her eyes remained fastened on him.

"Murder?"

"They're saying you murdered Jennie Ludlow."

"What are you talking about? Jennie was smoking in bed! The mattress caught fire! It was in the papers! Cade, what's going on?"

"All I know is what Davey told me. About him and Jennie." He patted her hand to express his sympathy. Then: "These folks here, they won't tell me a thing. Records are sealed."

"Why?"

"That's what we're going to find out this afternoon. At the arraignment. Now, I just want you to be patient for a little while."

He asked her a few questions. Yes, he understood that David had been in Los Angeles the night Jennie was killed. Yes, he understood the circumstances under which he had left. Emily was home, wasn't she? Anybody stop by? Telephone? No? Well, that was all right. Now, don't worry. Woman has a right to be alone in her own home at night. And the maid? What time did that nice maid of hers go to bed that night? Oh, that was maid's night out. Now, why get upset? Maids, don't they have a right to a day off, too? Just take it easy, Emmy. Take it easy.

Afterward, Cade went to a phone booth and called David to reassure him. By then, the wire services had the story. David had found that out because someone had called him.

"I wasn't taking any calls, but my girl said this one was urgent. It was Old Lady Prentice. Ever meet her? Well, she lives down the street." David's voice was strained with emotion. The news had stunned him. Like Emily, he had assumed Jennie had died in an accident. But now there was no time to talk about how he felt. Mrs. Prentice had asked to see Emily's lawyer right away, saying she had vital information for him.

"What kind of information?"

"I don't know. But she's not a woman who exaggerates. I think you should see her."

"Why don't you give me the address?"

Cade climbed the stairs of the old Maybeck house where Mrs. Prentice lived, and rang the bell. He was shown into a lobby and then, after giving his coat to the maid, conducted through double doors paneled with beveled glass, into a foyer and taken upstairs to a bedroom. Mrs. Alice Prentice was propped up in a fumed oak bed. She thanked Cade for coming and apologized for receiving him *"en négligée,"* explaining that she had just returned from a stay in the hospital.

"I hope you're recovered, ma'am."

"I'm not recovered, Mr. Burr. I'm dying. Excuse me." She rang a small silver bell and a maid entered. "Help me up, please," she said. The maid assisted her. Mrs. Prentice sat on the edge of the bed and gestured, first at a shawl, then at a pair of velvet slippers. She picked up a gold-headed cane and walked toward the door, leaning heavily on the maid's arm.

"I didn't mean to sound dramatic. But there's no saving me. I understand that I'll only last a few months. They tell me, however, that I will go easily. That part's good. Poor Miss Ludlow. The spirits of the murdered are always restless. A clairvoyant once told me that they sometimes have trouble comprehending that they are dead." She took a quick breath. "I'll give my deposition in the sitting room. Then we'll have tea." She made her way with an effort toward the door, then glanced back into the room. "That's my deathbed. It's strange to get up out of it. How old are you?"

"Eighty-two come September, ma'am."

"I'm eighty-nine. I don't hold with a lot of machinery and artificial methods to keep one's parts working. It's like the old Scottish proverb about crying back the dead. You know that superstition?"

"No, ma'am, I don't."

"Well, the whole notion was, you had to let them go. Unbolt the doors, make sure the bed wasn't lying athwart the planks and wait for the tide to go out. Point is, I mean to die as I've lived. I don't want anybody crying me back." She tapped Cade on the chest with the handle of her cane. "If they tell you you're dying, you ought to go home and do it in your own bed, where most of the important things in life happen."

They walked slowly out to the staircase, Mrs. Prentice shuffling over to a chair lift which carried her down the staircase, while Cade walked beside her.

"Now, what I'm going to tell you is plain and simple. I drove by the Blake house on the night of the murder."

"That was some weeks ago, Mrs. Prentice. How can you be sure it was that night?"

"Because I had been out to a dinner party that Monday. It's on my calendar. People talk. I'd heard that Dr. Blake was leaving his wife. He had gone to Los Angeles to some meeting, and I understood that he wasn't returning to her. That was the reason I was concerned about her. I looked up and saw Mrs. Blake sitting in her living room. I even know the exact time, since I asked my chauffeur. You'll want a statement from him."

"Yes, Mrs. Prentice."

"He's waiting. Well, when he told me, I decided it was too late to pay a call, so I just drove on. But according to the news reports, that murdered woman was still alive and screaming at ten-fifteen, five miles across town. And ten-fifteen, Mr. Cade, is the precise time I drove by Mrs. Blake's house and saw her there. Now, how do you take your tea, Mr. Burr?"

"With lots of whisky."

"I like you, sonny."

Cade met David in the hall shortly before the arraignment, later that afternoon. Gesturing toward the empty courtroom, Cade said, "You go in there and wait for me, Davey. I just have to go have a word with the judge before the proceedings."

"What happened? What did she tell you?"

Cade preferred to wait before saying anything. With the deposition Mrs. Prentice had given him in his pocket, it did not seem as if the whole thing would even come to arraignment. Of course, Emily could have solicited murder but (and this was a very important legal point in Cade's mind) that wasn't the charge, and if she were supposed to have acted in concert with someone else, then why wasn't there a double arraignment? He confidently expected the whole matter dropped.

David said, "What did she tell you, Cade?"

Cade decided there was no point in not being perfectly open with him. "Emily has an alibi. Mrs. Prentice gave me a deposition. She and her chauffeur happened to drive by the house and both of them saw Emily at exactly the time this murder was supposed to have happened."

"My God, you mean it's over?"

"Well, let's see what the judge has to say, shall we do that, Davey?"

Cade gave him a brief wave and then walked stolidly down the hall, turned a corner and knocked at the wide, heavy door of Judge Amos Manly's chambers.

14

Judge Amos Manly sat at his desk in chambers, leafing through the arraignment papers, his back to the high, arched windows. He paused in his reading, a delicate forefinger holding his place. The hooded eyes looked up, two points of light in a skeletal face.

"People versus Blake. One Eighty-seven. Cade? You defending?"

"I am the defense attorney, yes, Your Honor."

"Thought you'd retired."

"So did I."

"Hm."

Judge Manly glanced down at the place he had marked, frowned, then sat back, throwing his glasses on the desk. "Ready to plead?"

"No, I'm not, Your Honor."

"Why not?"

"Discovery proceedings haven't been completed. Petition for *duces tecum* there on your desk."

"What do you want, Cade?"

"Notes, documents, and other tangible evidence possessed by the prosecution. Names of prosecution witnesses. Police report on behavior of accused in the forty-eight hours since her incarceration. Coroner's report."

"Sounds like you don't know anything."

"That's right."

"Ask for any of this stuff?"

"All of it."

"Hm. Rufus? Any objection?"

"Yes, Your Honor."

"State the objection, please." Judge Manly rested his gaze on the district attorney, waiting for an answer. When the district attorney hesitated, Judge Manly asked, "You planning to prosecute this thing yourself, Rufus?"

"Yes, Your Honor."

"Hm." It made for problems. He didn't like Rufus Simonds. At that moment, almost as if Rufus had read his mind, the district attorney looked up at him. If Manly's dislike amounted to prejudice, he would have to disqualify himself. Manly looked briefly at the face, the dark hair, the strongly marked eyebrows, the powerful nose, the full lips. He had never tried a case with Rufus himself as prosecutor. If he said anything, it would have to be now. Their eyes met. No, it was only the theatrical flair one found so often in trial lawyers that bothered him. And the voice. It had an extraordinary range and belonged on the stage. Well, that didn't matter. A man had a right to his style. He would listen only to argument. It struck him that Rufus had still not stated his objection. Manly looked at him again. The voice spoke, now a dry rustle.

"Subject reports contain speculative material confidential in nature, referring to police theories, unapprehended crime partners, accomplices, et cetera. This material is probably not discoverable under the work-product theory of Hickman versus Taylor, 1947, 329, United States 495."

"Comment?"

"Well, it appears I'm being told something is a secret and when I try to find out why, I get the answer, 'Well, if we told you, then you'd know.' " Cade looked at them sleepily.

"Rufus?"

"If the requested material is made available to the defense, Your Honor, my office declines to be responsible for the consequences."

"Let me just have a look here for a moment." Manly carefully examined the papers in front of him. Once again, the bony forefinger hesitated at the same place. "Rufus, you've got a murder, a body, a suspect, a police report indicating motive, apparent opportunity, and a coroner's report indicating the time of death.

108

You've also got a warrant for the arrest of the accused. But there's something missing. Hasn't it struck you, Rufus?"

Cade thought, We also have an alibi. But he would wait to hear them out before playing that card.

"What's that, Your Honor?" asked Rufus.

"The murder weapon."

"I intend to disclose that during the course of the trial."

"Disclose it now."

Rufus shot a brief look in Cade's direction, then looked back at Manly, who said sharply, "Now, let's not have any glancing about. You know as well as I do that we can't have any private conversations on this subject." Rufus suddenly seemed young, almost too young. He was half Cade's age. As if to make sure he showed no prejudice, Manly said to Rufus, "Don't let old Cade there fool you. If he so much as caught you whispering to me in the corridor, he could have the whole case thrown out of court. And he'd do it, too. So, since I need to know and you have to tell me, let's have it now. Murder weapon?"

"There was not, in the strictest sense of the term, any murder weapon as such, may it please the Court."

Cade opened his eyes wide. "You just say there was no murder weapon?"

"He did."

"Move to dismiss. Complaint defective."

"As such," Rufus repeated quietly.

Manly said, "Let's hear about the 'as such.' How do you think Mrs. . . . uh"—he consulted his papers, refreshed his memory—"Mrs. Emily Blake killed Miss Jennie Ludlow?"

"By supernatural means."

"By supernatural means." Echoing the statement in a flat tone of voice, Manly tipped back in his black leather chair, looking at Rufus.

"Yes, sir."

Cade turned in his chair with an effort, studying Rufus. Then he said, "You know, I owe you an apology. I don't think I've ever appreciated the originality of your mind before today." Then, to Manly, he said, "Move to dismiss. The charge is incompetent."

Manly studied Rufus. "The statute against witchcraft in England was repealed in . . . let me see . . . 1725. As for the law here in this country, which of course came from there . . ." Swiftly, Manly swiveled around in his chair, pulled a thin blue book down from his shelf, opened it to the second page and read aloud: " 'Be it enacted, that if any person shall use, practice or exercise any invocation or conjuration of any evil and wicked spirit, or take up any dead man, woman or child out of his, her or their grave, to be employed or used in any manner of witchcraft, enchantment, charm or sorcery, whereby any person shall be killed, destroyed, wasted or consumed, that every such offender, being of any of the said offenses duly and lawfully convicted and attainted, shall suffer pains of death.' " His mouth formed itself into a hard line. Then he said without expression, "That's the only applicable law I can think of. Now, Rufus, if that's what you've got in mind, I think I should tell you that the Privy Council struck that law from the books in the Massachusetts Bay Colony in 1695. And I should also tell you that it has no counterpart in any state in the Union."

"The charge was brought under Section One Eighty-seven of the Penal Code, Your Honor."

"Straight Murder One."

"Yes, Your Honor. Murder is still a crime."

Manly told himself he must not even appear to acknowledge the innuendo. "Comes to the same thing, that your point?"

"Yes, Your Honor."

"And you intend to prove this in my court?"

"I will attempt to do that, yes, Your Honor."

Silence filled the room. It hung in the air like an unspoken question. Manly made a bridge of his fingers, determined to take as much time as he wanted to rule on the matter. Cade pulled off his glasses and polished them on his wide, flowered tie. Rufus sat motionless, waiting.

"When you go to the preliminary hearing, you're going to have to produce enough evidence to show that the accused should be bound over to trial. You know that as well as I do." He studied Rufus, thinking, Maybe he's had a nervous breakdown. It seemed unlikely. Rufus appeared composed and resolute.

"Yes, Your Honor."

110

"Myself, I'd like to hear that evidence now. Got any objection?"

Rufus said, "I will be glad to offer the court the evidence." He took a folder from his brief case, opened it and, glancing at his notes, said, "People will show that, on March 25th of this year, defendant participated in experiments involving telepathy and clairvoyance. Experiments were abruptly terminated when defendant refused to continue with them, but not before three attending professors had described her performance as 'supernormal.' Depositions have been obtained from all three.

"In the next instance, subpoenaed records show that defendant warned her psychiatrist, Dr. Lambert Jones, he could die of appendicitis. In a telephone call to his home that Friday, learning that Dr. Jones had left town for the weekend, defendant insisted he return immediately, threatening Mrs. Jones that otherwise her husband would be stricken with appendicitis and die. Thinking she was talking to a disturbed patient, Mrs. Jones disregarded this warning. Dr. Jones died on the following evening in the manner described. Depositions on file from the widow of Dr. Jones and the attending coroner in Humboldt County. In this connection, the people will draw the Court's attention to the fact that today, appendicitis is comparatively rare in this country, and death from ensuing peritonitis occurs in perhaps two hundred cases annually, that is, one in a million. Multiplying this by the number of days in the year gives us a chance factor of one in seventy-three billion.

"Thirdly, defendant repeated this performance in the case of the decedent, threatening her with death and naming in advance the date and nature of her demise. This information is contained in a diary belonging to the decedent, in her own handwriting. Although the People are well aware that this would customarily be regarded as inadmissible evidence, People plead that said document be admitted into evidence anyway, on the grounds that it clearly establishes defendant's foreknowledge of the crime of murder, that same crime she herself threatened to commit."

Rufus returned the folder to his briefcase. Cade and Manly sat motionless. Then Manly said, "Under the law, I do not have any choice except to order a preliminary hearing. Cade, I'm going to take your *duces tecum* under advisement. Rufus, you are hereby ordered to turn over all relevant prosecution documents to me so that I can make proper determination as to whether discovery at this point would prejudice People's case."

"Yes, Your Honor."

"Cade?"

Cade paused, thinking, remembering that the chief argument advanced against J. B. Rhine's research at Duke alleged that Rhine's results were nothing but statistical artifacts. But in the face of the evidence Rufus had offered, what judge would accept such reasoning? He weighed the odds, then decided. The case would undoubtedly go to trial. "No comment at this time, Your Honor," Cade said.

Manly said, "Very well. The *prima facie* case will warrant trial, in my opinion. Let me just say this much: I am going to try this case without prejudice. The record will show that. But I want to caution you, Rufus: If, at the close of the case for the prosecution, you have offered only a statistical argument, I will hold that you have wasted the Court's time and will then direct the jury to bring in a verdict of acquittal. Do you understand me?"

"Yes, Your Honor."

"We'll hear the arraignment."

The three men got to their feet. Manly let the other two go into the courtroom ahead of him. Walking alone to the window, he looked across the patch of park to Bufano's stainless steel statue of Sun Yat Sen. Above it, he could see the steep, tile roofs of Chinatown. There, fortunes were told every day by the I Ching, incense burned in the joss house, and devils were cast out by the miraculous power of ancient herbs. And here, Rufus actually intended to try a young woman for supernatural murder. *In my court!* He was glad he had not disqualified himself. The case would attract enormous publicity. He himself would listen impartially. Then, at the end, he would throw the whole goddamned thing out of court. And Rufus could go explain matters to the press. And to the people. At the next election. It would serve him right.

15

Cade walked into the courtroom, joining David. David looked at him, puzzled. He was obviously thinking about the alibi. Did Emily know? Not possible. David wouldn't have been allowed to see her. She wouldn't know. She wouldn't have gotten her hopes up.

Cade patted David's shoulder, his face showing nothing. They reacted to the sound of the bailiff's voice. Manly entered the courtroom, aware that less than a dozen people were there to answer the bailiff's demand that they rise. Manly crossed to the bench, thinking, If this thing comes to trial, I'll have to have a couple of dozen men from the sheriff's department here to keep order.

Spreading the skirts of his black robe and seating himself, Manly banged his gavel. Everyone sat down. A door at the side of the courtroom opened. David, sitting with Cade, looked over at it, then jumped up, a shocked look on his face. Mildred Theale had entered, escorting Emily. Manacled.

Cade pulled David back into his chair before he could say anything.

"That's just the beginning," Cade said to him in a low voice. "You want to help her, you keep hold of yourself, you hear me?"

David clenched his jaw, gripping the sides of the armchair in which he sat at the defense table, then jumped up and embraced Emily as the matron seated her. She tried to smile. She looked dazed. David felt his throat tighten. Emily stretched out her hands, touching his face.

Manly said, "We'll hear the charges read."

113

Cade was on his feet. "We'll waive the reading of the charges, Your Honor."

"How does the defendant plead?"

"The defendant pleads Not Guilty, Your Honor."

"Let the record so show."

David looked at Cade, at a loss. He started to say something. Obviously, he was thinking about the alibi. Cade shook his head.

"Later, Davey," he said quietly. A bailiff led David to a seat with the spectators. He turned when a hand was put on his shoulder, and he saw Marianne. She pulled him down beside her. Their eyes met. He saw the bewilderment in her face. He looked at her blankly. Her gloved hand took his, squeezing it. Her square, strong face was set. The gray eyes searched for Emily.

"May it please the Court," Cade was saying, "I ask that in the matter of bail—"

Rufus got to his feet.

"Objection. Your Honor, this being a capital offense, punishable by death, the prosecution requests that bail be denied."

David felt himself growing light-headed. This wasn't happening. This couldn't be happening. He got awkwardly to his feet and started to say something but Cade turned around at that moment and gave him a warning look, Marianne pulled on David's hand, and David sat down, saying in a louder voice than he intended, "It must be some kind of legal maneuver. It doesn't mean anything." Manly banged his gavel. David looked toward Emily. She was staring off into space.

Manly said, answering Rufus, "Overruled. Since the prosecution has yet to show that the alleged crime was committed in conjunction with any other crime, no capital offense has yet been established, and bailment is accordingly in order."

Cade got up slowly and said in what was almost a wondering tone, glancing at the papers in front of him, "Considering that all the records are sealed and that the prosecution has so far failed to show that my client is in any way a danger to herself or to society, having no felonious record, I ask that the defendant be released without bail, on her own recognizance."

Manly struck his gavel once, then saying, "So ordered. Trial to begin in this court on the fifteenth day of July of this year, the

defendant to present herself before the bench at that time."
Then, banging his gavel again, Manly said, "These arraignment
proceedings are hereby terminated."

Manly rose and started out. Those in the courtroom rose. Emily
started toward the side door. A bailiff stopped her, and Mildred
Theale removed Emily's manacles. This seemed to come as a
surprise to Emily. Making his way quickly toward her, David took
her in his arms. She looked up at him as if she could not quite
understand what was going on.

The three of them drove to the Blake house in silence—Emily,
David, and Cade. Esmeralda opened the door, her brown face
wrinkled, near tears. When she saw Emily, she stretched out her
arms and embraced her. Emily had to bend down to kiss her. The
maid began to cry. Emily hushed her, patting her face. Esmeralda
took Emily's hand and kissed it.

"Why don't you fix us some tea?" Emily said. Esmeralda nodded, wiping her eyes on her apron, gesturing them in. Esmeralda
hurried into the kitchen, and the three of them went into the
library. They all remained standing.

David said to Cade, "But I thought she had an alibi."

"What alibi?"

He remembered that Emily did not know anything about what
had happened. He explained about Mrs. Prentice. Emily turned
to Cade for some explanation.

David said, "Do they have to go through this anyway? I mean,
if it's quite clear that she couldn't have done it—"

"They're not saying she was there."

"I don't think I understand."

"They say this is something you did from a distance. Let's say,
by an act of will." Cade said this looking at Emily. She looked
back at him without any expression.

"I don't know what you're talking about," she said.

"The prosecution alleges that you committed murder by supernatural means."

David's mind raced. *That story she told me! That crazy story
she told me about a kid!* He had to get her out of there before
she said anything. He had to talk to her.

"That's the nuttiest thing I ever heard of!" He tried to laugh.

115

It sounded forced. "Honey," he said quickly, "you've been through enough. Why don't you get on upstairs and freshen up while I talk to Cade here?"

"Are you serious?" she asked Cade finally.

"*They* are."

"Cade, I really think she should go upstairs because—"

"Can they do that?" Emily asked.

"Yes."

David said, "It's some kind of mistake."

Cade answered, "That's what they allege. And the judge has no choice. You must understand, he has to proceed to trial. That's the law."

"They can't go ahead with it! Honey, let me talk to Cade."

She said, her eyes fastened on Cade, "Can they really do such a thing?"

"It seems so."

"Well, what can we *do?*" She was dazed.

"If they proceed, all we can do is defend."

"No wonder Emmy's upset! It's ludicrous! Who ever heard of anything like this?"

"It's happened."

"When? In Salem!" David said, trying to sound as if he were joking.

"There was a case like it back in . . . let me see . . . 1929. Fella named Blymyer was accused of killing a man named Rehmeyer."

"You seem to know all about it," Emily said.

"A case like that, it tends to stick in the mind."

David tried to take Emily's arm. She shook him off.

"There was another one—no, there were two—back in 1945 in England. Famous cases. Fella named Walton. And then some unidentified woman."

"And you're telling me they were both supernatural murders?" Emily twisted her hands.

"That's what was said."

"Who said it?"

"Ever hear of Dr. Margaret Murray?"

"She's an anthropologist."

"World-famous."

116

"Yes."

"Well, she's on record as saying they were witchcraft murders."

Emily continued to look at Cade without saying anything. David began to get angry.

"Are you telling me that people were convicted of witchcraft in 1945?"

"No, the cases never went to trial."

"For want of evidence?"

"That's right, Davey."

"You sound as if you're taking this seriously!" David's voice rose.

Cade said quietly, "I always take a murder charge seriously."

"Excuse me," said Emily. She started toward the door. "I'll be down in a few minutes." She left the room.

David breathed a quick sigh of relief. In a moment, he would excuse himself, follow her upstairs. Cade accepted a cup of tea from the maid. He did not say anything. His silence made David uncomfortable.

"I'd better go see how she is," David said finally.

Emily was just getting out of the shower, scrubbing her hair dry with a rough towel. David entered.

"You okay, honey?"

She said nothing. He thought about the story she had told him. *That crazy story.* It was just the kind of story they'd like to hear! *But the boy was dead.* The story was a fantasy, but he must make quite sure she never repeated it. He must make her understand how strange it would sound. He didn't know how to bring up the subject. He licked his lips, watching her nervously. She seemed stable enough. Now.

"I'm fine," she said almost coldly. He shot her a quick look, then, taking the towel from her, began drying her back.

"It's all right," he said awkwardly.

"What the hell makes you say it's all right?"

"Easy, now."

"Don't try that bedside manner on me! I'm not one of your goddamned patients, David!"

He tried to be calm. "I only meant that you haven't done anything."

"Whereas *you*—!" She broke off, irritated at herself. She began to dress. He sat down in the slipper chair, lacing his fingers.

"Okay," he sighed. He thought, Why not be direct? Why not treat her as a mature adult. That would tend to make her feel like one. She didn't need to have fantasies now. "Look. I want you to do something for me. For both of us. I don't want you to tell Cade what you told me. About that kid."

"Lupe."

"Yeah."

She had gotten into her pantyhose and bra and now had the hair drier on. She was holding it in her left hand, a brush in her right, watching herself in the mirror. Brush, brush, brush under the powerful stream of hot air. Hmmmmm. Hmmmmm. Then click.

"What are you talking about?"

"You know goddamned well what I'm talking about!" He could have bitten his tongue. What on earth had made him snap at her? He said gently, trying to smile it away, "We just don't want Cade to hear that crazy story. I mean, from what he says—"

"But that boy kept following me! That little boy! And he kept saying—" Her eyes were wide, searching his. He put his hands on her shoulders, squeezing them, returning her gaze with a look full of understanding. Tenderness.

"Trust me, okay? I mean, who needs to know about something that never happened?" She started to speak, eyes still on his but he went, "Sh, sh, sh! I know. *Some* of it happened, but then you sort of imagined the rest of it, just the way we said, right, honey?"

She nodded dumbly.

"So we just won't say anything at all." He gave her a long kiss, holding her tight until she caught her breath. They walked downstairs together, David with a protective arm around her.

16

They sat in the study having tea. Cade hadn't said a word about the trial, but had only talked about furniture, commenting at length on the new rug Emily had bought David for the study. "It's a fine Bokhara . . . A Kashan? You thought of buying him a Kashan? Emmy, you can't have a Kashan in a man's study. Much too la-dee-dah. Me, I like a Bokhara. Most masculine of all Oriental rugs. It's a good rug, Emmy. A shade new, but give it fifty years—no, Emmy, I mean it, I haven't got it to give but you have—and its rich glow will warm your declining years. Yes, a touch more, thank you—no, fine. I like a smoky Keemun."

David watched him, remembering almost like a schoolboy how Cade had once quoted Whitehead's remark to him—what was it? . . . that one should talk about unimportant things until everybody had gotten the temperature of the room. Now he saw its effect. Emily had come into the room full of anxiety, but old Cade, comfortable, affable Cade, had deflected emotion with small talk until Emily had been able to compose herself. Now she sat embroidering away, listening. She searched for a scarlet thread.

There was a pause. David said, "We really don't know what the hell's going on, Cade."

"I know you don't. These people in the district attorney's office, they got all the evidence sealed. Won't tell me a thing. Lucky I didn't have to go to the toilet. Mood they're in, they wouldn't have pointed the way."

"When will you know something?" Emily asked, snipping at her thread.

Cade answered mildly, "I've filed a petition of *duces tecum.* That means 'thou shalt bring with thee,' in case you ain't got your

Latin on the tip of your tongue. It's a subpoena demanding that the prosecution show its hand. See, they've got some things up their sleeve, and if we don't know what they are, it's kind of hard to refute them."

"You mean they don't have to tell you?"

"Davey, they've got a right to keep their *speculations* secret. Only, at this point, it appears their whole case is pure conjecture. 'Course, I don't know. They won't talk to me. Will you?"

"Emmy doesn't know anything. Isn't that right, honey?"

Emily said, "I don't know anything. I didn't kill her. I'm perfectly willing to take one of those tests—"

"A polygraph?"

"Yes. To prove that I'm telling the truth!"

"That isn't necessary, Emmy," said David.

"But why not?" she asked.

"I just . . . think it's demeaning."

"But I want to. Cade?"

Sipping his tea, Cade glanced at David, caught the slight shake of his head, blinked at him innocently and said, "Myself, I think Emmy's idea is a very good one."

Cade arranged by phone to have the test made the next day.

At police headquarters the following morning, Emily sat in a chair in a small room while a mild-mannered police doctor with a short graying beard fitted on the sensor devices of a polygraph. She winced, feeling the slight suction of the small rubber cups on her skin, feeling a thin plastic wire taped to an area just below her breastbone, to hold it in place, stiffened as air filled the rubber sleeve of the sphygmomanometer tightening slightly around her upper arm. The room smelled of disinfectant, and the cement walls were painted with light green, like the walls of an institution. She swallowed.

"My name is Dr. Phillips," he said, taking up a pen and consulting a list of typed questions he had had prepared. "Now, I'm just going to ask you simple questions, Mrs. Blake, all right? Nothing to get upset about. And as I told you, we can stop this anytime you like. You comfortable?"

"Yes."

"You understand that this is just a way of picking up cues. My father used to tell me that you could always tell when a poker player was bluffing because his ears got red—of course, that isn't always reliable—"

"Is this?"

"Yes. In most cases, yes." He pointed his pen at the polygraph. "Here, we're measuring changes in respiration, heart rate, and skin resistance. I'm going to be asking you matter-of-fact questions. The whole purpose of the test is to find out whether you have any guilty knowledge. If you haven't, your responses to the questions will be perfectly normal. All set?"

"I'd like to know whether you have any information about the charges against me."

"No, ma'am. And that's preferable. It's much better if I don't know anything about the case at all. Ready?" Emily nodded. He then began asking her commonplace questions about herself: her name, her age, her place of birth, residence, marital status, and occupation. That much settled, he said, "I'm now going to give you five addresses. One of them was the address of the deceased. Now, I want you to repeat each of them as I say it. I suppose you know the address of the deceased—"

"Of course I know it. It was in the newspapers. Besides, I visited her there."

"Just answer the questions as I ask them, if you please, Mrs. Blake." Dr. Phillips read the questions typed out on the sheet before him. He did not want information from Emily, he wanted only to find indications of guilty knowledge. He read her a list of addresses and she repeated them. He wrote something down and went on to the next question:

"Did you kill the deceased, Miss Jennie Ludlow?"

"I certainly did not!"

"Just answer yes or no, please."

"No."

Dr. Phillips knew nothing about the case excepting that Emily was charged with the murder of Jennie Ludlow. He knew Jennie's address and the date of her death, and that was almost the extent of his information. He confined himself to questions about the deceased, about whom Emily knew almost nothing, the house in which she had lived (roughly described in the police report), and what knowledge Emily might have about how she died. At the end of the inquiry, he took the typed sheet on which he had made inked notes, signed it, had it Xeroxed, and gave a copy to the waiting Cade.

That afternoon, Cade went to see Rufus in his office, threw the copy of the polygraph test results onto the desk in front of him, and folded his arms.

"Polygraph says Mrs. Blake was telling the truth. Says she didn't kill the deceased and doesn't know anything about her murder. Change your mind any?"

"We both know there are people who can pass a polygraph successfully. That's why the evidence isn't usually admissible in a court of law. That is, unless both sides agree—and I don't."

"But just between us, I thought it might alter your thinking."

"It doesn't."

Cade studied him. When Rufus only met his eyes, not answering, Cade got to his feet slowly. "Father of Lies, is that it? Just thought I'd ask." The eyes continued to meet his. Cade reminded himself of something, a scientific dictum he had learned years before and had schooled himself never to forget in any argument: down through the class *Mammalia*, averting the eyes is a sign that an animal does not want to fight. He watched Rufus steadily. The eyes never wavered. Rufus was not about to back down. He must find out why. Whatever made a man like Rufus reach such an outrageous, dangerous conclusion?

Cade said casually, flicking imaginary specks off his trousers, sitting down again, "Something bothers me. Once this thing hits the press, we're in for a whole hell of a lot of publicity. After that, there's no way back. Now, you're a bright man. You're one of the smartest young lawyers I've ever met. My daddy always taught me never to praise a man to his face, but here I'm just trying to state the facts. You're smart enough to know there's almost no way you can win. Let's say you lose. Not an unreasonable supposition. Now, what happens then? Three big things." And Cade ticked them off on his thick fingers. "One, the case gets thrown out of court. You don't convince the judge, there's no way he'll ever let anything like this go to a jury. Two, you end up looking like you're not playing with a full deck. And, three—given the kind of unfortunate publicity a trial like this is bound to attract—you destroy your career."

"I know all that."

"Well, you can quit anytime you like, sonny."

"I would if I could."

"What stops you?"

"The weight of the evidence."

There was a long pause. Cade took out a fine Dunhill pipe, filled it, tamped it, and lit it. Rufus waited patiently.

Then Cade said, "I want to ask you something, may I?" Rufus nodded his head, the dark eyes resting on him, the full lips closed in a resolute line. "I want to ask you this: what happens if you win? I mean, hell, man, we're talking about sorcery! You win and that gives a kind of governmental sanction to what you're doing. Lots of people interested in this kind of thing nowadays. Has it occurred to you that you might start a panic?"

"Yes."

"That don't bother you none?"

Rufus hesitated, then answered quietly, never changing his position in his leather armchair. "The kind of public hysteria you suggest already exists. Right now, there are millions of people all over the world who believe in the occult. The Russians are spending a fortune on such research. So are we. I'm sure you know that. All right, they've stopped calling it the 'occult.' Today, the acceptable term is 'psi phenomena.' It's the same thing. I'm afraid the belief is already there. I didn't start it."

"I know about psi research. Is that all you're talking about?"

"Names change. Such things used to be called 'the work of the Devil.' "

"You believe in the Devil?"

"The Devil's greatest trick is to persuade us that he doesn't exist."

Baudelaire, thought Cade.

"You're right," said Rufus. "I'm gambling my name, my position, my career." A look. Then: "How much are *you* gambling?"

"No further questions." Cade got up slowly, shook hands and shuffled out of the room.

123

17

Emily and David were home waiting for Cade, who had promised to come over as soon as he had seen Rufus. Marianne stopped by. After the arraignment the day before, David had taken Emily straight home. Marianne had been told nothing. She felt shut out.

"I want to know what the Christ this is all about," she said.

Emily started to say something. David gave her a warning look. Emily said, "I'm going to tell her."

"I thought we weren't going to talk about it to anybody."

"I can't go through this without Marianne!"

Emily told Marianne what the charges were. Marianne stared at her. Then she said, "I need a drink." She poured herself one, downing it greedily. She put down her glass and sighed with relief, saying, "Well, if that's all that's going on—"

David said irritably, "You seem to think this is some kind of a joke."

"It's bullshit!"

"Well, of course it's bullshit," he said, "but it's happening!"

"Oh, come on! The son of a bitch doesn't know his ass from Ninth Street."

"Go tell that to the judge."

"I won't have to. You're dealing with a nut. If a man in an institution saw that bill of particulars, the district attorney would be inside with him in ten minutes." She put a protective arm around Emily. "Honey, you've got nothing to worry about."

The doorbell rang. "That's the doorbell," said David.

"You have a remarkable grasp of the obvious."

124

"I'm trying to tell you to get the hell out of here. That's Cade here to see us."

"You don't have a problem," Marianne said, kissing Emily. "I'll see you tomorrow."

David showed Marianne out and brought Cade into the library. Emily said, "Care for a drink? It's almost five."

"When I want to know the time, I'll ask for it."

David started making drinks for them. Emily looked at Cade's face. "Didn't he believe me?"

Cade shook his head. "Didn't think he would."

"Well . . ." She felt at a loss. "You mean, I'm actually going to be put on trial?" Cade nodded. Suddenly, it was all quite real. Her hands were like ice. "When?"

"There's lots of motions we can make. What with your being pregnant, I think we can delay it about a year."

"A year." Emily stretched out a hand, took the drink David had made for her and tried to maintain her composure.

David said, "What about a change of venue? Then we could get the whole thing out of his hands."

"We have no grounds. There hasn't been any publicity. They've been very careful. And Manly, he's imposed a gag rule. Just as well. Once this thing comes out, there'll be lots of it."

"What'll we tell people?" David was trying to keep his voice even.

"Nothing."

"But they know I'm under indictment," Emily said. "There are bound to be questions."

"Don't answer them. Just say your attorney ordered you not to discuss the case. And don't."

"For a year." Emily had spoken quietly. Then she said, "How soon can I go to trial?"

"Usually, delay is on the side of the defendant."

"I'm pregnant. This whole thing is crazy. And I don't want any delay. How soon?"

"Oh, about six weeks."

"That's what I want." Emily set down her glass. "Excuse me," she said. Then she left the room abruptly, ending the conversation.

The following day, Cade entered Judge Manly's chambers at ten in the morning, nodded at Rufus, who was there already and, moments later, Manly entered the room, sat down in his high-backed chair behind the carved teak desk with the ball-and-claw feet, gave them both a scarcely perceptible nod and began to speak.

"In the matter of the petition *duces tecum,*" Manly said, clearing his throat softly, "I have examined the material in question. It is indeed highly speculative in nature, referring to police theories, unapprehended crime partners and is, in my judgment, not altogether discoverable under the work-product theory." He shoved a stack of papers toward Cade. "I've decided to make this much available to the defense. I'm giving Rufus a list of which portions I mean."

Cade was startled. It showed only in a sudden shifting of his eyes. He said, "Your Honor, you're asking me to proceed to trial without full information as to why the prosecution saw fit to accuse my client." Was he imagining it, or did he see a thin line of perspiration on Judge Manly's upper lip? Cade squinted. But Manly had swiveled around in his chair, gotten to his feet, pulling his black gown around him, and walked to the windows in round-toed squeaking black shoes. He stood there, hands behind his thin back, staring down at the traffic along Montgomery Street. He pulled out a handkerchief, snorted loudly into it and then stuffed it back into his sleeve, a gesture Manly had acquired in England. Cade remembered that he had been a Rhodes Scholar. Manly turned back to face him.

"Cade, look here," he began, then hesitated, forced to remember, as always, despite their old friendship, that in these situations he spoke *ex cathedra,* and that there were always legal constraints limiting what he could say. One slip and he could be forced to disqualify himself. He nodded then, as if agreeing with himself that this was an opinion he was free to offer, and said, "Cade, in

126

my opinion, he has a case. The material I've made available to you leaves no room for doubt."

The hearing was adjourned.

That afternoon, Cade sat down behind the huge rolltop desk in the room where he was staying at the Pacific Union Club, lowering the green shade on the brass lamp down to a comfortable height, tipped back in his chair and began to read through the documents Manly had made available to him, making notes from time to time on a yellow tablet.

He had a stack of books on the floor beside him which he had gotten that afternoon from the Mechanics' Library. He had stopped by there on his way back from chambers, making his way through thick bronze doors hung from a marble arch, then taking a cage elevator to the second floor. An old lady with frizzy hair and a green eyeshade had greeted him with a smile.

"Rose, come talk to me. I want help."

Together, they had made up a list. She said, "Most of these don't circulate."

"Oh?"

"People take them out and then don't bring them back."

"Is that so?"

"It's the same everywhere. We can't even get them on inter-library loan any more."

"But you'll trust *me*."

He had sent for Sam Willinger, a nondescript man of about fifty-five, with pale-blue eyes, bad teeth, thinning hair, and a worn blue suit. He had met Willinger years before in Tadich's Grill (in pioneer days, they served just fish and only opened when the temperature fell below sixty, so they had called themselves "the cold-weather restaurant," much the way the Blue Fox had advertised itself as "Just across the street from the San Francisco morgue"), and Cade had taken an instant liking to him. Willinger was a tireless detective who had no prejudice whatever. He never cared how anything came out. When he arrived at Cade's club, Cade scribbled something down, handed the paper to Willinger and said:

127

"Here. Go to work."

At five, Cade rang for a whisky and soda. He read almost without stopping for the next two days. Then Willinger returned, handing him a folder.

"That it?"

"So far."

Glancing at the papers inside, Cade said, "Understand there was a grave robbery about that time."

"The night of the murder."

"Um. Seems somebody stole the newly buried body of a young woman around here somewheres."

"Page six."

"Um-hm. They ever find her?"

"Most of her."

Cade searched for a paper of his own. "Get any details?"

"Grave opened. Body violated. Heart torn out."

"Make the papers?"

"Nope."

"Not surprised. Police like to discourage them from printing such stories, lest the details inflame the susceptible."

"I couldn't find any police report."

"It's confidential. I have a copy here. It says that the evidence suggests the casting of a death-spell. Which, of course, is the charge."

Willinger blinked. "A death-spell?"

"Ancient. Usually involves a Black Mass. Sodomy. Bestiality. Mutilation of animals. That sort of thing." Cade frowned, the bushy eyebrows drawing together in a look of concern. "Prosecution found evidence of the same in that cemetery. What's the name of it again?"

"San Bruno."

"Um."

Cade wheeled around abruptly in his chair, looked off into space and rubbed a thick hand over a bristly chin. Then, with a quick sigh, he said to Sam Willinger, handing him a list of hand-written questions, "Here. Come back with the answers."

Willinger continued his investigations, reporting to Cade every few days. Weeks went by. Then Willinger brought Cade a detailed report of something new. Cade looked at it. His face was grim. Early that evening, he called on Emily and David.

It was very stormy. On the news, a reporter described the situation in Golden Gate Park, where a hailstorm had destroyed a wing of the Conservatory. Pictures were shown as a commentator remarked that it had been built as a copy of the Royal Pavilion in Brighton during the Midwinter Carnival of 1898 and afterward maintained by the city when McLaren began building the park. To liven up his story, the newscaster read details of how the park was built, a carpet of lawn running five miles from the Haight district to the sea, laid down on the sand and watered with power from a windmill. McLaren had persuaded everybody in town to dump horse manure at the park's entrance, to help get things started. Then, after the Earthquake, thousands of people had lived there in tents for months, while Bernhardt performed in the Greek theater in Berkeley to raise funds for relief. The storm raged. The newscaster talked.

Emily had a headache and wasn't watching. David was restless. When Cade was shown in, David immediately shut off the television set. One look at Cade's face had made him uneasy. Cade waved away offers of a drink. He sat down, keeping his overcoat on, as if the chill of the weather had somehow made its way into the room.

He said, "Emmy, I'm afraid you weren't honest with me."

"What do you mean?"

"A witness will be compelled to testify that she took you to a necromancer."

"What?" David was shaken, alarmed.

"Someone who practices black magic." Cade kept his eyes on Emily. She looked away, rubbing her arms. Cade said, "A boy. Named Lupe Serpiente."

"My God, I only met him by accident!"

"And he said something to you. What?"

Thinking. So she told them that. Then: "He said Jennie's name." That's all she heard. That's all she could have repeated.

"Nothing else?"

129

"No." Her face betrayed nothing. She was sure of it.

David said angrily, "I heard all about it! I don't care about some damn kid—"

"I do, only because the prosecution knew about it and I didn't. You withheld evidence."

"I didn't think it mattered!"

He shifted ground suddenly. "I want to ask you something else, Emmy. On that day you followed Jennie to the beauty parlor, you happen to take a lock of hair belonging to the deceased?"

She avoided his eyes, not answering.

"Someone saw you put it in your purse. Just a little thing. But unusual. The kind of thing one remembers having seen. And someone remembered."

"Cade, you're beginning to sound as bad as them!" David's eyes were narrowed.

"I apologize. But you see, I got to meet them on their own ground." He paused, pursing his lips. "It's a curious belief, isn't it? You know, in the old days, Orthodox Jews never cut their hair, and when they trimmed their nails, they always burned the cuttings, lest some enemy get power over them. It's a strange superstition. But the strangest thing is, it's been found all over the world, down through history. Emmy, did you intend to give Lupe Serpiente that lock of hair?"

"She couldn't have!" David yelled, jumping to his feet. "The kid was dead!"

"How did you happen to know that, Davey boy?"

"Emmy said he'd been following her. Once she thought she'd seen him in the garden and called the police. Well, she was upset, so I looked into it and when I found out he was dead, I knew she didn't have to worry."

"Um-hm. So you already knew he was dead when you took that hair, Emmy? Or did you know?"

"No, I didn't know. Not until David told me."

"I see." Cade frowned, thinking. Then he said, "The police reports indicate the boy died the fifteenth of April. Jennie was killed on the twentieth." Another pause. Then: "See, at one time, they were trying to make the boy your accomplice. Good thing

130

he was already dead. We really don't need any more problems."

Cade got to his feet, shoving his big hands deep into the pockets of his overcoat.

"I want you to think about all of this, Emily. And if there's anything more that I need to know—anything you think someone else may find out—I beg you to tell me. That's all right, I'll let myself out."

When he was gone, Emily said, "My God, why don't you let me tell him?"

"I told you to keep that crazy goddamned fantasy to yourself! How the hell many times do I have to tell you? *It never happened!*"

The whole thing had frightened her. Her eyes were wide, and the iris had washed out so that the blue had become almost a pale green. The hand she had put to her mouth was trembling. He took her in his arms, holding her to him with all his strength. She thought, *This is real. Nothing else is real.* She shut her eyes, clinging to him, as if she could somehow lose herself in him.

The empaneling of the jury had begun. Rufus wanted to inquire into the religious beliefs of every prospective juryman. Cade tried to object on the grounds that such an inquiry was not the province of the courts, given the fundamental Constitutional separation of church and state. Manly ruled that it was not possible to approach the search for truth objectively without asking something about the nature of the beliefs of the jurors, and permitted Rufus to exclude atheists and Cade to exclude what he termed "zealots." Manly decided any extremist could be challenged for cause. Cade settled on a simple course of questioning. He made inquiries probing unconscious superstitions and tried in each case to choose jurors who were conservative, settled, and without undue imagination.

Rufus saw immediately what Cade was doing. He had no objection. Rufus himself asked the same sort of question of every prospective juror. His own examples, however, were very different.

To one elderly man with a lined face, a scrawny neck, and

rheumy blue eyes, Rufus said, "I am going to describe what reportedly happened to a man named Daniel Douglas Home." Rufus then went on to describe an act of levitation performed by Home. In front of witnesses, with all the lights on, Home was seen to raise himself up in the air, go headfirst out a third-story window and then float back into another room. All this occurred in the presence of reputable witnesses who were watching very carefully to see if some kind of trick was involved and who came to the unanimous conclusion that there wasn't. "Sir," asked Rufus, "would you believe such a story?"

"Hell, no."

"Even when I tell you this apparently happened hundreds of times in the presence of witnesses?" The old man shook his head. "What if I tell you that the witnesses include William Cullen Bryant, Nathaniel Hawthorne, Elizabeth Barrett Browning, Robert Browning, the King of Naples, Napoleon III, the Empress Eugenie, Queen Sophia of the Netherlands, the Czar of Russia, and even a delegate from Charles Darwin, Sir William Crookes —and that Mr. Home himself ended up working as a correspondent here in San Francisco for the *Chronicle,* which has all the records?"

Rufus took a breath, his gaze fixed on the startled eyes of the prospective juror.

"What I want to know is, if I present you with evidence of an occurrence like this—evidence you would certainly accept if this were straightforward testimony about an automobile accident— would you be prepared to accept it?"

"I wouldn't accept it if God Almighty came down and said it."

"Witness excused."

A number of potential jurors acceptable to Cade said there were no conceivable circumstances under which they could entertain such evidence. They were also excused. But a surprising number answered yes. Rufus accepted only them.

Together, Rufus and Cade empaneled a jury of sober citizens in the surprisingly short time of two weeks. Every juror professed to have an open mind, which meant, in this case, that every one was prepared to entertain ideas commonly called "superstitious," if the evidence warranted. None of the jurors had the slightest idea what the trial was about.

It began six weeks to the day after Emily told Cade she did not want any delay.

18

It began on the fifteenth of July at ten in the morning. Since there had been no pretrial publicity, there was little interest in the affair. The courtroom was only half full. Marianne had no trouble finding a place beside David, just behind the defense table where Emily sat.

Having seated himself, Manly turned to Cade, asking, "Is the defense ready?"

"Ready, Your Honor."

"Is the prosecution ready?"

"Ready, Your Honor."

"You may begin."

Emily looked across at the man who was to prosecute her for murder. She saw only a thickset man in a dark suit, with marked features and full red lips. She heard the beginning testimony. The morning was devoted to routine matters. Lieutenant Fonner was called to the stand and asked to answer questions about having been called to Jennie's house by neighbors the night of her death. He described finding the body and discovering the fact that all the doors and windows were locked. Cade had no questions for him. Fonner was followed by a dentist in a plaid suit, with a lantern jaw and a fixed smile, who exhibited two sets of X-rays and declared that from an examination of the teeth, he was confident that the deceased was his former patient, Miss Jennie Ludlow.

Dr. Viterbo was called. The coroner was plainly uneasy. Rufus questioned him quietly. Dr. Viterbo held forth on third-degree burns. Rufus allowed him to talk for a moment or two, then interrupted. "Thank you, sir. Now, would you tell us the condition of Miss Ludlow's body when you first found it?"

"Carbonized."

"I see. Under what circumstances would one expect to find a body in the condition in which you found Miss Ludlow's?"

This was the question Dr. Viterbo had been dreading. Now, under these circumstances, it no longer mattered. He said simply, "The remains looked as one would expect if the body had been cremated."

"Most of us think of cremation as occurring in moments. What actually is the case, Dr. Viterbo?"

"It takes about two hours at a temperature of fifteen hundred degrees Fahrenheit."

"And yet you say this occurred in eight minutes?"

"So far as I can determine, yes, sir."

"Can you explain that, Dr. Viterbo?"

"No, sir, I can't."

"Do you mean this is something outside your experience, Dr. Viterbo?"

Then the truth forced its way out. Dr. Viterbo said, greatly agitated, "It isn't a matter of opinion, sir! It's impossible!" There was a murmur of surprise from the courtroom. Manly rapped his gavel. The jurors sat forward in their chairs.

"Your witness," said Rufus.

"No questions, Your Honor," said Cade.

The witness was excused. Cade rose. "Your Honor," he said. "Prosecution has failed to show murder was committed. Yet that is the charge of which my client is accused. Move to dismiss. Charge is incompetent."

"Your Honor," said Rufus, "the People will indeed show murder was done."

"I object to the use of the future tense. Prosecution's own witness, the coroner, was unable to furnish evidence pointing to murder. I cannot understand accusing someone of a crime without first establishing the fact that a crime was committed. Will the Court please rule on my motion to dismiss?"

"Your Honor, learned counsel is well aware that the coroner's role is purely advisory. It is for the People to say whether murder was done."

"Do you so specify?"

135

"Yes, Your Honor."

"How was it done?"

"By supernatural means."

The reply was so unexpected, most people thought they had misunderstood. There was a bewildered hum in the courtroom. Taking advantage of the confusion, Cade rose, saying with mock surprise:

"Would learned counsel repeat his answer? I fear I must have misunderstood."

"By supernatural means," Rufus said again. This time, everyone was quite sure what he had said. The murmuring in the courtroom rose to a crescendo. Manly banged his gavel. A reporter raced for the door, on his way to a telephone.

"Your Honor," Cade said, "we do not know how to respond to that statement. First, I asked whether a crime had been committed. I was told that the People would stipulate that the deceased was in fact murdered. When I asked how, I was told 'by supernatural means.' He's saying he's basing his case on 'information denied to mortals.' No, listen here"—he had been interrupted by an uneasy tittering—"that's what the dictionary says, that's not me talking. Now, first off, I don't know where the prosecutor got hold of such information, and second, I fail to see how he plans to communicate it to the rest of us humans. Incompetent, Your Honor. May I respectfully remind the bench that it has not yet ruled on my motion?"

"Your Honor," said Rufus, "the People ask nothing more than an opportunity to show precisely how the defendant not only could but did commit such a crime. I remind the bench that should we fail to do that, the Court may throw out the case without ever submitting it to the jury."

"Mr. Simonds, I don't want you to tell me the law again, do you understand?"

"I beg the Court's pardon."

Manly took off his glasses and rubbed his eyes. Then he said, "Will you both approach the bench, please?" Cade and Rufus came toward him. In a low voice, a hand over the microphone, Manly said, "There's a young woman dead. So far, we don't seem to know exactly what happened. Rufus says he knows but needs

136

time to explain it. His language has landed him in some difficulties. Seems to me the bench has an obligation to the deceased. If Rufus here can shed light on how she died, we're bound to listen. Cade, I'm going to overrule you in this instance. Rufus, you're right. If the case you present doesn't have any merit, I am indeed going to throw it out of court." The men retired. Manly banged his gavel. "Let the prosecution state its case."

Cade sat down again in his chair. Rufus walked over to the jury. He spoke in a quiet, matter-of-fact voice.

"The People will show that the accused, Emily Blake, threatened the deceased, specifying in advance how, when, and where she would die. That is a matter of record in the decedent's own handwriting. With the permission of the court, I offer the diary of the decedent, Jennie Ludlow, in evidence, to be marked Exhibit 41."

Rufus handed the red-leather diary to a clerk and a voice said, "So noted."

The jurors looked at Rufus with their fullest attention.

He went on, saying, "That, the People will allege, is foreknowledge of murder. The People will offer, as ancillary proof, that the accused has exhibited supernormal powers in a controlled situation under strict scientific observation, and in at least one case, has predicted the time, place, and means of another death, where the odds were one in seventy-three billion."

Emily whispered to Cade, "It's that boy we talked about. He told me those things!" Cade nodded, putting a finger to his lips. She felt the weight of the jurors' eyes on her. She avoided looking at them, feeling unequal to it. She felt light-headed. David had given her a tranquilizer. Perhaps it was that. She thought, I mustn't faint. An absurd impulse to explain to them that it was all Lupe made her get to her feet.

"I just want to say—" she began. She heard the sound of the gavel. The room swam. Then she felt Cade's arm guiding her back down into her chair.

Judge Manly asked, "Does defense want to move for a recess?"

Cade asked Emily in a quiet voice, "You feeling all right?"

"Why? Am I pale?" Her voice sounded to her as if it were a long way off. She looked at Cade anxiously.

137

"You look fine, Emmy. You just tell me when you need a rest."

"I'm all right, Cade."

"No recess at this time, Your Honor," Cade said.

Rufus continued in the same measured tone. "Ladies and gentlemen," he said, "this is a case without precedent. I say that advisedly. Down through history, according to the best estimates, several hundred thousand people have been tried for witchcraft, found guilty, and sentenced to death. The youngest of all was a little French girl—Catherine Naguille—burned at the stake at the age of eleven. Someone gave her five pounds of flax to put under her dress so that her death would be swifter."

There was an audible gasp. Rufus paused. Emily looked at him with horrified eyes. A whisper began running through the courtroom. The spectators had suddenly reacted to the word "witchcraft" and one could hear the whispered syllables repeated again and again. Manly banged for order.

"We must take great care," Rufus said. "Here in this country, in Salem, in 1692, we had a series of notorious cases. Thirteen people were hanged as witches on the testimony of three adolescent girls."

"Objection," said Cade, getting to his feet. "Prosecution is offering a defective example. Those three adolescent girls are now thought to have been the victims of ergot poisoning, acquired from eating spoiled rye grain. Made them hallucinate. I respectfully refer the Court to a scholarly work on the subject to be found in the April issue of *Science* magazine, 1976."

"If I may finish the point I was making, Your Honor . . ." Rufus looked at Judge Manly, who nodded. Rufus then said, "On this one point, the People and the defense do not disagree. In the Salem cases, those accused were probably innocent. My point is that their deaths tainted the name of Salem, and in almost three hundred years, that memory has not been eradicated. The prosecution of witchcraft was also tainted. In almost three hundred years, we have not had one other case of witchcraft brought to trial in this country—despite the fact that last year alone, something like forty-six million copies of books and magazines on the subject were sold all over the world and that a conservative estimate on the number of people in this country today who believe in and practice witchcraft is something in excess of half a million. There are scientific laboratories all over the world—many of them subsidized by governments—studying what are called psi phenomena, and the consensus in the scientific community, here and abroad, is that such phenomena are real."

Rufus paused, looking into the faces of the jurors, waiting for his words to sink in. Then he said, "That means there are people who have the power of telepathy; there are people who have the power of psychokinesis—that is, to move objects at a distance; there are people who have the power of clairvoyance. I'm sure all of you know that the police very often employ the services of such people to help solve crimes. There are at least half a dozen other occult gifts for which no explanation can at present be offered." Now the voice deepened as Rufus turned and looked straight at Emily. "What I'm saying to you is that it is entirely possible that there are people who commit murder by occult means—*and that in almost three hundred years, because of our prejudices, not one of them has ever been brought to trial in this country!*"

A loud murmuring started in the courtroom. Manly banged his gavel. Rufus said, letting his voice gradually increase in volume:

"Ladies and gentlemen, the People will make a basic assumption: that there is such a thing as evil . . . thought of as an entity we call 'Satan,' 'the Devil,' 'the archfiend,' 'the king of the powers of darkness' . . . and that there are people who are able to summon up evil for their own terrible ends. And the People will show that Emily Blake is indeed herself such a person . . . that she is in fact a witch, that she has compacted with the Devil, that with his power and only with his power, she procured the hideous death by fire of the woman who had taken her husband away, the deceased, Jennie Ludlow."

As if on cue, a large woman seated with the spectators got to her feet, opened a big purse and pulled out a handful of religious tracts which she began distributing, talking to herself at the same time, then crying out, "I wouldn't be caught dead without Jesus!" As bailiffs ran toward her to evict her from the courtroom, a young man with fixed eyes ran up to Rufus, grabbed him by the lapels and threw him against a table, yelling out, "I'm going to cut off your fucking balls and make you chew them up and swallow them, you lousy creep!" A policeman lowered his head and charged toward him. Several women spectators began to scream. Manly banged his gavel repeatedly, ordering the court cleared.

Emily got up and hurried around the defense table, intercepting Rufus. "I'd like to speak to you," she said.

He walked away from her, as if unaware of her existence. Cade had come toward her.

She turned to him, saying, "He wouldn't talk to me!"

"He's not allowed to talk to you, Emmy. Ever." Cade steered her back. Her knees buckled. She fell against the defense table. David ran toward her, supporting her.

"My wife is ill!" he yelled out.

Marianne forced her way through the crowd, hands out-stretched, reaching toward Emily. Manly adjourned court until the next morning.

On the evening news, there were differing accounts of what had happened. One version had a college student brandishing a knife. Another had David attacking Rufus. The leading news commentator in the country editorialized from the East, saying that the prosecuting attorney was clearly in need of psychiatric help and expressing surprise that so distinguished a judge as Amos Manly would ever have allowed such an absurd case to come to trial. In general, there was an outcry demanding his removal.

On one station, several jurists were interviewed on the procedure necessary to remove a district attorney from office. Since he was an elected official, recall was suggested. Mention was also made of a notorious judge who had publicly abused defendants, urging them to plead guilty and, in the case of those charged with sex crimes, suggesting reprehensible means for dealing with them (emasculation, torture, etc.), and pointed reference was made to the years it had taken to remove him from office.

The truth was, there was no ready means to unseat Rufus. Interviewed briefly as he left the courtroom, Rufus blinked at the quartz lights, shaded his eyes, spoke in a soft voice of his duty and said, in answer to charges that he was deranged, "I do my duty as I see fit. The jury is quite free to find for the defendant."

David and Emily had gone with Cade to have dinner at Marianne's. David had insisted they not talk about the trial. Afterward, Cade had accompanied David and Emily home. There, they found a crowd of reporters and curiosity-seekers surrounding the house, held back by a cordon of police. They had waited outside for hours, undaunted by locked doors and drawn blinds. At times, they had chanted Emily's name. They were in a good mood. Wanting to get rid of them, David stood at the top of the stairs and signaled for their attention. A chorus of questions was shouted up at him by reporters as flash bulbs popped and television cameras were held up. His few words were drowned out by the voices of the crowd, yelling for Emily.

"This whole thing is crazy!" he shouted. "Will you people let us alone? We don't know anything!"

A cheer went up and David thought he had won them over, until he turned to go inside and saw that Emily was standing behind him in the doorway, under the glowing fanlight. She came forward, hands folded, looking down at the mob on the sidewalk crowding up against the wrought-iron railing in front of the house.

Voices died down, as if they expected her to speak. Instead, she looked out over them in silence, as cameras were pointed at her. Someone started jeering. The crowd joined in. A newsman climbed up onto a round stone pedestal at the foot of the stairs into which the low wrought-iron fence was fastened. At the same time, a lanky teenager climbed up beside him, a brick in one hand. Taking aim, he threw it at Emily, narrowly missing her. She seemed rooted to the spot, wide-eyed, oblivious. At the same time, the boy lost his footing, grabbed at the arm of the reporter, there was a struggle for balance and the teenaged boy fell across the fence, pierced through the eye by an iron prong. He began to scream in agony. The reporter wheeled around and then, almost as a reflex action, began snapping pictures of the boy. The mob rushed at the reporter. There was a near-riot. Emily rushed inside and slammed the door. Police officers rescued the maimed boy with David's help. The crowd edged back, hearing sirens. "Oh, Jesus!" screamed the boy. "Oh, Jesus, *help* me!"

The police finally cleared the area. Two plainclothesmen had been detailed to watch the house. They sat outside in the dark in an unmarked car. Police cars had orders to circle the block every fifteen minutes and detain and question anyone found loitering in the vicinity.

David went slowly up the stairs, shoulders sagging, and opened the front door with his key. He walked into the living room and found Emily standing there with a butcher knife in her hands. Her eyes narrowed. Slowly.

"Emmy?"

"Is anyone with you?" she asked, her voice unnaturally soft.

"Nobody. Emmy, what's going on?"

"Somebody tried to break in. The police got him."

"Emmy, put the knife down."

"Why? So you can protect me?"

He moved toward her, took the knife from her hands. She let go of it, saying in a low voice, "David, help me—"

"Shhh."

"David—!" Her voice began to rise sharply.

"Easy, honey."

She sank to her knees, still clutching him, a terrible cry of anguish wrung from her throat. "David, *he's out there!*" He looked at her, not understanding. *"Lupe! That boy! He's not dead, David! I saw him out there in that crowd!"*

19

David lay awake all night worrying about Emily's state of mind. She was three months pregnant. And obviously hallucinating again. Was there no way he could force a postponement of the trial?

He lay close to her, not wanting to move, even though the weight of her body had made his left arm go to sleep. Her face, as she slept, seemed troubled. The mouth was set. From time to time, he could hear her grinding her teeth. He spoke to her softly, kissing her, somehow entering into whatever dream she was having, so that he could feel her relax, could see the fine lines around her mouth disappear, lost in blessed sleep.

Christ, what should I do? What the hell can I do?

At eight o'clock the next morning, David was in the kitchen drinking coffee and leafing through the newspapers when the doorbell rang. Esmeralda went padding out to answer it. David stared at a picture of Emily standing at the top of the stairs, hands folded, staring out at the crowd. In the foreground, an arrow pointed to the shadowy figure of a teenaged boy in the act of climbing up onto the wrought-iron fence. A witness had made a remark about a "peculiar look" she had given him, just before the frightful accident. The papers were careful to make no comment on it at all. Marianne had telephoned several times, but David was in no mood to talk to her. He sat drinking his coffee, glancing through the paper. Then he looked up to see Cade standing in the doorway, his face set.

"Morning. Where's Emmy?"

"I guess she's still upstairs." He glanced at his watch. "I thought we weren't due in court for another hour."

"I want to talk to her. Now."

David sent Esmeralda for Emily while Cade helped himself to a cup of coffee from the earthenware drip pot on the stove. He drank it in silence, standing up at the counter. David said:

"What's wrong?"

"Emily appears to be taking matters into her own hands."

"What do you mean?"

"She called me at seven o'clock this morning. Didn't you know?"

"No." David looked up, puzzled. Then the door opened and Emily entered. She said good morning to Cade, thanked him for coming so promptly, gave David a quick kiss, and walked into the kitchen and poured herself coffee. Cade looked around.

"Where's that fat little maid of yours, honey?"

"Upstairs. I told her to start on the bedroom."

Cade took a quick breath, rubbed his thick hands together and said, "Now, Emmy, what's this about your planning to take the stand?"

"I want to do it. They can't stop me, can they?"

"No, Emmy."

"Can you?"

"No. But I don't want you to do it," he added slowly.

"Why not? Don't you trust me?"

"If I put you on the stand, then the district attorney gets to ask you questions, too. Got any idea what it's like to be examined by a prosecuting attorney who's out to hang you?"

"Don't," said David shortly.

"It's all right," said Emily. "No, Cade, I don't."

"Well, let me give you a sample. Just so's you'll know what you're in for. All right, Emmy?"

"Fine."

Cade took Emily's coffee cup from her hands and set it down on the table. Then he said softly, "How did you find out your husband was having an affair with the deceased?"

"My marriage has nothing to do with what happened."

"Oh? Seems to me it does. Appears to be right at the heart of the matter, since it furnishes motive. Question is, how did you find out? Answer the question, please."

"I won't."

"You'll be ordered to."

"I thought you couldn't force a wife to testify against her husband!"

"That's not testifying against him."

"Adultery is still against the law!" Almost surprised at her own cleverness, Emily said, "That would be accusing him of a crime, wouldn't it?"

"No, it isn't a crime any more. Answer the question."

"I won't."

"You'll be held in contempt."

"I'll pay the fine!"

"You won't just be fined. You'll be put in jail and kept there until you answer."

Suddenly, Emily drew away from him, the memory of jail still a fresh, raw recollection.

"Yes, in jail," Cade went on quietly. "And kept there without bail. And I should warn you that your continued silence would have a most unfortunate effect on the minds of the jurors. Now, answer the question."

"Cade!" She felt cornered, frightened.

"Leave her alone!"

"Answer the question. You don't have any choice. No choice you'd want."

"I guessed! And . . . well, he told me."

"And what he told you upset you so terribly, the one thing you wanted was to kill her."

"That isn't true!"

"Isn't it? Didn't you meet with a boy who offered to help you get rid of the woman? Didn't you then obtain a lock of her hair? Didn't you take it to him?"

"They don't know that!" David shouted.

"How do you know?"

"But he was dead! He was already dead!" David said loudly.

"Did you know that?" Cade asked her. She shrank from him. He said flatly, "No, I can't put you on the stand. He'd tear you to pieces."

She walked away from them toward the window, where she

145

stood looking out at a weeping cherry. It was in flower, and she watched a yellow hummingbird with a red crown hovering beside a blossom. For no reason, she remembered that their hearts beat at the rate of six hundred times a minute. She tried to lose herself in the picture of the bird in the tree, to think of nothing.

"Cade," she said finally, turning around to face him, "do you think I'm innocent?"

"Emmy, honey, I'm defending you!"

She let it go, aware that his answer was slightly off-center, and tried another tack.

"Cade—how do you think Jennie died?"

"I have no idea."

There it was again. Well, this time she would press. "But you must have thought about it."

"It's not up to me to offer the prosecution theories on how an alleged victim met her end."

"Could the district attorney be right? Not about me but about how she died?"

"Well, I'll give you the same answer Kant made. He said he did not feel himself authorized 'to reject all ghost stories; for however improbable one taken alone might appear, the mass of them taken together command some credence.' See, he's just saying he don't know. Well, neither do I. But that's not something on which the defense has to take a position, Emmy."

"But I want to, Cade. I want to tell them the truth. And the truth, Cade, is that Lupe killed her!"

"Emmy, Lupe is dead! He was already dead a week when Jennie was killed!"

"He is not dead. I saw him last night. Now, I insist on taking the stand!" Her voice was low, urgent. They were both staring at her. She felt suffocated, as if the room itself were closing in on her. Banging open the door, she hurried out. They could hear her running up the stairs.

David said, "Look, if it'll help—"

"It won't help! I don't want her on the stand!"

"How can you stop her?"

"Let me use your phone, may I?" Cade called a clerk in his office, told him to prepare a court order, gave him a number and told him to bring it to the courtroom when it was ready.

"What kind of an order?" David asked.

"For an exhumation."

"You don't believe her?"

"It's Emmy who doesn't believe *me*. But I think she will after she sees the body."

Cade finished his coffee, glanced at his watch and started for the door. David put a hand on his arm.

"When are you planning on this?"

"Today. After court adjourns. I'll get you the address. You two can meet me at the cemetery."

20

Court was reconvened at nine that morning. On the surface, everything appeared under control. The number of bailiffs had been doubled. Long lines of people had waited all night, and the courtroom was filled to capacity. Marianne sat with David. A projector stood on a table, and a large screen had been set up to one side. The lights had been turned out, and for some minutes, a procession of discalced Cistercians with lighted tapers had been shown in their monastery in Solesmes, chanting as they climbed a flight of worn shallow steps to the oratory. Then the projector was switched off, the lights in the courtroom were turned on again, and Rufus stepped forward, saying:

"I thank the Court for the opportunity to reacquaint members of the jury with the nature of the Gregorian chant. Please call Professor Matson."

A gaunt man in his mid-fifties was sworn in. He had a shock of lank, surprisingly blond hair, a large thin nose and a thin mouth drawn in what looked like a reproving straight line. His credentials, placed in evidence, established him as one of the world's leading musicologists, at present a Fellow at Lincoln College at Oxford.

Once Professor Matson was sworn in, Rufus asked to have the lights turned out again, and on the screen was projected an image of Emily, eyes glazed, sitting on the floor of the isolation cell in which they had locked her, combing her hair with her fingers and singing to herself. Emily gasped. She had not remembered the moment. Lupe! she thought. Cade was right! They must know about Lupe!

At the same time, Cade got to his feet and said, "I demand that those lights be switched back on!"

As soon as the lights were turned on again, and the operator once more turned off the projector, Cade turned to the bench with a look of outrage. But Emily had also gotten to her feet. She tried to go toward the bench. A bailiff blocked her way. She gave him a frightened smile and, twisting her hands, said to Manly, "May I say something? You see, I'd like to explain—"

Manly banged his gavel. "The defendant is out of order." Then, to Emily, he said, "If you want to address the Court, you will be given an opportunity at a later date."

"Sit down!" Cade whispered to her harshly, taking her arm. She tried to wrest free, moving slowly, the whole thing unreal, saying to Manly with a pleading smile, "I really feel that I ought to explain—"

"You sit down and let me handle things, you hear?" Cade's eyes were locked in hers. She read warning in them. Slowly, she surrendered, allowing Cade to lead her back to her seat. She turned to a bailiff and said timidly, "May I speak to my husband?"

Manly had heard this. When the bailiff looked toward him, he nodded. David came toward her. She took his bent head in her hands, whispering, "Oh, David, I love you. I just wanted you to know that I love you." Marianne reached forward, squeezed her hand.

David asked Emily, "Are you all right, honey? You want to ask Cade for a recess?"

She thought, We're both prisoners. We have to ask permission to come and go. She became aware that everyone was looking at them. Holding David's head close to her, she turned and looked around the courtroom, almost with surprise, as if she could not understand what she was doing there. She looked from face to face, as if searching for an answer. Then she saw something and an icy fear clutched her heart. With a slow, rustling sound, heads were turning away. No one met her eyes. She put a hand to her mouth. She could feel David trembling in her arms.

"I'm all right," she said. She forced a smile. "Really. I'm all right."

149

David resumed his seat and the trial continued. Cade got to his feet and took a step toward the bench, a look of real anger on his face.

"Defense has never had access to this videotape! I respectfully remind the Court of the Marcus decision—Supreme Court, 1961—I won't trouble quoting the whole thing, since I'm sure the Court is as familiar with it as I, but this evidence was obtained by unwarrantable search and seizure and I object to its use—"

"May it please the Court—" Rufus tried to interrupt.

"—and to any use of similar evidence likewise obtained, since it would be considered 'the fruit of a poisonous tree.' "

Manly banged his gavel, his face set.

"Sustained. The members of the jury will ignore the videotape."

"I humbly beg the Court's pardon," said Rufus. "People merely sought to show that defendant was familiar with a certain melody."

"Objection!"

"Sustained. I caution the prosecuting attorney."

During all this, Professor Matson had remained sitting stiffly in his chair in the witness box. Without warning, he started to leave the stand.

"You are not excused, sir," Manly said.

"May I just have a glass of water, please?" He had grown suddenly pale. Someone brought him water from the defense table. He reached for the glass, lost his grip on it, and it crashed to the floor. He leaned heavily on a low railing. A bailiff ran forward to assist him. He mumbled something. Manly ordered half an hour's recess and Professor Matson was led into an anteroom to lie down. When court reconvened, he came back in slowly. His color had returned but he avoided looking at Emily. He was seated again. Manly reminded him that he was still under oath, and Rufus once more approached the witness.

Taking a small velvet bag out of his pocket, Rufus took an antique recorder from it and offered the instrument to Professor Matson, saying, "I understand, sir, that you can play this instrument."

"Are we to be treated to another musical interlude?" Cade demanded.

"State your objection."

"Counsel has not shown relevance for this performance."

"I will show relevance, Your Honor."

"Proceed."

To the witness, Rufus then said, "Will you please play for us the passage we discussed?"

Professor Matson demurred. He did not want to do it. Pressed for a reason by Judge Manly, he refused to give one. Annoyed, Manly ordered him to comply. "I decline," he said.

Manly's jaw tightened. Rufus asked the Court to direct Professor Matson to do what had been asked, saying that his evidence was important. Again, Manly directed the witness to comply and once again, Professor Matson refused. Rufus asked Manly to characterize Matson as a reluctant witness. Manly did so, saying to the professor:

"I will have no alternative but to find you in contempt. This being a capital case in which the prosecution has described your evidence as material, I will have to order you confined in jail until such time as you cooperate."

Professor Matson gave Manly an uneasy look, saying, "But I gave my word—"

Rufus interrupted, saying, "You told us that. We sought permission and obtained it." Rufus took a parchment letter with a thick red seal from his table and entered it into evidence, identifying it as a letter from the Holy See. There was a susurrus of surprise from the spectators. *Bang.*

"Professor—" began Manly in a warning tone.

Professor Matson yielded with obvious reluctance. He put the small recorder to his lips, tested it, and after one or two false starts, played a melody. It was identical to the one Emily had been humming on the videotape. The murmuring in the courtroom indicated that a number of people recognized that the two melodies were the same. David looked quickly at the back of Emily's head, wanting her to turn so he could see her face. She did not move. Cade watched her out of the corner of his eye. She leaned

151

forward, listening intently to the flutelike sound, her mouth half open. As soon as the brief, haunting song was finished, Professor Matson handed the small instrument back to Rufus, who put it away in the velvet bag, then returned it to an inner coat pocket as he cleared his throat. There was a pause. Rufus leaned on the railing of the witness box, rubbing his eyes with his fingers, giving the impression that he had forgotten for a moment what he wanted to say. Marianne pressed David's fingers nervously.

Rufus asked softly, "Will you identify that melody, Professor?"

"It's called 'The Invocation.'" Professor Matson's voice was thin and clear. Unaccented, it still betrayed the influence of another language.

"Will you place it in context for us?"

"The liturgy of the Roman Catholic Church is based on Gregorian chants."

"How old are these chants?"

"Our records go back fifteen hundred years. The chants, as in the case of the monks of Solesmes, may in fact go back to the Temple of Solomon. We have no idea how music was written then—or, indeed, whether it ever was. It may have been handed down from time immemorial, just as the Bible was originally an oral tradition."

"And what you just played for us? Would that be sung in church?"

"No, it would not." Professor Matson took out a handkerchief and blotted his face. Fine beads of perspiration popped out on his skin.

"Explain why not, please."

"The Church liturgy is based on eight of these chants. What I just played is the ninth."

"When is it used?"

"It is never used. In fact, when I heard the young lady humming it—"

"Objection!"

"Strike that response! That part referring to the defendant." Then, to Professor Matson, Manly said, "Witness will confine himself to answering questions."

"I do beg your pardon," the professor said.

152

"Let me ask you the question in another way. Professor, would it surprise you if you heard me singing it?"

"It would astonish me."

"Why?"

"The original is in the archives of the Vatican. The manuscript was personally sealed by Pope Gregory the Great with the Ring of the Fisherman almost fifteen hundred years ago. It has, to my certain knowledge, never been copied."

"How did you come to see it?"

"I had Papal permission to inspect those particular archives. The manuscript on which those particular numes are written—"

"Numes?"

"Notes. The Gregorian melody. That manuscript is secret. I am the only person who has seen it in fifteen hundred years. I personally saw it sealed after I looked at it and, at the Vatican's request, I have never written it down nor played it for anyone. The manuscript has not been opened since I saw it. The Vatican itself will testify to that."

"Did the Vatican give a reason for this secrecy?"

"Yes."

"What was that reason?"

"The chant is profane."

"Profane?"

"As contrasted with sacred. From the Latin *pro fanem,* meaning 'before the temple,' therefore, outside it—therefore, unholy."

"Unholy."

"Yes."

"What was the original purpose of the chant?"

"To call up the Devil."

There was absolute silence.

Then Cade said, "Move for a mistrial. Counsel deliberately pursued a line of questioning which he knew involved inadmissible evidence damaging to my client—"

"Damaging?" asked Rufus softly.

"In the minds of the credulous, sir!"

"Address your remarks to the bench, gentlemen."

"Will Your Honor rule on my motion?"

"Would you gentlemen approach the bench?"

153

Cade and Rufus made their way over to Manly, who pushed aside his small microphone, clasped his hands and leaned forward, speaking in a low voice.

"Cade, with respect to your motion for a mistrial, I remind you that you petitioned me for a writ of *mandamus* before pleadings. It was your view that *mandamus* will lie to compel the trial court to order the prosecution to permit defense counsel to inspect or make copies of statements in possession of the police or the prosecution." He paused, sighing and rubbing his jaw. "No such statements are involved here."

"My objection, sustained by the Court, was to a videotape of the defendant humming to herself while incarcerated."

"Yes, well, I think that was intended as demonstrative evidence by the prosecution and, as such, would lie outside the scope of your petition for *mandamus*."

"I remind the Court that it sustained my objection."

"The Court agrees with defense counsel that the exhibition of that videotape, together with the sound of the accused humming that particular and peculiar melody"—an emphatic pause—"comes perilously close to self-incrimination. But in this Court's view, the error is not incurable, and I'm going to rule in favor of an admonition to the jury to disregard." Then, almost impatiently, he added: "I mean, Christ, how the hell could somebody humming some damn melody be grounds to throw a capital case out of court?"

"Oh, my God," said the voice of a woman juror. All three men turned to look. Emily had gotten to her feet and was doing a slow, graceful dance in front of the courtroom, humming The Invocation. She raised her voice, looking almost insolently around the courtroom, singing *La la la!* and struggling slowly with a matron and a bailiff who were trying to restrain her. Then she began to laugh. She looked around as if to make sure to include all of them and laughed mockingly. David rushed up the aisle toward her and tried to take her in his arms. The courtroom filled with a strange murmuring sound, almost like bees swarming, Emily's mocking laughter growing louder and louder.

"May we have a recess!" Cade said. "My client is clearly not in possession of her faculties at the present time."

154

Manly banged his gavel and ordered an adjournment until the following day, allowing for a motion for further postponement, should the defendant require more time to recover herself.

David, his arms around her, Marianne joining them, led her from the courtroom. Bailiffs did not have to hold back the crowds. Everyone had moved clear of the aisle down which they were walking.

21

David drove Emily home. Marianne sat with them in the front seat, Emily clutching her, hiding her face in Marianne's musty blue knitted dress. When she felt David make a left and start up the steep hill toward their house, she asked, still hiding her face in Marianne's breast:

"Are those people still there?"

Ahead, David could see an even larger crowd around the house. Police, recognizing his car, beckoned him on, making way for him. David glanced quickly at Marianne.

"Just ignore them," Marianne said to Emily.

"I don't want to look at them," Emily whispered. "I don't want them to see me."

"Here, put these on," Marianne said, pulling out a pair of dark glasses and thrusting them into Emily's hand.

"They're prescription, aren't they?"

"What the hell is the difference?" Marianne pulled off her long wool scarf. "And take this." Emily put on the dark glasses, bound the scarf around her head so that it concealed half her face and, as David parked the car in front and scrambled out, police holding back a crowd with men wearing badges reading "Press" standing in front, aiming cameras at them, Marianne helped Emily from the car and the two of them hurried her upstairs into the house.

Once inside, David said to Marianne, "I'm going to give her a shot," and ran upstairs to prepare one. Emily, still clinging to Marianne, sagged with relief when the door slammed shut behind them.

"I don't want a shot," Emily said. "Anyway, not that kind." Pushing Marianne away, Emily reached out a hand and touched

156

Esmeralda's face. Esmeralda murmured something to her in Spanish, wiping her hands on her apron and looking up at her with her spaniel's eyes. She wondered how much Esmeralda understood about what was going on, then remembered she listened to the news on television in Spanish. She asked Esmeralda anyway, speaking in Spanish and using the familiar. Esmeralda nodded, then took Emily's hand and kissed it. Emily pressed a cheek against the top of fat little Esmeralda's head for a moment, then went on into the library and poured herself a drink. Marianne followed her.

"If he's going to give you something, you shouldn't drink that."

"He's not going to give me anything."

"Let's put you to bed."

"Let's not." Emily downed her drink, poured another. Marianne went to her, took her hands in hers and pulled her down onto a little sofa.

"You're letting it get to you."

"You noticed."

"Look, you have to fight."

"It's *him!* I tried to tell them but they wouldn't let me talk!"

David had come into the room. He met Marianne's questioning eyes over Emily's bent shoulder and nodded briefly, standing there irresolute, hypodermic in hand.

Marianne said, "She says she doesn't want it, David."

"Well, I think she needs it."

"Oh, I think Emily can decide whether she needs something. Right, honey?" Emily nodded, still bent over, her face almost in her lap. "See, she's fine now," Marianne said. "She can handle it."

"Look, she couldn't handle it in court—"

"All right, I lost my head!" Emily looked up at him defiantly. She got to her feet, the drink in her hand, took a sip and then, looking levelly from one of them to the other, said, "I lost my head because this whole damned thing is ridiculous! It's absurd!" She tried to sound convincing but her voice faltered. Reacting to something in David's eyes, she said shrilly, "Stop looking at me that way!"

"Honey, please, you were hysterical."

157

"Are you blaming me?"

"Darling—" He put the hypodermic down on a table, and going to her, enfolded her in his arms.

"I want to get away!" she said, her voice rising.

"We'll get away."

"I mean, *now!*"

"We've got to live through it."

The exchange called, saying Roberta was on the phone wanting to talk to her mother. Marianne said, starting out, "I'll take it in the other room."

Emily burst out, "I don't *want* to live through it! I didn't do it! *He* did! How can I get through to you, David? *He's* the one who played that melody! That's where I heard it! He was whistling it! You heard what they said about it! I *couldn't* have known it! I heard it from him! He's doing it all! He's the one who killed her! Why won't you *believe* me?"

"Emmy," he said gently, holding her by the shoulders, trying as hard as he could to make her listen to him, "the boy's dead." She just stared at him. He tried to keep the impatience out of his voice. "If you get up in court and try to blame this whole thing on some dead kid, Christ, think how it will *sound!*"

She continued to meet his eyes, implacable. "He's not dead!"

"You just don't believe me, do you?" Then, when she didn't answer but only kept looking at him, almost as if she were suppressing anger, he said, "Emmy, I can prove it to you! Do you want me to?"

"What are you talking about?"

"Cade got an exhumation order."

"He what?"

"You heard me. He wants to give you a chance to see for yourself."

"You think I'm crazy. That's what you think, isn't it?"

"I don't think anything of the sort. I think you're confused. As a matter of fact, we were going to go out there today, but after what happened—"

"You mean, after how I behaved in court, don't you, David?"

"I mean, after we saw that it was all too much for you—"

"He's doing it!" she yelled.

158

"You want proof?" He had raised his voice without meaning to. Marianne had just come back into the room.

"It's all right," she said. "She's next door with a friend. I can stay if you need me." She looked from one to the other, then asked, "Proof of what?"

"Yes," Emily said to David, "I want proof."

Picking up the phone, David called Cade.

They had to make their way through the crowd again. This time, Emily wore a camel's-hair coat with a wide collar which she had turned up, dark glasses, a scarf, and a big Garbo hat. She went down the stairs, a gloved hand holding Marianne's arm, while David ran ahead to start the car. They hurried to get in. As they started to drive away, the crowd broke through the lines and surrounded the car. Emily got a look at a wall of faces pressed against the windows of the car, noses flattened, expressions avid, blurred, insatiably curious. She buried her face in Marianne's dress, twisting the material in her fingers.

David said, furious, "Jesus, I wish I had the guts to run right over them!" They drove away. Emily felt panic rising in her throat. Her hands tightened, gripping Marianne's dress. She could not bring herself to look up.

"It's all right," Marianne crooned to her, "it's all right, baby, just don't think about anything, don't look at anything, just rest." Emily lay on her breast. David drove with one hand, unfolding a piece of paper with directions on it at the same time and trying to read it. Marianne stroked Emily's hair, soothing her. Emily's breathing became deep and regular. Marianne wondered if she was asleep.

Then David stopped the car. "I see them," he said. "I'll go ahead. You bring her." He leaned over, giving Emily a little kiss and pinching her cheek. "No reporters. No crowds. Very quiet. There's Cade."

David jumped out, slammed the door, and they heard his footsteps running away. Slowly, Marianne sat Emily up.

"Okay now? Sure you're up to this?"

"I'm fine."

They got out of the car in front of a stone columbarium with pointed arches. An official in a dark suit stood on the steps, rubbing his hands slowly, nodding to them. Emily started toward him.

"No, this way," said Marianne.

She turned. On the path ahead, she saw Cade standing with several men from the coroner's office and the cemetery. Emily and Marianne joined them. The group formed a respectful half-circle, walking with them, Cade leading the way. The path wound its way through a stand of yew trees, cutting across a well-kept lawn.

"This way, please," said an unidentified man from the cemetery association. "Interment was in an older section, and I'm afraid at present it hasn't quite had the attention it deserves."

Then they came to a break in the yew trees, and the path led them into an unkempt sweep of grounds. It was an exposed location and the wind blew. Emily grabbed her hat, head bent, following the footsteps of the others.

"Right over here," the voice said.

She looked up. Then she saw it. The weed-choked eminence. The fallen headstones, like a ruined city. The small stone houses of the dead, with the low doorways, through which one was obliged to go with bent head, bronze doors still proof against the salt air.

"Here we are."

No, it couldn't be. It was a trick of the mind, as is déjà vu, when what is happening seems familiar because the mind has misfiled information, made what happened milliseconds ago seem to belong far in the past. She tried to tell herself it was no more than that. Then she glanced to her left and saw the rusted gate in the wall, the steep cobblestone street leading down to a part of the city she had never seen. Until that horrible moment. That horrible moment that had never happened.

Her jaw went slack and she began to make a noise like an animal, a guttural throaty sound—David thought it was almost like the sound made by an epileptic in a seizure—and Marianne said:

"What's the matter? What is it?"

David ran toward them. "Come on," he said, trying to act as

160

if nothing had happened, "we'll walk together."

She tried to explain, to tell him, but the words wouldn't come. Now they were walking toward a low stone vault. She said nothing. Her head lolled toward his. Carefully, he took off her dark glasses to look at her eyes. They were glazed, unseeing. "Emmy? Honey?"

Her muscles went stiff, rigid. Marianne said, "Let's take her back to the car."

"No, I want to see," Emily said in a strange voice.

"Are you sure?"

David said to Marianne, with an impatience he could no longer hide, "I just want her to see for herself!"

They went forward a few steps. Toward the little stone house. Ruined. Graffiti scrawled all over the walls. Men wearing masks and black gloves were sliding a coffin out of the vault. They set it down at the bottom of a short flight of stone stairs. Emily looked up and read the name "Serpiente" over the low door. Cade nodded.

Quickly, the black-gloved men unscrewed the lid of the coffin, wrenching it open. In it, pillowed in pink silk, lay the body of a boy, dressed in a dark suit with a white flower in its lapel. The skin looked artificial from the cosmetics with which it was covered, and the dark curly hair was carefully arranged around the head.

Cade took out a death certificate, offering it to Emily. "April fifteenth," he said, pointing to a date. "That the boy?"

"Yes," Marianne said, her eyes riveted on the mouth. The familiar harelip was there but there was something odd about the mouth.

Staring at it, Marianne said in a low voice, "Why is he smiling?"

The man from the cemetery association who had led them there spoke into her ear. "Decay does that." He had not meant to be heard but his voice carried. Emily reacted, hearing him. At the same time, a workman dropped his screwdriver. It rolled out of his reach. He went to retrieve it, bending over, shoving open the small door of the vault with his back. In the pale, misty

161

daylight, Emily could see a shelf to the left. It was exactly as she had remembered it. *No, it wasn't déjà vu.*

Oh, my God!

She backed away, then tried to run, slipping on the wet grass and then falling, striking her head on one of the sunken gravestones. She tried to scramble to her feet, a hand to her head. Wet. She was bleeding. On her knees, she looked down, seeing her own blood sinking into the earth of the burial ground.

Arms held her. Then she heard herself beginning to cry out, a low, desperate, prolonged sound she did not even recognize, but that she felt reverberate through her whole being. She cried out repeatedly, as if the sound were a way of walling off pain, of blocking out what she simply could not bear. She felt David's and Marianne's arms supporting her, heard a confusion of voices, alarmed and concerned, but she did not care, she did not care about anything except blocking all of it out for as long as she could with repeated, terrible cries. It was a raw, tearing, long drawn-out sound, the last thing she remembered. After that, she lost consciousness.

They ran toward her, all of them except Cade, who stood muffled in his heavy coat, white hair blowing in the wind, staring off at a weatherworn sign on the rusty gate, which bore the old name of the cemetery: San Bruno.

22

David had arranged to have her taken to a hospital for observation. Emily did not want to go. Then, when she found out David had asked her gynecologist to meet them there, she was apprehensive.

"Is something wrong?"

"Wouldn't I tell you?"

"You're worried about the baby. My God, am I going to lose it?"

"Sweetheart, it's just a checkup. Routine. Okay?"

Her skull was X-rayed. Then a neurologist examined her, an athletic-looking youngish man with square, regular features and a German accent.

"Your head hurts you now?"

"Yes."

"Where does it hurt you, please?"

"Here."

"You are pointing to the spot?"

"Yes."

"Tell me what side it is."

"The left side."

"The left side, very good."

A spasm of pain made her close her eyes.

"Shall I explain to you why it hurts you?" the neurologist said, his fingers exploring the surface of the wound. "You have a bruise there, on the inside of the brain case, a swelling. Since there is no place for tissue to expand, it pushes inward, and the pressure on the brain makes your head ache. When the swelling goes down, the ache will disappear."

She rolled her eyes up toward the doctor. There were yellowish flecks in the irises and her skin was livid.

"Is my skull fractured?" she asked in a careful voice.

"No. You have only a concussion."

"A concussion."

"Any blow is a concussion. The brain, you see, is like a bowl of jello, and when you strike the head with sufficient force, the brain is thrown violently in the direction of the blow, inside the skull." He sighed. "How many fingers am I holding up?"

"Two."

"Now, tell me what you had for breakfast."

"I haven't had any breakfast."

"Why not?"

"Because . . . no, I had some toast and coffee."

"What time is it?"

"I don't know."

"What time do you think it is?"

"It must be getting close to six."

Her gynecologist entered the room. She saw him, standing to one side.

"Look away, please," the neurologist said. "Now, where do you feel the pressure when I touch you? Now."

"My right knee."

"Now?"

"My left foot."

"What is two times twelve?"

"Twenty-four."

He said to the gynecologist, not turning toward him, "Fascinating, isn't it, that the test for a rational mind is composed of a series of foolish questions?" Then, to Emily, "Watch my fingers."

Monotonously, the examination continued. Unsnapping a pocket flashlight, he peered into each of her pupils. "The eyes, you see," he said in a soft rapid murmur, "are indeed the windows of the soul, inasmuch as they are actually visible parts of the brain." He finished examining her, then put his flashlight and little mallet away, telling her gynecologist that she was all right. Then the neurologist gave her a quick, polite nod and left the room.

164

The gynecologist gave her a pelvic, ordered routine blood tests and a urinalysis, took her blood pressure, and then examined her breasts. His name was Dr. Susskind, and women liked him because he was fatherly and old-fashioned. He bent over her, and she looked at the pink scalp under the thinning gray hair, at the long-lobed ears, enlarged with age, and felt strangely comforted. She could feel the rough texture of a Donegal tweed cuff under his white jacket as he examined her breasts. His hand hesitated over something.

"That hurt you?"

"No."

"Sensitive?"

"No. Not at all."

He straightened up. "Any pains in the tummy?"

She shook her head. Then: "Am I all right?"

"Seem fine."

"I don't want to lose the baby."

"No reason you should."

"I lost the last one."

"When you were what? Ten weeks along?"

"Yes. But I lost one before."

"Also in the first trimester, wasn't it?"

"Yes."

"Well, that kind of thing—a spontaneous miscarriage in the first trimester—that generally means an abnormal pregnancy."

"Why did it happen?"

"I told you before. Could have been some genetic mismatching."

"Could this be the same thing?"

"My guess is, if it were, you would have aborted by now. The first trimester is the tricky part. The one you're about to enter is what we regard as the stablest part of any pregnancy. You're over the part where you get to feeling punk and not far enough along for any discomfort."

"Could I lose it because of the trial?"

He hesitated. She pressed him. He said, choosing his words carefully, "There's always the risk of an emotional trauma having

165

an effect on the pregnancy itself. Why don't you let me ask for a medical postponement?"

"For how long?"

"Another month and you'll be on firmer ground. Those fifth and sixth months are pretty easy. Or if you like, I'm sure I could ask for postponement till after delivery." She frowned, trying to decide. David had given her a shot on the way there. It had made her drowsy. "Look, why don't you let me do it? I can't postpone the arrival of your baby, but I can sure as hell postpone that trial for you. Want me to?"

She made up her mind. "No."

"Sure?"

"I just don't want it *there*"—she made a weak gesture—"sort of waiting for me. All that time that I'm waiting for the baby. I mean, I just can't *stand* the idea!" Her voice had risen. He put a firm, gnarled hand on her shoulder.

"I want you to be calm. Now, I'm going to tell you something. I lost my wife two years ago." He stopped talking suddenly, remembered pain tightening his throat. There was a silence. Sharp-edged. Then he said in an uneven voice, "Emmy, there are some things you just have to get through."

Marianne entered. They had let her come in for a moment. She went to Emily and kissed her wordlessly. Dr. Susskind squeezed Emily's shoulder, turned away, and left the room quickly. As he opened the door, she saw the shoulder of a uniformed policeman standing in the corridor just outside, his back toward her. A nurse entered, a fresh-faced Irish girl, who began to take her pulse, asking at the same time if it was an American holiday because she had to get to the bank. Emily didn't think it was a holiday. The girl was relieved.

"In this country, it's terrible. The bank closes if you fart out loud."

Emily looked toward the door, remembering the uniform. "What are they doing out there? Are they afraid I'll run away?"

The girl blushed but gave her a smile. "I think they're here to keep away the unwanted."

"I wish they could."

"Pardon me?"

166

"Nothing." Emily set her jaw.

"Talk is, you're a witch," said the girl in a lilting, matter-of-fact brogue.

"Is that what you think?"

"Me? How would I know?"

Emily looked at her with dislike.

Later, the nurse was hurrying out to the bank when she met David in the corridor. He asked about his wife.

"Oh, she's just fine, now." The nurse was rubbing her hand. It was reddened. He took it, glancing at it. "It keeps stinging. Like nettles," she said, the end of the phrase rising with the brogue's inflection. "Well, and I suppose I spilled something on it." She pulled her hand away, staring at it, then remembered something. "Oh, there's a doctor called here for you. I told the desk but you know what they're like. Did you get the message?"

"Dr. Burns?"

"That's the man. He said he could see you at four."

David glanced at his watch, saw that he had ten minutes to make the appointment and thanked her, starting away. She followed him.

"You don't think it's a bit of glass?"

"No." Together, they walked quickly toward the elevators. "When did you notice it?"

"Just now. We don't get time to get sick. Around here, the only thing they know how to run is the nurses. Right into the ground."

"I'm sure it's nothing." David got into the elevator, giving her a brief smile.

The tall, stooped psychiatrist listened to David attentively. David's eyes again took in the thatch of white hair, the white mustache, again examined the old scar around the left eye. It had left a depression in the flesh near the socket, so that there was something uneven in his glance. If he were a patient, David would have asked him about it. David went on talking, telling Dr. Burns about the exhumation and the effect the whole thing had had on Emily.

"Only a mild concussion?"

"Yes."

167

David then asked him if Emily's behavior seemed normal, and Burns shrugged, saying mildly, "To be honest, I don't know what normal behavior would be under such circumstances. What you're telling me is that she became hysterical, fell down, and struck her head. Doesn't that strike you as understandable, to say the least?"

"It's the pattern that bothers me."

"I take it that she still doesn't want to see me."

David shook his head slowly. "I told her you knew the whole story. I mean, Jesus, this is no time for secrets—but—well, no." He shook his head again. "She said she doesn't want to talk to anybody."

"How well do you think she's coping? What's your impression?"

"I don't know."

"Apart from what you've told me, have there been any other dramatic changes in her behavior?"

"No. But I still think there's something wrong with her." When Burns didn't answer, David said, "I'm sure you've thought about my wife's case. I'd like you to share your speculations with me." His language sounded stilted to him, and he shifted in his seat uncomfortably. Burns took a moment to make up his mind, then swiveled around in his chair, reached for a book and opened it.

"Your wife's case reminded me of something. Now, I want to be very careful about this. I'm not saying her illness is morbid—"

"Then you do think she's ill?"

"Well, I do think she's exhibiting a neurotic syndrome. But I don't know that it's going to get any worse." A quick breath. "It's very difficult for me to discuss a patient I've never met. I'm sure you appreciate that, Doctor. This is pure speculation."

"Yes, I understand."

"What you described put me in mind of this. Are you familiar with the works of Oesterreich?" He opened the book to a place he had marked.

"No."

"He died in—let me see—1949. But in his field, he has never

168

been surpassed. I'd like you to read this particular passage." He pushed the open book across to David, who began reading.

" '. . . but there are yet other ways in which this condition may arise. One of these begins with a hallucination: the new person is at first corporeally represented as some little distance away. Then it draws near to the individual and suddenly seizes upon her in order to "incarnate" itself into her.

" 'In this group belongs the case of the maid of Orlach, who was obviously a creature of very limited intelligence.

" 'From the 25th of August onwards the black spirit subjected her to more and more violent temptations; he no longer remained under disguises outside of her, but made himself master, as soon as he appeared, of her whole interior. He entered into her and henceforward uttered by her mouth demoniac discourses . . .

" 'From the 24th of August the black monk always appears to her in the same way. In the midst of her work she sees him in human form . . . Then she hears as if he spoke a few brief words to her, for example generally: "Won't you yet give me an answer? Take care, I shall torment you!" and other similar things. As she stubbornly refuses to answer him . . . he always continues: "Well, I shall now enter into you!" ' "

David turned the book over and read the title: *Possession Demoniacal and Otherwise* by Oesterreich.

"Are you telling me my wife is possessed?"

"Since I don't believe in anything of the sort—and neither, for that matter, does Oesterreich—I couldn't be telling you that. It sounds like what used to be called 'possession'—in its earliest stages. But we think of possession today as conversion neurosis. I'm sure you're familiar with the concept. I am guilty of something. I can't accept responsibility for that guilt. Therefore, I will invent somebody else who is to blame."

"Well, at least you're not suggesting an exorcism."

"Certainly not!"

"You sound as if you don't approve of such things."

"I certainly don't approve of the way they attract attention. Did you know that at Loudun they had as many as 7,000 spectators? Once a fight broke out between the Catholics and the Protestants. Over reserved seats!"

169

"We've got enough of a sideshow going on as it is."

"Yes."

"I wish she'd talk to you."

"I think we'll have to leave that up to her."

"I don't know what to do. I mean, if you're right—"

"Oesterreich says that possession is usually cured by the faith of the possessed. If she has faith in you—well, I think that's going to be enough to get her through it."

"Thank you."

Dr. Burns spread his hands. David frowned, not yet finished. He took a deep breath and then said, "What about . . . well, all these odd things. Knowing things she couldn't possibly know . . . foretelling the future—"

"Are you sure those things happened?"

"Well—"

"I'd be a little skeptical, myself. Oesterreich rejects all supernatural explanations, and so do I. That's all I can say. Now you've heard from both of us!" The phone rang. He answered it, then excused himself to take a brief call in his private office.

Alone, David opened the book, about to consult the index, when he happened to catch sight of the last paragraph. It was a brief statement about what Oesterreich chose to call "parapsychology." It ended with the statement: "We must defer an answer to these questions until we know more of parapsychic phenomena, their frequency and conditions of origin. The purely negative reply which so greatly facilitated for rationalism the historical criticism of all these accounts is frankly no longer possible today."

He read it through slowly, twice, to make sure he had understood it, then put down the book and left the office without saying goodbye.

23

Emily lay in her hospital bed that night after David had gone, comforted by the feel of starched sheets, nurses, routine. She would not let herself think about the trial. She would pretend that there was no tomorrow. She forced herself to think about the past. David. Heidelberg. On that first day, he had taken her for a ride on a little steamer down the Neckar. She remembered the river, green from the trees lining its banks, as they glided under the towers of small castles. Beyond Hirschorn, she remembered, the river made a three-quarter turn around the base of a conical hill, the slopes of which were irregularly divided into patches of cultivation in different shades of green. On its summit, like a crude crown, she had seen the walled city of Dilsberg. Across the river was a monastery, set on a low hill. Then came Heidelberg. First, they had seen the thirteenth-century walls of the university, built at the water's edge. Traffic on the river got heavier. There were barges, lighted pleasure boats, sculls, and a one-man ferry hooked to an overhead cable and propelled across the placid Neckar by the flow of the current. Halfway up the forest-clad slopes of the Königstuhl was a red castle. One night, in the forest there, they had made love.

She began to sob. She could not stop. "You all know that wild grief that seizes us when we remember former happiness." Who had said it? No, she would not let herself think about the trial. She would force herself to remember the writer's name. It came all too easily: Jünger. And with it, a blank mind. Again. No. Think of something. Anything. Quick. Wait. He was dead. She knew that now. It had never happened. It was all right.

She awoke remembering that he was dead. It had all been a bad dream. Now she could smile. Her heart was light.

Court was reconvened the following day. Rufus called Dr. Len Sawyer to the stand. Dr. Sawyer, a dermatologist like David, was in his early forties, husky, with short dark hair and a face like a clenched fist. Rufus spoke to him in a flat, matter-of-fact voice:

"Dr. Sawyer, have you from time to time removed marks from the skin of the accused?"

"Yes. Several times."

"What were they?"

"Nevi."

"In layman's language, please."

"Moles. No problem. Didn't even bleed."

"What color?"

"Reddish. Sometimes a bit on the blue side." Dr. Sawyer appeared puzzled at this line of questioning. He did not know why he had been called as a witness, protested his ignorance of the proceedings and asked that the doctor-patient relationship he had with the accused be respected as confidential but was overruled, in consonance with a recent California law.

"You say, several times. Why not all at once?"

"Well, they recurred."

"On March fifteenth of this year, the defendant consulted you professionally. Her reason?"

Dr. Sawyer protested but was told to answer. Reluctantly, he said, "The patient had a little something on the skin of her breast she wanted removed."

"Did you remove it?"

"No, sir."

"Why not?"

"The trade-off would have been unacceptable."

"Would you clarify that?"

"In my specialty, you have to weigh how the condition looks compared with how the scar would look after surgery."

Offering in evidence photographs Dr. Sawyer had routinely taken of Emily's skin, Rufus nodded to the projectionist, who flicked a switch. A slide was projected showing her rounded breasts.

At that moment, hunched in her chair in the dark, Emily felt herself go ice-cold. A terrible apprehension seized her.

The slide was replaced by a second slide, showing an extreme close-up of the left nipple. There was visible what looked like a beauty mark along the milk line. Rufus asked:

"Is this what the defendant wanted you to remove?"

"Yes, sir."

"What is it?"

"A polythelia."

"I would like you to put that in words all of us understand."

"Oh, it looks like a beauty mark."

"What *is* it?"

"A nipple. An extra nipple."

Emily felt the hairs prickling at the back of her neck.

There was a murmur of astonishment. The projector was shut off, the lights were switched back on, and Rufus said in a low voice to the clerk, "People's Exhibit Numbers 55 and 56." Then to Dr. Sawyer, he said, "Did you find breast tissue under the nipple?"

"Yes."

"In your judgment, would it be capable of secreting milk?"

"Mrs. Blake has changes in her breasts during menstrual periods, like all women. They become full and tender."

"Does she lactate?"

"Yes. It's a rare phenomenon, but during her menses, she produces very small quantities of milk. Of course, now during her pregnancy—"

"I am speaking about earlier. Does the milk flow from all three nipples?"

There was an awkward pause, after which Dr. Sawyer replied, "Yes, sir. That is what brought her to me in the first place."

A ripple of amazement went through the courtroom. Emily felt her face go hot with shame. She turned involuntarily to look at David and caught his eyes on her, dark with anger for her sake, and then he was on his feet and at her side, comforting her. Dr. Sawyer looked at Emily sympathetically. A sob broke from her.

173

She clapped a hand over her face. David held her to him. She sobbed in his arms.

Dr. Sawyer said indignantly, "How anybody could look at that poor woman crying her eyes out and think for one moment—!"

Instantly, Rufus interrupted coldly, "Let the record show the defendant is not crying but sobbing. Tears are not possible to a witch."

Emily lifted her face and gave Rufus a shocked look. Instantly, David snatched her back in his arms. But he was not quick enough. The jurors had seen that her eyes were dry.

"I can't cry!" she whispered to him, frantic. "David, I can't cry!"

"People don't cry when they're scared, Emmy! They can't!" He whispered in her ear, stroking her hair. A bailiff asked him to resume his seat, tapping him on the shoulder and pointing.

"I won't listen to that lovely woman slandered!" said Dr. Sawyer.

Rufus replied, in a quiet voice that managed to make itself heard throughout the courtroom, "Satan never works more like a devil than when he looks most like an angel of light."

Cade drawled, not bothering to rise, "Sounds just like Reverend Wigglesworth in the *Day of Doom* when he describes the blessed in heaven as 'looking down with eternal joy on the torments of the damned.' "

Manly gavelled, saying angrily, "Strike that whole exchange! You people want a mistrial, you're going to get it!"

"I beg the Court's pardon," Rufus answered. "Dr. Sawyer," he turned now to the witness box, walking toward it, meanwhile massaging his hands as if he were cold, "was this extra nipple ever sensitive?"

"Absolutely not!" Dr. Sawyer responded, evidently sure that he had scored a point for his patient. "It was anesthetic, as a matter of fact. She had no feeling at all in that area."

"Are you familiar with the term 'witch's mark'?"

"I am not." Dr. Sawyer was taken aback.

"The term 'Devil's mark'?"

"No."

"I am going to read to you something from a work by Michael

174

Dalton, who described the sign—that is, the witch's mark—as"—and here, Rufus began reading from a small, tattered book he pulled out of his pocket—" '. . . some big or little Teat upon their body, and in some secret place where he (the Devil) sucketh them, appearing as a man, woman, or a boy.' "

Emily screamed. She tried to stop herself, pressing her hands to her mouth and looking up with terrified eyes. Rufus glanced in her direction, then continued:

" 'And besides their sucking, the Devil leaveth other marks upon their body, sometimes like a blew spot or a red spot, like a flea-biting; *all which for a time may be taken away but will come again to their old form.* And these the devil's marks be *insensible* and *being pricked will not bleed,* and be often in their secretest parts, and therefore require diligent and careful search.' Dr. Sawyer, do you notice any correspondence between your testimony about the condition of the accused and the passage I just read to you?"

There was another commotion in the courtroom. Manly banged angrily with his gavel.

Dr. Sawyer sighed and said, "I refuse to comment on the work of some superstitious idiot."

"And yet, this searching for witch's marks was conducted by no less an authority than the great William Harvey. Did you know that, Dr. Sawyer?"

"No, I didn't."

"Would you tell the Court what William Harvey is responsible for?"

"He discovered the circulation of the blood," said Dr. Sawyer slowly.

"Hardly the work of a superstitious idiot," murmured Rufus. Then in a matter-of-fact voice, he said to Cade, "Your witness."

Emily thought, I have to lie down. I must ask them for a recess. Instead of speaking to Cade, who had gotten to his feet, she turned around intending to catch David's eye. At that moment, she saw that he was staring at her in shock. Her eyes wavered. She thought, I am going to faint. She did not care. She put her arms on the defense table and slumped forward, telling herself it did not matter. Nothing mattered. Cade was speaking but she could scarcely hear him. Her hands were shrunken with cold. She rubbed them together, feeling the bones. Her head swam.

"Dr. Sawyer," said Cade, "William Harvey did indeed discover the circulation of the blood, a most remarkable finding, considering when he made it. Do you happen to recollect the century?"

"About four hundred years ago."

"Yes. If memory serves, William Harvey was born in 1578. Hardly a fool, but a child of his age all the same. No further questions." He turned and then saw that Emily had collapsed. A matron held smelling salts under her nose. Manly adjourned court for the rest of the day. David drove home slowly with Emily. Neither spoke until they got into the house.

Then Emily said, "I didn't scratch myself."

She walked slowly upstairs and lay down, trying to keep her mind a blank. Someone had told her to concentrate on the number one, to say it and try to see it as if it were written over the center of one's forehead, as a way of blocking out all thought. She did that now. In a little while, she fell into what seemed like a drugged sleep. Finding her that way, David put her to bed.

She did not wake up until it was dark and quite late. David wasn't there. She pulled on a robe and crept downstairs, seeing a light coming from under the library door. She knocked, then went in. David was sprawled in an armchair, fast asleep. He snored. A glass still dangled from his hand. She went to take it and he dropped it, then woke up. He looked at her, trying to focus his eyes. She saw that he was very drunk.

"Emmy," he said thickly.

She tried to get him upstairs. When he passed out in her arms, she struggled with him, lowering him onto the couch, got a quilt to cover him with and then went back upstairs to bed. Alone.

24

The next day was Saturday. Recess. Desperate, David turned to Marianne for help, asking her to take Emily on a retreat. After all, Emily had been raised a Catholic, and he thought such a weekend might give her comfort. He suggested this to Marianne almost impatiently. He himself had an active dislike of religion and did not even believe in sin, which he dismissed as nothing but disturbed behavior.

Marianne said quietly, "There *is* such a thing as sin."

"Bullshit. I know every so-called sin in the book, and if you want my opinion—"

"Do you know about the Black Mass at Sainte-Secaire? It involved an act that was so unspeakable, you couldn't get absolution from the priest or even the bishop. You had to go to Rome, to the Pope himself. I think you still do."

David asked, curious, "What was the sin?"

Marianne gave him a sidelong look and answered, "You know, I'm not going to tell you!"

In the morning, David started out of the house, swearing under his breath, wondering why the hell all this had to happen. Rotten luck. What was luck, anyway? He thought about luck. Funny word, luck. What did it mean? Luck was the character of one's fate, good or bad. But luck also meant whatever happened by chance, which implied, of course, that one's life exhibited design. Every event was at once cause and effect, but luck stood outside the high walls of necessity. Luck was significant accident. Luck was what, after all, did not have to happen. Luck was an outlaw. And life, he decided, was a bag of shit. As he started the car, he saw Marianne arriving, waved to her and drove away.

Marianne rang the front doorbell and asked Esmeralda if Mrs. Blake was ready. With a shake of the head, she gestured toward the living room. The door was ajar. Marianne walked over to it. Through the crack, she could see Emily sitting cross-legged on the floor, reading a letter. Marianne called her name. Emily, absorbed, did not seem to hear her. Marianne pushed the door open slowly, then gasped. Emily was seated on the floor in the middle of the room in what looked like an avalanche of mail. There were half-emptied sacks surrounding her.

"Jesus."

Emily glanced up at her briefly, blankly.

"You reading that stuff?"

"Some of it."

"What is it, hate mail?"

Wordlessly, Emily handed her the letter she was reading. It was postmarked Urbana, Ohio, written in a round, childish scrawl in violet ink on binder paper by a woman identifying herself as widowed and sixty-four. It begged Emily for help. Emily showed her another, printed in block letters, cursing her for all the world's evil and saying that the sender was praying "to Almighty God that you and your kind get burned alive at the stake."

"Don't read any more."

Emily kept reading, her face a mask of indifference. She read rapidly, compulsively, through one letter after another. Marianne heard the doorbell ring, and then Esmeralda showed in a small, swarthy mailman who dumped another sack of mail on the floor, then introduced himself as Ali Marrakesh.

"Where are you from?" asked Marianne in a dangerous voice.

"Tunis." A broad smile. Long yellowing crooked teeth. He pulled a pad of government forms from his back pocket, tore one off, turned it over and, advancing toward Emily with the stub of a pencil, asked for her autograph. Emily did not look up.

Marianne said, "I know a few words of Arabic."

"Oh, the lady speaks Arabic!"

"Would you like to hear some?"

"Yes, indeed, missus!"

"I empty my bowels upon the graves of your parents," said Marianne in perfect Arabic, "while bats defecate upon your

178

household gods." The mailman's expression did not change but his face became suffused with blood, as if his collar had suddenly become too tight. "Now, get back on your camel and get your ass out of here, buster!"

The mailman looked at her with round, incredulous eyes, then turned and stormed out of the house, banging the door behind him. Marianne turned her attention back to Emily, who had still not looked up.

"Front and center. We're leaving." Then, when Emily still showed no reaction, Marianne went to her, seized her roughly by the arm and dragged her to her feet. "And I mean now!"

Emily stared at her like a frightened little girl. Marianne led her upstairs, packed a few things for her, and the two of them drove away minutes later.

"I want you to put the seat back and sleep," Marianne said. They had crossed the Gate Bridge and were headed north, through the hills of Marin. Emily did as she was told. Marianne pulled a car robe from the back seat and shoved it at her. Emily snuggled down under it, making herself comfortable on the deep leather bucket seat of Marianne's old Volvo. She was docile now, like a child. Marianne wondered if she had been taking sedatives. She stole a look at Emily's face. Her color was good. It was pink in repose, and the thick blond lashes caught the sunlight as they drove, the rounded blond brows, the thick gold hair. Emily slept for an hour. The fresh air blowing in on them was now scented with pine. They had begun to climb up into the mountains of the Cascades. Marianne shifted into low. Emily stirred.

"Where are we going, Mommy?"

"Away."

"Good."

Ahead of them on the mountain road, Marianne could see an inn. Should they stop for a meal? She decided not to, driving past it. At that point, Emily sat up.

"Accident," she said.

"Where?" Marianne squinted ahead. "I don't see it."

"I want to stop." She turned around in her seat, saw the inn and said, "Back up. I want to go there."

Marianne pulled over to the side, onto the shoulder.

179

"I packed a lunch. A nice lunch." She did not want to tell
Emily that wherever they went, she would be recognized, that
there would be curious crowds. "Don't you want the nice lunch
I packed?"

"Let's see the nice lunch."

Marianne got an old Abercrombie & Fitch picnic hamper out
of the trunk, spread a checkered cloth on the meadow grass under
the trees and, when Emily sat down beside her, triumphantly
pulled something out of the basket.

"Look. Blood sausage. Like we used to get in Heidelberg,
remember?"

"Full of sodium nitrite. Bad."

Marianne set her mouth. "Look, during my lifetime, I have
been threatened by fallout in my milk, DDT in my vegetables,
DES in my meat, aerosol in the ozone, and red dye in my lipstick,
not to mention whatever the hell is in my cigarettes. Now, Emily,
I have had it. You are free to choose your risks. Let me choose
mine." She bit into the sausage defiantly. Emily grinned, reaching
for some herself. Marianne snatched it away. "I forgot. You're
pregnant. Drink your milk first."

They had lunch in silence, then stretched out in the tall grasses
for a break, while Marianne smoked and stared into the blue.
Then they started off.

Around the next curve, traffic slowed down. They could make
out flashing red lights. Marianne said, "Jeez, you must have eyes
like a hawk." The traffic threaded its way through one lane, past
a couple of cars splintered together in a head-on collision. Marianne could see blood all over the highway. She averted her eyes,
then looked around for an ambulance. A highway patrolman in
the middle of the road said, "Keep moving, lady." But now she
could see bodies sprawled in the road, glass everywhere. She said,
"Where's the ambulance?"

"We're taking care of that, ma'am. Now, just keep driving."

"But where the Christ is it?"

"Lady, this only happened five minutes ago. Now, will you keep
it moving, please?"

She drove slowly, looking straight ahead. Then, when she got
past the flares, and the traffic began to accelerate, she looked at

Emily out of the corner of her eye, wondering whether Emily had heard. But Emily was fast asleep again.

It had been a long drive, and it was almost dark when Marianne parked the car in the village. Emily woke up, looking around.

"Where are we?"

"Maria de Merced."

"You're kidding."

"No. I telephoned. We're going on a retreat. Now, grab your suitcase." They got out of the car.

"But I'm not a practicing Catholic any more."

"They don't care."

Carrying their luggage, they followed a path through the forest, slipping on frozen cow tracks, no sound except for the trickle of water that ran off the melting snow. The path curved out over the face of a hill. Below, the city glittered. They heard the thin sound of bells. Then they got to the monastery. There were hundreds of tourists outside the walls. The buses that brought them were parked under Gothic arches.

The church was open to the public and Marianne insisted on stopping there first. They went in, crowding through a Romanesque entrance, past an Etruscan-like recumbent figure of the Virgin, a smile carved into the painted stone face. A bell jangled. Monks with thin beards and shaved pates shuffled in through a low doorway. They began to intone the Mass in quavering voices. The crowd pressed Emily against a statue. Under the dusty vestments, the wood was split, and the painted expression on its face had cracked and peeled. She tried to steady herself. A statue of St. Patrick fell forward against her, like a drunk in a bar. She propped it up again, then noticed the carved snakes at its feet. Snakes, she thought. Serpents. Serpiente. Coincidence. She must not think about it. She must not think about it.

After Marianne had genuflected and blessed herself, they left the church and walked toward the cloister, where Marianne pulled on a bell rope. Then a panel set low in the wall slid open. A simian-looking head twisted around, and observant unfeeling eyes, like an animal's, looked up at them. When Marianne gave her name, the massive door swung open on confusion. The hall was crowded with visitors, all of them women.

A brother led them upstairs, down a cocoa-matted hall, showed them to a room with carved dark furniture upholstered in red velvet. He pointed at printed rules nailed to the door, then left. The window opened on the exercise yard. Emily looked out. Below her, she could see eight brothers in Franciscan habits walking together, four abreast. They marched in two squads facing each other, taking turns walking backward. One brother read aloud in a rapid monotone, no sound but the susurrus of Latin, the creak of sandals, the rattle of scapulars. From the forest came an odor of incense cedar.

Dinner would be in an hour. They lay down for a nap. Emily told herself she must not let herself think about the trial. She constructed a fantasy and tried to lose herself in a web of dreams. When this was over, they would travel. They would go to Vienna. She remembered reading that the Turks had fought their way inside the walls before retreating, leaving behind a legacy of lilacs and coffee houses. They would visit Innsbruck, with its glacial river white from rock ground to dust. Then, Spain. Traced through rocky canyons like fossil outlines were the ghosts of dead rivers. They would visit Punella, a town with no vegetation, no public buildings, where the windowless houses dug out of muddy red earth looked like huge bubbles that slowly rise to the surface of a volcano.

She longed to travel. To run. Anywhere.

There was a knock at the door. Marianne opened it, and a wizened old man in Franciscan habit indicated in sign language that there was a telephone call, then pointing at Emily. Marianne was perplexed.

"I didn't tell anyone where we were going and you didn't know."

"Maybe it's David. I mean, if something happened—"

"Yes, and maybe it's some goddamned reporter." Since the monk didn't speak, she seemed oblivious to the fact that he might be able to hear. Now he gestured to Emily to follow him. She started out. Marianne intercepted her, saying, "No, let me." The two of them followed the old monk down the hall. Several brothers walked by them, glances averted. At first, Emily reacted. She was offended, dismayed. Then she remembered: custody of the eyes. They walked on, following the little monk. Hearing music, Emily glanced through the open door of a small auditorium as they passed it. Two priests on benches, listening, while a third played the piano. He played mechanically, with an almost spastic grasping at the keys. She remembered that there was an Order in which by custom the Mass was sung badly.

The telephone was in the front hall, in a glass booth like a sedan chair. Marianne went in and sat down on a worn velvet cushion, picking up the receiver of the old-fashioned instrument and speaking into the mouthpiece. "Yes?" she said.

"Mrs. Blake?" came the operator's voice. It was faint, interrupted by a sound that was like cellophane crackling.

"Who is calling Mrs. Blake, please?"

"One moment, please." Then: "It's a Mr. Jiles."

Leaning out of the booth, a hand over the telephone's mouthpiece, Marianne asked Emily, "Know anybody named Jiles?" Then, when Emily shook her head, Marianne said, "It must be a mistake."

"One moment, please," said the operator again. More crackling. Then the operator's voice, saying, "I'm sorry. I think it's *Giles.*" There was some interference on the line, and the operator finally returned and said with a quick sigh, "Ma'am, I will spell the name. G-i-l-l-e-s d-e R-a-i-s."

"Baron Gilles de Rais?" asked Marianne, with a touch of sarcasm.

"That is correct, ma'am," said the operator, relieved.

"Would you tell the baron for me—" began Marianne, warming up, but the operator interrupted her again.

"Ma'am, I'm sorry but a lot of our lines are down. This is a very bad connection or I'd ask the party to call back, but I'm not sure the party can get through again. Are you Mrs. Anne Blake? Because my party says he's waiting for you."

"I'm afraid you've got a wrong number."

"My party is very definite, ma'am."

"So am I. Tell your party there is no one here by that name.

183

And I don't think there's anybody there by that name, either."
Marianne hung up the phone impatiently, struggling out of the
narrow glass booth.

"Who was it?"

"Some joker."

"Well, who?"

"He identified himself as 'Gilles de Rais.' 'Baron Gilles de
Rais.' "

"I don't know any Baron Gilles de Rais."

"You wouldn't want to."

"Do you know him?"

"Oh, for Christ's sake, he was friends with Joan of Arc."

"What?"

"I told you, it's some joker. He was one of the worst men who
ever lived. He says he's waiting to meet you."

"And he was friends with Joan of Arc?"

"Well, you know, she was burnt as a witch, and there are a lot
of scholars who still think she was, and for that reason—oh, Jesus
Shit Christ, am I sorry!" She looked around. Fortunately, the hall
was empty. "Anyway, it has nothing to do with you."

"He asked for me?"

"In the first place, nobody knows we're here and in the second
place, no, he did not ask for you. It's some screw-up."

"I thought you said—"

"He's looking for *Anne* Blake."

Emily went absolutely white. Marianne grabbed at her.

"I want to lie down," she said. "I have to lie down."

Marianne took her upstairs. They both lay down again to rest.
When Marianne awoke, Emily was not in the room. Nervous, she
went looking for her and found her in what a sign on the door
described as "Parlor." The room was lined with books, and Emily
was seated at a desk, her head in her hands, all the expression and
color washed out of her face, a large book open in front of her.
Marianne went over to her, concerned, leaned over her shoulder,
and when she saw what Emily was reading, she tried to take the
book away from her. Emily wouldn't let her. She kept reading.
Marianne read, too. She couldn't help herself. It was a passage
from a scholarly work by Tondriau and Villeneuve.

184

"Rais, Gilles de: Gilles de Laval, the Baron of Rays . . ."
Duray! No!
". . . grand-nephew of Du Guesclin, Marshal of France, was a pederast, satanist, necrophiliac and disemboweller. He was raised by his grandfather Jean de Craon, who schooled him in depravity at an early age. A group of procurers and villains made themselves available to find young 'victims' and the Baron would first ravish the boys and later kill them."

See, I used to live with this guy, Mr. Duray, but oh, Christ, lady, he was a awful bugger! He hadn't said it, she imagined it. But how was that possible?

"De Rais massacred so many children that it is impossible to give an exact estimate. Demonologist Michelet mentions two hundred, while Bernelle and Huysmans claim that the number reached eight hundred. The butchery and perversion had satanic accompaniments; de Rais insisted that the children be brought to him in chains or bound and thank him before they were killed."

Hey, how about I come live with you?

"Before massacring them, de Rais would play out a scene reminiscent of something from a de Sade novel; he would invite them to sit upon his knee. The victims would then relax, thinking that they were saved; with the care of an artist, the baron would then purposely cut their throats. Whilst the blood spouted over him, he would look at them lovingly, drinking in their last breaths, before ravishing them with all the fury of some enraged monster. After de Rais had raped them, he would often find pleasure in dismembering the corpse, beheading it sometimes or reducing the brain to pulp. This was carried out in the presence of his friends whilst he laughed to the point of tears. He was arrested on 13 September 1440, and executed the following year."

"Let's go upstairs now, okay, honey?" Marianne put her hands on Emily's shoulders, pulling her up. Emily moved slowly, obeying Marianne with a childlike wish to please. Marianne led her back to their room.

Emily asked wonderingly, "Why did you bring me here?"

"I thought maybe you'd like to talk to a priest."

"Oh."

A bell rang. They went downstairs to a silent dinner of soup

185

served at a long refectory table, the only sound the voice of a monk reading to them from St. Augustine's *Civitas Dei:*

". . . where all around me boiled a cauldron of unholy loves."

After dinner, they went down to see the Guest Father. He walked with them in the long twilight in the terraced gardens overlooking a river. He showed them the fruit trees and talked rapidly, interrupting himself with brief, sacred exclamations, clasping fine-boned hands. Perspiration ran down Emily's face. He noticed it. Was she not well? They went inside. He showed them an album of photographs from a trip he had taken to Spain, pictures of girls holding oranges. Emily felt a terrible longing to cry out to him, You have got to help me! Oblivious, he showed her another photograph of dark-eyed girls holding up more oranges, this time just outside Valencia. Suddenly, to her horror, she began to laugh. Hysterically. She turned away, trying to pretend that she was coughing. Marianne quickly led her away, excusing them.

They went to bed very early, fell fast asleep in the thin pure mountain air. Emily dreamed that she was awake. The room was the same, excepting that there was something wrong with its composition, as if some blind center of herself had made an error, so that it was disorienting to find herself there. The room's character had changed. How, it was difficult to say. It was a question of mood, of resonance. The light was altered. It was, if anything, brighter, even harsh, but she was unable to make out details. Lately, she had had the same dream again and again. There was a set pattern. It filled her with a sense of blank expectation. Nevertheless, she was unable to remember it in advance.

She became aware that she was afraid. Her heart pounded. It was as if some terrible knowledge of an ultimate horror had escaped long enough to race across the dark fields of the sleeping mind. A bar of light appeared suddenly under the door. The terror that seized her dissolved away the dream. Then it seemed to her that the dream still existed. She had only exercised her prerogative to step outside the circle of its enchantment. The dream's landscape stretched below her, now only a memory of itself, but a memory she could examine from within. It was possible for her to walk through its world again, as through a set after a performance; more than that, simple acquiescence would set it all in motion again. Now, detached, analytical, she moved slowly through the charade a second time. Here were its elements. It was ingenious, nothing more. The conjurer's trick exposed, it held no interest for her. And then (a misstep? had she touched something?) the trap was sprung. She was once again the dream's prisoner. She opened her mouth. The sound of her own voice waked her.

She struggled to her feet, remembering a line she had read—what was it?—that "the real horror is that there is no horror."

Slowly, she made her way toward the bathroom. It was simple, even primitive. It had no running water. Instead, a pitcher in a basin, a candlestick. With shaking fingers, Emily lit the candle, a wave of nausea coming over her. Was she pale? She must see. She looked in the framed mirror that hung over a chest of drawers. It was dark. *Through a glass darkly.* She leaned forward, straining to see herself. The candle flared up. The reflection wavered back at her, frightened, imploring. But not her face. Lupe's.

The splintering crash wrenched Marianne from her sleep. She sat bolt upright, looked around, then raced for the bathroom. There was another crash. Then she heard footsteps running in the hall. Another crash. Marianne grasped the long metal handle to the bathroom, threw open the door. There was Emily, the basin in her hands, her face contorted with rage, smashing at the mirror again and again.

Quick. The door. No, it's all right. My friend is ill. Not now. Please. She ran back to Emily, seizing hold of her. The two of them struggled. Emily's eyes were wild, and her arms kept flailing, even after Marianne had dragged her back into the bedroom, flung her down on the bed. She forced tranquilizers into her mouth, held a glass to her lips. More knocking. *Not now!* Marianne packed their things in five minutes. They left, Marianne half-dragging Emily down the long, dark corridor, calling out to the shadowy figures of hooded monks appearing everywhere, "My friend is ill! Try to understand! My friend is ill!"

The drive back was a nightmare. Marianne drove, hanging on to Emily, who alternately slept and then sat bolt upright, talking incomprehensibly, struggling with the arm with which Marianne held her. Twice, Emily tried to throw herself out of the speeding car.

Then, the house. David, white-faced, in a robe, all of them caught in the glare of flash bulbs by the photographers who waited, never sleeping, never sleeping. Marianne stayed with them, sleeping on the sofa in the library, while Emily, heavily sedated, slept through what little was left of the night and all of Sunday.

She did not know that her behavior at the convent had attracted the attention of all the other members of the retreat. That the press had gotten wind of it. That the details were known by everyone the following morning. Including Rufus, who immediately dispatched Fonner to Maria de Merced Monastery to investigate.

25

Monday morning, she seemed to have no recollection of what had happened. Docile again, she let herself be led down past the cordoned-off yelling mob of the curious to the guarded car. Then the three of them drove to the courthouse.

They were off to go skiing, Emily and David. Rufus talked, Cade interrupted, but she did not listen, would not let herself pay attention. She took David's hand and they boarded the German train, all private compartments herringboned on either side of an aisle, each with little blue upholstered reclining chairs. A waiter entered, spread a starched white cloth over a collapsible table, brought them frosted drinks and a dinner of trout, parsleyed new potatoes, rounds of lemon, a light Moselle. And the salad? Would they take watercress? Endive? *Gewiss. Und Brötchen dazu. Schön.* The waiter boned the fish. Through the window, they could see lighted oblongs of fresh-drifted snow.

Rufus had the projectionist showing slides. In some part of her mind, she heard him speak of the devil-dancers of Ceylon, possession by Meh Suh, the Mother of Colors, in China, the *Phi* of the Siamese, Marco Polo's thirteenth-century account of devil conjurers in Cathay, the Greek prophetess who became possessed after drinking sacrificial blood, the demon-masks of ancient Incas, hereditary possession among the natives of Fiji, the double-souled among the New Guinea Vindessi, Melanesian ghost-possession, death by suggestion performed by Tibetan priests.

*　　　　*　　　　*

She must force herself not to listen to anything. David. David in her arms in their berth, as the cold Alpine air blew in on them, made them drowsy. Then came the climb upward, the grade ever steeper, flanked by the gorge's walls. To the steady labored chugging of the train, now double-engined, was added the fabled *Rauschen* of mountain torrents.

Morning. Skis banged along the corridor. Goggled and booted, they climbed down into the icy air, boarded a *Seilbahn*. Bobbing like a cork, the gondola slid forward, pulled along a cable like a pencil line drawn across the white landscape, swooping sharply upward, over the tops of trees, over crevasses. The mist blew, the car sailed straight into a cloud of it, there was only the black line of the cable disappearing ahead. Then the landing platform of the lodge appeared, jutting out of sheer rock. Everything was buried under great slopes of snow, the trees were gone. Past the timber line, there was an abrupt silence.

Now Rufus had the projectionist showing slides of the tympana of various mediaeval cathedrals, each one depicting The Last Judgment, devils and gargoyles. His voice continued, relentless. There was no escaping it.

But I will escape.

Don't listen. The lodge had oak-planked floors, fires blazing on stone hearths. Outside, they could see a big bowl of snow surrounded by peaks. There were the skiers, bright-sweatered, arms raised as, one by one, like divers, they plunged down the sides of the glistening hollow.

The slopes were all dusted with fresh powder snow. They went right out. Looking back, they could make out the line of their tracks all the way from the ski hut. It was a good day, not too hot, they kept at it, slogging up the practice hill and gliding down. The ski instructor punched a gloved fist into a palm and shouted to hear his own voice through earmuffs. Emily felt the crust of snow give under the sharp edge of the waxed skis as she zigzagged back and forth across the alp's face. At the bottom, she stopped to look at the view, the range of peaks running south across the bright sky toward Italy, the ski trails plunging down into the forest, no sound except the uninterrupted oiled clicking of the chair lift.

Click-click-click. Sh. She leaned on her elbows, face in her hands. Her eyes closed. She would not listen. To anything. Click-click-click.

Rufus nodded at the projectionist, who began putting away his equipment. The lights had been switched back on. Rufus said:

"I think we have shown that these phenomena are universal. They are found throughout history, in all times, in all places, in all cultures. I now want to direct your attention to the religious background of the accused."

Father Timothy was called. After he was sworn in and seated, Rufus introduced him as the Guest Father of Maria de Merced and thanked him for coming there on such brief notice.

"Before proceeding with this witness," Rufus continued, "I would like to place in evidence this documentation, showing that the accused was born and baptized a Roman Catholic." Rufus handed certain papers to the Court Clerk, murmuring a number.

"So noted," Manly said.

"Objection. Irrelevant," Cade growled, on his feet.

"I must insist, Your Honor, that the religion of the defendant is indeed relevant."

"That piece of paper don't say anything about her religion now."

"Does counsel mean to suggest that the defendant has abjured her faith?"

"Objection. Incompetent. Prejudicial."

"The jury will disregard the prosecutor's last remark," said Manly, striking his gavel.

"Your Honor," Cade pursued, "one of the cornerstones of American Constitutional law is separation of church and state. I find it intolerable that the prosecution should seek to lay the foundation for any argument in the private religious convictions of any person."

Rufus said quietly, "With the Court's permission: if it could be shown that an accused was a member of a satanic sect devoted to sex perversion, bestiality, ritual murder, and cannibalism—and there are such sects in our country, that is

191

well-documented—would Your Honor not admit information on that sect as relevant?"

Cade was on his feet, shaking with indignation. "You comparing the Catholic Church with some assemblage of depraved orgiasts?"

"The Devil has the largest congregation in the world," Rufus murmured, riding over the whisper of surprise that rose from the courtroom. "And the law that applies here—"

"Don't you quote me the law again, do you understand?" Suddenly, Manly's face was mottled with fury. Rufus noted it quickly and made him an apologetic answer:

"I beg the Court's pardon. My position here is painful. It is difficult. As I said at the outset, this is not a case I ever wanted to prosecute. But once embarked on this course—"

Manly was not interested. "Get to the point!" he snapped.

"The religion of the accused is relevant. I ask only for an opportunity to show it."

"All right, I'm going to let you go forward and reserve judgment!"

"Thank you, Your Honor." Rufus walked slowly over to the witness box, lacing his hands, then taking a book from a table. He opened the volume and handed it to the witness.

"Father Timothy, I have here a copy of the baptismal ceremony. Would you read a few lines of it for us, please?"

Father Timothy took the open book, adjusted his metal-framed glasses and began reading: " *'Exorciso te immunde spiritus! Exi ab ea!'* " His voice droned on.

"Would you translate that into English for us, Father?"

"Pardon me," Father Timothy said. Then, turning to Judge Manly, he protested in a soft voice, "Your Honor, I don't feel that one of the sacraments of Holy Mother Church should become the subject of a legal dispute in a civil court."

"This is a criminal court," Manly corrected him.

"I meant only to contrast it with a canonical body. Perhaps 'secular' would have been a better word."

"You've just been asked to translate two lines of Latin. I don't see why you shouldn't answer the question," said Judge Manly irritably.

"Very well, Your Honor." Reading from the text, Father Timothy translated slowly, " 'I exorcise thee, thou unclean spirit! Go thou far away from this servant of God! Come out of her! Hear thy doom, O Devil, Satan accursed!' "

"These are the words pronounced by a Catholic priest over a baby at the time of baptism?" asked Rufus. There was an indignant stir in the courtroom.

"Yes."

"Are they meant seriously?"

"I don't understand."

"Father, we are discussing here one of the seven sacraments of the Catholic Church. Now, are the words you have just translated for us nothing but a vain and archaic fancy or are they meant to be taken literally?"

"The ceremony of baptism is an ancient custom."

"I didn't ask that."

Emily began to tremble uncontrollably. Cade looked at her, then put a hand on hers. She covered her face with her other hand. He saw that it was covered with cuts and scratches. Seeing him looking at it, she pulled it away, then averted her face.

"Mother Church teaches us that we are born in Original Sin."

"Your Honor, will the bench direct the witness to answer the question?"

"Witness will answer the question put to him," ruled Manly.

"Some would interpret the language as metaphor," Father Timothy replied.

"All language is metaphor," Rufus said sharply. "You're evading the question. I'll put it another way: isn't the whole ceremony of baptism an exorcism, intended to drive a demon out of the newborn?"

"Originally, that was the intention, yes."

"I mean now, Father."

"Customs survive that no longer mean what they meant. They have today a different interpretation."

"You're not answering me."

"I plead incompetence."

"I beg pardon?"

"Your question should be addressed to the College of Cardinals. I would not presume to answer for them."

"I am going to read something else. In speaking of the Devil, this writer says, '. . . so we know that this dark and disturbing spirit *really exists* and that he still acts with treacherous cunning; he is the secret enemy that sows errors in human history. He is the treacherous and cunning enchanter, who finds his way into us by way of the senses, the imagination. The question of the Devil and the influence he can exert on individual persons is a very important chapter of Catholic doctrine given little attention today.' That statement says the Devil *literally* exists. Would you agree with that, Father?"

"I would have to agree with it, Mr. Prosecutor."

"I see that you recognize the quotation. For the benefit of the Court, would you tell us who said it?"

"Pope Paul the Sixth. In a speech His Holiness made several years ago."

"In the eyes of the Roman Catholic Church, then, the Devil continues to be a reality? Not an abstraction, not a metaphor, not an image—" Suddenly, Rufus spoke in a new tone, his voice ringing with authority: "Reality. Both the Devil— and his followers."

"Yes."

"Therefore, it follows as the night does day that the defendant herself believes in the reality of the Devil, being a true member of the Catholic Church. To the best of your knowledge."

"The Catholic Church has millions upon millions of members. I cannot say that all of them agree upon everything."

"They must agree upon doctrine, Father, or stand in peril of excommunication. You teach these things. Have you any reason to believe that the accused does not accept them?"

"I don't know the accused."

"Very true." Rufus paused. After a moment, he took a piece of paper from his desk and held it up. "I am going to read you something, and then I am going to ask you a single question. Will you bear with me?" Father Timothy nodded his head.

Rufus said, "Dr. Margaret Murray, whose credentials I have already entered into the record, was recently and for many years a Professor of Egyptology at the University of London. It is

194

generally acknowledged that she is the world's leading authority on witchcraft. Her extraordinary career as a scholar is too well known to require any endorsement from me. Indeed, it would be presumptuous for me to attempt to embellish so remarkable a record. Dr. Murray, in the text I have already entered into the record, points out that she studied the names of thousands of witches over the centuries and that there was what she called 'a pattern too positive to be ignored. First, there are no Anglo-Saxon names among them, but Christian and pre-Christian names of Celtic and Latin origins predominate. Finally, in compiling a list of several hundred of witches' names, it can be said that all these names fall under eight headings with only dialectical and slight variations.' Now, I am going to read you Dr. Murray's list:

" 'Elizabeth
" 'Christine
" 'Margaret
" 'Alice
" 'Mary
" 'Ellen
" 'Joan
" 'Anne.' "

Rufus paused, looking around the courtroom. Then, with a sudden gesture, he snatched the last piece of evidence he had entered into the record from the Court Clerk and thrust it at Father Timothy, who took it, surprised. "Here, Father Timothy, is the baptismal certificate of the defendant, Mrs. Blake. She tells us that her first name is Emily and that her maiden name was Emily Jans. Will you read the name on the baptismal certificate for us, please?"

"Anne Emily Jans."

Sensation. Gavelling.

"Yes. Anne Emily Jans. Quite right. A name she has, for her own reasons, chosen to suppress. The night before last, was there a long-distance call to your monastery for Anne Blake? Not Emily Blake but Anne Blake?"

"I . . . I don't know."

"There was." Rufus produced documents, handed them to the Court Clerk. "Records from the telephone company in the county where Maria de Merced Monastery is situated. The call is recorded. People's Exhibit Number 158."

"So noted."

"The caller identified himself with the name of the most notorious satanist in all history: Gilles de Rais. The record shows it. And the caller asked for Mrs. Blake by her Christian name, a name not even her husband nor her best friend knew was hers. They were questioned briefly this morning. Not only were they puzzled, both of them vehemently denied that that was her name." Another few papers. "People's Exhibits Numbers 159 and 160."

"So noted."

"This much established, I want to ask you a question, Father Timothy. First, was the defendant a guest at your monastery's retreat for women this past weekend?"

"Yes. Yes, she was."

"Did she make the arrangements?"

"No. Her friend did."

"Did you have any conversation with her?"

"I had . . . a very brief conversation with her. Just before dinner."

"On what subject?"

"Oranges."

Tittering. Another call for order.

"Is that all?"

"Yes."

"What was her behavior like?" Then, when Father Timothy appeared to hesitate: "I remind you that you are under oath. We know very well what her behavior was like. We are asking you only for confirmation. Confirmation the law insists that you give."

"She became . . . well, she was overcome with laughter."

"Laughter?"

"Yes."

"Are you telling me that she became hysterical?"

"It is not up to me to interpret the lady's behavior."

"When did Mrs. Blake depart?"

Pause. Then: "Saturday night."

"At what time?"

196

"Late."

"How late?"

"At about midnight."

"Isn't that rather unusual?"

"Yes."

"Why did she choose to leave at midnight?"

"I don't know."

"What preceded her departure?"

"I can't answer that. It would be hearsay."

"Other witnesses will be able to furnish us details of that sudden departure. Now, Father Timothy, the following morning, something unusual was discovered on your premises, specifically in your public church. Will you tell us the nature of what was found?"

"Desecrations."

"Describe them, please."

A pause. Another look to the bench. Then, reluctantly: "The recumbent stone statue of the Virgin for whom our church is named had been defiled."

"How?"

"I must protest. Myself, I know of no connection between the visit of the lady to our church and what happened, and therefore—"

"It is up to us to establish connections, Father. Exactly how had the statue been defiled?"

"With a stone image of the Devil."

"From where?"

"It had been wrenched—we cannot imagine how, since it must weigh five hundred pounds—from the façade of the church itself."

"And where was this statue of the Devil?"

"It was so positioned as to give the impression that the Virgin was giving it the *osculum infame.*"

"Meaning?"

"In the Black Mass, it is customary for participants to place a kiss . . . on the Devil's posterior."

"And where was this stone Devil?"

"Seated. On the mouth of the Virgin."

197

"Hysterical laughter. A midnight departure. And desecrations. Have there ever been any other desecrations at your church, Father?"

"There have not."

"No further questions."

Emily had clasped her hands as if in prayer, leaning her elbows on the defense table. Her face was chalk-white, and she did not seem to be hearing anything that was going on. When Cade rose to cross-examine the witness, murmuring an apology as he tried to make his way behind Emily's chair, she did not hear him. He hesitated, then turned and went around the table in the other direction. He approached the witness stand slowly, thoughtfully.

"Father Timothy," he said. "My client here is on trial for murder. She is accused of having committed it by supernatural means. The district attorney himself is on record as having referred to her as a witch. Now, I'd like to ask you a question on that subject." A long, deep breath. When Cade was sure he had everyone's attention, he asked, "Father Timothy, does the Bible there mention witchcraft?"

"Yes, it does."

"How is it described?"

"It isn't."

"Oh?"

"The Bible just names the offense."

"Specify."

"Exodus 22:18. 'Thou shalt not suffer a witch to live.' "

"Does it define the offense?"

"Never."

"So, as far as you know, the Good Book could have been talking about playing marbles or jacks, isn't that so? I mean, the Bible also says that a man shall be put to death for cursing his mother and father, isn't that so?"

"Yes."

"So, it could have been some offense that meant a lot to them but wouldn't be a matter of life or death to us, isn't that true? We're talking about witchcraft now. The Bible could have meant something we would look on as harmless—like casting a horoscope—ain't that the truth? I remind you you're under oath."

198

"Yes. Yes, that's perfectly true."

"So my client is being accused of something even your own religion can't define. Father Timothy—"

Here, Cade was interrupted by a bailiff who touched him on the elbow and nodded toward Emily.

"Excuse me, Your Honor," Cade said. He went over to Emily, bent down, and looked into her face. She was sitting perfectly still, hands folded in her lap, expressionless. She stared straight ahead at nothing. Cade saw what had attracted the bailiff's attention. She sat there like a shell of herself, she was composed, she was breathing regularly but her eyes did not blink. Cade frowned, passed a hand in front of her face. No reaction. He spoke her name. She gave no sign that she had heard him. He took her hand, holding it gently, then pressing the palm hard down onto the table. It was like the hand of someone unconscious.

"Your Honor," he said, "I'm going to ask for a recess."

David drove her home, his face working, Marianne holding her. She seemed oblivious of her surroundings, of all of them.

26

When David started to turn left at the foot of the hill leading to their house, he saw that the street had been blocked with a barricade. A yellow light flashed from it. There were two police cars drawn up, blocking access. When David hesitated, his car now blocking the opposite lanes of the street, a policeman got out of a squad car and waved him away. David hit the horn. The policeman waved him away impatiently. David continued blowing the horn. Marianne looked at Emily. She did not seem to hear it. The policeman, wearing a helmet and boots, strode over to the car, stooped down and said to David:

"Can't you see the road's closed? Now, keep moving."

"Will you let me through, please? I live there."

"Can I see some I.D.?" Then the policeman caught sight of Emily, recognized her and said, "Never mind." He straightened up, beckoning to another officer, who came running toward them with a walkie-talkie. "I don't know whether you can get through now, Doctor," he said. Then, to the other officer, "Give me that thing." He took it and spoke into it, identifying himself. "Can you hold that tear gas?" he asked. "They want to come through."

"What the hell is going on, do you mind telling me?"

"Just a moment, sir." Then, into the walkie-talkie, "I know they weren't supposed to be back this early but they are. Now, can you hold the tear gas?" He crouched down near David's open window, facing straight ahead, not meeting their eyes. "See, they've got a SWAT squad up there, guys from the Humane Society—" David gave him a surprised look but at that moment, the walkie-talkie crackled into life, the policeman listened, nodded, said, "Okay, right now," and waved to the other to move the barricade, then pointing at David's car and gesturing, indicating they were to let him through. "Okay, sir," he said, "but when you get in the house, keep all windows closed."

"I want to know what's going on." But the officer had already started walking away. He did not appear to be listening. David drove slowly past the barricade and the men swung it back into position behind him.

The street was deserted. It was very quiet. Then, as they climbed the hill, they began to hear it, a relentless, inhuman moaning, like the voices of damned souls. It was everywhere. A moment later, the house came into view. The SWAT team was standing by, holding tear-gas guns. There were two ambulances from the Humane Society, the window spaces in the back covered with wire mesh. The members of the SWAT team were wearing gas masks, and so were the men standing next to the ambulances. In front of the house was what looked like an infestation of black cats. They were everywhere, scrambling up onto window sills, crawling up the banisters, all over the stairs and particularly on the threshold, where they were most thickly congregated— scrawny black, yellow-eyed alley cats, cauterwauling, fighting and scratching as if trying to force their way into the house. The stench was terrible. Their cries shattered the quiet of the neighborhood. A fire truck was drawn up ahead, and a fireman with a hose was trying to wash them away from the house. As soon as the stream of water moved, the cats returned to the same place.

"Oh, my God in heaven!" whispered Marianne. She put a hand over Emily's unseeing eyes.

David slammed on the brakes. A policeman hurried over to the car, waving him inside, his face anonymous under his gas mask, and David yelled, "What is this, some lousy, stinking practical joke?"

"Get in the house, sir. Immediately. All of you." His voice sounded hollow through the mask. He opened the door for David, who jumped out, ran around to help Marianne and Emily, and then turned and saw with horror and loathing that the cats were all coming toward them. Toward Emily.

"In the house! Now!" The policeman grabbed his arm, he hung on to Emily, Marianne supporting her on the other side, and while the firemen washed the plague of cats away from their path with a high-pressure nozzle, the three of them scrambled up the slippery stairs, soaking wet from the water, got into the house and banged shut the door, locking it.

Emily stood in the hall, her face showing nothing. David grabbed her and yelled out to Marianne, "Get on the phone and get hold of Clarence Burns—he's a doctor—you'll find his number in my address book there in the study—and tell him to get over here right now!" Then, lifting Emily in his arms, he carried her upstairs and into the bedroom.

In a little while, he came downstairs, looking white and pinched. Marianne said, making him a stiff drink and handing it to him, "He's on his way. How is she?"

"Pretty much the same. I gave her a shot. I didn't want to do it until he'd seen her but—well, Christ, I didn't know what to do."

"Is she sleeping?"

"No. But her eyes are normal again. Thank God."

Marianne squeezed his arm.

"What the hell's going on out there?"

"They said the tear gas will clear up in about fifteen minutes."

"Are they gone? I mean, those goddamn cats?"

"Yeah."

"I don't know why the hell they didn't take one of those lousy automatic weapons they keep parading around with and blow the little fuckers to kingdom come!"

"They just shot them with tear gas. Then they threw nets over them and hauled them away."

"Lousy practical joke."

"Yeah."

They didn't look at each other.

"You want a drink? Help yourself."

She shook her head, pulling on her coat. "I have to go out."

"She might ask for you."

"I have an errand to run."

"Well, Jesus, can't somebody else do it for you?"

"No. Look, I'll be back in an hour, okay?"

"See you."

Her car wasn't there. She borrowed David's. He stood at the hall window, watching her drive off. The wet front steps sparkled in the late afternoon sun. He went back upstairs to Emily, sitting beside her, holding her limp hand. It was half an hour before Dr. Burns arrived. David went downstairs to let him in, then took him into the library to talk.

He had sent Esmeralda up to sit with her, not wanting Emily to be alone. A little later, after David had told Burns what had happened since Emily had left the hospital, the two men went upstairs to the bedroom. Esmeralda rose, folding her soft plump hands and looking at David with sympathy.

Burns had declined a drink. Seeing Esmeralda, David said, "Would you like her to make you some tea?" Burns shook his head.

"Nothing, thanks, Esmeralda."

She nodded, padding away. Burns bent over Emily, pulled out a pocket flashlight, and lifting up her eyelids with his thumb, peered into her eyes. He pressed the eyelid over the eyeball. She did not react. He tried her reflexes. They were normal.

"How long has she been catatonic?"

"I guess for about an hour and a half."

"Mrs. Blake," he said. "Can you hear me? I'm Dr. Burns. Your husband sent for me. I'm a psychiatrist. I'd like to help you. You don't have to say anything, just squeeze my hand." No reaction. He put her hand back on the coverlet, patting it, and walked over to the windows. David followed him.

"What do you think?"

"How often is she seeing him now, every day?"

"I—I don't know."

"Well, it's oftener, isn't it?"

"Yes."

"Any other change in her behavior? Before this?"

"On the trip, Marianne said she was . . . well, childlike."

"Neurotic withdrawal." Burns nodded, as if agreeing with himself. He squinted, looking out the window at the still garden. David stole a glance at the disfigured eye, and in part of his mind, began speculating on the nature of the injuries to the epithelial layer and whether a skin graft would have any real chance of being successful. He decided it wouldn't. Burns said reflectively:

"Here's what we know. She's being tried for murder. She says she's innocent. But in such circumstances, part of her feels guilty for having wished that woman dead in the first place. The very fact that no one seems to know exactly how the murder was committed would very naturally contribute to her unconscious conviction that she did it. Being unable to accept such an idea, she tries to reject it by blaming someone else, an invented person. Does she have any brothers?"

"No. She was an only child."

"Are her parents living?"

"No, they died in an accident when she was quite young."

"And she was reared by whom?"

"Oh, a succession of people."

"You mean, in an institution?"

David was puzzled. Then: "You mean, in an orphanage? No, she's quite well-to-do. She was reared by servants, governesses, that sort of thing."

"What I meant was, is there someone who could tell us anything at all about her childhood?"

"I can't think of anyone. They're scattered all over the place. And when she was twelve, she was sent away to boarding school. I think there was an uncle guardian but he died."

"I'm looking for some counterpart of the boy—what does she call him? Lupe? Some youthful counterpart. Some Mexican child."

"She went to school in the East. There aren't a lot of Mexicans living there. Then, Switzerland."

"Hm. Well, I think the immediate thing is to reach her. See, the problem is, she's involved in a bizarre trial, and as I get the picture—now, correct me if I'm wrong—everything she's doing is *helping* them. When you tell me, for instance, that she saw him in a mirror . . ." Dr. Burns shifted his weight uncomfortably, folding his arms. "Well . . . let's just say, from a practical point of view, that I think she'd be better off just insisting on her innocence and not . . . well, agreeing with them, so to speak, that it was a supernatural crime and at the same time trying to offer them an alternate suspect."

"And the things that are going on?"

"Well, I would like her as much as possible to ignore them."

Ignore. Ignore the fact that a five-hundred-pound stone devil with a bare ass somehow ended up sitting on the stone face of a statue of the Virgin lying on a slab in the church? David wondered if Dr. Burns could read his expression. He asked, "How do you account for them?"

"Well, some of them seem to be nothing more than practical jokes. The practical jokes of a very sick mind. You see, cases like this tend to excite disturbed personalities, just the way pyromaniacs are their most dangerous at the time of a forest fire. In a case like this, one would *expect* all sorts of disturbed behavior to surface. A thing gets in the air and, well, it's extraordinary how many people are willing to believe it. The important thing is for your wife to understand that so she can cope with it."

"But *some* of the things . . ." David trailed off but he kept his eyes fixed on Dr. Burns.

"You mean, the seemingly inexplicable?" David nodded. Burns said, "Do you know about the Piper case?" David shook his head. Burns went on, "It was really quite famous. A case of somnambulistic possession here in this country in the last century. William James was convinced that the woman had supernormal faculties. She was under constant investigation by detectives for several years. There was never any evidence of fraud. Yet, she seemed to be able to tell people things she had no way of knowing—I don't mean things she could have gotten by reading their minds—it seems to me a degree of telepathy in some persons is too well documented to be argued with at this stage of the game—*but things that hadn't happened yet, which later occurred.*"

"I see."

"But the point is, there have been thousands of mediums, so-called. Houdini exposed every one he ever met. Why is she the only one—oh, I shouldn't say the only one, names like Eusapia Palladino come to mind—but one of the few whose gift seems authentic?"

"I don't know."

"Well, neither do I. But I don't think it's a useful avenue to pursue. Do you see what I mean? Example: if someone comes to a doctor with a runny nose, general malaise, perhaps a slight temperature, some sneezing and coughing, well, the doctor, if he's got any common sense, is going to presume that the man has a *cold*. Not a supernatural cold, not some arcane disease, just a common cold. In the majority of the cases, the doctor tells the patient to go home to bed with some aspirin and a hot-water bottle, the whole thing is treated as a cold, it runs its course and that's the end of that. What I'm saying is that your wife is exhibiting all the familiar symptoms of conversion neurosis, and I don't really see any reason not to treat it that way."

David looked down at his shoes, frowning. Dr. Burns excused himself and went back over to Emily, sitting down again next to the bed and taking her hand.

"Mrs. Blake, can you hear me? This is Dr. Burns speaking. I'm here to help you. You'd like me to help you, wouldn't you? If you can't speak, just try squeezing my hand."

Slowly, Emily's hand clasped his. David saw this and locked his fingers together, watching them both.

Dr. Burns said, "The first thing I'm going to do is draw the blinds. I think we'd both like it if it weren't so bright in here." Dr. Burns put down her hand, got up and started toward the windows. David was ahead of him, already drawing the blinds. Dr. Burns said to him in a low voice, "I'm going to try hypnotizing her."

"I thought you said that wasn't possible. In cases like this."

"Most of the time. Maybe the odds will be with us."

Dr. Burns crossed back to the bed, sat down again, and once more took Emily's hand. "Here I am again. That's better, isn't it?" He nodded to David, who extinguished the lights, all except for a dim night light. "Mrs. Blake," he said, "you're suffering a great deal of pain, aren't you?" A pause. Then, another squeeze. "I know you are. And I think I can help you. Will you let me help you, Mrs. Blake?" Nothing. Again: "Will you let me help you, Mrs. Blake?" Another squeeze. Burns said softly, "In order to help you, I'd like to put you under hypnosis. Will you let me do that?" No answer. He waited patiently, still holding her hand gently in his. "It'll be very easy. It's a pleasant sensation, just like drifting off to sleep, hearing the rain falling on the windows. But

I can't do it unless you want me to. Do you want me to do it?"
She squeezed his hand, this time visibly. Dr. Burns said, "That's
good. Then, let's just think about the rain, shall we? Just keep
listening to the rain pattering on the windows. It's a soft rain. A
spring rain. Oh, it's a very gentle rain, and you know something?
It's putting you to sleep. You hear that soft rain falling, and all
you want to do is go to sleep. Just go to sleep. Listen to the gentle
sound of the rain. Such a soft sound. So soothing. It's putting you
to sleep, isn't it? Just let the sound of the rain put you to sleep."
    Her breathing had grown deep and regular, and her eyes were
closed. David could see the subtle change of expression as the
muscles of her face slowly relaxed. Her thick blond hair framed
her face and now the skin was once again rosy. Dr. Burns said:
    "Open your eyes, Mrs. Blake."
    Emily opened her eyes. The lids fluttered for a moment. The
eyes were luminous again. The vacant stare was gone.
    Dr. Burns said, "Look at me, Mrs. Blake."
    Emily turned slowly to look at him.
    "I'm Dr. Burns. I'm here to help you. You're going to let me
help you now, aren't you, Mrs. Blake?"
    She nodded slowly.
    "We're going to talk about what's troubling you so that we can
make things better for you. You've had a very bad time. People
have said very cruel things about you. They say you killed someone. Did you kill someone, Mrs. Blake?"
    Her eyes widened in fear.
    "Don't be afraid. Remember, I'm here to help you get better.
Did you kill someone, Mrs. Blake? You can speak now."
    "No," she said.
    "Good. Very good. No need to be troubled. Deep sleep. Deep
sleep, Mrs. Blake. Your first name is Emily, isn't it? May I call
you Emily?"
    "Yes."
    "Now, I want you to tell me about Miss Ludlow. How did Miss
Ludlow die?"
    "She burned to death."
    "Do you know how that happened, Emily?"
    "No. No, I don't."

207

"Of course you don't, since you didn't kill her. We both know that. Now, I want you to talk to me about Lupe. Who is Lupe?" She gave him a frightened look, trying to raise herself up. He put his other hand on her shoulder, easing her down onto the bed again, saying, "There isn't anything to be alarmed about. I just want you to keep listening to the sound of my voice and to answer my questions. Who is Lupe?"

"A boy."

"A boy you knew a long time ago?"

"No, I met him with Marianne."

"Yes, of course. I thought perhaps he reminded you of someone. Does he seem to remind you of someone, Emily?"

"No."

Dr. Burns frowned, pursing his lips. He studied her. "Where does Lupe live?"

"He's dead."

"How do you know he's dead?"

The eyes rolled. She became greatly agitated. He soothed her, stroking her hand, reassuring her, then repeated the question.

"I saw him."

"I see." He paused, studying her. "But then, when you think you see him now—say, in a mirror—"

She became terribly upset, sitting up, clutching at his arm, then holding up a hand as if to shield her eyes, which were now reddening.

"Let's turn that light off," Dr. Burns said quietly to David. "She may have suffered a little retinal hyperaesthesia. I'd have an eye man check her out, if I were you."

David turned off the night light. The room was now quite dark. Dr. Burns took hold of Emily by the shoulders and said, "I want you to be very calm. You are now feeling calm. You are going to lie down again." Her muscles relaxed, and he lay her back on her pillows. "Now, just listen to the sound of my voice, telling you to be calm. Lupe is dead. He can't do you any harm. As a matter of fact, he never did anyone any harm, did he?"

"He killed Jennie!"

"He couldn't have done that because at the time she was killed, he was already dead. Lupe is dead, Emily. He didn't kill Jennie

208

and you didn't kill Jennie, do you understand?"

David listened intently for some response. He bent forward, listening for some change in her breathing. At the same time, he became aware of a faint odor: garlic.

"What's that smell?" he said.

"A little garlic. Something she's been eating."

Downstairs, the front door opened and closed. Neither of them heard it.

"Emily," continued Dr. Burns in a soothing voice, "when you wake up, you will have no recollection of any of this. The only thing you will remember is that you did not kill Jennie and you have no idea who did."

Laughter. Then a soft voice said something disgusting. In Spanish.

"What did she say?" asked Burns.

"What the Christ is going on? That isn't Emily's voice!"

"Never mind that. What did she say?"

"I don't *know!* And I'm telling you that that voice—!"

"Buenos días, Doctor!" said the voice out of the darkness, a child's voice. "Your wife here, she's one hell of a fuck! Hey, turn on the lights and let's see his face! I bet he looks like he just shit in his pants!" Smothered laughter. Faint. Mocking. And the voice accented. A Spanish accent.

"That isn't Emily!" said David.

"That's it. The alter ego. Classic case." In an authoritative voice, Burns said, "I want to talk to Lupe now. Are you Lupe?"

Snickering. A coarse answer in Spanish. Then: "Hey, doc, what happened to your eye, huh? That motherfucker with a bow and arrow. Lousy fucking toy to give a kid."

David heard Burns's quick, surprised intake of breath. "Is it true?" he asked Burns. *"Is it true?"*

"She's reading my mind. You notice how she had to bring up the subject first so I'd think about it."

At that moment, the door to the bedroom opened. Marianne stood there. A shaft of light from the hall illuminated the figure on the bed. David let out a cry of horror. Marianne gasped. Her hands flew to her mouth. The face was Lupe's, stamped somehow into Emily's flesh. The same face David had seen in the coffin.

209

The head on the pillows lolled, turned toward him. The eyes met his. The blue eyes darkened, as if from some extraordinary excitement, so that the blue iris now seemed almost black. The face began to change more, not just the expression but what underlay it, the whole play of musculature and the repertory of glances, so that she seemed to be an altogether different person. The complexion became yellowish. The face grinned. An indentation began to appear below the nose. It formed itself into a line, pulling up the mouth and giving it the trace of a sneer. Forming a harelip. Now it was Lupe's face. Completely. It looked at David. Winked.

Marianne screamed.

At that moment, the figure on the bed went completely limp, and the face of Lupe simply dissolved away. Into Emily's. The breathing was shallow, irregular, alternating with periods during which she appeared to stop breathing altogether, then sucked air in deeply. *Cheyne-Stokes,* thought David. *Jesus, he's got to bring her out of it.*

"Emily," said Dr. Burns. "It's time to wake up now. When I finish counting to three, you will be awake. I'm going to start counting, now. One, two, three . . ."

She opened her eyes and looked around slowly at all of them. Marianne hugged her. Dr. Burns patted Emily's hand.

"Feeling better now?"

"Yes. Yes, thank you."

"This is Dr. Burns, honey," said David.

She nodded, then asked, "What's wrong? What happened?"

"You just had a little spell. It's over now."

"I see."

"You're feeling better now, aren't you?"

"I guess so."

"I'm going to give you something to make you sleep. Then I'll arrange to see you tomorrow, all right?"

"All right."

Dr. Burns went downstairs with David, who sent Esmeralda back up to sit with Emily.

"Better give her a rest now," David had said to Marianne.

"Yeah, okay."

Alone with Burns, David said, his face ashen, *"What in God's name happened?"* Burns shook his head. David yelled, "You saw it! We both saw it! That's the face of that boy! That boy she keeps talking about! Now, explain that one—Doctor!"

Burns frowned, looking at the floor. Then he said gently, "There are well-authenticated cases—in your own field—where subjects have been able to make marks appear on the skin. Stigmata. In some cases, actual writing. Would you call that supernatural?"

"No. No, I wouldn't."

"Why not? I mean, if nobody knows how it's done—"

"Well . . . the skin develops embryonically from nervous tissue. It's extremely susceptible to suggestion. Are you trying to say this is the same thing?"

"I'm simply suggesting the possibility."

They did not discuss it any further.

27

An hour later, Marianne came down the hall from the room where she had left her suitcase, and tapped on Emily's door.

"Yes?"

She went in. Emily was still in bed. She was sitting up in a bathrobe, a steaming pot of tea at her elbow.

"I thought Esmeralda was sitting with you."

"I'm all right now. I sent her downstairs to fix dinner."

"Where's David?"

"He went to the office for a couple of hours."

"You okay? You sure?"

"Positive."

"Okay."

Marianne went to the closet, walked in and came out dragging a madras dress and a pair of sandals. She threw them on the bed.

"Here. Get dressed."

"Where are we going?" Emily got into the dress, slipping on the sandals.

"Down the hall. I just don't want to see you schlepping around in a bathrobe. I look bad enough." She looked down at her bunchy skirt and found a fresh stain. "Oh, balls!" She scraped ineffectually at it with broken nails. "It's bad enough to drag around twelve pounds of tits. But why in hell did God have to make me a slob?"

She started out the door. Emily followed her, curious. Marianne marched down the hall to the guest room and they went in. A banged-up leather suitcase with torn stickers lay on the bed.

"You staying over?"

"Tonight."

"What about Roberta?"

"She's at a friend's. She's bringing her to the convent tomorrow at eight. I'm picking her up then. That is to say, you are."

"One more time."

"I have had it. I have fucking-A-well had it. Who was that horse's ass David showed up with?"

"Dr. Burns. David told me about him."

"A shrink."

"Marianne, he's not a horse's ass."

"I can tell a horse's ass at twenty paces."

"For Christ's sake, he's the dean of psychiatry at the university!"

"I don't care. I want you to listen to me." Marianne took her hands, pulled her toward the bed and they sat down together. "I saw what just happened in there!"

"What happened?"

Marianne brushed a hand over her unkempt hair, looking away, trying to think.

"Well, tell me!"

"It doesn't matter." Marianne got to her feet and walked up and down in front of her restlessly. "I don't know what the hell is going on. And I don't know what that asshole of a district attorney is up to, but what I know is *you can't take any more!*"

Emily began to tremble uncontrollably. She hugged herself, trying to stop. She said in an unsteady voice, "Marianne, I didn't do it! I told them I didn't! Why don't they believe me?"

"That's why you're going away."

Emily looked at her quickly, shocked.

Marianne said, "I mean it. They've got the ACLU working on this, lawyers' organizations, Christ knows what else. That D.A. is going to end up on the funny farm. But I don't want you to end up there with him. You get the picture?"

Emily tried to whisper a prayer to herself but her heart was dry. There was no God. If there were, how could He allow such things to happen? Abruptly, she remembered that someone had once described the earth as a "prison-planet." Was that the answer? Why was Marianne looking at her that way?

Emily asked carefully, "You think I'm that bad off?"

"I'd be."

Their eyes met.

Emily said, "All right, what do I do?"

Marianne opened the suitcase and dragged out more stained clothes, then a ratty brown wig. One passport with a picture of Marianne and Roberta. Airline tickets.

"My car is outside. When it gets dark, I want you to put on this crap, go downstairs, get in my car and drive to my house. In the morning, pick up Roberta at eight o'clock. She'll be on the playground."

"Does she know about this?"

"No. See, she was at her girl friend's and I asked them over the phone if she could spend the night there. I didn't have any chance to talk to her. Tell her yourself. She's smart. She'll understand."

"You want me to run away."

"I've made all the arrangements. Remember that trip I wanted to make to Peru? Here are the tickets. Her things and mine are packed in this suitcase."

"Peru?"

"Yeah. Nice innocent place."

"But the passport—"

"Bullshit. The picture is a picture of Roberta and me. A lousy picture. They'll never know the difference. What the Christ do they care? Good old Peru. Who the hell would want to go to Peru?"

"But Marianne! They'll start looking for me!"

"Listen, stupid! I thought about that! I booked you on Pan Am, via *Rio*. You change planes there. You get off the plane, understand? Only, you aren't ever going to get back on the other one. Just stay there and wait."

"I can't! I can't go live in Rio the rest of my life! And David? Oh, God, you're marvelous to have thought of all this, I can't ever tell you how grateful I am, really, Marianne, but to ask David to spend the whole rest of his life in Peru—"

"Rio!"

"Rio! It might as well be Kamchatka or Reykjavik! How in hell could he practice?"

"Not the rest of his life! Not the rest of yours! Just long enough for them to catch up with this guy. Honey, they're going to take him away to the laughing academy, don't you understand that? It's only a question of time. But it's time you don't have. *You can't take any more,* don't you see that, baby?"

"I'll be all right. Honest."

"Even when they take you into protective custody? Because that's what I hear they're going to do."

Something snapped. Emily began sobbing into her hands. Marianne rushed to her side, flinging an arm around her and holding her.

"Okay?"

"Okay."

Emily went downstairs, wondering whether David had returned yet. Marianne followed her, impatient."Why did he have to go to the office today, anyway?"

Emily said, "He still has a practice."

"After all this?"

"More than ever."

"How do you figure it?"

They had something to. eat. When it was dark, Marianne said: "Okay. Now."

"But David's not back."

"Well, I'll tell him when he gets here."

Slowly, almost dazed, Emily put on the greasy skirt, the stained blouse. She put the passport and the tickets in her purse, then put on the wig. And Marianne's pancake make-up. A big hat. A scarf. And a coat.

She left unrecognized, driving away in Marianne's car.

David returned late, exhausted. He went upstairs and saw Marianne wandering down the hall in a dirty wrapper.

"Where's Emily?"

"Asleep."

He opened the door to the bedroom, saw that it was empty.

"She's in with me. I didn't want her to be alone so I put her in the other bed. You don't want me to wake her up now, do you?"

"No. No, of course not."

"Good night, David."
"Good night, Marianne."

At exactly eight o'clock in the morning, Emily drove up to the convent schoolgrounds in Marianne's old Volvo. In the distance, she could see Roberta in her beige jumper and flowered shirt running from another car toward a group of children. Emily got out and waved. Roberta waved back, then began running toward her. Emily backed toward the Volvo, holding open the passenger door of the front seat.

Roberta had grabbed a volleyball and was running with it, half a dozen other little girls running after her. Emily started to get back into the car. She would drive away as soon as Roberta got in. Then Roberta stopped running. Stood still, staring in her direction. She thought, *She knows I'm not her mother.* If Roberta came closer, she could explain.

Roberta hung back, staring at her. Now the other children were watching her also. She waited. Silence. Eyes fixed on her. There was nothing she could do but depend on the sound of her voice, which she was sure Roberta would recognize.

"Roberta!" she called.

Roberta didn't move.

"Roberta, honey!" she called again, taking a step toward her. Roberta backed away. Emily thought, I have to let her see who I am. She cursed the wig, cursed Marianne's clothes. She should have put them all on in the car, after explaining things to Roberta.

Impasse. The child wouldn't come toward her. In the distance, she could see a nun, football in hand, standing stock still watching them. It was her move. She knew it. She walked slowly over toward Roberta.

"Hi, honey," she said.

Roberta didn't answer but shrank away.

"Isn't this a funny get-up! Your mother and I decided to change clothes as a game!" *Christ, the other kids had heard that! But what the hell was she supposed to say?*

216

"Roberta, honey—" she began, walking toward her. Now Roberta was standing perfectly still. Well, it was all right. She would simply take the child by the hand and lead her away. She came closer.

"Witch," said Roberta.

Emily stopped moving. She looked at the child, her own godchild, incredulous.

"Witch," hissed Roberta. "Witch, witch, witch!" She began making convulsive movements, chanting the name over and over in an ecstasy of rage. The other children joined in, Roberta their leader, all of them repeating the terrible name again and again, till the air was filled with a litany of hate. A nun began to run toward them.

Emily said, "Roberta! Roberta, stop it! Stop it!"

Their eyes met. Then Roberta let out a strangled cry, staggered backward as if some invisible force had been hurled against her, and was flung to the ground. Her muscles went rigid. Emily, in a panic, ran toward her. At the same time, Roberta began to thrash about wildly, flopping her arms back and forth like the arms of a doll. Her teeth were locked. Foam appeared at the corners of her mouth. Her eyes rolled and she emitted terrible, protracted screams of agony. One of her arms snapped back at a grotesque angle, as if it somehow weren't part of her. It was clearly broken. Now it began to look as if the same thing had happened to her clavicle. She was moaning, sobbing and crying through clenched bloodied teeth, gasping for breath, twitching and flailing uncontrollably, and the nun threw herself on top of her, pinning her to the ground to keep her from injuring herself further, calling out at the same time to another nun, who ran up and fluttered to the ground next to her like a fallen bird:

"Call an ambulance! For God's sake, Sister, call an ambulance!"

Emily tried to come closer, to help, to comfort, but the sight of her seemed to agitate Roberta even further, so that the nun was obliged to call out:

"Please get away! Please, please get away!"

And at the same time, Emily heard a sound. Everywhere. A

murmuring. Increasing in volume. And the sound she heard was the sound of anger. Words ran through the air, like rags fluttering in the wind. The same words. *It's her! It's her!* She was kneeling on the hard ground near the stricken child. She looked up. A semicircle of strangers had formed around her. Flinty-eyed. Murmuring. The air thick with the hum of fury. Then, far off, coming rapidly closer, the sound of sirens.

28

She kept thinking, I have to go to her, but when she tried again, Roberta worsened dramatically, flinging herself back and forth, despite the efforts of the two nuns holding her down, a froth of blood at her mouth, and strangled sounds coming from her throat between clenched teeth, while she banged her head violently, again and again, on the hard gravel of the path. One of the nuns turned around, still struggling with Roberta, and cried out to Emily, "Please, *please* don't come any closer!"

She felt herself impaled by a ring of glances, glances that were quickly averted as soon as she looked around. She thought, desperate, I must call Marianne. There was a pay phone at the edge of the playground. She began rummaging in her bag for a coin.

Just then, a policeman came up and touched her on the elbow. Startled, she let out a little cry, dropping the bag. It lay at her feet, open. She could see the edge of the passport case and the airline tickets stuffed into one side. The policeman stooped to pick it up. Another policeman, heavy-set with a thick neck and a red face, came striding up to talk to him, and the first officer took a step toward him, Emily's bag still in his hands. She thought of the suitcase in the trunk, filled with clothes for herself and Roberta. *They'll know I'm running away.* That meant they would put her in jail for the rest of the trial. At the thought of it, the unspeakable recollection of those padded walls, the hours of begging, yelling, screaming for help when no one came, cold fear gripped her. The policemen were still talking in an undertone. She looked at them helplessly, her face slack.

The red-faced one said, raising his voice, "Them clothes don't fit and she's wearing a wig. Now, you tell me why."

219

The second policeman glanced around, then jerking his head at the crowd, said, "Well, can you blame her?"

They looked at each other for a beat longer. Then they reacted to the sound of an approaching ambulance siren. The second policeman stepped out into the street to direct traffic. The first policeman said, "I'm sorry but I think you'd better come with us, Mrs. Blake."

"Where?" Her voice was a croak.

"Home. If you go out unescorted, we can't handle the crowds." He handed her purse back to her. She walked unsteadily to the car, Marianne's car, then followed a squad car back to her own house.

David was waiting for her. He grabbed her by the arms when she came in, slamming the door behind her.

"Are you crazy?"

He knew. She must have told him. Well, she had to.

"Where's Marianne?"

"They came for her and took her to the hospital. Was Roberta in some kind of an accident?"

"No." She walked slowly through the hall into the kitchen, pulling off the hat and wig, got out of the coat and asked Esmeralda to make her some strong coffee, then sat down at the breakfast-room table, her head in her hands. David sat down next to her, gently massaging the back of her neck, giving her a tender kiss on the ear. She made him call the hospital repeatedly. There was no word yet. Bewildered, he asked what had happened to Roberta. She told him briefly, almost listlessly, then turned, searching his face for some reaction. He grimaced.

"Kids!"

"I'm telling you, she broke her arm!"

"Hysteria. Typical." Then: "They don't know? I mean, what you were planning to do?"

"No. I don't think so." Then she said with alarm, "But the suitcase! It's still in the car!"

"Marianne's suitcase. Marianne's car. Where's the rest of the stuff?" She took the passport and the airline tickets out of her purse and handed them to him. He grabbed them, almost yanking

220

them away from her, went over toward the kitchen and put them on the passthrough.

"Shouldn't we put them away?"

"Why? They're hers. She left them here. We're not trying to hide anything."

True. She wasn't thinking. Esmeralda carried over a cup of steaming coffee, and she began to sip it greedily.

"I don't know what was in your mind."

"Well, Marianne said—"

"I know what she said. What's she trying to do, get you locked up? You're just handing them their case on a silver platter. How do you think it would look if you ran away?"

She tried to remember Marianne's explanation. It had all seemed so reasonable. "You see, Marianne feels once they get rid of that district attorney—"

"Honey, he's accused you of murder. He's got a case. All he has to do now is show how you did it. And according to Cade, that's the one thing he'll never do." He clasped his hands. Tight. The way he always did when he was trying to suppress real annoyance. "I don't get it. It's an awfully stupid move for a smart lady. And Marianne is a very smart lady."

"Whereas I—"

"Oh, come on. With the strain you're under, you could do anything." He grinned at her, then grabbing her by the scruff of the neck and giving her a playful shake. Then his face clouded in thought. He rubbed a forefinger over his upper lip. She stretched out a hand, touching it herself, feeling the thick bristles under the skin.

"You know what that little indentation is for?"

"What?"

"Come on, you're a skin doctor. You're supposed to know."

"I don't know. Tell me."

"Well, before a baby is born, it knows all sort of secrets about where it came from. But those secrets aren't supposed to be told in this life. So, at the last minute, your guardian angel places a finger there—just like that—and says, Sh!"

He nuzzled her. She rubbed her head against his, feeling a wave

221

of comfort, security. She sipped her coffee. Over the lip of her cup, she saw that his face was once again shadowed, perplexed.

"What is it?"

"Nothing."

"No, come on. Tell me."

He paused, reflecting, and then said too casually, "How come Marianne always seems to be around when these things happen?"

She looked at him with open-mouthed surprise. Then her face hardened. "What are you trying to say?"

"I should have kept my mouth shut."

"She wasn't around this morning!"

"But she's the one who set the whole thing in motion."

"What the hell are you talking about?"

"I'm sorry, I'm sorry! I guess we're both strung out."

"She's around because she's with me all the time! She's literally the only friend who's stuck by me. And this is the thanks she gets."

"Okay, okay!"

Something was wrong with his smile. She looked away, drumming her fingers on the table. He glanced at his watch. They would have to leave for court in about an hour. Something tugged at the back of her mind. She tried to remember what it was, then gave it up. She sipped at her coffee. His dark eyes rested on her. She put down her cup and asked, "David, what happens if I lose?"

"Oh, don't even talk about it!"

"I think we should." She tried to keep her voice steady.

"It's crazy."

"Crazy things have happened."

"Well, I'm sure it would be reversed on appeal."

"That means I'd have to go through this all over again." She took an uneven breath. "I can't stand any more."

Neither of them said anything for what seemed a long time. Then David said, looking away, "Remember, there's always another way out."

Yes. That's what was at the back of her mind. The reason he had called in Burns. "You mean, Not guilty by reason of insanity. That is what you mean, isn't it?"

"I just meant there's always a way out."

"Is that what your doctor friend suggested?"

"I don't think we should talk about it any more."

"Is that what he suggested?"

David got up and paced the floor, hands plunged deep in his pockets. "I brought it up."

"Oh."

"Well, honey, you don't know what was going on upstairs in that room!"

"Tell me."

"I said, I don't think we should talk about it any more!"

"What did he say when you brought it up?" He didn't answer. "David, I asked you a question!"

"He said he'd be willing to support such a plea." He wiped his mouth nervously with a fresh-ironed handkerchief. "It's just that I was looking for a way out, and with testimony from a man of his stature—"

"—that would convince them."

"Yes. I guess it would."

"And Cade's reaction?"

"Well, Cade said—" He saw too late that he had stepped into a trap. She was eyeing him. "All right, I asked him! He's your attorney and I had to have his opinion. I told him everything!"

So Cade knew. Finally. And believed—what? "What did he say?"

"That such a plea would just terminate the proceedings."

"And what would happen to me?"

He folded his lips, shrugged, hands still in his pockets.

"I'd be locked up, wouldn't I?"

"Not necessarily."

"But it is possible, isn't it, David?"

"Well—maybe for a little while. You'd be . . . you know, hospitalized. Maybe for a few months. Less time than an appeal would take. Honey, it's an avenue we just had to explore. It's only a question of sparing you."

"I suppose they'd even let me go to a private sanitarium."

"I think so."

223

"An expensive one. Which, fortunately, I can afford." Her voice was light, casual. He did not see what she was driving at. He said, shrugging:

"Well, some of those places are like deluxe hotels. But I don't know why we're even bothering to discuss—"

"After what I've been through, I could probably use the rest. But you'd miss me, wouldn't you?" A change in tone made him react with surprise. She went on: "Unless, of course, you met another Jennie. In which case, you might want to keep me locked up indefinitely." She gave him a cold smile. "I mean, there is a lot of money involved, let's face it."

He drew himself up, looking at her as if from a distance neither of them could ever hope to cross. "Excuse me," he said. He walked out of the room. She heard him close the door of the library behind him.

She sat where she was, feeling battered by too many emotions. "I mustn't think about it," she said to herself. "I mustn't think about anything at all." She went over to the kitchen television, turned it on, switching to a soap opera, and then sat down and watched it for fifteen minutes, absorbing nothing. Then the program was interrupted by a news bulletin. The screen showed a throng of reporters with microphones, lights, and cameras hurrying down a hospital corridor after a doctor in a white jacket with *Dr. Mill* written on a plastic card pinned to the pocket. The reporters surrounded him, trapping him, all of them trying to question him at once. He was a short man with a youngish face and wisps of prematurely gray hair, and he blinked repeatedly in the glare of the lights. Voices called out, What is Roberta's true condition, Doctor? Why are they putting her arm in a cast? Is there a drug problem, Doctor? Can we talk to her mother? Doctor, would you turn this way, please? Nervously, he shielded his eyes from the lights, then held up a hand for silence. Now there was a close shot of him, half a dozen microphones in front of his face. Emily got to her feet, watching the set intently. David strode in, already in the midst of a peace-making speech. She motioned him to be quiet. He broke off, going over to watch the small set with her.

"The family—uh, that is, Mrs. Milner—has authorized me to

224

make the following statement . . ." He cleared his throat nervously. "The child, Roberta, is here under observation. Tests thus far completed show the child to be physically normal in every respect. Mrs. Milner would like me to take this opportunity to thank all those who have called, inquiring about her welfare."

"Is it true that she has a number of broken bones, Doctor?" a voice asked. The doctor answered that the preliminary X-rays indicated fractures and breaks, and detailed some of them quickly in medical terms. The voice of a well-known reporter interrupted impatiently, asking:

"Doctor, what about the so-called 'crying out'? Isn't that the denunciation of a witch?"

"I have no further comment." He tried to move away. Another reporter moved in on him, cornering him.

"Doctor, we understand that the child was heard by many people here in the hospital saying that Mrs. Blake was tormenting her. Do you have any comment on that?"

"I have no comment to make at all."

"Doctor, does Roberta think Mrs. Blake is a witch?"

The doctor fought his way through the crowd, stepping into an office with a glazed door and banging it shut behind him.

A reporter turned to face the network's camera and said, "And that, ladies and gentlemen, is the news about the so-called 'spellbound child' at the U.C. Hospital this morning." Another voice announced that they were now rejoining the program in progress, and David turned off the set.

Emily had walked away, her arms folded across her breast, the tip of a shoe tracing the grouting of the quarry tile. She licked her lips. She looked at him out of the tail of her eye.

"I'm sorry. Can you ever forgive me?" she burst out.

"Who gives a shit?" He moved toward her. "Isn't that why people like us get married? So there's somebody you can say anything to—and nothing changes?" He rubbed his palms awkwardly on his jacket. "I mean, that's just one reason but—"

Then her arms were around his neck and she was hugging him to her with all her strength. "Hold me." He put both arms around her, his face in her neck, murmuring reassurance. She said, "I'm afraid."

225

"No, no, no, no."

"David, I don't know how to fight any more."

"He hasn't won a goddamned thing."

"But he has. In most people's eyes." She tried to make herself push it all away. She pulled up his cuff, looking at his watch. "I'd better change." She started out of the room, then stopped. She was afraid to be alone. "Keep me company," she said. He went with her. They heard the phone ringing, the familiar brief ring before the exchange intercepted the call. When they got upstairs, it jangled again, repeatedly. They had let somebody ring through.

David answered it, then held it out to Emily, saying, "Marianne."

She cradled the phone on her neck, undressing at the same time. They were late. "Oh, God. How is she?"

"They're running some more tests." Marianne's voice sounded empty, as if all the emotion had run out of it.

"I know you want me to tell you what happened, but I don't know," said Emily, her throat suddenly dry, constricted. "I just went there the way we'd planned—"

"—and I so appreciate your offering to pick her up," Marianne said rapidly, interrupting her. "I suppose I was stupid, asking you to go dressed as me, but I just didn't want all those God-awful people closing in on you, do you understand what I'm saying?"

"Yes. I understand."

A pause. A long pause. Had the line gone dead?

"Marianne?"

"They're going to ask you something. I just want you to know it wasn't my idea." There was a click. Emily looked at the receiver, then handed it back to David, who replaced it as she finished getting out of Marianne's clothes. She took a three-minute shower, brushed her hair, put on some cologne, and then went to her closet to get out the suit she had taken to wearing to court. It was comfortable and anonymous, a full dark skirt with a matching top with bell sleeves and a cowl. She had worn it so often, cartoonists had done sketches of her in it. She didn't care. It had begun to give her an absurd sense of security. The suit wasn't there. She called Esmeralda, who sponged it and pressed

226

it for her every day, and asked for it. Esmeralda was puzzled. Yes, she had cleaned it for the *señora*. Yes, she had brought it back upstairs and hung it in the closet, as always. Esmeralda looked in the closet herself. She was at a loss. No, she didn't know where it was. She offered to look for it. There wasn't time. Impatiently, Emily chose an Oxford gray dress with a wide, loose turtleneck, pulling it over her head as if it would somehow protect her from the arrow-like glances that came from all sides, as if its dark cloth could somehow shield her.

She went back into the bathroom and put on lipstick, a pale shade, pressing her lips together. She could see David's reflection in the mirror behind her. She said, meeting his eyes in the mirror:

"What happened on Friday? When that doctor was here."

"We'll talk about it later, okay?"

"No, now. Exactly what happened up here?"

"You were out of it and I called in Burns."

"And?"

"Well, he tried to hypnotize you."

"Why?"

David did not want to say. She forced him to tell her, and he explained Burns's theory reluctantly.

"I see. Then what happened?"

"He . . . made a suggestion to you that you were not guilty."

"I never thought I was."

"Well—"

"And that's all that happened?"

"Yes."

She knew he wasn't telling her the whole truth, but quite suddenly she felt unequal to more. She gave him a quick, bright smile. "Would you excuse me for a moment?"

He left her alone, closing the door. She turned on the water to disguise the sound of what she was going to do. Then, opening drawers and cabinets, she searched until she found what she was looking for: a bottle of Seconal. In another drawer, she found a box of coffee-blacks she had saved for some reason, each one wrapped in a twist of silver paper. She opened all of them, throwing the candies down the toilet and wrapping up the Seconal pills. Then she put the whole little pile of wrapped pills back in the box, put it in her purse, and put the bottle containing the remainder into the front of her pantyhose, at her crotch. The matrons didn't search you there. She knew. Flushing the toilet, she turned off the water and came out of the bathroom, giving David a shiny smile. He helped her into her coat.

"I'm all ready," she said.

They left for the courthouse.

29

When they got outside the door, there was a mob gathered in the street, larger than before, ominously quiet, so that they hadn't realized anyone was there. Emily stood perfectly still, her gloved fingers laced together to keep them from trembling. She had always been afraid of crowds. The size of this one made her feel light-headed. She looked down as from a scaffold at the faceless throng, held back by a police cordon. David took her arm. Then she heard it, low at first, almost like the slithering of a snake, then growing in volume until it was everywhere, inescapable, as if it were a sound made by the very air itself: an unspeakable hissing. They started down the stairs. A policeman ran up to help them, taking David's arm.

At the street, he led them toward a car, a limousine.

"We always go in my car," David said.

"You're to take this one, today," the young officer said. Emily hung back, seeing something that made her want to run.

"I think my wife would rather take my car."

"Sorry, sir. Orders. Just a precaution." He stepped toward the limousine, reaching for the door handle. Emily thought, I can't. I can't. It was the windows that had frightened her. They were black.

"Come on," David said. He helped her into the depths of the back seat. Then the door swung closed like the door of a cell. There was a click, and she knew the driver had locked it from the front seat. The car started, began to move forward slowly. She looked out, surprised that from inside she could see everything.

There were people on all sides, staring unseeing in her direction, unafraid because they could not see her eyes. Now, as the

229

limousine moved slowly through the dense crowd, she saw their unaverted faces, all of them staring sightlessly in her direction, the eyes wide with fear or narrowed with suspicion and hatred. In that sea of faces, she read her verdict. Hell-hounded, desperate, she saw now exactly what he was doing, the dead child in whom no one believed, the demon child. She tried to pray. Her mind remained a blank. A fragment of a line echoed in her memory:

> *"But wherefore could I not pronounce 'Amen'?*
> *I had most need of blessing and 'Amen'*
> *Stuck in my throat."*

She reached into her purse and touched the box of coffee-blacks, as if it were an amulet. Then she closed her eyes, gave herself up to the oiled motion of the black limousine, thought of nothing. An escort of motorcycle policemen led the limousine down Bush Street. Cars pulled aside to let it pass. Headlights on, the long black car moved soundlessly down the boulevard. Like a hearse.

Now they were in court again. She sat at the defense table, forearms resting on it, trying not to listen, oblivious of the newspaper artist sketching her with quick, covert strokes. She heard voices rising and falling, motions, countermotions, a meaningless dialogue of legal terms punctuated by a sound of mallet on wood that began to seem as if it were pounding on her skull. She looked around, counting chairs, tables, railings. Every stick of furniture was a bar in her cage. Then Judge Manly said in a new tone of voice, pointed with anger, so that she looked up now and began to listen, her attention captured:

"Out of the question!"

"Your Honor, hear me," said Rufus. "This is analgous to a sex offense. In such cases, we accept as testimony the finger of a minor pointed at the accused in answer to a question."

What on earth were they talking about? Suddenly, Emily sat up, apprehensive, her head on one side, listening intently. She concentrated her attention on the argument, hearing Cade's answer:

230

"That, sir, is a repugnant comparison!"

Manly said to Rufus, "What the prosecution is asking has no precedent."

"It had, sir," replied Rufus unemotionally, "in the courts of Oyer and Terminer."

"In the Salem witchcraft trials?!" Cade was beside himself.

"The test of touch," Rufus said quietly.

Manly replied, "Sir, are you asking this Court to admit spectral evidence? Even the Salem judges questioned *that!*"

Rufus said in a deferential tone, his hands making a supplicating gesture, "May I remind the Court that spectral evidence consists of remarks like 'Your shape came to my room last night,' et cetera. People will certainly ask for nothing of the sort, since no conceivable alibi can be furnished for such a charge."

"That, I believe, is the first thing we've agreed on!" Cade was angry and contemptuous and took no trouble to conceal it. Rufus said mildly:

"But here, Your Honor, we have a simple test."

"I know what the test is," Manly said irritably.

"I beg the Court's indulgence!" Rufus said, growing suddenly emotional. "I am obliged to prove a supernatural crime! Is it so unreasonable that I be afforded at least this small demonstration of her powers?"

Manly reflected, the hooded eyes half-closed in the skeletal face, tips of the long fingers touching, as if in prayer. Then he put his hands flat on the desk and leaned back, looking around at all of them. He had evidently made up his mind about something. He turned, addressing the jury:

"As you have heard, prosecution has introduced into evidence affidavits stating that when the defendant went this morning to pick up the child of a friend, the child reacted with fear, called defendant a witch, and then suffered some kind of seizure, during which she injured herself grievously. Child is now suffering from an unremitting hysterical episode. Sedatives have been administered, with no effect. Best medical opinion suggests that further dosage would be dangerous." He consulted his notes. His mouth tightened into a straight line. He paused, then continued:

"Pulse rate at present is a hundred and seventy. Pulse is weak."

There was a murmur of alarm. He rapped his knuckles on the desk like a schoolmaster. The courtroom grew quiet. Emily was overcome by a sudden giddiness. She gripped the edge of the defense table, thinking, Is that what they were saying all this time? Why didn't I listen? My God, why didn't I listen? She thought of Marianne with a wave of longing, a terrible, irresistible sympathy. Judge Manly said in a flat voice:

"Prognosis is grave. We are given to understand that if this condition persists, death will supervene."

Commotion. Emily felt spangles of cold perspiration on her face. How could she tell them that she hadn't done it?

"Prosecution is asking for 'the test of touch.' Now, I'm going to explain that. The theory was that if the so-called witch touched the afflicted, her devil would inevitably be drawn back to her, and that that touch alone would break the spell. Prosecution is asking for me to adjourn this Court to U.C. hospital for the purposes of making such a test, on the extraordinary grounds that it may serve to save a child's life. But I must point out that, should such an incredible event occur, prosecution would then seek to use it as evidence against the accused." His face hardened. "Denied." Down came the gavel.

There was an uproar. Manly gavelled for order, and when several people scrambled into the aisles, creating a disturbance, bailiffs promptly evicted them from the courtroom. It was quiet again. Very quiet. Rufus was on his feet, asking:

"Will the Court accept a motion for adjournment to the hospital for the purposes of hearing the child's unsupported accusation?"

"That, I must allow. So ordered." The gavel. A hollow, wooden sound that she felt would punctuate her days for the rest of her life.

Manly was getting to his feet. Everyone rose. Cade took her arm. She heard the blurred litany of the bailiffs, then was led outside.

The black car again. This time, with Cade. Crowds. Always crowds. They had just gotten the news. It traveled by whispers, so that the air shook with sibilance, a hissing like the steam from a thousand cauldrons. She covered her eyes, let Cade lead her like a child to the car. She would think of nothing. She would not let herself hear or think. She clapped her hands over her ears, shutting her eyes, rode hunched forward, longed for oblivion.

Motion. Stopping. Crouching, making her way out of the black car, eyes closed, a hand on Cade's arm. Walking. Steps. The pneumatic sound of doors opening. A rubbery floor. The slight jar of elevator doors closing. Being lifted up, up. How strange the world was when one couldn't see it. When one didn't look but let oneself be led. A kind of escape. *Oh, God, let me escape!*

Then she almost tripped over something as they got out of the elevator. She opened her eyes. A corridor. Why was it so familiar? Oh, yes. She had seen it on television. Behind her, footsteps. Many footsteps. She turned quickly. Oh, yes. The jury. Court stenographers. Bailiffs. Then Manly and Rufus.

They all crowded into a brightly lit room. Not a private room. A ward? No, of course not. An operating room. It was the only place large enough to accommodate them. Then she heard it— a sound that tore her apart, strangled, inhuman crying, like an animal's. A respirator. Suspended bottles for intravenous feeding. Then the wall of backs opened and there before her, strapped to the table, immobilized in traction, thin arms heavy with casts, lay Roberta, a chalk-faced Marianne hovering over her. Marianne wept. A small, lost sound. Her mascara had run, and there were clownish black lines and smudges on her square face. Her hands were clasped helplessly. Roberta's eyes were rolled up in her head, showing only the whites. Then they moved, searching the room, while she continued to groan and scream through teeth clenched over a padded splint that had been forced into her mouth to keep her from swallowing her tongue. A nurse mopped bloody mucous from her cracked lips. The eyes began to move rapidly, back and forth, back and forth. Then they found Emily's. A piercing scream filled the room. Rufus said, greatly agitated:

"Your Honor, I *beg* you—!"

Manly deliberately turned his back on Rufus, walking to the far side of the room, the bailiffs herding the jury after him. He said to the jury in a low voice:

233

"I remind you that we came to this hospital only for the purpose of hearing an accusation."

"I say that scream was accusation enough!"

His tone was improper and Manly let him know it with a look. Without his flowing robes, Manly looked thin and pinched in his black suit.

He said quietly, "The jury is free to decide whether the child's scream had the character of an accusation."

More screaming. Marianne's voice, sobbing. A doctor was heard, in a sudden lull, saying, "Pulse a hundred ninety."

"Emily, *please!*" Marianne cried out desperately. Cade seized Emily's arm, saying:

"The defendant will not be called as a witness in this trial in any capacity!"

Now they heard the huffing sound of a respirator, the urgent murmur of the voices of doctors. Dr. Mill looked up, glancing in Manly's direction, saying, "I'll have to ask that the room be cleared now."

Bailiffs herded them toward the door. Marianne rushed up, crying out hysterically, "She's dying! Don't you understand?"

"Your Honor, I beg you in the name of God—!" Rufus said loudly. "Mrs. Blake can save the child's life!"

"I have not forbidden the defendant to act!" Manly, under the strain, had lost his temper.

"Defendant is not a witness!" shouted Cade.

Manly turned on him and said in a rapid angry voice, "In any criminal case, whether the defendant testifies or not, his or her failure to explain or to deny by his testimony any evidence or facts in the case against him may be commented on by the Court and considered by the jury! The choice is hers!"

Emily looked around wildly, her mouth gaping open. Then she felt Marianne's hands, pulling at her arm. Marianne, to whom she never said no. Manly was too quick for her.

"Stop her!" he ordered.

Bailiffs intercepted them, wrenching Emily away from Marianne. Manly asked, staring at Emily:

"Do you want to participate in such a test?"

Emily said yes, moving her mouth but no sound came out.

234

"Very well," he said. "Cover the child's eyes." A thick rolled towel was taken out of a sterilizer and laid over Roberta's eyes. A doctor held it in place. Roberta's agonized cries pierced their ears continually. Manly pointed at a nurse. A bailiff led her to Roberta's side, taking her hand and placing it on the child. The screaming continued. This was repeated a second time with Mildred Theale, the matron, who approached the child with extreme reluctance. Touch. Pause. More screaming. Then a doctor's voice. The anaesthesiologist.

"She's fibrillating. Patient is expiring. Get these people the hell out of here!"

Wild-eyed, Marianne pulled at Emily with an imploring look. Together, they went toward the blindfolded figure of the dying girl. Marianne took Emily's hand, holding her arm by the wrist, and placed it on Roberta's forehead. Silence. Absolute silence. Roberta had stopped screaming.

"She's converted," the anaesthesiologist said. "Pulse rate regular. A hundred ninety . . . No, a hundred eighty. Slowing." Nobody moved. "A hundred fifty," he said. "Marked slowing. Way down now. Down to a hundred. Normalizing."

The white-coated figures crowded around the table. Emily backed away. A step at a time. "Normal," said the voice. The nurse removed the towel from Roberta's eyes. Roberta looked around.

"Mommy?" she said.

Marianne ran toward her, embraced her, sobbing. There was a murmur of awe. At a sign from the doctor, Manly nodded and the bailiffs escorted the group out of the room.

Emily stayed where she was, backed up against an instrument table, her face bloodless, her eyes fixed, incredulous. With her left arm, she massaged her right, then looked down at her hand. She looked to the side, thinking carefully. He was everywhere now. In some part of herself, she had known it would happen. Marianne understood. Marianne knew.

She looked up, a desperate smile on her face, and caught Marianne's eyes. For a second. Then Marianne averted her glance, and she felt her world ending.

Cade returned, taking her arm. She let herself be led away.

235

30

On the way home, the limousine driver turned on the radio, unaware that the speakers were on in the back. They heard news bulletins about Roberta's miraculous recovery and announcements of an upcoming interview with a faith healer. David pressed the intercom button and asked the driver to change the station. He tried several stations. Variants of the same bulletin were being repeated on all of them.

"It's the news hour," said the driver. "Twelve o'clock."

"Turn the radio off, please," said David.

"Yes, sir."

It clicked to silence. They drove home, not talking, looking straight ahead. She thought, Nothing matters. What curious, bizarre lives they all led, playing to an empty house, gesturing. She saw workmen repairing a cobbled street, lifting the stones out of the ground, one by one, exposing the yellowish clay underneath, and she thought what a thin veneer on the earth a city is.

"I think you should eat something."

She shook her head. "I'm not hungry." Opening the thick, plate-glass door in the dining room, she walked slowly into the garden, gray under leaden skies, following the gravel path toward the pergola built against the high wall at the very back, counting her steps, weighing immutable alternatives: conviction, an asylum, suicide.

She sat down heavily on a stone bench. Next to it was a huge boulder in the top of which had been carved a little basin many years before. Once, they had kept tiny, tiny goldfish in it. Not any longer. Now, nothing. There was water in it, a little bit from last night's rain. She stared into it, trying to read her future. She heard the crunch of footsteps on the gravel. David. He came up and sat down beside her, taking her hands.

"I love you."

"Poor David."

"We're going to come out of this, Emily."

"Are we?"

"You've got to believe it."

"We'll never get out of it. He won't let us."

"He?"

"Lupe!"

"Don't!"

She turned, looking at him full, almost with surprise.

"Yes, Lupe. Don't you understand what he wants? *Don't you see it yet?"*

"Emmy, *please—"*

He wouldn't let her talk about it. Ever. Well, what did it matter? Again, she heard the importuning voice somewhere in her head, incoherent, scratching. Always the same question. And some mute, inaccessible part of her said no.

They sat in complete silence. For a long time. Emily finally said:

"We used to talk. Remember?"

Yes, she thought. Once they had both talked a great deal. Their world hung motionless in the blue air while they talked and talked, and the universe, opening itself like some incomprehensible flower, had blossomed forth upon emptiness and eternity's desert. Stars exploded and the liquid crystals of protein molecules strung themselves into creatures, played for time, while an ineluctable tongue of spirit, flamelike, licked at the events on which it lived.

Yes. Once they had talked. Now it was different. Perhaps because words tipped the scales. Shaped what one felt. She was sick of talk.

She looked around the enclosed garden, up at the tops of the trees nodding in a slight wind, at a Monarch butterfly pollinating a jasmine blossom. She thought for no reason of Haldane's remark, that the eye was the right size. The rods and cones have

237

the diameter of a light wave. Smaller, the eye would be inefficient. Larger, useless. Yes, how perfectly every part of the universe was fitted together. One was irresistibly drawn to seeing it as design.

But if that were so, then why this agony? Why must she suffer torment? No, there was no design. The Infinite was not only purposeless but blind.

David looked at his wife, thinking, My God, I can't help her. I have to pretend to be able to. But I can't. Not now. He squeezed her hand, squinting up at the sky. "It's going to rain."

"I don't care."

The first drops fell. She watched them plashing in the little basin. Then looked again. The drops were red. They looked like tiny bundles of filaments, loosely held together in a globe, a sort of gelatinous growth, like algae.

"It isn't rain," she said, looking up into the leafy arbor stretched across the pergola over their heads. Something must be falling from the trees. Then, more drops. Red drops. She noticed an odor in the air, a familiar smell. Now David was squinting into the basin, a look of surprise on his face.

"Well, I'll be damned," he said.

She sniffed the air. "David? It smells like blood!"

"Yeah."

"Well, what is it?"

"Nostocacaea."

"What?"

"Nostocacaea. Think of 'lost acacia.' It rhymes with that. Hm. I've read about it but I've never seen it before." He dipped a hand into the basin, caught one of the gelatinous drops in his palm, and sniffed at it with scientific curiosity.

"Well, what is it?"

"Oh, nothing. Some kind of fresh-water algae."

There was a rumble of thunder, then the rain started coming down, filling the stone basin quickly with clear water, washing away the slimy little strands and filaments.

"Come on," he said, grabbing her hand, "we'd better run for it."

They ran through the garden back into the house. Esmeralda had left lunch on the table. She looked at them hopefully, making a little gesture with her plump hands. David sat down to eat.

"Come on, honey."

"I can't." The sight of food made her ill. Letting him eat, she wandered out of the room. The phone rang. The exchange picked up, then let it ring through. David answered it. It was a pharmacy asking about renewing a prescription. David screwed up his face, trying to remember the patient, meanwhile eating a salad. Then it came back to him.

"All right," he said with his mouth full. "Fine." He gave them his registration number, and handed the phone back to Esmeralda to hang up. Finishing his luncheon, he drank the glass of fruit juice at his place, then blotted his lips and went in the other room, searching for Emily.

More thunder. Some sheet lightning. Then a real downpour. He thought of the mob keeping vigil outside the house. Would this drive them away? Would anything? Ever? He found Emily in the library on a stool, pulling down the Index volume of the *Britannica*. She turned toward him.

"What did you say the name of that stuff was?"

"Forget it."

"Tell me the name of it, please." There was something familiar about it, something she couldn't place.

"I don't remember."

"It's a name like 'acacia,' she said. " 'Lost acacia,' you said." Then it came to her: "Nostacacaea." Quickly, she leafed through the Index volume, found a reference and took down another book from the set of the encyclopedia, opening it. She found the reference. "Here it is." She started reading: " '. . . so named by Paracelsus—' Paracelsus? Greece?"

He reached for the book. "Switzerland. Sixteenth-century physician. Come on, be with me. I don't want to look things up now."

"Just a minute." She found her place, continued reading. " 'Nostoc, so named by Paracelsus for the genus Nostocacaea—a kind of bundle of filaments loosely held together in a globe, a sort of gelatinous growth, smelling of blood, which has been observed to fall repeatedly throughout history, occasionally in great quantities, in many parts of the world . . .' Well, there. That's exactly what it is. Strange." She was about to close the

239

volume when her eye caught sight of the final sentence. She looked at it, not reading it aloud. "It is sometimes called 'witches' blood.' "

She put the book back on the shelf. At that instant, there was a splintering crash. Then another. David ran into the hall. Climbing down from her stool, she ran after him. A rock came crashing through the fanlight over the door. David dragged her out of the way.

Now the house rang with repeated blows. They ran to a side window. David looked out. In the pouring rain, he could see a mob in the street, hurling rocks, debris, bottles, everything they could lay hands on, stoning the house. A policeman fired a warning shot into the air, dispersing the crowd, while another radioed for reinforcements.

Emily tried to get to the window herself. David wouldn't let her look. He held her in his arms. They heard the shattering of an upstairs window. Emily covered her ears, shaking with dread as he held her. Sirens. Coming closer.

There was a pounding at the door. A voice called out, Police. Open up. David got their coats. By the time they were led out of the house, a line of police with night sticks were holding the crowd back.

A television news camera was aimed at her by a man running alongside them.

A newscaster yelled at him, "Go wide!"

"Back off! I'm holding her in a tight close-up!"

"I said, go wide! Get this whole scene!"

"It's a fantastic close-up!"

"Close-ups are like pussy! Great when you can't get it all the time! Now, go wide, you bastard! Get me that crowd!"

The limousine again. They started away quickly, this time with a siren. But not quickly enough. A rock crashed through the side window, showering them both with pebbled glass. Emily began unwrapping a coffee-black and putting it in her mouth. Then another.

*   *   *

Now there were armed guards outside the courtroom, wearing slickers, standing in the downpour, crowds still milling in the street despite the rain.

"Oyez, oyez, pray rise for His Honor, Judge Amos Manly," intoned a bailiff. The afternoon session of court began. Emily's head had begun to shake with a palsied kind of motion. She leaned her elbow on the table and rested her chin on her fist, trying to steady herself. She thought, I cannot bear any more. I simply cannot bear any more. They are torturing me. Yes, it was torture. She thought of strappado, the hideous punishment inflicted on witches. When they fainted in agony, the torture was stopped, delayed, until the victim was revived. *That is what they will do to me if I faint. I mustn't faint.* The rain was driving now, tattering needle-like on the windowpanes. She tried to lose herself in the sound of the rain. Another coffee-black. Why not all of them?

Emily said she was sick. She got up, clutching her purse. There was a five-minute recess while she went to the bathroom. The matron accompanied her, taking her to a facility next to a holding cell, where there were no doors on the cabinets. She tried to be alone. The matron suspected something.

"I'll hold your purse."

"No!"

The matron searched it, found the box of coffee-blacks and unwrapped one. She recognized it.

"Very clever."

The matron confiscated the Seconal, searched her, found the bottle and took that, and then escorted her back into the courtroom.

The rain was torrential now. Never-ending. A tropical storm, the end of a hurricane in the Pacific, now spending itself over San Francisco.

Rufus said, opening a small, vellum-covered book, "Murder was done by the casting of a death-spell. In cases of murder by witchcraft, we are obliged to demonstrate two things: that the accused is a witch—and the means by which she committed murder." He walked toward the jury box and then turned, so that he was facing

241

in Emily's direction. She tried not to look at him, at the same time feeling the weight of his gaze.

"I have here a list of ancient questions," he said. "People are well aware that defendant is not to be called as a witness. But I will ask these questions anyway, in the hope that the accused will answer them in her heart."

He opened the book, glanced down at it and then read each of the questions in an unemotional voice, pausing only when the sound of the storm made it impossible to be heard:

" 'How long have you been a witch?

" 'Why did you become a witch?

" 'In what manner did you become one?

" 'What is the name of your incubus?

" 'How did you make a pact with him and on what conditions?

" 'What music was played?

" 'What did your incubus do for you in exchange for coition?

" 'What mark has he put upon your body?

" 'What harm have you done to your victim and how did you do it?

" 'Why did you do this harm?

" 'What storms have you raised and with whose help?

" 'What children have you enchanted and why have you done it?

" 'What limits has the Devil placed on your evil doings?' "

Rufus closed the book, walked over to the prosecution's table and laid the book down on it carefully. Emily looked at him without flinching. She would not look away. Now she heard a pounding at the doors of the courtroom but she did not look away. She was determined to keep her eyes on him.

"The accused knows the answer to every question I have asked! What is her answer? Silence! She refuses to allow herself to be questioned!"

A bailiff had opened a door, admitting a police lieutenant. He was making his way along a side aisle toward the bench. Outside they could now hear voices, shouting over the storm.

Rufus had been unaware of the hurried, whispered conversation behind him, between the police lieutenant and Judge Manly. A rap of the gavel attracted his attention.

242

Manly said, "Will both counsels approach the bench?"

Cade got up slowly, lumbered over, and stood beside Rufus. Manly said to them in a low voice:

"We've got a riot out there. I'm going to have to call a recess."

At that moment, there was a splintering sound at the back of the courtroom. A yelling mob was trying to break down the doors. From outside, they could hear the rat-tat-tat of automatic weapons. Women in the courtroom began screaming hysterically. A walkie-talkie carried by a guard crackled into life.

A voice said, "We are firing warning shots."

Now there was the sound of running feet and more yelling outside in the corridor. The voice on the walkie-talkie said, "They are retreating, repeat, they are retreating. Am to relay request that courtroom be cleared. Do you read me?"

Manly gavelled a recess and ordered the guards into action.

Rufus began gathering together all the evidence on the prosecution's table and heaping it into the boxes out of which he had taken it. Members of his staff helped him, working swiftly, efficiently. The yelling outside was louder than ever.

There was a stampede. The guards were prepared. They had their weapons ready. The spectators were kept under control at gunpoint. They were allowed to leave the courtroom two by two. Then the doors were bolted. Manly declared a recess, at the same time ordering Emily taken into protective custody.

She fled to David's arms, cringing away from the matron who came toward her.

"I beg you not to let them take me!" she cried out, clinging to him.

"Get away from her!" David said, backing toward the door, dragging her with him. "I swear to God, I'll kill the first one who comes near her!"

Men from the sheriff's office ran toward them, grabbing them, attempting to pull them apart. He hung on to her, struggling to protect her, while a matron pried her clutched fingers loose from his coat. David flung himself on a deputy, fighting to get hold of his gun. It took three men to pin him down and handcuff him.

243

Manly said, "Take him home."

A sheriff protested.

Manly said, "I told you to take him home. Now, I mean it."

They led David away.

31

Emily was locked in a cell by herself on the sixth floor of the city jail. It was a floor on which there were only holding cells for the criminally insane. It was deserted. She was left alone.

Drums. First, muffled. Slow. A dead march. Then, slowly, inexorably, the tempo increased.

The cell had a small barred window looking down on the intersection of Sixth and Bryant. The rain had stopped. Far below, she saw gangs of teenagers dragging things into the middle of the street. The drumming accelerated. Faintly, she could hear the boys calling to each other, then came the sound of jeering from upturned faces, looking toward her.

More drumming. Faster. Faster.

Now she saw what they were doing. They had erected a huge stake and were piling wood, sticks, twigs, everything, around the bottom of it. An old cart with wooden wheels came around the corner and was dragged down the middle of the street by a dozen boys. Lashed to the front of it was the figure of a woman. Upright. Tottering. She recognized it instantly. It was dressed in black, a full skirt, with a long-sleeved black top. And a cowl. Her clothes. Stolen.

Drumming. Racing now. Intolerable.

The stiff figure of the woman was dragged from the wagon by ropes tied to its wrists and around its neck. Boys clambered up onto the pyre, dragging it after them. They lashed it to the stake, then looked up in her direction, pointing at the figure and yelling.

The drumming was now a tattoo, a blur of sound.

Two other boys were pouring something from cans all over the wood. Gasoline. The first boys jumped down from the pyre.

245

Someone threw a match on it, and the whole thing exploded in flames.

She watched herself burned in effigy. Cheering.

Silence.

Her head throbbed. She clung to the cold bars of the window, watching the flames. Footsteps. Slow. She did not turn around. A grating of metal. The lock clicked open. An oiled rumbling as the heavy barred door was slid back, then slammed shut. She turned around and saw him standing there, waiting.

Lupe. With the sightless, staring eyes of the dead. His dirty child's hands stretched out blindly, reaching for her. She began to scream. It was unspeakable, loathsome. She had to get away. Seizing the bars of the window, she began banging her head against them violently, trying to knock herself unconscious. It was no use. Something in her fought for life. Breath. Sanity.

A matron heard the screaming and began running down the long corridor toward the single occupied cell. When she got there, Emily had lost consciousness. She lay on the floor of the locked cell. Alone.

The matron said afterward that she was sure she heard Emily's hysterical voice shouting, as if she were talking to someone. The only words the matron could remember hearing were, Yes! Yes, anything! *Anything!*

Cade sat at the big rolltop desk in his room, documents spread out under the pool of light cast by the green-shaded lamp. It was ten o'clock that night. Within a matter of days, the prosecution would rest, and it would be up to Cade to begin presenting the case for the defense.

He had worked out his strategy. He would accuse Rufus of having done nothing but excite popular superstition, meanwhile offering only circumstantial evidence. Rufus would answer— Cade could hear him, could even imagine the cadence of his phrases, "I remind learned counsel that all evidence, save only direct eyewitness testimony, is circumstantial. Does learned counsel mean to suggest we may only try for murder those caught in the act?"

Cade had his answer ready. He would begin in an offhand way, amiably, walking up and down in front of the jury box, leaning on the rail and talking to the jurors one at a time, as if to friends. Of course, he would end up ridiculing the prosecution's whole case—hell, if he had his way, he'd have the whole courtroom in an uproar of laughter. That was the way to handle Rufus. With ridicule.

Demons.

The word returned to him again and again.

Demons.

He wasn't just fighting Rufus. He was fighting superstition. And it was growing.

Open before him was the Bible. Once again, he read the curious statement in Genesis vi, 2: "Now when men began to multiply over all the world and had daughters born to them, the

247

angels noticed that the daughters of men were beautiful, and they married any one of them that they chose . . . Giants arose on earth, as well as afterwards whenever angels had intercourse with the daughters of men and had children born to them."

A strange statement. What did it mean? He looked at an explanation, supposedly written by Clement I and paraphrased in an old Catholic encyclopedia by a writer who doubted both the source and the interpretation. But the argument itself remained strangely compelling:

"According to his account, the angels were not overpowered with the passion of sensual love while they were yet in their purely spiritual state; but when they looked down and witnessed the wickedness and ingratitude of men whose sins were defiling the fair creation of God, they asked of their Creator that they might be endowed with bodies like unto men, so that, coming down to earth, they might set things right and lead a righteous life in the visible creation. Their wish was granted, they were clothed in bodies and came down to dwell on earth. But now they found that with their raiment of mortal flesh, they had acquired also the weakness and passions which had wrought such havoc in men; and they too, like the sons of men, became enamored of the beauty of women and, forgetting the noble purpose of their descent to earth, gave themselves up to the gratification of their lust, and so rushed headlong to their ruin. The offspring of their union with the daughters of men were the giants—the mighty men of superhuman build and superhuman powers, as became the sons of incarnate angels, yet at the same time mortal, like their mortal mothers. *And when these giants perished in the Flood their disembodied souls wandered through the world as the race of demons.*"

He shook his big head, wanting to dismiss the whole idea. Ordinarily, he would have said, The man's a damn fool. But the man was Pope Clement. And the letter was said to have been written to St. James, *the Lord's brother.*

Demons. Everywhere. By Talmudic computation, seven million, four hundred and five thousand, nine hundred and twenty-six.

"Certain learned men have declared that magic did not exist

at all except in the belief of men, who imputed to witchcraft the natural effects whose causes are obscure. But this is contrary to the authority of the saints, who say that demons have power over the bodies and imagination of men, when they are so permitted by God."

And that was St. Thomas Aquinas.

He couldn't accept it.

He rubbed his eyes, trying to push the thought away. It returned anyway, waiting somewhere in the shadows of the room. He did not care, he would not think about it. He had devoted his life to reason and to law. He would not allow a shadow of doubt on that point. He was too old to change. His weapon was humor. When he got to his feet to present the defense, he would make a laughingstock out of Rufus. He, Cade, would ridicule the whole case out of court. Rufus had no arguments Cade couldn't counter. Except one. And that, he was sure, Rufus couldn't present.

Then he heard the doorbell. Late. Not expecting anyone. A knock. And Sam Willinger came in. Looking, if anything, more unkempt than ever.

"Want a drink, Sam?"

"Better pour one for yourself."

What was Ring Lardner's remark? "He was a man of few words, most of them ill-chosen." That was Sam. Cade picked up a ship's decanter and splashed whisky into a couple of glasses. Sam emptied his, still wearing his hat.

"What's going on?"

"That Rufus. Got a real surprise coming up."

"That so?"

"Yeah."

"Let's have it."

"Tomorrow, he's going to show how that woman was murdered."

After Sam Willinger left, Cade sat at his desk, a look of incredulity on his face. That was the one piece of evidence he couldn't counter. For the very simple reason that it was *impossible*. It had to be.

He tried to think. He felt suddenly very old. And now, something in him was afraid of the shadows.

249

33

The next morning, the streets around the courthouse had been cleared, and armed guards were stationed in front of the building, riot guns in their hands, their faces expressionless. The sky was dark but the rain had stopped. The streets were strangely quiet.

Emily was led into the courtroom by a side door. David was waiting for her. He took her in his arms, kissing her and stroking her hair, as he led her toward the defense table. Then he saw the bruises on her forehead. He touched them gently, looking at her for some explanation.

"It's nothing," she said.

"But what happened?"

"Nothing happened."

She gave him a brief, flickering smile, and for a moment seemed more like her old self. Cade had gotten to his feet. He took her gently by the hands, seating her beside him at the defense table. David moved back to a seat in the courtroom. Cade kept hold of Emily's hands.

"You all right, honey?"

"I'm all right, Cade." Was it her imagination or did the gnarled old hands seem to have a slight tremor? Then a bailiff announced Manly, the air was filled with the familiar rustling as everyone rose, Manly seated himself, more rustling, coughing here and there, and then silence, as the staff of the district attorney began conferring with bailiffs in whispers. Fonner approached the bench and conferred briefly with Judge Manly, Manly nodded, Fonner gestured, and two associates of the district attorney began carrying in a sheeted piece of furniture. They set it down in the small square in front of the jury box, then removed the sheet. It was an armchair, slightly scorched. Emily recognized it. She sat very still, locking her fingers together to keep from trembling. Her knuckles whitened.

Fonner was called to the stand by an assistant to the district attorney and asked to identify the armchair.

"It's the one in which we found the body of the deceased." A ripple of interest went through the courtroom. Necks craned. There was a pause, during which one could hear the familiar murmuring as the chair was entered into evidence, the equally familiar response of the Court Clerk:

"So noted."

Cade looked around. Rufus had not yet entered the courtroom. His chair was conspicuously empty. Manly sensed a theatrical gesture, resented it.

"Where is the district attorney?" he asked an assistant.

"On his way here, Your Honor."

"He's late."

"In order not to take up the Court's time unnecessarily, may we continue introducing certain articles into evidence?"

"Proceed."

The assistant district attorney nodded at the bailiff stationed at the side door, it was opened again, and two men entered, carrying a sheeted figure. It was placed in the chair.

After the men had left the courtroom, Benjamin Leopold, the assistant district attorney, went over to the figure in the armchair and pulled off the sheet.

It was Jennie.

Emily screamed. A short, involuntary scream of terror. David felt all the blood leaving his face. Weakness overcame him. He gripped the arms of his chair, trying to control himself.

Not Jennie. A wax figure as lifelike as something in a Hollywood museum. But to David and Emily, who had known Jennie, the figure was agonizingly real. David could imagine a scent in the air. Silvery. Like incense.

There was a stir in the courtroom. Manly banged his gavel, his

251

jaw set. This was exactly the sort of thing he had been afraid Rufus would do in court. Yes, and the delayed entry. The suspense.

"Cover the figure!" Manly ordered. Hastily, a sheet was thrown over it again. Manly wasn't satisfied. Calling over the assistant district attorney, Manly pointed at the prosecution's table and demanded to know why preparations for the day's session in court were incomplete. Boxes of evidence had not even been carried in yet.

"I am afraid that the People are not ready," Manly said in a tight voice, his neck reddening with anger. "Where is the district attorney?"

"On his way, Your Honor."

"Did you telephone to make sure?"

"Yes, Your Honor."

Manly did not like being kept waiting. He ordered a fifteen-minute adjournment. At the end of that time, he sent for the assistant district attorney, Benjamin Leopold.

"When you talked to him on the phone, did he say he was leaving?"

"Your Honor, I didn't talk to him."

"Well, who did?"

"No one answered the phone, Your Honor, so I assumed—"

"Bailiff," Manly interrupted, "get me a marshal."

The adjournment was continued for another fifteen minutes while a marshal was sent to the house of the district attorney.

The adjournment was extended several times. After two hours, it was noon, and it seemed fairly clear that court would have to be adjourned for the luncheon recess. David and Emily sat with Cade in the small room set aside for the defense. Cade was restless. He went back into the courtroom several times to find out what he could, but the clerks told him nothing. David had gone out several times and brought back coffee, but Emily herself had touched nothing. She seemed to have drawn into herself. At times, her eyes remained closed, almost as if she were sleeping.

Then a bailiff entered and David got up, expecting that they were adjourning for lunch.

"Where would you like to eat?" he asked Emily.

252

"We're not adjourning yet," the bailiff said.

They went back into the courtroom and sat down again. Manly entered. A bailiff announced him again. There was still no sign of Rufus. Manly sat down, called the court to order and then, having done that, seemed to hesitate as if changing his mind. He got to his feet.

"I'd like counsel for the defense to join me in chambers. If you please. This Court will stand adjourned for half an hour."

Someone called his attention to the time. He drew his mouth into a straight line and said, "We are not adjourning for luncheon at present." A bang of the gavel. He made his way down from the dais toward a green baize door, Cade lumbering after him.

Cade entered Manly's chambers. Silence. Heads turned. He saw Manly, Leopold, the assistant district attorney, Viterbo, and Fonner, all looking at him. Leopold was round-faced, with a retreating hairline and a curved smile, almost like a sheep's. He was a man of probity, in Cade's view. One could imagine him, on Yom Kippur, striking his breast in synagogue, in repentance for the year's sins, eyes glistening with tears of regret. He had made enemies in his career, because he lacked manners, tact. He was a man incapable of falsehood. Manly said:

"Cade, sit down. We have a problem."

Cade settled his bulk into a chair Fonner pulled out for him. There was an ominous silence. Then Manly said:

"Rufus is dead."

Cade said, "My God, what happened?"

Manly nodded at Viterbo, who opened an envelope with shaking fingers and slid several photographs onto the desk. One was enough. It showed a body sprawled in a chair behind a desk. Charred. Beyond recognition.

They all looked at it in horror. Manly said to Viterbo:

"Have you been able to make positive identification?"

Viterbo pulled some dental X-rays from his brief case. "Yes. We got hold of his dentist. It's Rufus, all right."

Manly said, shaken, "I am, of course, ordering a complete investigation." He looked at Fonner. "I'm putting you in charge." The eyes in the skeletal face turned toward Leopold. "I presume you're ready to carry on in his place?" When Leopold hesitated,

253

Manly said, the strain showing in the irritation of his voice, "You've been here every day! You've been working with him! I ask you again, are you prepared to continue?"

"Yes, Your Honor."

"Very well. I'm adjourning court until tomorrow afternoon, at two o'clock." To Viterbo, he said, "I'd like to seal the coroner's records for the time being. Can you do that for me?"

Viterbo shook his head. "People already know. I mean, hell, there was just the marshal at his house when they broke in."

"God Almighty."

Before anyone could ask him anything, Manly rose, in a gesture of dismissal. Fonner ducked his head and hurried out, followed by a bewildered Leopold. Cade hesitated, then, aware that it would be improper for him to meet with the judge without the presence of the district attorney or his representative, murmured a simple Excuse me, and followed them slowly out of the room.

In the anteroom, Cade spoke briefly to Emily and David. Emily looked at him with round, incredulous eyes, but David's face was full of hostility.

"Suicide, right? The son of a bitch never had a case in the first place! When he realized it, he killed himself, right? Right!"

"Died like Jennie."

Emily shrank away, white with fear. David started asking him questions. Cade interrupted, saying, "I don't know a damn thing."

Emily could only think of one thing: would they take her back to jail, back into protective custody? She said to Cade, a hand on his arm, her voice cracked, dry:

"Will they let me go home now?"

"I already got me a writ of habeas corpus. Yeah. They'll let you go home."

She sagged with relief. That was all that mattered, all she could think about. The death of Rufus was something she could not absorb. Not yet.

Back in court, Manly took the bench.

"Owing to the unfortunate death of the prosecuting attorney last night—"

There was a roar of amazement. The spectators, afraid of losing

254

their seats, had remained in the courtroom for hours. This was the first they had heard of what by now was known all over the city, everywhere.

"—I am adjourning these proceedings until tomorrow afternoon at two o'clock, at which time the assistant district attorney, Mr. Benjamin Leopold, will resume for the People."

When Manly got to his feet and the bailiff called out, "All rise," they remained seated, too stunned to move.

34

The next day, proceedings were again delayed. Cade was called into chambers. Leopold was there ahead of him.

"Mr. Leopold seems to have a problem," Manly said. He gave Leopold an opaque look of inquiry.

Leopold said, "The fact is, Your Honor . . ." He faltered, trying to remember the speech he had carefully rehearsed. "Your Honor," he said, "the People request an adjournment until such time as they can prepare their case."

"Mr. Leopold!" Manly was suddenly furious. "We are under great pressure! There are riots in the streets! No, I can't give you a postponement! Why should I?"

Leopold tugged at his collar, trying to loosen it. He said in an unsteady voice, "If People proceed, it will have to be on material already presented."

Now Manly no longer troubled to control himself. "Mr. Leopold," he said in a cutting voice, "this Court has been patient. People promised to show how murder was done. Are you now prepared to produce that evidence?"

"No, Your Honor."

"Why not?"

There was a painful pause. Then Leopold said, "Your Honor, all the remaining evidence People intended to offer was taken from the files by Rufus Simonds."

"On what authority? What the Christ did he do a thing like that for?"

"I can't answer that, Your Honor."

Cade got to his feet, hanging on to the back of his chair. Manly looked at him quickly.

256

"Something wrong, Cade?"

His heart was racing. He could feel the beginnings of a fibrillation. He knew all about it. Wandering pacemaker causing occasional arrhythmia. Didn't mean a damn thing but he might have to lie down and this was a hell of a time to interrupt proceedings.

"I could do with a glass of water."

Manly sent for one and Cade covertly swallowed some Inderal. He thought, Give me twenty minutes. I'll be okay.

Manly turned back to Leopold, the hooded eyes piercing in the skeletal face.

"Well, where the hell *is* the evidence?"

"Destroyed."

Now it began, paroxysmal, like a trapped bird beating its wings against the bars of his chest. He knew it would pass. He longed to lie down. He thought, almost as if it had never occurred to him before, I'm an old man. Once, one of his grandnephews, a little boy, had come into the room when he was lying down in the middle of the day and asked what he was doing in bed. I'm old, he had said. How did you get old? the child had asked him. And he had answered, Well, one night you go to sleep and when you wake up in the morning, you're an old man. He had meant it as a joke but by God, he thought, it was the exact truth. Son of a bitch.

They were all looking at him.

Manly said, "Cade, you all right?"

"Hell, half the time I'm sick abed on two chairs. Now, let's just go on."

Manly said, trying to get it straight, *"Destroyed?* What evidence? How much of it?"

"All of it."

There was a shocked silence. Then Manly said, "Destroyed how?"

"By fire. Incinerated."

"Same way?"

Leopold nodded, acutely aware that perspiration was running down his face.

Manly said, "In this Court's opinion, it's in the public interest

257

that this case come to some legal conclusion. Now, I'm of a mind to *order* you to continue. If I do that, what course of action are you prepared to follow?"

Leopold drew himself up and said, "In that event, Your Honor, the People will have to rest their case."

"Unacceptable!"

"People have spoken," said Cade. A little pain. Not much. He would have to lie down.

Leopold said, "That's all I can do. I'm sorry."

Manly rose. They returned to the courtroom.

The room was jammed. When the bailiff finally announced that Judge Manly was entering, the whole room jumped to its feet. Manly seated himself. He looked around at a world of staring eyes, then at the captain of the guards he had summoned to keep order in court. The guard nodded to him. Manly said:

"Will the defendant rise and face the Court, please?"

Emily got to her feet, looking around in fear. She saw no hint of sympathy anywhere. Cade squeezed her hand. She threw back her head and faced Manly bravely.

"Mrs. Emily Blake," Manly said, glancing again at the captain, "I am reliably informed that no further evidence will be forthcoming from the prosecution."

A rising murmur of incredulous voices, a rush of anger. Gavelling.

"The fire in which the district attorney died was more widespread than was thought at first. The rest of the trial evidence has been destroyed."

A howl of rage from hundreds of voices at once. Silenced suddenly by the lowered rifles of the men standing guard.

"Under those circumstances, since the People are unable even to show how murder was done—"

Now, threatened violence. The guards closed in, rifles at the ready, holding back the spectators.

"—I have no choice but to dismiss the charges against the defendant."

His thanks to the jury were lost in an uproar of fury. Guards
258

seized Emily and David by the arms and rushed them out of the courtroom, which had now become an inferno of malevolence.

An hour later, while they were packing, Cade arrived.

The three of them huddled around a fire in the living room. Emily clung to David, looking at Cade, bewildered.

"Is it over?" she asked.

David said to Cade, "What the hell just happened?"

Cade didn't say anything for a few moments. Emily's question began to echo in her head. *Is it over? Why hadn't he answered her?* She twisted her hands, looking at Cade with a trembling jaw. "They'll all think I did it! And that's what you think, too, isn't it?"

"What difference does it make what anyone thinks!" David burst out. "It's all over now!"

"Is it?" Cade felt calm. His pulse was normal again. He told himself that it was important not to have any undue excitement. What lay ahead of them now was strenuous. He looked up, seeing David's eyes on him. A flat stare. Emily, intercepting it, answered Cade's question, saying:

"No, it isn't over."

"Who killed Rufus, Emmy?"

Absolute silence. Then:

"Lupe."

"I don't think we should talk about it any more," David said, feeling shaken. "We have to pack now. We have to get out of town."

"Not yet."

"What's this 'not yet'? For Christ's sake, Cade, we're not safe in this town any more!"

"You're not going to be safe anywhere. Not till this whole thing is settled."

"What are you talking about?"

"Emmy knows. Don't you, honey?"

She did not look at either of them.

Cade said, "Davey, let me ask you something. You believe your wife? I mean, this whole story she's been telling us all along?"

259

David's eyes moved as he tried to pick his way carefully through treacherous words. "I know she believes what she's saying."

"Don't you, Davy?" David answered him with a look of hostility. Cade said evenly, "Because if you don't, that means you think she's insane."

"Don't you dare say such a thing to me!"

"Definition of insanity is being unable to distinguish between reality and fantasy, and you know it. Now, if you don't think she's guilty—"

"Well, of course I don't!"

"—that leaves only one choice. Me, I got to believe what she's saying is true. I don't mean that she just thinks it's true. I mean, that it *is*." Cade turned and looked at Emily steadily, the old eyes still a strong blue under the jutting brows, the lined face resolute. "Emmy," he said, "I believe your story. It don't make sense. It don't square with anything I think. But I am prepared to take you at your word."

Emily looked at him for a long moment without saying anything, searching his face. Then, throwing herself in his arms, she began to cry uncontrollably, hugging him. "Cade!" she said. "Oh, Cade! Cade!"

He patted her awkwardly, then, like a grandfather, pulled out a huge handkerchief and shoved it at her. She blew her nose, and David came over and put his arms around her, stroking her hair.

"It's going to be all right," he said. "Everything's going to be all right now, honey."

Cade poked David with a stubby forefinger and asked, "You prepared to believe her?"

Emily turned her glistening eyes on David, questioning him. He took a quick breath. "Well, Christ, I believe *something's* going on! But I don't know what!"

"Not what I asked you. Now, looky here. You're a doctor. You got a scientific mind. Well, that's all right. William James, he was a scientist. Man was practically running the medical school at Harvard when I went there. And he said we believe in all sorts of laws of nature 'which we cannot ourselves understand, merely because men whom we admire and trust vouch for them.' True, ain't it? Well, how about Emmy here? You admire and trust *her*. What are you gonna do if she vouches for something?"

Now they were both looking at him, waiting. He met his wife's eyes. For the first time, as he searched their unflinching blue depths, he realized that he had somehow always pushed the whole thing away, had loved her, cherished her, blamed himself for what had happened, and tried to help her but that he had never given her the one thing she wanted: belief. His mind had rebelled. David, who had always hated superstition. Had despised the occult. Now he made himself look at Cade. Cade, who was made of the same stuff as David. A phrase from his childhood days in Sunday school came into his mind. *Help thou mine unbelief.* Something in him surrendered. He turned to his wife then and said:

"All right, I believe you."

Wordlessly, Emily went to him, put her arms around his neck and held him for a long moment. When she let go and turned back to face Cade, there was a look of relief in her eyes neither of them had seen since before the arrest, before Jennie, before any of it.

"It's not over," Cade said in a quiet voice. "Not yet. But it's going to be. If you do what I tell you to do."

Emily felt a sudden sick sense of foreboding. She heard herself ask in an unnaturally casual voice, "What, Cade?"

"I want you to call him. That boy. Tonight."

"What are you talking about?"

"I've read a little bit about all of this. He opened that door. So far, he's been left to come and go as he pleases. But if you *make* him come—"

"I can't do that!"

"You can, Emmy."

"What makes you say such a thing?"

"He wants something from you. What is it?"

"I don't know!"

"But it's true, isn't it? It must be, or he wouldn't keep coming back."

"Well—I—I suppose it's true."

261

"He wants to possess you. That's it, isn't it, Emily? But he can't. Not ever. Not without your consent. You know that, don't you?"

"Yes. Yes, I know that." She was suddenly afraid.

"Well, so long as that door stays open and he goes on wanting what he wants, my money says, if you call him, he's got to come."

She said, greatly agitated, "I can't!"

"Just listen to me—"

"No!" Her face was rigid with fear. "I can't! I can't!"

"I think you can."

"No, really, I don't know how! I've never called him. I've never been to see him except that one time in the alley I told you about and then, that time in the cemetery, *that time you yourself told me I couldn't have seen him because he was dead!*"

"But you know you can call him up, Emmy."

"I can't! I can't!" She turned away, terribly overwrought. David saw something in her face. He went to her, taking her hands, trying to read her expression.

"What does he mean, honey?" David asked.

"He taught you a song," Cade said flatly. "Wasn't that the reason he taught it to you?"

There was absolute silence. Emily began to tremble so much, she had to hang on to the back of a chair for support.

"You remember the song, don't you, Emmy?" Cade asked her in a soft voice. "That chant. Remember?"

"I can't! I won't!"

David was taking quick, shallow breaths, looking from one to the other. Something snapped. He yelled out, "All right, I believe her! We both said we believe her! What the hell do you want to see him for?"

"To get rid of him." He had spoken in a matter-of-fact voice. Now he took Emily's hands and said to her gently, "I'm your friend, Emmy. Right now, I may be the best friend you've got. You let me help you. You call him up. He'll come. My guess is, he's got to come. Then you leave things to me. Emmy?"

She leaned on him for support, her face ashen. Then her whole body yielded and she said, "All right, Cade."

He picked up his brief case, saying to David, "Get me my coat.

Get coats for all of us. Heaviest coats you've got." David looked at him blankly, then went to the front hall closet and returned with Cade's heavy Irish tweed overcoat, a fur coat for Emily, and a thick camel's-hair coat of his own.

"I'll get your purse," he said, starting out.

"We won't need that, Davey."

"Well, if we're going out—"

"We're not going out. We're going upstairs. You've got a way up to the attic, haven't you?"

"Why the attic?"

"Just let's go on up there. Come on. Now."

Silently, the three of them went up the staircase to the bedroom floor, down to the end of the corridor and then up the narrow staircase to the empty attic. It was large but the roof sloped, so the only standing room was a small space in the center. Cade had taken something out of his brief case.

"What is that, chalk?"

"Bloodstone." Huffing and stooping, Cade drew a circle on the floor about eight feet in diameter, then made a triangle inside, writing down what looked like letters in an unfamiliar script. Then he got to his feet, sighed and arched his back. A cold trickle of perspiration suddenly ran down David's spine.

"Just give me a hand here," Cade said. Same voice. Flat. Matter-of-fact. He had pulled a small brazier out of his brief case. He handed it to David, pulling him away from the circle and waving Emily back. "Just hold that a second." Cade now took out a little bag of charcoal, emptied it into the brazier, crumpled paper into it and then lit it with a match. The paper seemed to be soaked with something because it began to flame brightly. Then, when it died down, the coals were glowing. David still held it. Cade put a pinch of incense on the coals. The attic now filled with the clean, pungent odor of camphor. He seemed very concerned about the coals and blew on them several times to make sure they were glowing. Then he removed a couple of candles from his brief case.

"Now, I'm going to tell you both something. Once we go in that circle, no talking. I mean, none. You can't say one word, neither of you. You both understand that?"

They stared at him.

"Just the chanting. Emmy, all by herself. I'll be reading a few things aloud. Old things. A bit from King Solomon, something from the Chaldeans. Nothing to bother your heads about. Don't even need to listen." The unlit candles still in his hand, Cade fumbled in a pocket and took out a very small worn book. It looked old, ancient. When he opened it to a place he had marked, David saw that it had been written by hand.

"Now, we're gonna hold hands," he said. "The three of us. That's important. Don't matter what happens, don't anybody let go. That clear?" He saw David's look and added, "Oh, he's coming. But, here's the thing. I don't want you to have any conversation with him at all. Even when he asks you questions. Or threatens you. Leave the talking to me." He looked at each of them in turn to make sure they had understood, lit both candles, switched off the lights, then stepped into the circle, indicating that they were to enter it with him. Bending down, he dripped tallow on the floor, then stood both candles upright, after which he reached up, taking the brazier from David's hands, shook it, filling the air with incense, then set it down. Slowly, with David's help, Cade got to his feet, and then, taking the little book out of his pocket again, he indicated that they should now join hands. Then he read:

" 'Lord God ADONAY, Whose Names are HEIE, ACER, HEIE—that is to say, I AM THAT I AM—Who hast formed man out of nothing to thine own image and likeness, deign, I pray Thee, to bless and sanctify this Pentacle. By the Name of ON, which Adam heard and spake; by the Name of JOTH, which Jacob learned from the Angel on the night of his wrestling; by the Name of God AGLA which Lot heard and was saved with his family; by the Name ZEBAOTH, which Moses named, and all the rivers and waters in the land of Egypt ran blood; by the Names ALPHA and OMEGA, which Daniel uttered, and destroyed Bel and the Dragon; by the Dreadful Day of Judgment; by the changing Sea of Glass which is before the face of the Divine Majesty, I invoke, conjure and command thee to appear and show thyself before this circle, O Spirit Lupe!' "

He nodded at Emily. Slowly, clutching their hands, her eyes

264

half-closed, she began to hum the antique melody, and then to chant it, rocking slowly back and forth as she did, repeating and repeating the ancient music that sounded at the same time Gregorian and obscene. *La la la.* She was back in the cemetery now, on that fog-blown day when she had heard it first. Now, she was on the coarse strand at China Beach and the same sound was echoing faintly from a cave up on the cliffs. Now, in a filthy alley, hearing it whistled, as if hearing it mocked. Yes, he had taught it to her, and now, suddenly, she was on the floor of that cramped padded cell with the high ceiling, unable even to bang on a table or pound on a wall, feeling again the incredible almost primeval helplessness of not being able to make a loud noise, her voice muffled by her little prison, so that all she could do was sit on the floor combing her hair with her fingers and repeat the strange chant he had taught her, *la la la,* always the same weaving seductive melody, and now, here she was, chanting it again, lost in the sorcery of those syllables, *la la la.*

The house was suddenly cold, colder than she had ever remembered it, with a cold that seemed to seep under the door and into the room. She broke off singing suddenly. Her head moved, as if she were shaking it, a quick, involuntary movement, and they felt her shudder. Cade said:

"He's here, isn't he? Don't answer me, Emmy. Just make a sign."

She nodded, incapable of speech.

"Where?"

She moved her head, indicating the door. Cade looked there. Nothing. Empty space. Cade glanced at the tattered little volume in his hand, then started reading:

" 'He who forges the image, he who enchants—
The spiteful face, the evil eye,
The mischievous mouth, the mischievous tongue,
The mischievous lips, the mischievous words—' "

Suddenly, a jar on a shelf rose into the air and hurled itself in an arc across the attic, smashing itself to pieces against the wall. Cade went on as if nothing had happened:

265

"'Spirit of the Sky, remember!
Spirit of the Earth, remember!'"

Emily began to writhe, pulling at their hands, as if trying to free herself from both of them, a strangled sound coming from her throat. She became stronger. David and Cade clutched her hands, trying to hang on to her. Her strength was suddenly extraordinary, astounding. She seemed as if she were being wrenched away from them by some invisible force.

Cade hung on to her with all his strength as he began reading again:

"'They are seven, they are seven.
In the valley of the abyss, they are seven.
In the numberless stars of heaven, they are seven.
In the abyss, in the depths, they grow in power—'"

A whole shelf of bottles was hurled to the floor with such terrible force, the glass seemed to explode. Emily, her eyes dragged toward the sight, opened her mouth in a silent, frightful scream. David began to shake almost convulsively. Cade clung to him, still holding open the tattered little volume, and continued reading:

"'They are not male, they are not female.
They dry up the moistness of the waves.
They do not love women, they have not
begotten offspring—'"

A kerosene can stored in a metal cabinet suddenly exploded, fell to the floor, and the boards began to blaze. Emily tried to scream and wrest free, but Cade yanked her savagely toward him, still hanging on to her damp hand, and got hold of her hair so that he could pull her head toward him, make her look away. Cade said, the voice rising, falling,

"'They are the enemies of God.
They who have revolted cause the gods to tremble.
266

They spread terror over the highways, and advance
with whistling roar.
They are evil, they are evil.
They are seven, they are seven, and again, they are
twice seven!' "

A black wind that extinguished all the light outside the circle
roared through the attic, obliterating the flames and drowning out
Cade's words. Then everything was still again, there was the floor,
unburned, and they heard Cade's voice, saying:

" 'Spirit of the Sky, remember them!
Spirit of the Earth, remember them!
Conjure them!' "

Absolute silence. They hung on to each other, their hands
soaking wet.

A cold mist seemed to seep under the door and through the
cracks beneath the window sashes, moving, moving, as if it were
somehow gathering itself into that one empty square in front of
the closed door to the stairway. David thought, It's fog. Of course.
He remembered now. He had once been in a theater in London
when the fog crept into the auditorium and became so dense, the
screen itself became invisible, the film was projected onto a waver-
ing curtain, blurred, hardly recognizable, and then the lights had
gone on, the performance was canceled. It was fog. *But how could
fog accumulate in one part of the room?* He found himself saying
in a part of his being, *Don't let it happen. Don't let it be true.*
Then wisps of it began to dissolve away. And now, he could see
it. No. It wasn't happening. He was imagining it. But he shot a
quick, incredulous look at Cade's face, and Emily's, both of them
straining forward, watching, and knew in that moment that they
saw it too.

The door was opening. And someone was coming in.

Lupe.

Barefoot. In rags. His child's hands stretched out toward Emily.
His child's face, with the soft, luminous eyes, pleading with her.
The harelip mouth half-open in a silent cry.

267

The child's lips moved, saying something. Emily leaned forward, straining as if to hear. She turned away, a look of stark terror on her face.

"No!" she cried out. "No!"

Cade yelled at her, "Don't! Don't listen to him and don't talk to him!" Then looking directly at Lupe, Cade said in a strong voice:

> " 'I take refuge with the Lord
> of the Daybreak from the evil
> of the blowers upon knots
> and from the evil of the
> envious one when he envies.' "

The child turned his frightened eyes on Cade, then held out an imploring hand, turning it palm upward, and they saw that it was bleeding. Both hands. The palms dripped blood.

Cade's voice deepened. " 'Harken unto my prayer. Free her from her bewitchment. Loosen her sin. Let there be turned aside whatever evil may come to cut off her life.' "

Emily shuddered and groaned. Lupe pulled up his shirt. He was bleeding, slowly, slowly, thick red blood from a wound in his side.

"Demon!" yelled Cade.

The child began to cry. Now his feet were bleeding. He stretched out his bloody hands toward David, in agony. Cade felt David lunge toward the wounded child and hurled his shoulder at David to stop him, saying:

"Demon!" Then, as if from the depths of an ancient memory, Cade began saying, with the force of a curse:

"Aglon Tetragram Vaycheon Stimulamaton—"

The child staggered backward as if struck violently in the face. There were marks on his soft cheek, harsh red marks as if from a terrible blow. Emily cried out:

"My God, don't *do* that!"

"Demon!" yelled Cade.

The child came toward them, shoulders hunched, sobbing, the grimy hands reaching out, then stopped, by an invisible barrier.

"Ezphares!" yelled Cade.

268

The child was flung to the floor as if struck by a giant. He cried out in anguish, a little boy's cry of pain that pierced the heart. Emily cried out again, "He's only a baby! He's a little boy!"

"Be *silent!*"

She was on her knees, still gripping both of them by the hands, crying and begging, saying, "Can't we talk to him? Maybe he doesn't understand! Do we have to hurt him?"

"Emmy, he's not a child! He was never a child!"

She sobbed, her mouth contorted with pity and with pain. "All right, he's a ghost! He's dead! But I can't *stand* this!"

The child crawled toward her, the angelic face bewildered, filled with pain. "Lady, I'm sorry! Please, lady! Please, lady, I'm sorry!"

"Cade!"

"Don't look at him, Emmy, and don't talk to him! He's not a child! You want to know what he is? I'll show you, Emmy!

"Retragsammaton Olyarum Irion—"

Then the wounded child scrambled to his feet, a look of abject terror on his face, tried to run for the door, but Cade impaled him with another word:

"Esytion!"

Lupe stood there as if rooted to the spot. He seemed to grow in stature, in dignity. The bleeding had stopped.

"Existion!"

A quick, indrawn breath. David's. For Lupe was older now. Taller. The lines of the jaw had hardened.

"Eronya!"

Emily took a step backward, cowering against David, icy with fear. Lupe was a grown man. With a classic face. A face she was sure she had once seen on a statue.

"Onera Erasym Mozm!"

Older. Before their eyes, he began to age. His hair whitened. The eyes, which had looked at them first with pleading, then dignity, then reproach, were now dimmed with age. He did not seem to know it. He took a step toward their circle again. He limped now. And the outstretched hands were gnarled, the nails long, blackened. Like talons.

"Messias Soter Emanuel—"

269

Old. Incredibly old. The teeth were gone now, the hair. The lips dribbled saliva. And the twisted limbs would no longer support the body. He had sunk to his knees, the head thrown back, the mouth open, the stringy neck, like a mummy's neck, reduced to the size of a wrist.

"Sabaoth Adonay!"

Putrescence. What lay before them now was a rotting corpse. The air was filled with an unspeakable stench. Before their eyes, the body was decomposing. David retched. But the eyes continued to look at them. Emily cried out, "My God, he's dying!"

"He can't die, Emmy," Cade said. Then:

" 'O Lord God, Almighty and Ineffable, Who art seated above the heavens, Who beholdest the depths, grant me, unworthy sinner that I am, that those things which I conceive in my mind may also be executed by me, through Thee, O Living Lord, Who livest and reignest for ever! Amen.' "

The loathsome, decaying mass on the floor began to spread itself into a pool of stench. Emily was sobbing now and David, his head bent close to hers, as if they were taking refuge in one another, was rubbing her cheek with his, their fingers twisted together.

Then it was gone. It was over. It seemed as if they went on standing there forever. Then Cade let go of their hands, walked out of the circle, switched the lights back on.

"It's over," he said. "Emmy, it's all over. We won, Emmy."

They were downstairs now. In the front hall. Outside, guards were still protecting the house. Cade was ready to leave. He looked suddenly very old, very tired. Emily came toward him, putting her arms around him. She tried to say something, to thank him. All that came out was tears. She clung to him, sobbing. With relief. It was finally over. David put his arms around her. Cade embraced them both.

"I'll see you to your car," David said.

Cade shook his head. "Don't go out that door." Cade took a long breath, then explained. "Manly, he has reason to think you're in danger." Another breath. Labored. "He's called in the FBI. They'll be coming here for you today. You're going to be settled in another town, given new identities."

David said, trying to think, "I thought we'd just go away. For a couple of months. Just until this whole thing dies down."

Cade looked at him steadily. "It's your choice, of course. But if I were you, I'd listen to Manly."

Then he was gone. Out of their lives. They packed a few things. An hour later, FBI agents arrived and took them to the airport, where they boarded a private jet. They were flown to Boston as Dr. and Mrs. David Oxley, then taken by car to a village in New England, where an old Colonial house had been found for them. Their arrival attracted no attention. It seemed perfectly natural for a doctor newly transferred to a leading Boston hospital to buy a house in the country.

Dr. and Mrs. Oxley settled down to a new life, making new friends. Of course, they had had to give up their old ones. But the past was so full of pain, they felt only relief. It was over, they told each other. It was over at last.

They could not even thank Cade. Cade, whom a maid at the Pacific Union Club found the next morning, sitting up in bed smiling, the eyes fixed in death.

35

David and Emily were happy again together. She seemed to him, if anything, more beautiful, rosy, golden, content. By agreement, they never talked about what had happened. At times, Emily would remember, he would see it in her face, but he would hush her with the words "It's not good for the baby," and she would make herself push the memories away. Once she said, remembering with pain:

"But why me?"

And David had answered almost impatiently, "Hell, every patient asks that! You ought to know better! Every one of us who finds out he's got some incurable disease is forever asking, Why me? Emmy, honey, nobody ever has an answer to that question. Now, forget it, okay?"

"Can I ask a favor?"

"What?"

"To see Marianne."

His face clouded. They hadn't spoken, Emily and Marianne, since that one terrible day in the hospital. Marianne's name brought back memories. David wasn't sure seeing Marianne again was a good idea.

"She couldn't help it," she said, reading his thoughts. "And I want to see her."

"We don't even know where she is."

"She's in Heidelberg. She went back."

"Jesus Christ, you've been writing to her?"

"Well, she wrote to me first."

"How did she find out where we are?"

"The Army, I suppose. Somehow, they know everything. What

272

difference does it make? You know she'd never tell anybody. And I want to see her."

"Well, hell, we can't go to Heidelberg! You're due in three weeks!"

"She's coming back on leave."

"Then, what are you asking me for?" He was nettled.

"I—I don't like springing things on you. She wants to come. But only if you want her. Just to be with me."

"Oh, honey! Of course she can come!"

Emily cabled, inviting Marianne. A week later, David went to the Boston airport to pick her up. He left early because there had been a snowstorm and the roads were icy.

It was the fifth of January. The witching time, Emily remembered, not wanting to think about it. The end of those twelve days between Christmas and Epiphany. The Witch Huntsman now swooped through the air, the powers of evil were let loose, werewolves prowled and the witches worked their will. She had read all of it in Frazer. In the woods of northern Germany, people used to burn pine logs all night long to keep away evil spirits. She had secretly counted the days, praying that the baby would not be born then. But now, it was Twelfth Night. The next day she knew she would be safe. Superstition. Ridiculous. It was important not to tell David. David, who wanted to forget the terrible past.

David met Marianne and drove her back. She looked worse than ever. Her hair had been done in unbecoming bangs.

"Tell me I look like Glenda Jackson."

He gave her a look.

"Lie to me! For chrissakes, lie to me!"

"How on earth did you find us?"

Marianne stared at him. "Well, I couldn't. I mean, not until Emily wrote to me."

David was puzzled. Emily had been very definite about Marianne's writing first.

They arrived at the house. Marianne crunched through the snow, then stumbled up the stairs, arms outstretched. Emily, big with child, surrendered herself to the comfort of those familiar strong arms.

They were friends again. Marianne scuffed into the house,

273

coughing and laughing. Emily had begun to cry as soon as she saw her. They hugged each other.

Marianne said, "How about a nice crying drunk? Oh, Jesus Shit Christ, it's been five months and it seems like five years!"

When Emily went upstairs to dress, she found David at her desk, going through letters.

"What are you looking for?"

"Marianne's letters. Didn't you keep them?"

"They're right here." Emily opened a drawer, pulled out a handful of envelopes, and handing them to him, went in to shower. David looked through the envelopes. The first one was postmarked September 11th. He opened it and read through it quickly. It was warm, personal, full of gossip and mischief. One line caught his eye:

"I was afraid you'd never forgive me."

He put it down impatiently and then, when Emily was out of the shower, he went into the bathroom and said to her:

"Why didn't you tell me you'd written to her first?"

She looked at him blankly, a blue stare. He went in and got the letter and showed it to her. She reread it, not sure what he was talking about. He said impatiently, pointing at the phrase:

"You must have written her that you'd forgiven her."

"No, I didn't."

"She says you did."

A little knot of fear. Ridiculous. A misunderstanding.

"Emmy, listen to me. Have you written to anybody else we used to know?"

"No."

"Sure?"

"Of course I'm sure."

"Okay. I can understand about Marianne but I don't want you to get carried away."

"Just a minute. I didn't write to Marianne first." She was suddenly defensive, afraid.

He didn't want to upset her. Impulsively, he kissed her smooth, wet forehead, helped her dry her back, saying, "Forget I said anything."

From downstairs, Marianne called out to ask if they were ready.

274

David went to join her. Emily looked at the letter again. Now that she thought about it, how would Marianne know she had forgiven her for what had happened? She had no way of knowing what she felt. A sense of uneasiness came over her. She toweled her head furiously, trying to shake it off. She had lived with fear too long. It was a habit. She would have to break herself of it.

She found herself wondering again about how they had met. She remembered the *Kaserne,* Army headquarters in Heidelberg. In her mind's eye, she saw herself entering the compound. Snow covered the parade ground in the quadrangle's center. The sky was dark with rain clouds and a storm flag flew from the mast. In the oblong three-story buildings, with huge numerals like children's toys stuck on the outside, lights glowed from behind a thousand windows. A sentry guarded the Command Building, where a scrambled line connected Headquarters with the Pentagon. Marianne was hurrying across the parade field. They had waved to each other, hadn't they? Then somehow they must already have met. But when was the first time?

She heard a train whistle, a lonely far-off sound. She remembered something. What was it? Odd how the mind remembered remembering, like a word on the tip of one's tongue.

It came back in fragments. She had gone to the Casino for lunch. Inside the compound. It was one of the days when films were shown and she had her sandwich served at a little table in the theater and ate in the dark.

She had watched the screen, absorbed. From time to time, the doors at either side would open to admit patrons, and when rays of daylight fell on the screen, the filmed characters would fade like ghosts at dawn, become once again two-dimensional, and she would remember that they were only pictures of characters in a play. They were not people, they were fixed attitudes, like the toy figures in the Strasbourg clock. She could not follow the plot. She had thought how little of a man went into that chain of events one calls a story, asking herself what the characters had been doing between the scenes, what other actions, irrelevant to this tale, made up that day of their lives, in how many other roles were they also appearing?

"Honey?"

275

"Coming!"

The three of them went out to dinner together, seafood and lots of white wine. Marianne talked incessantly. Her old lover Vince was still there in Heidelberg. Waiting. Now she had a new lover, a burly sergeant.

"I've got a dinky little apartment. They gave it to me because of my rating. My typist is a three, the Secretary of State is an eighteen, and I'm a seven. Isn't that something? Ours is the only community in the world where one's relative social position is determined with mathematical exactitude. Anyway, Bob stays there. It's against Army regulations. He comes and goes at what I suppose are odd hours for a nonresident: that is, he leaves at eight in the morning and comes back at six at night. Now they're having unannounced inspections. Last week, the sergeant wouldn't leave until he'd looked in the linen closet and down the lightwell. I finally offered to let him smell the bed."

Pain. Sharp. Brief. Don't say anything.

Marianne went on: "Vince is being generous. He says he's prepared to wait. How do you like that? Christ, I said, haven't you got any pride? Next, you'll be wanting to help him off the bed after he screws me! But he just looked at me in that way he has, you know, when he just sort of stares at you. I told him off. I called him a dirty little Christer, but it didn't bother him. I've got to get away from all that suffocating patience and generosity, my God, all that *waiting,* and me the whole time living in a crummy two-room apartment, jumping in and out of bed between inspections. I mean, *Jesus!*"

Emily excused herself and went to the lavatory. It was a pretty room, with flocked wallpaper, burnished wood paneling, and a huge framed mirror in front of a dressing table. She had a brief contraction, nothing serious, but she wanted to be alone for a minute. A train whistle, again. Yes. Yes, of course! When she left the Casino that day, an old woman ran by her. The sound of a train. Deaf, the old woman had run under the barrier as it was being lowered. She was cut to pieces. Emily had seen it all. A stopped train, the diner at the crossroads, people with napkins at their chins looking out at the crowd, not understanding; beneath their car, like hell under the earth in a Renaissance painting, that

276

stained bundle of rags. Then she had turned away, sickened, and looked straight at the Hexenturm. The Witches' Tower. *Don't look at it. It's bad luck!* But she had looked anyway. Just in time to see a woman coming out of it. Coming out of a door she thought she had remembered seeing boarded up. Yes, there was a sign on it warning tourists away. The building was falling down. It was dangerous. The woman was dressed in black. The woman came toward her, taking quick steps. They had looked at each other briefly. The woman smiled.

It was Marianne. That was where they had met.

She had forgotten it all, repressed it, because of the horror of that accident she had witnessed. She had never wanted to remember that bundle of rags.

The door to the ladies' room opened. Marianne came in. "Are you all right?"

"Oh, yes. Yes, I'm all right."

"We were worried about you. Why are you standing here staring off into space?"

Another pain. Sharp. *Don't let it show!*

"I'll be right out!" Emily said, forcing a smile.

"I'll wait for you."

She walked back to the table with Marianne. Slowly.

"How long are you staying?" David asked her.

Brandy had been served. Warming hers in her hands, Marianne said, "Well, I thought I'd be here for the birth of the baby."

"It's not due for two weeks," Emily said. She felt another contraction coming on, gripped the sides of her chair and tried not to let her face reveal anything.

"Well, if you don't want me—"

"Don't be silly," said David. "We have loads of room."

"I was going to stay in Boston—" Marianne began.

"Stay with us," David said. A waiter brought the check. While David conferred with him, Emily said:

"I've remembered where we met. The Hexenturm."

Marianne gave her a bright smile. It could have meant anything or nothing. She went on talking about why she had come. "It's just that after all you've been through—"

277

David interrupted quietly, saying, "We never talk about it."

"I understand. Oh, I'm so ashamed. I should have tried to see you. I could have helped."

"It's all right."

"I didn't think it could get any worse. But my God, when they locked you up that night, and he came to see you—!"

Emily's blood froze. She had never told anyone about that, not even David. She remained perfectly still, her face showing nothing. David, preoccupied with a credit card, hadn't heard. Marianne's face wore a bright, expectant smile.

Another pain. Stronger now.

"David," she said, "may we go now?"

He got to his feet instantly. They drove back to the house. The road was icy, drifts of snow piled on either side. David turned on the radio. There were reports of closed roads, power outages. He said to Marianne:

"See? Now you'll have to stay."

Marianne. Who had first taken her to Lupe. Who was always there. Dear, helpful Marianne. What was it David had said? It seemed ages ago. She remembered now: *Why is she always around when these things happen?* Marianne, who had told David that Emily had written to her first, telling her their address. What did she want? *What the hell did she want?* Fear, like a dybbuk, crept into her heart. The important thing was to hide it, to go on smiling.

They were back at the house. Upstairs. Marianne said, "I want to see the widow's walk!"

"It's dark, you're both drunk, now cut it out! You can see it tomorrow! Emily has to get to bed!" Laughter. Embraces. Quick kisses. Another pain beginning.

Once the house was quiet, Emily pulled on a fur coat, took the keys and crept down the stairs. *I've got to get away,* she said to herself. *I've simply got to get away!*

She got to the car. Darkness. Icy cold. The car doors were frozen shut. She crept back to the house, ran a pan of hot water in the kitchen, then carried it out and sponged it all over the door's edges. She tried again. The door opened. Quickly, she slid into the chill car, inserted the key and prayed that it would start.

278

Harum, harum. Harum, harum, harum. Harum harum harum harum harum. A light went on upstairs. Her heart raced. She floored the accelerator and tried again. The motor caught. The car moved. She started away from the house, down the long treelined driveway. Behind her, in the rear-view mirror, she could see more light from the house as the front door opened. Marianne and David were running out after her. She heard faint voices. The engine was sputtering. She put it in neutral, trying to race the engine to warm it up. They were getting closer. Another pain. She did not think she could bear more pain like that. She jammed the car into drive. The motor died. She heard them running toward her, crying out. She began to cry in fear.

David wrenched open the door, grabbing her. "My God, what is it?"

"David!"

"Come on. In the house. Quick."

He helped her out of the car. Past Marianne. Who was standing there, all concern, hands stretched out. No, no, she mustn't let Marianne touch her. Fighting pain, she let David hurry her into the house. She collapsed on the doorstep. David swept her up into his arms, carried her upstairs. When he put her down on the bed, she saw Marianne blotting out the light in the doorway and she screamed.

"Is it bad?" he asked.

"Get her out of here!"

"Honey, baby, talk to me." He took her hands, looked earnestly into her face. "What kind of pain?"

"David, it's coming!"

"Now, take it easy. We're all packed and ready to go."

Marianne came into the room a few steps. "How far is the hospital?" she asked.

"Thirty miles."

"Thirty *miles?*"

"She isn't due for another two weeks. Now, will you calm down?"

She saw it now. The horror. Marianne was there to deliver her into those unspeakable hands. Lupe's hands.

Emily screamed, *"Get her out of here!"*

279

"She's out of her head," David said under his breath, motioning Marianne out of the way. The contraction was violent. David put a hand on her stomach, palpating her. Then he said:

"Now, it's all right."

"Get her out of here!"

"Look, I think it's better if I leave."

"What are you going to do, walk to Boston?"

"I meant, go to my room."

"Not now. I need you." David got a pair of sterile rubber gloves out of a box in the bathroom, powdered them, slipped them on, then checked Emily quickly. He said soothingly to her:

"Perfectly normal. Try to relax, okay?"

He walked away toward the bathroom, beckoning Marianne. "What's the matter?"

"Christ, she's so dilated, it could come any minute!"

"What can I do?"

"I've got a bag in the car. She's prepared for natural childbirth, so we ought to be able to make it." The words tumbled out. He was trying to think. "Look, when it comes on this fast, it usually means an easy delivery. Now, go get me that bag."

Marianne ran downstairs while David propped Emily's legs up with pillows.

"David, *listen* to me—!" She tried to tell him, but the pain was unbearable. She was struggling for breath. "Am I going to have it *here?*"

"Now, it doesn't matter! Babies have been born everywhere, lots of babies! You haven't had any problems. Don't worry."

One more contraction. So bad, she had to grip the sides of the bed. She tried to smile at him, saying, "I'm—I'm trying to relax!" She made an effort to remember what she had been taught in the classes she took. The breathing. Yes, the breathing. Panting.

"Should I pant?"

"Not yet."

"Should I bear down?"

"I'll tell you when to bear down." *Where the Christ was Marianne?* Then she came running into the room, his bag in her hand. He grabbed it.

Marianne again. *Don't look at her. And don't listen to any-*

280

thing she says. Oh, God, don't ever look at her again!

Another pain. It seemed unnaturally long. Agonizingly long. Emily's face was bathed in perspiration. When she relaxed between contractions, he held her in his arms, soothing her. But the pain seemed quite bad. He seized his chance, took Marianne aside. Something warned him to act. "Call an ambulance," he said.

"What's the matter?"

"Just do what I tell you to do."

Marianne ran downstairs. Emily began to suffer agonizing pains. David gave her a shot. It didn't help. He thought, I should give her a caudal. But he didn't have the medicine he needed. Marianne came back. There was something in her face he didn't like. On the pretext of wanting cold cloths, he sent Marianne into the bathroom, then followed her.

"What is it?" he asked.

"They've had three accidents. Way the hell out. They don't have an ambulance anywhere around. Shall we take her by car? I could drive. You could be in the back."

Emily screamed.

"What's *wrong?*" Marianne asked.

"I don't *know!* Maybe nothing."

How could he tell her about a doctor's instincts? How could he explain? It was as if the practice of medicine began where the textbooks left off. He hurried to Emily, bundling her up.

"I'm going to carry you to the car."

"Why?"

"Call me old-fashioned. I still like hospitals."

He picked her up, feeling her muscles contract in his arms, and brought her quickly downstairs to the car, where Marianne had put pillows and blankets in the back seat. It was very cold out. January. Frost. Marianne had the motor running.

Emily saw her. She let out a scream of terror. "Don't let her near me!" She struggled, hysterical. But David wasn't listening. All he knew was that the baby was coming, they had thirty miles to drive on an icy road, and Emily was out of her head with pain. She tried to tell him what was the matter but he wasn't hearing her. *And Marianne didn't even turn around.*

"Which way?"

"I'll tell you. Straight ahead until we hit the main road."

What bothered him now was that the pains were erratic. He couldn't time them. She had dilated without warning, the baby was obviously well down, he could feel that, but something was wrong. He struggled to hide his feelings. *Think about something else.* All he could think of was ice, ice everywhere, the whole of the New England countryside in the grip of a silent winter. He remembered a course he had taken once in med school, where they had been taught not to say, Wow. Wow, Jesus Christ, Oh, my God, anything. The patient watched you. If your face showed any sign—

"David—!

She was very pale, her pulse was irregular and her face was bathed in sweat. She was frightened. She wasn't bleeding. Not so far as he could tell. He took her blood pressure, struggling on his knees in front of the back seat in the lurching car. It was weak.

"David?"

"Yes, honey?"

"Where are we going?"

She was out of it. In some incredible way, she had forgotten what was happening to her. He was afraid. Then he looked up.

"Jesus! Marianne!"

"What's the matter?"

"Not this road! Oh, shit, I'm sorry! Turn around! Now!"

Marianne wrenched the wheel around so hard, the tires spun in the loose gravel. The frozen gravel. Where the hell were they? Miles from nowhere. What was she doing?

Then Marianne panicked. And drove off the road. The car jolted down a slope, then rammed into a tree. *Oh, God, it's going to turn over!* But it didn't. They were at a crazy angle. The baby was coming. He couldn't deliver it there. He scrambled out of the car, then, with Marianne's help, got Emily out, pulled out the bedding, the pillows, and the car seats. The baby was coming. In seconds. He lay Emily on the bedding, pulling off his coat in the freezing weather, trying to keep her warm. Emily was screaming, out of her head. The shot hadn't helped, and he couldn't risk more until after the baby had come. The flashlight was dim. He couldn't see. He felt the wet head, grasped it in his right hand, rotating it gently. He heard the cry, the unexpected, absurd, incredible cry of another voice, a new being. Emily was panting now, released. He had to attend to her, get her into the car. Then, up on the road, he saw the headlights of another car. A pickup truck.

He clutched the crying baby in his arms, trying to warm it, while Marianne ran toward the road, waving her arms. The pickup stopped, then swung around. Emily was coming out of it. She knew where she was, knew somehow what had happened to them.

"Is it all right?"

"Yes!"

"I can hear it crying! Oh, God, is it perfect? Is it all right?"

"I'm sure it's perfect!"

Marianne was running back toward them, stumbling through the packed snow. Emily turned her head, her teeth chattering. There was no light at all but there, up ahead on the road, was blessed help. She could see them backing the pickup around, swinging toward them down a whitened lane. Now the headlights blinded them. Emily looked away.

And into the face of the baby.

She let out a cry of horror.

And in that face, Emily read her fate. She clawed at David, straining, trying to pull herself up, trying to see, to make sure. Then, flinging herself on him, she suddenly remembered saying an eternity ago:

"Anything! Anything!" *My God, my God, what did I promise him?*

"What is it? Oh, God, what's *wrong?*" he cried.

Now she could see the baby's face clearly. *Her* baby's face. With the large, dark, luminous eyes. The El Greco face. The face that haunted her dreams.

And the harelip.

Lupe!

The men were running down the embankment now, flashlights waving.

"Kill it!" she screamed.

283

They ran toward her, beefy workers' arms stretched out to help her.

"Kill it!"

She heard the confused murmur of voices, all reassuring, felt herself lifted and carried up toward their truck, toward warmth, toward rescue. But all she could think of was that thing in David's arms. Then she looked up and saw the thin smile of triumph on Marianne's face.

That's why she was there! To protect that—*thing!* But that meant Marianne had done it. All of it.

She heard herself crying out, *"Why, Marianne? Why!"*

"Don't you understand? He freed me from Matthew! I owe him! And otherwise he would have taken Roberta!"

Realization and horror flooded through Emily's being. "Kill HER!" she screamed.

But they would never kill the baby. They would never kill Marianne. They would never listen to Emily.

Ever.

Author's Note

All quotations cited in the text are authentic. Their sources are given in the text itself, with the following exceptions: In the final scene, Cade's first speech, in which he consecrates the Pentacles, is adapted by the author from several medieval grimoires. The second speech is a Chaldean Incantation from the Royal Library at Nineveh, dating from the second millennium B.C. His third speech is quoted from a Chaldean magical text from a Bilingual Tablet in the British Museum. Cade's fourth speech comes from Chapter 113 of the Koran.

The magical words in an unknown language used by Cade to Lupe are from the *Grand Clavicle of Solomon,* by ancient tradition used to torture demons.

The set of questions asked of Emily by Rufus are from *La Sorcellerie à Colmar,* adapted by the author, and in varying forms, they have existed all over Europe for centuries.

Descriptions of deaths by spontaneous combustion are found not only in the newspaper articles cited in the text but in numerous sources, apart from the familiar references to be found in Charles Fort's *Book of the Damned.*

There are, as the text indicates, many descriptions of Home's extraordinary feats of levitation. The most recent account of them is in Colin Wilson's excellent book *The Occult,* Random House, New York, 1971.

The description of the tests administered by Professor Hindley is taken from tests conducted over a period of many years by Dr. J. B. Rhine at Duke University.

About the Author

GENE THOMPSON was born and raised in San Francisco, where his family has lived for almost a century. After graduating from the University of California at Berkeley, he worked and studied in Europe for some years. He now lives in California with his wife, also a writer, and their four children.